ROSE BY ANY OTHER NAME

MAUREEN McCARTHY

◆ ◆ ◆

Roaring Brook Press
New York

Published by Roaring Brook Press
Roaring Brook Press is a division of Holtzbrinck Publishing
Holdings Limited Partnership
175 Fifth Avenue, New York, New York 10010
www.roaringbrookpress.com

First published in Australia by Allen & Unwin

Library of Congress Cataloging-in-Publication Data
McCarthy, Maureen, 1953-
Rose by any other name / Maureen McCarthy. —1st American ed.
p. cm.
Summary: During a road trip with her mother from Melbourne to Fairy Point, Australia,
to see her dying grandmother, nineteen-year-old Rose gains a
new perspective on events of the previous year, when family problems,
the end of a long-term friendship, and bad personal choices
dramatically transformed her near-perfect life.
ISBN-13: 978-1-59643-372-4
ISBN-10: 1-59643-372-8
[1. Self-actualization (Psychology)—Fiction. 2. Family life—Australia—Fiction. 3. Family
problems—Fiction. 4. Interpersonal relations—Fiction.
5. Automobile travel—Fiction. 6. Australia—Fiction.] I. Title.
PZ7.M12818Ros 2008
[Fic]—dc22   2007018406

10 9 8 7 6 5 4 3 2 1

Roaring Brook Press books are available for special promotions and premiums. For details
contact: Director of Special Markets, Holtzbrinck Publishers.

Book design by Robin Hoffmann | Brand X Studios
Printed in the United States of America

First American Edition March 2008

For Patrice and Ramona,
who saw me through the bleak times.
Thanks for all the love and laughter,
the walks, the meals, and the talk.

Thanks to Vince, too,
for his love and support.

**And special thanks
to my son Patrick,**
a surfer, a musician, and a law student
to boot, for sharing all you know about
the great sixties and seventies bands
and musicians and for introducing me
to some of their present-day counter-
parts. Thanks for passing on your passion for the ocean, Pat. It gave me
inspiration for this novel.

Warm thanks to Erica Wagner at Allen
& Unwin for her belief in me when I
had none. And many thanks to Eva
Mills, too, for her enthusiasm for the
project and for her meticulous attention
to detail throughout the editing process.

◆ ◆ ◆

I'M ROSE. Rose Greta Patrice O'Neil. Rose. Not short for Rosemary, Rosa, or Rosanne. Just Rose. The name is an embarrassment. I'm not beautiful or delicate or sweet smelling. I'm not even pretty.

So it's Rose. My father told me that they took one look at me when I was born and decided on Rose because I was pink and scrunched up, and I exuded an air of superiority. Well, okay, thanks, Dad. But I've seen the photos, and I don't look anywhere near as superior as my three older sisters. Hilda. Cynthia. Dorothy. All of them were stunners and they still are. He said it to make me feel better. He is a lawyer. They know how to use words.

I never expected *love* to come when it did. Nor the way it came. Nor the complete mess it made of my life. I wasn't hanging out for it either, like some people. My life was fine. Great family. Excellent grades. I got on with people in my own way, and I had a best friend to laugh with and bitch with.

But love found me. It came straight at me like a howling wind. Knocked me to the ground, made me blind, chucked me in the air. And when I crashed, well . . . I thought everything was over.

But things are never *over* even when they're over. I learned that. They change. You think they won't but they do. Everything changes all the time. That trip I took with my mother was the beginning of things changing for me . . .

◆ ◆ ◆

ROAD TRIP

I can't believe I'm doing this. Can't believe she talked me into it. Had me feeling awkward, obliged, *and* compliant all within about a minute. I should have held firm. Should have said no.

I glance at myself in the rear-view mirror, so pale and . . . *mean looking* with my chopped-off hair and blunt, freckled nose. Mouth like a piece of string. Nineteen years old and I'm sitting stiff as a plank behind the steering wheel, waiting to start the engine. *For God's sake ease up! Chill out.* When exactly did I get like this? I poke my head out the window and look up at the summer sky, so deep and clear and blue, as innocent as a kid's drawing. *Nothing can be that simple*, I want to yell. *Don't lie to me!*

"Ready then?" I ask without turning around.

"Yep. I'm ready."

I pull down the seat belt, slip the buckle in, and settle it tight across my chest. *Concentrate on what you're doing, Rose*, I tell myself. Just concentrate on what you're doing and everything will work out. Turn the key. Okay. It starts first go. So it should. It's just been serviced. The lighted dashboard tells me I have plenty of petrol. Oil is fine too. The blinkers are working perfectly. Even the temperature gauge is smiling back at me with the black needle hovering slap bang in the green band. *Sweet.* This engine blew once, right in the middle of Punt Road. I lifted up the hood without thinking and . . . whoa! The cap blew off. Boiling water everywhere. Black smoke. Stinking fumes. The works. Lucky I didn't get badly burned. No one stopped. They just scooted past like I was a terrorist fussing over a dud bomb. Since then, I get scared if that needle goes anywhere near the red.

My bag is in the back. Wet suit. Surfboard tied to the roof. What a laugh. I haven't even *seen* the ocean inside a year, much less considered surfing! (I do *dream* about it though.) I've got the old rubber mattress. Pillow. Sleeping bag. There is some satisfaction in knowing that I'm ready for anything. I push the turn signal down and pull away from the curb. Clutch down and I slam it into second gear. We're off.

"Rose, I think I might have forgotten my credit card."

I step on the brake and stare straight ahead, hands gripping the wheel. *You've got to be joking!*

"Well?" I say, shitty as hell and not bothering to hide it. "Have you or haven't you?" I turn and see that she is looking at *me* instead of checking in her bag.

"Don't snap, darling," she says, before bending to search in her big, bright orange, ridiculous straw bag. "It's not *that* important."

"Sorry," I mutter, thinking that it really is every bit *that* important. The only way I agreed to her coming was when she said she'd stay in a motel if I decide to sleep a night in the van (which I've already decided to do although I haven't told her). How will she pay for it without her card?

"But you'll need it."

"I know."

"Any idea where it might be?" I ask through gritted teeth.

"Yep." She slides open the van door. "I'm pretty sure it's on the kitchen table. Won't be a jiffy." She hesitates a moment, smiles, and stretches out one hand, as though she's about to run it across the top of my chopped-off, inch-long, totally in-your-face hair. Thankfully, she thinks better of it and pulls away.

"I can't get used to it!" she says lightly, pretending that she's open to liking it when she does. I shrug sourly, as though her problem with my hair isn't any concern of mine. As though I'm completely at home with my new, weird, aggro image, when in fact I'm totally freaked out by it and I can't wait for my hair to grow back.

"Don't go without me!" she calls gaily.

"I won't."

I watch my mother jump out and run back toward our huge double-fronted family home on Alfred Crescent in North Fitzroy. She is dressed in well-cut red linen pants, a loose white cotton blouse with a frill around the wide neck, heeled sandals, and those long beaded aqua earrings that I like and wish I'd accepted when she offered them to me some months ago. Her dyed red hair is up in a loose bun and she looks good for her age. Fifty-two years old now. My sisters threw her a party last month, and I didn't even pretend I had something else on. Parties and me don't connect these days, and I think everyone understands that now.

I back the van into a parking spot just outside our gate and watch as she pushes open the wisteria-covered wrought-iron gate and makes her way up the pathway to the front door. I'm gripped with a sudden mad impulse to run after her before she disappears inside. To grab her and hug her tight, tell her I love her, just in case I never see her again. But the moment passes, thankfully. It's gone . . . almost before it registers. *Anyway, as though that's going to happen! As though she's going to disappear into thin air. God, Rose, get a grip.*

The rambling garden around our family home is wonderful at this time of year. It's filled with leafy trees and bright, chaotic climbing plants: clematis, sweet pea, and roses that cover the fence and creep up along the edge of the house steps. There are ferns and little pockets of bright summer flowers too. It's all so lovely that it could make your throat close up if you let it, which I don't.

I got this van last summer. Only two and a half thousand bucks. I'd saved most of the money over the previous year. There was a year or two left on the tires, six months on the registration, and the engine—according to the mechanic who checked it out for me—was in good shape. I'm not sorry. When the shit hit the fan I still had the van, which was something.

I turn off the engine and look at my watch. Five minutes already. The credit card is obviously not on the table. Then again, knowing my mother, she's probably in there pulling together half a dozen other things she's forgotten or thinks she needs. Or she might be making a last phone call, or taking one, or . . .

It's eight thirty on a weekday morning. We're going to be caught in rush hour traffic on our way out of the city, and there is no one to blame but myself. I was meant to be here over an hour ago to pick her up. I slept in later than I'd planned, and when I did get up, I messed around. Went to ring her at least three times and tell her that I'd changed my mind about her coming with me. After all, she has her own car. A top-model, stylish Saab, with air-conditioning, bucket seats, automatic gears, and a great sound system. Dad bought it for her when she turned fifty. Driving the Saab the shorter way through Colac and Camperdown, she could be in Port Fairy inside four hours. She'd be able to book into a motel before nightfall and be rested when she goes to see Grandma Greta.

Whereas I'm going the long way, around the steep and winding coastal road through the Great Otway National

Park, where it's sixty kilometers an hour for *hours*. I told her this. I was frank and uncompromising about my plans. I'm going to stop when I feel like it. I'm going to walk on the beach. Look at the cliffs. Chill out. Put my feet in the water. Have a swim if I can bring myself to. I don't care if Grandma does die before I get there. I mean it. She's eighty-six. According to my sister Dorothy (who is already down there), she wants to die. Where is the tragedy if someone of eighty-six dies when she wants to? I can't see the point of fond farewells and last goodbyes.

But when I got here this morning, my mother was waiting for me on the front veranda. Suitase at her feet and that wide straw sunhat on her head, looking so keen. What could I say? I just gulped, got out, walked over, and said, "Hi, Mum. You ready?"

"I've been ready for ages!" she said, and kissed me on both cheeks.

Ah! Here she is and yes, she's carrying a brown paper bag as well as, hopefully, her credit card.

"Sorry love," she puffs as she climbs in.

"You get it?"

"Yep." She grins at me. "And the lunch I so carefully packed for us."

"Where was that?"

"On the table, too." She laughs, and I can tell she wants me to join in. To indulge her zany forgetfulness with at least a smile. *Oh, there goes Mum again. Dithering along, messing up the practicalities . . .* But I turn away and start the engine again. I pull out and nose my way into the St. Georges Road traffic without giving even a hint of a smile. I actually *like* attention to detail. Taking proper care of the small bits and pieces of whatever's going on is what life is about, as far as I'm concerned. Why should I agree that leaving a specially prepared lunch to go to waste is something to laugh about?

"So what exactly did Dorothy tell you?" Mum opens up the conversation in this intimate aren't-we-going-to-have-fun-together kind of way that immediately gets my back up. "About Gran, I mean."

We are heading around the zoo now and the traffic is diabolical. Everyone is coming into the city to work and all the roads and intersections are congested. I keep myself from losing it by clinging to the thought that we're going the other way. Once we're over the West Gate Bridge, it will be okay. Just got to get out of this.

"Dorothy said Gran is fading fast and wants to see me," I say sharply.

"But why *you*?" Mum asks, then quickly tries to correct the impression that her nose is out of joint. "Not that it's strange to want to see you, but why you particularly? Why not . . . everyone else?" she finishes lamely. I don't take offense because I don't know the answer. I'm intrigued too. *Why me?* I have never had a particularly special relationship with my father's mother, Greta. Hilda, the eldest sister, was always her favorite, and the other two also seemed to shine more in her eyes than I did. But I am fond of her in a way. I guess we all are. She is a wiry old bird, bossy as hell and full of punch. Or was. She's on her last legs now. Demanded to be allowed to go home from the hospital to die in her bed. Her words, not mine. So I guess she figures her time is up.

My grandfather was a fisherman who drowned at sea when Dad was just a baby. Gran has lived in the same little cottage in Port Fairy all her life. It's where my father, who is an only child, grew up. Four small rooms with a dark hallway leading down to the kitchen. Never renovated but on a huge block. We used to spend our summers there when we were little.

As soon as my sister Dorothy heard that Gran wanted to go home to die, and that there was no one around to stay in the house with her, she managed to negotiate some time off from her glamorous television job and went straight there to look after her. Pretty heroic, considering how difficult Gran can be. Then again, the grand gesture is what Dorothy's good at. Theatrics is her game.

Dorothy is the sister nearest to me. Twenty-three years old and a bit of a flake compared to the rest of us. Not dumb. She consistently came out on top in just about every subject at university, and she was studying for her Masters in Classics until last year. I don't know anyone else who speaks fluent Latin and Greek, or who knows everything there is to know about everything that happened before 500 AD. It's just that Dorothy has real trouble with most of what's happened since, if you get my drift.

But that's all changing too. Dot's life did a total flip last year when she was plucked off the street—literally—to act in a soap opera. All of my three sisters are very good-looking, but Dot is quite simply gorgeous. I'm not kidding. She's got these huge, deep lavender eyes with lashes like long Japanese paintbrushes. Her hair is thick and dark and curly. She has fairer skin than the rest of us and the loveliest mouth, like a rosebud. (*She* is the one that should have been called Rose!) Even before she was on TV, people used to gape at her in the street.

"Gran wants to *give* you something?" Mum murmurs.

"Yeah."

"Any idea *what*?"

"Dot didn't say," I reply shortly.

"Maybe she's going to leave you all her money." Mum smiles.

"Maybe," I say dryly. We both know that there is no money. Gran has lived on the old-age pension for the last twenty years, and the cottage is already in Dad's name.

"Maybe you'll get the Collection," Mum says lightly, after a careful little pause. This gives me a nasty jolt. *Shit! I never thought of that.*

In my consternation I forget to take my foot off the clutch slowly enough, and the van lurches forward, almost hitting a little red Mazda pushing into the main stream from a side road. I wave in the driver irritably. *Damn it. Mum's probably right! The Collection. Yeah, that'll be it. So I'm on a six-hour drive for something I seriously don't want!*

"It's very precious to Gran," Mum adds cajolingly, like this might make me change my mind. Like I might suddenly start loving a heap of cheap old rubbish because some crazy biddy in her eighties has held it dear for fifty years.

"You might end up really . . . valuing it." Mum's voice peters out when I turn and give her my best withering look, daring her to continue. *Yeah right, Mum!*

"Oh well," she sighs, "stranger things have happened."

Naturally, I've been hoping for something nice, an antique bracelet, maybe, or a ring that Gran had been secretly hoarding all these years for her youngest grandchild. But no . . . I try to shrug off this secret hope. Better to expect the worst.

"Do you know this, like, for sure?" I ask after a few moments have elapsed. "Did Dot give you a hint?" Mum shakes her head so vigorously that I reckon she has a fair idea but doesn't want to hit me with the full, 100 percent horrible truth in one hit. Mum is the family diplomat, very good at breaking bad news.

"I'm only guessing," she says.

"Well, I don't want it," I mutter sourly.

"But there is no way you could throw it away," she says insistently. "I mean, *if* she leaves it to you, you can't just . . . dump it."

I don't reply because she's right. No way could you toss the Collection in the bin. It is so much a part of Gran and that little house that it would be an extremely sacrilegious and violent act. People don't mess with Gran or they cop it. I'm not normally superstitious, but if I threw the Collection away, I know I'd live the rest of my life in fear that she'd get back at me somehow—even after she was dead.

The Collection consists of about two dozen cheap, kitschy porcelain cats in a variety of inane postures, with mawkish expressions, insipid colors, and broken-off tails with patchy paint. Think the worst and you'll be right on the mark. Gran has always displayed them in her best room, on top of the crystal cabinet. A cat lover all her life, each one commemorates the passing of one of her real cats, who were all named after someone Gran admired, like Nelson Mandela or Bert Newton. So they all have personalities and names and histories . . . right back to the 1940s. Gran is not senile, or crazy in any other aspect of her life, but she dusts and rearranges these cats daily . . . *and talks to them.* If she manages to get you in the best room (which, incidentally, is hardly ever used for anything else) for a guided viewing of the Collection, you won't get out again inside two hours.

"What will you do with it?" Mum is all innocence. "I mean, if she gives it to you?"

"Leave the country. Slit my wrists."

"Now Rose!" Mum laughs uneasily. She's not sure if I'm joking, and neither am I.

At last the light turns green and we inch forward a few feet toward the Flemington Road intersection. I hold my breath and step on the accelerator. *Don't let the lights turn red again so soon.* They hold and we're across.

"What is Dot actually *doing* down there?" I think of flannels and bedpans and Dorothy's slight frame trying to lift Gran's bulky body. It's hard to imagine my dippy, hothouse flower of a sister in any kind of practical role at all, much less that of nurse.

"Not sure," Mum says.

"Bathing her maybe?"

"Goodness!" Mum is shocked at the thought. "I can't imagine it."

"Feeding her?"

"Maybe." Mum begins to chew her thumb, a sign that she's thinking hard. "Dot said she just wanted to be there."

"Oh well," I say hastily. "Good for her."

I guess we're both flummoxed. Dot doesn't usually do practical life very well.

"Maybe the tablecloth is in doubt?" I suggest. I mean it as a joke, but Mum nods seriously.

"That could be it."

Even though Gran's cottage is packed to the rafters with all kinds of junk, there are only three things that anyone wants. They are all wedding presents given to my grandparents in 1945: the crystal cabinet in the front room, which is all polished cut glass and deep shiny wood; an almost complete set of Royal Doulton 1920s yellowing dishes with little green flowers around the edges; and this incredibly lovely embroidered linen tablecloth, covered in birds and flowers from Chinese mythology. My three older sisters have had these things assigned for years. Hilda gets the dishes—although why she wants them so badly is a mystery. She and her husband could afford a dozen sets twice as good. Cynthia is desperate for the cabinet, for her surgical instruments.

And Dorothy believes the tablecloth is rightfully hers because the embroidered Chinese bird motif is her *sign*. As the fourth sister, it's always been understood that I miss out, but I honestly don't mind. I'll probably end up doing better than all of them anyway, as each of my sisters feels so guilty about me not getting one of the Big Three that they're always promising to make it up to me in "other ways" when the time comes. Over the years, I've secretly figured that I should be able to play this number for all it's worth when the time comes—and get something out of them that I really want!

For all I know, Gran wanting to give me something may have thrown a serious spanner into their settled arrangement. General gnashing of teeth and forming of secret alliances might already have begun. Then again, if they know *I've* been given the Collection, the three of them will be lying around weak with relief that they missed out, which makes me doubly pissed off.

"The council provides a nurse," Mum says after a while. "Dot is probably just keeping Gran company. Reading to her. Giving her medicine, making tea. That kind of thing."

"Right."

"It should be Cynthia," Mum muses. "After all, she's the doctor."

"You have *got* to be kidding!" I splutter incredulously.

"Yes, of course," Mum mumbles quickly, "only joking."

They are only fifteen months apart, but Cynthia and Dorothy are chalk and cheese. Dot is all airy-fairy and convinced that the world would be a better place if everyone spoke Latin and rode their bikes to work. Cynthia is efficiency plus, or thinks she is. She's twenty-four and will soon be a qualified doctor, which fills the rest of us with total pity for any patient she'll ever come across. I'm not kidding. She's the doctor who, if you went in with the flu, would tell you to go home and start making your will because you've most likely got a brain tumor. Once Mum had tinea between her toes, and Cynthia diagnosed her with some totally weird African skin disease. She didn't hold back with the bad news, either. By the time Mum got to her own doctor—who had never heard of the African disease—Cynthia had her believing that she would be covered from head to foot with pus-filled blisters that might or might not respond to some new cortisone ointment that would have to be flown in from America.

Dad reckons Cynthia will settle down once she gets to the hospitals for some hands-on experience with real people. But the rest of us seriously doubt anyone under Cynthia's care will even survive. Just how many *real people* will have to die or be sent absolutely crazy before she *settles down* is what we'd like to know!

So we've just come off the Bolte Bridge, with its two tall concrete pylons. The flat brown river and city buildings are on our left and a mass of factories is on our right. We travel along in silence for a few kilometers, past service stations and spare-parts manufacturers, drive-in food joints and masses of nerve-wracking, heavy traffic. Then I see the onramp for the West Gate Bridge curving up ahead like a long-forgotten promise about to come true. I wind down the window and let a rush of fresh breeze hit me in the face. *Yes.* I signal, pull over to the right, and join the stream of cars and big, noisy semis and trucks making their way up onto the bridge.

Once up there, everything shifts again. You can see all around in every direction. Oil refineries and factories, and huge container ships docked around the port. In the distance, great tracts of housing estates. And beneath us, the river is laid out like an ancient brown limb still flickering with life. Brightly colored boats are tied up along the edges, like toys. I think of my ex-best friend Zoe. So often it was the both of us up here, looking down across the city on our way to the coast. Her mother, sour and mostly silent, would take us as far as Geelong, chain smoking the whole way, and drop us off at the bus stop. We didn't care about the sourness or the smoking. Zoe and I would be in the backseat with the windows open, humming, grinning, giving each other the thumbs up. *Soon we'll be there*, was what we were thinking. *Soon we'll be drinking cocoa and reading trashy magazines, eating grilled cheese or chips from the shop, and getting our things together for the half-hour walk down to the waves.*

I had my first surf on my sixteenth birthday. Zoe and I had just come in from a swim, and we were looking longingly at the surfers skimming in on the waves, when this funny little guy came out of the water with his board under his arm. His blond hair hung in his eyes like old seaweed, and his long faded shorts had slid halfway down his bum.

"Hey, girls." He grinned as he passed us. "How's it goin'?"

"How long does it take to learn?" I remember asking him.

"Depends." He frowned. "On how much you want to."

His name was Charlie, and within half an hour he was offering to teach us. By the end of that summer, we both had boards.

As we come off the bridge, I switch on the radio. I'm desperate for some music, but there are just weather reports and traffic updates and the same news headlines that I'd heard at seven o'clock that morning.

"I need music," I mutter.

"Need?" Mum asks, amused.

"Yeah," I say gruffly, and begin to flip through the CDs. "You don't mind, do you?" A certain edge creeps into my voice. *You'd better not mind, because this is my trip, my van, and I don't even really want you here . . .*

"Of course not."

I'm still thinking of Zoe, so I flip on an ancient Doors album just for the hell of it. "Break on Through (to the Other Side)" comes roaring out of the speakers.

"Well, I certainly don't mind listening to this!" Mum coos, throwing her head back, closing her eyes, and putting both feet up on the dashboard. "This is *my* music."

"No it's not!" I snap before I even think. "Music is music. It doesn't belong to any one generation!" Mum just smiles and says nothing. And I wonder again what has gotten into me. When exactly did I turn into such an uptight . . . bitch?

Zoe and I were the only girls in our grade at school to take music seriously. Most of the other girls were into the big easy-listening bands or all the techno crap. Worse still, Britney and Kylie and the rest of the soft-porn stars. They read the trash magazines and kept up with the dresses and the love lives and the publicity stunts.

But from the time Zoe and I were about fifteen, we thought all that was complete shit. We loved the old stuff from the sixties and seventies and, of course, the great current bands who still know what rock is about. There is a heap of good, hard rock around, but you've got to know where to look for it. The big stores don't always carry the stuff we're interested in.

At about sixteen, we started sneaking into pubs to listen to the new bands around Melbourne. We got hauled up for our IDs, but never got into too much trouble. Coppers would turn a blind eye because they knew we didn't drink. We were there for the music. We'd often listen to the likes of Black Sabbath and Pearl Jam, or maybe the Peppers or the Clash, just to get us in the mood before we went to see live bands.

"God, Rose!" Mum breaks into my thoughts with a sudden laugh. "This stuff takes me way back."

"Yeah," I say sharply, but I don't comment in case she takes it as a cue to start reminiscing. I'm actually wishing like hell I'd put on something she didn't understand, something tougher and more complex. She's right. This *is* her music. Why the hell am I playing stuff from the *sixties*?

"Do you ever hear from Zoe?" my mother asks. I shrug casually, but the question freaks me out. *I didn't mention Zoe, did I? How come she knows what I'm thinking about?* Anyway, my mother knows the answer. She knows I don't see Zoe, so why ask?

"I miss her," Mum says quietly.

"Yeah, well," is all I can manage as I slip into fifth gear and step on the accelerator. "I'd get over *that*, if I were you."

Don'tcha just hate someone bringing up something or someone you are trying your best not to think about . . .

The road opens out before us, almost completely flat all the way to Geelong. For miles and miles, it feels a bit like we're skidding across this shiny plate of dreamland. Through the industrial suburbs, factories and giant storehouses, engineering plants and nests of refineries that sit there like pieces from a giant's toyshop. Those huge steel girders holding up the power lines, the acres of housing estates, all that industry and people living different lives. It enthralls me in a way. The road cuts through it all like a major artery bringing blood in and out. We are flanked at different points by huge sound barriers and then after a while wide banks of grass and native shrubs and trees.

When at last we are out on the straight open road, the tight ball that's been sitting inside my chest all morning unravels a fraction. I try to think of some nice thing to say to Mum to make up for biting off her head about music, but . . . I can't. I'm sitting on 100 and the van is purring beneath me like a big lazy cat. It's weirdly intoxicating to be thundering past the green signs pointing off to other places. Pity the poor bastards going to Werribee or Hoppers Crossing or any of the other shitty boring places! Above me the sky glows deep blue and cloudless in the bright light of morning. There are storms predicted for the late afternoon along the western coast, but I don't believe it for a minute. *This is okay. I can think of a lot worse places to be.*

"You want to stop for a quick coffee in Geelong?" I ask. It's the nicest thing I can come up with under the circumstances. I don't want to stop, but Mum loves her morning coffee.

"Okay," she says brightly, and rolls down her window and begins to hum a little. Is she trying to tell me she's enjoying it all so much, that life is a breeze and she hasn't a care in the world? Naturally I find it irritating. Life hasn't been a breeze for my mother for some time, so why pretend?

My thoughts are cut short by a fancy BMW pulling out in front of us, almost making me crash into the back of it. I slam on the brakes.

"Shit," I mutter, and Mum murmurs in agreement and smiles at me in this dry, offhand way that makes me think I might have imagined her previous false note. Maybe she isn't acting at all. Maybe she really is feeling good. I've spent virtually no time with my mother over the last ten months, so how would I know?

Sometimes I wonder if I've imagined everything. Truly, I do.

Don'tcha just hate it . . . when every thought you have is somehow undermined by an opposing thought? You think you've got the situation tied up and then this sneaking little doubt rolls in, making you question the way you see . . . everything?

Ah no. No. That's not going to work. Too complicated, too introspective. Can't make a piece out of that. Or can I?

21

◆ ◆ ◆

DON'TCHA JUST HATE IT . . . is the subtitle Roger gave me for the three-hundred-word column I write every week for the music paper *Sauce*—it's free and can be picked up in your nearest bar or café! Roger's the owner and editor of the paper, and the twin brother of Danny, who owns the café where I waitress.

I approached Roger about three months ago, when I found out what he did—music being the one thing left in my life I still loved. But he told me there were way too many experienced rock journalists around who couldn't get work, and suggested I try something else. I thought he meant try some other occupation like picking fruit or answering phones, but I didn't take offense. They're nice guys, both of them: early forties, fat, friendly, nerdy and fast-talking, always out for a quick buck. But I like them all right, because both of them are quick to see the funny side of anything going on, and they're always nice to me. I appreciate that because I don't see many people these days.

A couple of weeks after being given the dud news about my chances of writing for his paper, Roger comes around to the café to see his brother. He gives me one of his hearty shoulder squeezes, tells me I'm looking good and that I'm the best waitress his brother has ever had. Then he asks me for two *specials*, which means espresso coffee bitter and strong enough to give an ordinary person a heart attack. When I bring them over to where the brothers are seated, near the window in the café, I can see they are engrossed in a serious conversation—unusual because they usually jostle and laugh and slam each other around like guys half their age. So I put down the coffee, prepared to depart quickly. But Roger looks up with one of his wary smiles and motions to the spare chair.

"Hey Rose," he says, "have a seat. How's life?"

"Okay." I shrug, not wanting to sit down, because although the lunchtime crowd has gone, there is still plenty of clearing up to do behind the counter.

"Just okay?"

"Just okay." I smile back at him. "You know how it is."

"No, I don't." He is looking at me seriously now. "How is it, Rose?"

I stand there smiling stupidly, determined not to give anything away. The fact that nothing much is happening in my life is entirely my own fault. I know that. In a weird way, it's exactly how I want it, too. Anyway, boring people with oh-woe-is-me details is not my style.

"Come on," he insists. "Sit down, why don't you?"

I sit down and give one of my hey-guys-I'm-already-bored-with-this-conversation groans, then I cross my arms tight across my chest, throw my head back, and look at the ceiling.

"What's up?" Roger asks me.

"Well," I say, watching a fat blowfly make its way slowly across the greasy blistered paint above me, "don'tcha just hate it when every day seems more or less like . . . every other day?" I wait, still looking at the fly, but nobody says anything, so I eventually sit up again and stare at them. Roger is nodding up and down like an old sage, and Danny is lining up the sugar packets in a straight line across the table—a sure sign he's thinking hard about something. I find myself suddenly shy, hoping he's not thinking about *me* or what I've just said, because I don't want sympathy. I don't want anything to change at all between me and these two guys. I enjoy their daggy humor and all that breezy couldn't-give-a-shit chatter. It makes me feel like I'm a part of things without having to give anything away.

After a bit of a pause, Roger looks up. "So, write a column about it," he says to me.

"About what?" I say.

"About the things you hate," he replies. "It's exactly what we need, a short dark piece every week from the young female point of view."

"The things I hate?"

"What do you reckon?"

I shrug, trying to get my head around what he might mean. "All the things that piss you off," he adds, winking broadly at his brother. And suddenly he throws his hands in the air and starts yelling. "The price of bloody drinks in bars, Rose! Guys that don't come through! Ya family." He pauses for a moment and looks out the window before turning back to me. "George Bush and the friggin' war. High heels that crack your ankles. The way lipsticks melt! I don't know, Rose! Girl things. Big things and small things and every bloody thing in between!"

I nod slowly, a bit taken aback.

"Think you can?"

"Why me?"

"I heard you were smart," he says.

"Well . . ." I shrug, pleased. Danny must have told him about my VCE score. "It sure sounds a lot easier than writing about the things I love."

"That's the spirit!" he says, clapping me on the back, and the three of us suddenly crack up laughing. He pulls out his card. "Here. Just e-mail it to me in the next couple of days, and we'll take it from there."

In case you're thinking it involves good money and working in some groovy little office full of cool, like-minded music freaks, or free tickets to concerts where I meet famous people backstage—then think again. I e-mail Roger my piece every week, and I never see anyone. I don't have contact with older, more experienced journalists who could show me the ropes or how to do things better. *And* I have to pick up my copy of the paper from the local café, just like everyone else. Nor do I get any feedback, except for the occasional phone call from Roger telling me that I've stuffed up in some way. Maybe I've gone over my word limit or, more commonly, this week's "rave" isn't quite up to last week's. He's always telling me to crank things up a bit. I never know what the hell he's talking about, so I just do what I do, and each week when I pick up my copy of the paper, there's my piece under the name of "Ms. Angst."

I should add that every week, I half expect to not find it there, to have been given the heave-ho. It's not that I'd mind that much. I'm *not* one of those people who has always wanted to be a writer. The pay is crap (I still have to work as many hours waitressing as I used to), and churning out those three hundred words takes me more time than I care to admit. At the start of every week, I think, *Well, this is it, I've got nothing to write about*. But by the time Thursday comes around, I've usually had a bash at two or three subjects. I pick one and spend most of Friday—my day off from the café—polishing it up and sending it off.

So don't freak when you see the *Don'tcha just hate it . . .* line. It's only me chewing over a possible little diatribe for Roger.

◆　◆　◆

"LET'S HAVE OUR COFFEE down by the water," Mum suggests. Then she adds in a more hesitant, cloying tone that makes me want to heave, "That is, if you still want to stop?"

"Yeah, okay," I say.

So we take the exit and travel the few kilometers along the boulevard to the newly reconstructed precinct of shops and coffeehouses set along the bay. I pull the van into one of the parking lots that looks out over the water. Between the parking lot and the water there is a long, quite wide grassy area with small trees and a crazy pathway zigzagging down to a wooden pier and restaurant. Seats are dotted along the edge.

"Last time I was here it was a weekend," Mum muses, "and there were at least six brides all having their photos taken."

"When was that?" I ask shortly.

"Must have been a couple of years ago." She frowns. "Your father and I were on our way down to see Gran for Easter. People get married on any day now." Her wistful tone jerks me into fresh wariness. I reach for the door and slide it open.

"I'll get the coffee," I say, and point to the seat right in front of us. "Why don't you go sit out there and I'll bring it over?" I'm determined that this trip will not degenerate into any kind of getting-to-know-you-again experience. Ditto for meaningful conversations about wedding days, past or present, and romantic outings with my father.

26

"No, Rose," she says firmly, opening the other door. "Let me, please. I'd like the walk. Want anything to eat?"

"Okay then," I say with a shrug, happy for her to do it because I'm low on cash, "just the coffee will do."

Mum heads across the road to the nearest café, and I wander over to the lawn and look out at the oily, murky brown water. It's nice with the breeze and the sun shining. I'm wearing jeans with a faded denim jacket over an old pea-green T-shirt. It's warm enough to take off the jacket, but I prefer to stay covered. I dig my hands into the pockets of my jeans and edge back to the seat in front of the car, shut my eyes, and turn my face up into the sun.

Last time I was here, Zoe was with me. We missed the bus and had about three hours to kill, so we walked on the pier and ate pizza. Must have been about fifteen months ago. It was cold. I can see her sitting under that large plane tree down near the water, big legs crossed.

"Am I okay?" I remember her asking me that day. "Do you *really* think I'm going to make it?"

"Of course you're okay, Zoe," I replied automatically, slumping down beside her, opening the pizza box and handing her a slice on one of the napkins, "and you'll make it for sure."

I always answered these questions as though she'd never asked them before, when in fact, especially if we hadn't seen each other for a few days, she would often begin conversations this way. Zoe just can't do polite conversation starters like, "How are you? Isn't it a great day?" or "What have you been doing?"

"Do you really love me?" often came next. I know it sounds gruesome. But I didn't mind because I knew she really had to know. It wasn't a put-on. Most of the time she was such fun, but this stuff had to be faced and resolved before we could go on with anything else. I was her best friend, so who else was going to do it?

"Do I love you?" I would often joke. "What do you reckon, Zoe? That I hang around for your money?"

Zoe lives in Bayswater. Her mother lives on some sickness pension. They often don't have money for proper food because cigarettes and dope and those two stupid mongrel dogs are more important. Like me, she won a scholarship to that big posh school on the other side of town. But unlike me, she really needed that place to get where she wanted to go. For me, deciding to go there was just a way to piss off my older sisters, who'd all attended our excellent local state high school. Zoe's life had never been easy. Yet we were best friends from the first day in that place.

"But will any one guy ever *fall in love* with me?" she often persisted.

"Of course."

Zoe is the ultimate romantic, so this bit, along with getting to the top of her chosen career, was high on her list.

"How will I meet him?"

"For fuck's sake, Zoe. You're only eighteen!"

Zoe is beautiful in a big, in-your-face, over-the-top kind of way. I think so, anyway. Wonderful green eyes that sort of glitter in certain lights if she's excited or angry. Heavy black lashes and eyebrows, a wide mouth always laughing—or crying—and short, curly fair hair, which is usually dyed a few shades lighter than her natural color, sometimes with a slash of purple in it too, or orange and silver if she's in the mood. But she's heavy. I don't know how much she weighs, but she has big thighs and bum and breasts. I was always telling her that in another age, she would have been considered right on the money because she is so curvy. Her middle, waist, and belly are proportionally quite slim. But that look is not right for now, and I guesss it plays on her mind a lot. She's always trying to lose the weight, going on and off diets.

Of course, all that might have changed by now. I haven't seen her in a while. She might have lost it all.

Right through school, medicine was Zoe's one goal. And when she knew she had gotten in to the med school at Monash at the end of our senior year, it was like all her Christmases had come at once. She had leukemia when she was a kid and was in and out of the hospital for about six years, from the time she was eight. Apparently it was touch and go whether she'd actually survive or not. I don't know if her being fat is related to the childhood illness or not. We never talked about it.

It was during her time in the hospital that she fell in love with the whole world of doctors and surgery and advanced medical treatments. The doctors were her heroes. When other little kids were mucking around with their mates, playing dolls and computer games, Zoe was fighting for her life, and those doctors were the ones who saved her. Her plan was to eventually become an oncologist, and it probably still is. Unlike me, who has just frittered away my first year out of school by working long hours in a nothing job that pays badly (and will probably repeat the performance again this year because I can't see myself at university or going overseas), Zoe will have finished her first year at university by now and be gearing up for the second. I'll bet anything that she's done really well on her exams. There was never anything else but medicine for Zoe.

Apart from guys, that is.

I was never into guys in the same way, which is ironic when you think about what happened later. But Zoe fell in love easily and often, and she was always in some cataclysmic state about someone. She had no qualms at all about ringing guys up and asking them out. Sneaking off to see them. No qualms at all about sleeping with them either. Her heart got broken on a regular basis, but she bounced back quickly. That's how it was when I knew her, anyway.

"One hot latte." Mum is back with the coffee, smiling. She hands me mine, sits down beside me, and holds out a brown paper bag.

"Want some?" I peer in at the delicious-looking pastries she's chosen, and my mouth immediately waters. I was so taken up with travel angst this morning, I'd forgotten to eat anything.

"Thanks." I break off a piece of date slice and pop it into my mouth. The sweetness explodes on my tongue like a sugar bomb, and I'm suddenly starving. I pull the rest of it out and gobble it up quickly.

"Sorry!" I say, a bit embarrassed, pulling the top off my coffee. "I said I didn't want anything, but this is so . . . nice."

"Have another one." She smiles at me.

"You sure?" I choose the fresh blueberry muffin next, and its warm, light texture gives me a sudden longing for all that home cooking that I don't have anymore. At home my sisters are always making something delicious to eat. I miss it. Barry, the twenty-five-year-old tight-arse I live with now, literally doesn't know how to boil an egg. I know because I've seen him try. The other one—I call him Stuttering Stan because he can hardly speak a full sentence—not only doesn't cook, he resents anyone who does. He's one of those skinny, pale, sick-looking vegans who thinks everyone should live on nuts and fruit the way he does.

"Is it hot enough?" Mum asks, watching anxiously as I take the first sip of coffee.

"It's perfect." I smile at her, touched. I haven't lived at home for nearly a year, but she remembers how I like my coffee. "Thanks, Mum."

We both look out over the water. At the groups of people wandering along, at the sailboats tied up against the wharf. The crap that is usually lurking like a hungry dog around the edges of my mind has backed off momentarily, and a fizzy lightness invades my head. I like being away from the café. On the road, in the van. Doing something different. *Thanks, Gran*, I think to myself, then I feel mean and try to backtrack. Gran is probably about to die. She doesn't need me feeling happy about it.

"Before, when I asked if you've spoken to Zoe, there was a reason," Mum says quietly, not looking at me. My self-protective antenna immediately begins its high-pitched warning hum. More like a warning screech, really. *Don't go there, Mum, please. Things are fine now. Please just don't go there.*

"Oh yeah?" I say, as nonchalantly as I'm able, thinking, *Hold on tight, Rose, hold tight.* I do not want anyone, especially my mother, knowing exactly how much all this stuff still affects me. I bought one of those self-help books in a secondhand bookshop that's near the house I share with those two morons out in Hurstbridge, and as far as I'm concerned, I'm doing okay. I've gotten myself through the first couple of stages—denial, anger—all on my own. Now I figure it's time to move on, to forget it all. That's the one I'm working on now. *Forgetting.* I don't want to go backward.

"Did you know she's in the hospital?" my mother asks. There is a two-second pause as I feel the words crash their way into my skull. *Hospital?*

"What?" I whisper.

"The hospital," my mother murmurs back.

My heart begins to race. It lurches forward in my chest like an old car. *Chug, chug.* It's going to give out any second and leave me stranded by the wayside, no way forward. Wrecked completely.

"So you didn't know?"

"No."

"Rose, I know you . . . don't like talking about this," Mum says in a monotone, "about Zoe, I mean. But I thought I should tell you. I thought you'd be angry if we all knew and you were left in the dark."

"Right," I mumble, goose bumps rising along my forearms under the jacket. "Thanks."

A chill seems to be coming from deep down inside me. I pull the denim jacket tighter around me, suddenly feeling weak with shock. I know. I know what is coming next and, more than anything, I don't want to hear it.

"The cancer is back," Mum says.

"Cancer?" I speak the word, but it is hard to get my head around it. Cancer. The cancer is back. Okay, we always knew there was a chance of that happening, but . . . I didn't seriously consider it. She has been through so much already. So much of her childhood obliterated, lying in bed with IVs in her, all the drugs and nausea and not knowing if she was going to live or die. The doctors told her that if she stayed clear for ten years, then the chances of it recurring were minimal. When I first met her at fifteen, at the beginning of freshman year, she'd just come out of years of treatment. I want to beat my fists against something hard, a brick wall maybe, or the roof of my van. *Enough is enough.* She's twenty now. How much should one person have to endure? I know it's only been five years, but . . . Someone is laughing at us. *Five years is not ten years, is it?* Five years is worth nothing.

I turn to my mother, who is staring out at the water.

"It's in her blood?"

"I don't know," Mum says. "All I know is that she's been in the hospital for a few weeks of treatment."

A few weeks!

"So has it worked?" I ask quickly. "Is she going to get better?"

"I don't know," Mum says. "I don't know any details."

We sit quietly for a while, maybe two feet apart. I sip my coffee and stare at the brown water. I hate it now. The water. The bay. I hate the gaudy bright day around me, the breeze and the boats. Even the half-eaten muffin in my hand. Everything. This news has broken into my life like a burglar, sawing my heart open, exposing all the secret chambers. I can't seem to find a way to stem the flood of memory and . . . pain. I close off one seeping pipe and another one opens up somewhere else. I never thought this would happen. And I know she never thought it would happen either. Zoe considered herself cured. We both did. I forget about Mum beside me. It doesn't matter what she says now. I'm tumbling backward, away from the present at a crazy pace.

"You know it's been over a year now," Mum says quietly.

"Yes," I mumble.

"Maybe it's time for . . . " She peters out. "Some kind of . . ."

"What?" I come up to the surface and crank out one of my nasty, tight sneers. "For us to be best buddies again?"

"No . . . no." She stumbles on awkwardly. "I just feel it's time you stopped punishing yourself. It's what everyone thinks." She is looking at me, and I hate it. I hate it so much I want to stand up and grab her by both shoulders and shake her, but I stay sitting because I don't want her to know what this is doing to me. "All your sisters . . . and me. There has to be some way to . . . stop all this." She waves one hand helplessly in the air. "Even if it's just to help Zoe!"

Tears well up in my throat and I gulp them down. *Help Zoe? What about me? I need help. Why aren't they thinking about me? Am I some kind of monster that's beyond help?*

"Mum," I say, standing up. "No one knows . . . what happened."

"We have a fair idea, Rose," she says.

"No, you *don't*!" I try to smile, but my mouth isn't working. "That's where you're wrong." I can feel a tremor around the edges of my lips and I can't control it. But at least I'm not shouting, and I don't *think* I sound too angry or desperate. There are only a few people who know about . . . the full particulars of what went on last summer, and Mum isn't one of them. Ditto for my sisters and the rest of my family. I don't want them to know. It's none of their business.

"You all think you know everything," I say, completely exasperated, "but you don't."

"Okay." Mum bites her lip. "I won't mention it again, Rose."

"Thanks." I pull the jacket tight around me. "I'll just have a bit of a walk, okay? Only be a few minutes."

"Take as much time as you need," she says, still looking away, biting her thumb. "No hurry."

I walk to the end of the pier and stand staring out onto the water. It's blue now. Clear blue and lovely. How strange that the water changes color depending on what the clouds are doing overhead. Does that mean that it's not really blue at all? Or brown, or . . .? What exactly is color? Why didn't I pay more attention in science class?

Memories come rushing in. But it's okay. Out on the pier in the sun and the breeze I can manage them. It's when I'm in bed at three a.m., in that horrible house with those two strangers, that . . . I sometimes freak. There are a lot of trees around that house, and small twigs and branches are always falling onto the tin roof. When the wind blows, a branch scrapes across my window and I wake, thinking that someone is trying to get in. There are often scurrying sounds, too, of small animals up there in the ceiling. Barry reckons they're mice. He got up there once with a ladder and chucked a bit of poison about. It didn't make any difference, but I suppose I should give him credit for trying.

The three of us are like ghosts passing each other in the hallway. A polite murmur of hello on the way to the bathroom in the mornings. Short, sharp nods in the kitchen as we make coffee and disappear with it into our rooms. I hate the buzz of Stan's television, that blue light under his door. He's in there half the night watching . . . what? There is only a wall between us. Barry sniffs constantly. *Blow your nose!* I want to yell. *Have a cough! Get some medicine!* But I don't say anything. It's weird to think that the only people I spend time with these days are strangers.

I know I'm fucking up my life, but I don't know how to turn things around. Late at night is when it all gets to be too much.

But right now I'm seeing it from a distance, trying to pick a starting point.

Well . . . I suppose I'd have to say it all began with Nat. Meeting Nathaniel Cummins at the beginning of the summer, before the results came out. And Zoe's father, of course. I'd never met him before, although I'd heard about him. But even that feels like it happened to someone else. In a sense it did, of course. I was someone else then, someone else entirely.

◆ ◆ ◆

LAST SUMMER, MELBOURNE

"We saw him!"

"Rose. Come and look!"

"Quick—out the window!"

Here I am at the kitchen table, minding my own business, reading the paper, drinking coffee and wondering what life in Pakistan would be like. Would a girl my age have to cover her head all the time? What if the scarf blew off? Would she be blamed for that? I mark where I'm up to with my finger and look up.

"Who?" I ask, very cool and above it all.

"Him!"

I sigh in the studiously bored way I keep for my three older sisters before turning back to the paper. But they surround me, waiting to see if anyone knows his name. None of them do, of course, because neither do I.

"You know!" Hilda says in hushed, reverential tones. *"Him!"*

"Come on, Rose!" Cynthia snaps. "The guy you met."

It's hard holding my bland, I-couldn't-give-a-damn expression, but I manage. Just. I get plenty of practice. My sisters often get hysterical over the tiniest things.

"The guy I met?" I ask with a slow frown, knowing I'm driving them crazy but unable to stop myself. "Hmmm . . . I wonder who you mean?"

36

It's a bit like playing one of those stupid video games. You want to stop and do something more productive with your time, but you can't quite pull yourself away because you feel you're on the point of a meaningless minor victory.

There are raised eyebrows and sighs of frustration all around.

"Stop being so obtuse!"

"Don't pretend you don't know!"

"Come and see."

Hilda, the eldest, is very straight. She always plays by the rules and can't understand it when other people don't. She can usually be counted on to be a smidgen more sensible than the other two, but this time she's joined the all-important quest to get the youngest sister—that's me—hooked up to a guy because, *get out your hankies*, I've just turned eighteen and have yet to display any serious interest in males. The other two must have filled her in on the perfectly uneventful meeting I'd had the day before with a good-looking guy who lives in the big student house at the end of our street.

Very nice, I thought at the time. Nice looking. Nice of him to do that for Mum. Nice guy. Just that. *Nice.*

After Mum had gone inside, he and I stood talking in the street for a while, mainly about Melbourne University, where I hope to be studying next year. But the crazy sisters had caught sight of him, and the fact that I'd been smiling as we talked. All too stupid to even recount, but they demanded to know all about him. Caught at a weak moment, I made the mistake of telling them a few snippets of the conversation. And so it's *on* as far as my sisters are concerned.

Good-looking, lives nearby, a student at the same university as I'm going to attend, so . . . I must be dying to see him again, right?

Well, no. Sorry. Not really. Not at all, actually.

"Don't cut yourself off, Rose," Hilda says, in her self-appointed role of the concerned eldest sister taking charge of a delicate operation. *Cut myself off?* "You have a tendency to do that, you know," she adds, looking around at the others for support. They nod, all eyes on me.

"I'm reading the paper," I reply, turning back to the article.

"He's just standing there . . . waiting," she says.

"Waiting?" I croak in disbelief, and look up. "Waiting for what?"

"For you to come out," she ploughs on determinedly, although I can tell that even she knows she's being crazy. "Why don't you at least saunter down there and check out . . . the situation?"

"The *situation* is a bus stop, Hilda!" I say. "People tend to stand at bus stops because they want to catch buses. That's probably a radical concept for you to take in, but why don't you give it a try?"

Hilda is the only one who doesn't live with us anymore. Not officially, anyway. She is twenty-seven and married and has eighteen-month-old twin boys. But she lives only a few streets away and is always over at the family house: using the phone; dropping off the kids for us—mainly Mum—to mind; making weird, healthy concoctions for the boys that they refuse to eat; and, of course, filling us in on what David thinks about everything. Her husband, David, is nice enough, in spite of the fact that he is ten years older than my sister, is a stockbroker, and is never home because he's so busy making piles of money. But listen to Hilda and you could be forgiven for thinking he might be the next savior of mankind, if only he didn't have to work late.

"He knows you live here, Rosie."

"It's a bus stop, Hilda," I say again, calmly. "It's very normal to wait at a bus stop."

They look at each other and roll their eyes, all agreeing, no doubt, that there has to be something seriously wrong with me. One by one they plonk themselves down opposite me at the table. I can tell they're about to embark on one of their confidential sisterly advice sessions, so I glare at them and turn back to my paper. There is nothing I hate more, and they know it. Then Cynthia jumps up again and goes to the front window. She pushes back the flimsy curtain and peers out. Our renovated Victorian family home is built on a rise, so you can see through the trees in the front garden and onto the road.

"Still there," she calls over in a meaningful whisper. "You could go out there now and invite him to your party." Cynthia is plumper than the rest of us. She has dark curly hair, and when she gets serious, like now, her brown eyes seem to bore through you, as though she's trying to mesmerize you into agreeing with her. I look away. Honestly, once she becomes a doctor, that look will freak out so many sick people.

"I could do that," I say slowly, "*if* I was having a party."

"You *have* to have a party, Rose," she snaps.

"No, I don't."

"But you've just turned eighteen!" Hilda weighs in. "And finished school. We *all* had parties when we were eighteen!"

"I don't want one."

"You've got big things to celebrate, Rose," Cynthia declares from the window, just as though she is summing up an important argument about a world-shattering event that will change the course of history forever. "You've turned eighteen. School is over. University is around the corner. Big stuff, kiddo. Come on! This is when your adult life begins. You've been waiting for this all your life!"

"I have?"

"You hated that school."

"So?"

"So, now you're finished with it!"

"I don't want a party."

Cynthia has always fancied herself as the ultimate organizer. Someone who can personally make anything happen—from the annual street party to food distribution in the Third World. I'm sure she wants me to have a party so that she has a legitimate reason to boss the rest of us around.

"What about Zoe?" Hilda ventures breathlessly, looking past me to the other two, who nod furiously. "Zoe needs a party even if you don't!"

I don't say anything because they have me pinned there. My best friend, Zoe, probably *would* get right off on an end-of-school party. And I know there is no way her own tight-arsed mother will throw her one. But I'm not going to give in that easily. My sisters use these tactics all the time.

Another thing. The sisters assume everything in my life belongs to them. Within a month or two of Zoe first coming over to stay at our place, it was, *Ask Zoe this. Tell Zoe that. Would Zoe like to come?* Zoe just about always does like to come because her own home life is so horrible. She is away with a relative in Albury this week, but when she's in Melbourne, she practically lives at our place. But that isn't the point. She doesn't belong to the sisters.

The big point is that Zoe and I have plans for the summer already, and they don't include formal end-of-school parties where our classmates come along dressed up in expensive clothes in order to throw up in the backyard. No way. The two of us, Zoe and me that is, are going down the coast in my van, which is waiting for me in a used-car lot in Preston. Only a few more pay checks and it's all mine.

40

I can't wait to get back out on the ocean. It's been the thought that's sustained me through the slog of senior year. We'll take off as soon as I have my hands on the van—probably mid-December. Stay at Zoe's dad's place for a few days and then travel on around the coast, sleep in the back of the van, cook our meals over fires, meet whoever . . . before we both start university.

That's the plan, anyway. The fact that neither of us has any experience lighting fires or sleeping in vans, or even much driving experience for that matter, is beside the point. I've got my license now. We'll learn.

Cynthia is still looking out the window.

"He's so good-looking," she murmurs. "Just right for you, Rose. Have the party, invite him, and you'll get to know him."

I shake my head. What more can I say? *En masse* the sisters are simply unstoppable. I go back to reading the article about terror-training camps in Pakistan. But it's hard to concentrate.

"I give up." Dorothy gives a huge frustrated sigh, slumps forward, and buries her face in her perfectly manicured white hands as though this tiny domestic situation is the big calamity of her life.

"Well good," I say sharply, "I wish you would."

Dad intercepts this impasse by pushing his way through the kitchen door. He's carrying his battered old bulging briefcase with one hand and holding a cell phone to his ear with the other. He nods to us, frowning, as he listens to whoever is on the other end of the phone. Dad's wearing one of his court suits: dark, beautifully cut Italian, but a bit old and rumpled. The loosened tie and the shadows under his eyes tell me that he must have been up late, working on a case. It's unusual for him to be home this early. It's only just turned five, and Dad is hardly ever home before seven or eight.

"Hi, girls," he says without smiling. He switches off the phone, slips it into his pocket, and goes to the fridge. Dad is good-looking for someone in his fifties. Tall and a bit stooped, he has a long straight nose and beautiful deep-set brown eyes. His hair is still thick and wavy but peppered through with gray, and—luckily, because we've all inherited it—he has smooth olive skin.

"You're home early," Hilda addresses his back. Dad says nothing as he pulls the milk carton out of the fridge and pours himself a glass.

"You have a win?" I ask, the way I always do. It's our thing.

"Winning is what it's all about, Rosie my girl," he said to me when I was about ten, "that's what they're paying me for." I've never forgotten it.

"A few days to go yet, love," Dad mumbles with a sigh. He stands looking out the window with his back to us. "So, where is your mother?" We look at each other. It isn't like Dad to be so distracted.

"Upstairs, I think," Hilda says, and then, very sympathetically, "Tired, Daddy?"

"Yes, darling, I am a bit tired," he says in a slightly warmer way but still not turning around. Hilda gets up and switches on the kettle.

"You want a cup of tea?"

Dad shakes his head. Hilda often calls him Daddy, which tends to drive the rest of us bananas, although on this day, not one of us bothers to pull her up about it. It's unusual for us to see our father in such a morose mood.

As the eldest, Hilda has perfected the helpless little girl number, right down to the last eyelash flutter and pout. She does the same thing with her own husband but refrains when the rest of us are around because we give her hell. Especially Cynthia.

"Try to *act* like a grown-up," Cynthia snarls every time she hears Hilda's breathless-and-innocent routine, "even if you're not!"

Almost from the time I can remember, I've wanted to be a lawyer like Dad. I've always adored Mum, and I idealized each of my sisters at different times too, but it was Dad I wanted to emulate. When he realized I was serious, he let me in on his world in all kinds of ways. Took me to his office. Showed me briefs. Told me stuff he never told the others about the criminal underworld, about big corporations and the behind-the-scenes world of politics and business. If he has a particularly interesting case I often go down to the courts to listen to him. When I do, I'm sometimes so proud of him that I get a mad urge to stand up and tell everyone in the courtroom that they're listening to *my* father. I almost choke with pride—I'm not kidding—he's that good.

He is never nasty when he's interrogating a witness, never sarcastic or rude or overly personal, just sharp and logical and relentless with detail. I particularly love hearing him sum up a case. Even if it's something I don't understand, like a big corporate takeover or a business scam where the legal language is so technical that it's virtually indecipherable, I still enjoy it. He walks up and down in front of the jury, talking to them quietly in exactly the same warm, intimate way he talks to us. It's a gift, I reckon, and I'm nervous about not having it when my turn comes.

He always takes me out for coffee afterward, or for lunch if he has time, and he'll introduce me to other lawyers.

"You'll be seeing her around here in a few years," he tells them with a twinkle in his eyes—even when I was only thirteen and in my school uniform. They'd smile and nod kindly and pat me on the head. But Dad meant it. Then and now. He has always taken me seriously. I think he is tickled pink that one of his girls is going to follow in his footsteps. Especially with me being the "surprise" and all. Not that they rub it in, but Hilda remembers Mum saying that three kids made a perfect family. Well, I'm number four. It would have been better for them if I'd been a boy, I guess . . . but here I am, a fourth girl, and there's not much anyone can do about it.

Dad puts his glass on the sink and slips out of the room, leaving us all quiet for a moment, listening to his feet climbing the stairs.

"Mum won't appreciate being interrupted," Cynthia says softly, frowning. "She's trying to organize a temporary visa for that Sudanese family."

Mum teaches English to newly arrived migrants and refugees. She brings work home sometimes and has her own little office upstairs, all set up with a phone, fax, desk, and filing cabinets. But if the rest of us are home, she brings her work downstairs. She likes to be right in the middle of whatever is happening.

She tends to get very involved with her students, and sometimes this is a complete drag for the rest of us. She is always bringing people home. Once we had an Afghan family of six living in the front living room for nearly a month. Crying babies, wailing music, weird food—way too much, actually. But that kind of thing is an exception. Usually people stay for a few days until proper accommodation comes up, and they're incredibly grateful and polite. So it's no big deal.

Dad's got this huge profile as a left-wing lawyer. He's always being interviewed on the radio and is asked to speak for different causes, like prison reform, union rights, or detention centers. On the other hand, the family's wealth comes from him representing the big end of town in their financial dealings, and he's quite open about that. Company takeovers, industrial litigation, property developments—that sort of thing.

"I wouldn't be able to do the important stuff if I didn't take on the boring jobs to finance it," he often says, a bit mischievously. But I think he secretly loves it all. The law is endlessly interesting to him.

"I'm off." Hilda stands up. "Got to pick up the twins."

"Has Ryan's tooth come through yet?" Cynthia asks.

"Nope." Hilda sighs, her face crumbling a bit in that exhausted, resigned smile that so many young mothers seem to have. "We've been up all night."

The *we* would be Hilda and baby Ryan. I doubt Dave, the mighty gladiator, would be part of anything as lowly as sore gums in the middle of the night. Not when there was a million bucks to be made the next day. But I shouldn't be so bitchy. His work creates a brilliant lifestyle for my sister. They have the most stunning converted warehouse to live in, full of fantastic stuff. They have a beach house, and they go on amazing holidays. Hilda is a fully qualified architect and could have an army of nannies if she wanted, but she chooses not to. "I don't want strangers looking after my babies!" she tells her girlfriends who are already back at work and urging her to do the same. "I love looking after the boys." But Ryan and Cormac take their toll. Hilda is the least robust of us, and she often looks completely beat.

"I've got tomorrow morning off," Cynthia says suddenly. "Let me have them for a few hours."

Hilda's face slowly brightens. "Really?"

"Of course! Plan something."

"I think I'll just go to sleep!"

"I'll help too," Dorothy chimes in.

"And I'll be home from work in the afternoon," I say. "I can take over then."

So you see, in spite of all our differences, when push comes to shove, we help each other out.

We can't hear what they are saying, but our parents' raised voices are audible through the door. A bit unusual. Our parents hardly ever argue. Instinctively, the four of us wait for them to come bursting into the kitchen. But soon we hear the front door slam and, not long after that, the car starting outside. We look at each other. Dad must have gone out again, but it's odd that he didn't come in to say goodbye. A couple of doors slam upstairs, and then there is the creaking of the pipes at the side of the house as water runs into the old claw-foot bath. We grin at each other. A bath is Mum's tried-and-true way to ease tension. If she gets stressed or has an argument with someone, she'll stay in the bath for an hour, and then come back downstairs completely revived.

"They must have had a fight," Hilda murmurs with a wry smile.

◆ ◆ ◆

THE NEXT DAY, I'm walking home from my summer job at a local café, eating an ice cream, and I run into that guy again, the one from the student house down the street. When I see him walking toward me, carrying a plastic bag of groceries, I turn away and pretend I don't see him. It's embarrassing being caught stuffing my face. But he approaches anyway.

"Hey!" he says.

"Oh, hello!" I fake surprise. He's caught me slurping a chocolate-chip doubleheader like a greedy dog. I should have gotten a single cone, but free ice cream (any kind we want!) at the end of a six-hour shift is the one perk of my horrible job. All through the long, hot hours dealing with boring, patronizing, inconsiderate people, I'd been consoling myself with thoughts of four scoops instead of two. This guy looks at it dripping onto my hands and is obviously amused.

"Hate ice cream, do you?"

I find myself blushing. Cynthia is right. He is very good-looking! How could she tell from that distance and through the trees? Straight nose, wide face, and big, perfect smile. Lots of money has been spent on those teeth. I know because it was the same with mine. My mouth was so full of plated silver bars and wires I could barely talk, much less eat anything but mush, for about four years. Dressed in a snow-white T-shirt, long cotton beach pants, and flip-flops, he looks completely comfortable inside his tall, muscular body. A mite edgy though, moving his weight from one foot to the other, as if he might sprint off at any minute. Part of me wishes he would. I'm in my sweaty black T-shirt, short black skirt, and plain sandals. My long dark hair, which is usually my best feature, is greasy and tied back in an elastic band, and I haven't plucked my eyebrows for yonks. I remember the conversation with my sisters the day before. I'm meant to say something sassy at this point, so . . . I have a go.

"I've been in the coal mines," I say, "and this is the inducement to go down again tomorrow."

"Say no more." He grins again, looking right at me this time. "You heading home?" I nod, and we begin to walk off together. Relief washes through me. It's much easier not looking directly at someone you find attractive, at least when they're paying attention to you.

"Want some?" I ask politely, for something to say. I hold out my ice cream, not thinking for a moment that he'll take me up on the offer because it's so obviously been slurped over by me.

"Thanks." He stops, puts his hand over mine, and takes a big suck of my ice cream, on both sides. He leaves his hand on mine for a second longer than he needs to. I'm too surprised to feel pleased. But I do get a zap of something that feels like electricity shooting up my legs.

"I was hoping I'd run into you again," he says suddenly.

What? I'm now seriously overcome with shyness. How do you respond to something like that? I frantically try to imagine what Cynthia or Dorothy would say. Should it be, *Oh yeah, me too*, or something more cool and offhand like, *Oh really? Are you hard up for friends?*

In the end, I cough and pretend I don't hear him.

"So you liked that school?" he asks. I turn and look at him in surprise. I don't remember mentioning what school I went to.

"I've seen you in your school uniform," he says, as though reading my thoughts. I do my best to ignore the rather flattering realization that he must have noticed me well before I'd set eyes on him.

"No, I hated it," I say. "Right from the start, I hated it. I don't know why I stayed there for so long."

"Really?" He seems surprised. "Why?"

Damn. I wish he hadn't asked me that! I don't know him well enough to go into details. Then I think, *What the hell? All those magazines tell you to be yourself.* Okay. I take a breath. Go for broke. Be myself. What is there to lose?

"There was a very tense social scene there," I say, then take a fresh mouthful of ice cream to give myself an extra second or two to come up with something lighter. "I didn't like it at all. Too many little Britney look-alikes for me."

"So why did you stay?" he asks, frowning seriously.

"Well, I won a scholarship, and . . ." I shrug, wishing like hell I hadn't brought up the Britney thing. He probably loves that blond, cute, bubbly look. What guy doesn't? How do you do this stuff? All I've done so far is sound like a twisted, jealous bitch. "And I guess I wanted to do well, so I ended up staying," I mumble on. "My best friend was there, too. I mean, it was good from the academic point of view." My voice is trailing away stupidly. "I guess."

"My sister went to that school."

"Is she still there?" I ask very politely, thinking *please* make her an *older* sister who went there ten years ago! Or at the very least make her a seventh grader. Someone I couldn't possibly know.

"No, she's just finished too," he says. "Like you."

"Oh?" I smile to show that I think that's a pleasant coincidence. But I'm desperate to change the subject because I've got this sinking feeling I'm going to find out something really unpleasant. At least make her one of the nerds or a sporty type who was completely oblivious to what really went on. Within the social hierarchy, I mean. I search around for something to say.

"Did she like it?" I ask weakly.

"Yeah, she loved it."

I nod as though that is a perfectly reasonable answer.

"Alisha," he says shortly, then quickly flings one arm out to stop me from walking straight into busy traffic. "Alisha Cummins."

Alisha Cummins! Oh shit! If any girl epitomized all that I hated about that place, it was Alisha Cummins. Not only did she look and play the part of the teen queen, gushy and insincere, but under all that, she was nasty. Most of her friends were not all that bright. They tittered and giggled and played along with whatever they thought was the current definition of cool. But Alisha *was* bright, and she ruled. Fair and tall, with perfect skin, she must have done a lot of ballet when she was younger because she moved like a swan. She and her cronies gave it to anyone who didn't toe the line.

"You know her?"

"Yeah, I know her," I say, feeling flat and dull now. *My luck, huh? Within the first five minutes of meeting this attractive guy, I find out he's closely related to someone I loathe.* "Your sister is . . . *not* my favorite person," I say quietly. We've turned into my street now, and I just want to get away from him. I know it probably seems like an overreaction, as if I've caught a dose of my sisters' theatrics, but even the mention of that girl brings up such a . . . taste in my mouth. I'm not good at pretense.

"She's got big problems," her brother goes on, uneasily.

"Really?" I almost laugh and try to imagine Alisha's problems. A gap in her diary? Not enough suntan oil? Daddy put his foot down about a spending spree?

50

"Yeah," he sighs, "she's got a lot of stuff to work out."

"Well, I guess we're all in the same boat there," I mumble, not looking at him. "Got to rush now. See you around."

"Why?" I see he is genuinely startled, but I don't care and start to walk off.

"Why do you have to go?" he calls after me. I stop and turn around. "Why do you have to rush?"

I hesitate, and say the first thing that comes into my head: "I've got to do something for my mum."

"What exactly?" He's amused now. He can tell I'm lying, and it's embarrassing. But I can't backtrack without losing more face.

"My turn to cook dinner."

"Gee, you must eat early."

It's about three in the afternoon. I feel myself flushing all over again. I hardly ever blush, and I've done it twice within the last ten minutes.

"Yeah. Special dinner," I mumble, not meeting his eyes. There is an awkward pause. "Complicated dishes."

"I'm not my sister, you know," he says.

I don't know what to say to that. Part of me knows it's completely fair enough, but I stand there looking around like a kid caught doing something naughty. He comes over and stands in front of me again.

"I don't even know your name," he says softly.

"Rose O'Neil," I mutter.

"Well, I'm Nathaniel." He holds out his hand, and what can I do but take it? "Everyone just calls me Nat," he goes on. "We're having a house-warming party next Friday, and I want you to come."

"Why?" I pull my hand away, shocked. I so don't want to go to his friggin' party! Then I look over to our house, where Mum is walking through the front gate with a bundle of books under her arm. She waves gaily before disappearing into the house, and I almost groan because I know I'll be in for another sisterly advice session as soon as I'm inside.

"A lot of reasons," he says, "but one big one." I look up, curious, and he smiles. "The first time I saw you, Rose O'Neil, you were riding your bike through the Edinburgh Gardens in red boots, your hair was flying out behind you, and you were . . . singing. You had this kind of . . . defiance about you. I thought to myself, *Jeez, that is one cool chick. I'd like to get to know her."*

I am actually touched by this admission, but I quickly squash the feeling. So . . . I sing on my bike. *Big deal!* I'm glad he saw me in Cynthia's red boots, though. I love those boots. I pinch them when I know she won't be home.

"You saw me," I say in a bored voice, not meeting his eyes, "but did you hear me?" I can hold a tune and that is about it. My singing voice is thin and ordinary. Anyway, I'm not stupid. Some guys are experts at these cute little flattering tactics.

"Yeah, I heard you."

"Poor you," I say.

"My sister won't be there," he pleads with a grin. "She's in Sydney."

"You're in a different crowd than me," I say. "I'm just out of school. I probably wouldn't fit in."

"You'll fit in."

"What makes you so sure?" In fact, Alisha's presence was a huge issue for me. Now I know that she won't be there, I wouldn't mind going. He grins and shakes his head as though he can't work me out but thinks I'm funny anyway.

"I just know it," he whispers. I look up to see if he's serious, and he gives me one of his charming grins. "If you don't like it, then it's not as though you're going to have to go far to get home."

"Well, maybe I will," I say, edging away. He leans forward and touches my hand briefly.

"Say you'll come? Between eight and nine on Friday. The big corner house, right?"

"Okay."

♦ ♦ ♦

I DON'T FINALLY DECIDE to go to the party until about an hour before it's due to begin. All afternoon I tell myself there are a million reasons not to go. For a start, I won't know anyone. Second, I hate his sister. Third, he has to be fake because he's way too good-looking, and fourth . . . At about this point I know I'm scraping the barrel. Too good-looking? Come on, Rose!

Of course, the sisters won't let me go out in the boring outfit I had in mind. Dorothy takes charge and I have to say that, when she is done, I walk out that door feeling . . . pretty good. But nervous, too. Afraid that I've overdone it. My hair is tied back in a tight knot, they've smeared aqua and gold shadow around my eyes, and my body is packed into this really gorgeous little purple skirt. More like a square of sequined material, actually. Dot knows how to drape it around my hips and pin it just so. On top, I'm wearing a black silk blouse of Cynthia's that she found in a thrift shop, which has tiny buttons down the front and a wide, low, embroidered neckline. Under the skirt, I'm wearing lace tights that stop at the ankles. I refuse to wear Cynthia's stilettos because I know I'll fall over in them, so, much to their disappointment, I settle on my black ballet flats.

The whole look is way too exotic for me, but for some reason—very unusual for me—I let the sisters take over. I leave the house feeling excited. Not that it translates into confidence as I walk up the street toward that thumping electronic sound—the kind of music I really hate, but never mind. This is a student party. What if I am way overdressed? What if they all look at me and snigger, *Who the hell is the try-hard?*

I have to force myself not to turn back.

But there is no need to worry. I walk in the front gate and he is standing near the doorway, talking to a couple of guys and three girls. He pulls away from his friends and jumps down from the porch onto the grass.

"Hey, Rose!" he says warmly, as if he really is pleased to see me. "I was hoping you'd come."

"Thanks." I smile at him. He takes a step back and grins.

"Wow! You look . . . different!" I smile gamely. "Really good," he adds quickly. I can tell he means it, so I give a little prayer of thanks for the sisters, glad now that they'd made me dress up. I sense the little crowd behind us eyeing me up and down curiously, but I don't dare turn to them.

"Yeah, well . . ."

He laughs, takes my elbow, and steers me inside. We pass more people, and I get more looks. I'm not used to this. I tend to dress way down. I make a point of not calling attention to myself. As we get farther down the wide passageway and into the hub of the house, the music—bland electronic filler that is Muzak as far as I'm concerned—gets louder and louder. By the time we hit the huge crowded living room, we're shouting at each other.

"So, this is it." He waves at the posters on the tattered papered walls, and the DJ with all his equipment in the corner. "Our house. We've been cleaning up all day for this. What do you reckon?"

"Great." I smile. "When did you move in?"

"About four months ago. But we all had exams, so we couldn't have a party till now."

"Who else lives here?"

"There are five of us." He points to a plump girl with red hair sitting on one of the couches. "Mally!" She hears her name and looks over. "That's Mal, everyone's pal."

"Get lost, Cummins," she shouts, and gives me a wave.

"And Luke and Pete." Nat points to two guys who are doing something to the lighting system in the corner. "And there's Petra. Her room is out the back." He takes my elbow again and leads me through the throng, out to a big, bright kitchen. Fewer people are out here and most of them are busy organizing food and drinks.

"We're all students," Nat explains, "like most of the people here, actually." He grimaces. "Bit boring, huh?"

I'm surprised by this. *Boring?* I don't know what he means. I can't wait for university.

"At least you've got something in common," I mumble lamely.

"Too much." He frowns briefly as he pulls glasses from a brown cardboard box. "I like to mix with different people." He gestures at everyone in the room. "We all went to private schools. We're all white and Anglo and basically from rich backgrounds." He looks directly at me in a kind of challenging way and then smiles self-consciously. "Well . . . richish. Upper middle class. Know what I mean?"

"Yeah, I do," I say, surprised. "I know exactly what you mean."

"Drink?"

"Oh, sorry!" I remember the bottle back in the fridge at home. "I should have . . ."

"Hey," he laughs, "we've got plenty. What'll you have?"

Nat is the host, or one of them, so I'm expecting that after introducing me to a few people, he'll be off any minute to get drinks, greet friends, and generally do what has to be done. There are a lot of people here, and a lot of drinks to pour. He does it all—with ease—but keeps coming back to me, explaining who people are and where they fit in, introducing me, asking me bits and pieces about my family and work. After about an hour, with my second glass of Stoli in my hand, I realize with a rush of heady delight that this totally charming, genuine, fantastic-looking guy is actually interested in *me*.

A new crowd arrives, and there are more introductions, more jokes, and more drinks offered. Mally comes in and puts trays of little pies in the oven.

"Half an hour"—she punches Nat's arm—"and we'll serve these."

"Sure," he agrees. "Let's go out the back," he says to me, grabbing my hand.

So we take our drinks out into the soft still night, park ourselves on the old slatted seat, and he rolls himself a cigarette.

"Smart girl," he says when I refuse one.

"How long have you smoked?"

"Couple of years." He takes a drag and sends the smoke out into the night air. "But I'm gonna give it up soon."

"That's what everyone says." I smile.

"I started when I was at home," he muses. "My little rebellion against the old man's rule. He absolutely hates cigarettes."

"Do you see them much?"

"About once a week. Mum would go to pieces if it was any less," he sighs. "I go home for Sunday lunch usually.

"I just got so sick of it," he says when we get into why he moved away from home, "family breathing down my neck the whole time."

I nod and try to imagine moving out myself, then back away from the idea so fast it's scary. My family breathes down my neck the whole time, too. Does this make me a cowardly, dependent person?

"Maybe they breathe in a totally different way from mine." Nat grins when I try to explain. "Sounds to me like you all get on."

"Yeah, we do," I say, frowning a bit, "but my sisters are on my case the whole time. I mean it. It does get annoying."

"I just had to." His mouth is tense, and I get a strong sense that the decision to move out might have been pretty fraught. "Even though home is the more comfortable option."

"There is something admirable about moving out, away from your comfort zone," I say seriously.

"Well, I'm glad you find something admirable about me." He smiles into my eyes and I blush a bit because he's flirting and I don't quite know where to look. So I look at my watch and laugh.

"And I've only known you an hour," I quip.

"Just think what you're going to find out in the *next* hour!"

"What? You've got more . . . admirable qualities up your sleeve?" I go all wide-eyed and innocent.

"Too right!" he says. We are both laughing now. "Hang around, babe! There is no end to my admirable qualities."

Hey! I think. *I can do this. I'm getting good at it.*

Nat and I are getting on so well that, amazingly enough, I more or less forget about the Alisha factor. When he tells me about his two older brothers and one younger sister—all of them intent on pleasing their father, a magistrate—I simply nod and listen to what he tells me, forgetting for a moment that this is a family that Zoe and I used to wonder about and ridicule. Oh sure, Alisha is there in the back of my head. I know who he's talking about when he says in passing that his parents actually encourage his little sister to get sucked into all the materialistic crap that he hates, but I conveniently push it to the side.

I can hear the party heating up inside. In spite of the crappy music, I want to go back in there and dance, but he seems keen to keep talking.

"So, tell me about yourself, Rose," he says. "What are you hoping to do?"

I can hardly believe this, but within a few minutes I'm, like, spilling all the beans. I'm appalled with myself—*even while I'm doing it*—but I can't seem to stop! I've never had a nice guy pay me any attention before, so it's the novelty factor, I guess. When we're out together, Zoe is the one they all talk to. She knows how to tease and flirt and get them feeling good, and . . . that's okay. I honestly don't mind.

So even though I've only had two drinks, I start telling him everything.

About Dad the lawyer and how great he is. About wanting to be a lawyer myself. About all those egotistical dreams of doing important work: walking the world stage as an ambassador for the UN, or working in the Third World with Amnesty International. And I don't stop there. I tell him my views on international politics. What's happening in the Middle East. Asia. Africa. He doesn't look at me while I'm talking, just sits there staring up at the sky, smoking while I rave on.

At last I stop and still he looks up and says nothing. *God, this is excruciating! I've bored him into a stupor!* I mentally kick myself. Forget about all those smart, wily tricks of Zoe's; *any* halfway intelligent girl knows you shouldn't blab on about yourself! I am about to apologize, to at least backtrack a little and try to inject a bit of humor into the conversation, when he turns to me.

"You'll do it," he declares with one of his slow smiles.

"I might not even get into university!" I snort derisively. "I can't believe I just . . . said all that stuff! It's so embarrassing. I mean . . ."

"One way or another, you'll do it," he declares again, very seriously, "and so will I. We'll both get to where we want to be."

"How do you know?"

"I just do."

This is my cue to ask him about his ambitions, his dreams. I'm about to do this when he leans over and kisses me on the mouth.

Lightly, sweetly. Then he puts both his arms around me, draws me closer and does it again.

"Hey, Rose," he says into my ear, "you feel like a dance?"

"Yeah," I say. We both get up, and I'm glad that we're in the dark, because my legs feel incredibly wobbly. "I'd love to."

I take a look at my watch when we hit the light of the kitchen and start to laugh. He turns around.

"What are you laughing at?"

"It's only half past ten!"

"So?"

I just look back at him, and he starts laughing too.

"You're not used to picking up before midnight, eh?" He puts his arm around my waist and pulls me into the middle of the throng. "Is that it?"

"I'm not used to picking up at all," I shout back, but I don't think he hears me and maybe that's just as well. Some guy is screaming into his other ear about noise level complaints from next door.

Once inside and among the crowd, I suddenly don't give a damn about the crud music. I just want to dance. He's the same. So we go for it, big-time. Moving in and out around the others a bit, showing off, smiling, and always ending up together. When the music stops, we hug each other, breathless and sweaty, laughing into each other's faces.

Just after midnight she arrives, like a magical moment in a horror film, a black version of the Cinderella story. Instead of the fairy godmother, the evil witch appears. Nat looks over my shoulder, frowns, his attention caught, so I turn around. Alisha is in the doorway with two friends from last year standing on either side of her like bodyguards. Alisha, Ingrid, and Sally Crawley, all of them staring at us.

"My sister." Nat gives a wave, picks up my hand, and, in spite of the fact that I pull back, insists on dragging me through the crowd over to where she is standing. Unfortunately, just at that moment the music stops.

"Nat!" Her eyes sweep over me before going straight back to her brother's face.

"I thought you were in Sydney," he says, pecking her cheek in a perfunctory way.

"Came back early."

"This is Rose." Nat introduces me with a smile, still holding my hand.

"We know Rose," Alisha says, not even pretending to smile.

Nat hesitates, as though perplexed more than anything. He's obviously forgotten! The tension is so taut for a couple of seconds that I almost blurt it out myself. Just to get it over with. But I manage to hold back.

"Alisha," I say calmly. Although I am completely rattled, I know it would be suicide to let it show, so I stare straight back into her eyes as though there is nothing even vaguely odd about the situation. She gives one of her breathy, hollow laughs.

"What . . . are you doing *here*?"

"Your brother invited me," I say lightly.

"When did you two meet?" Ingrid pipes up, sounding seriously affronted. I almost laugh. Silly little Ingrid! God, I can see her standing outside the seniors' locker room, squealing appreciatively at some sick joke Alisha has just made at some other girl's expense. The ultimate hanger-on. She can't help herself. Brain-dead. This will give her something to talk about for the next year.

"Rose lives up the road." Nat has just picked up the vibe. He points to the kitchen. "Make yourselves at home"— he tightens his grip on my hand—"then come and dance." With that he pulls me back into the throng of dancers.

"Hey, I'm sorry." Nat pulls me closer. "I told you she wouldn't be here."

"It's okay," I say shortly. I keep telling myself, *It's okay*. But the whole spark of being here has disappeared. And it must show on my face, because he lifts up my chin with one hand.

"What's up?"

"Nothing . . . really." I try to laugh.

"There is."

He looks so concerned that I do laugh, and it suddenly all seems so ridiculous that I want to get away. Why get into such a flap about someone you've only known for a couple of hours! I look at my watch, but he beats me to it.

"You're not going?"

"I have work tomorrow," I say. "I'll be wrecked as it is."

"Is this like having to cook the dinner?" He smiles.

"No. Really," I laugh with embarrassment, "I have to get up at six."

"I'll walk you home then."

This surprises me. About to tell him that of course he shouldn't and that he must stay to look after his guests, I stop myself. Walking out on his arm will look a lot better in front of his sister. I won't have to feel like a cowering dog crawling away to lick my wounds. Yeah, this is a good idea. Let him walk me home.

"Okay," I say.

Once we're outside, the mood shifts again. Upward this time, amazingly. Within a few minutes of being out on the street, the little scene with Alisha fades away. Nat takes my hand and we walk over to my place, talking about nothing much, but laughing easily. It's a beautiful night. Warm without being hot. The big, fat yellow moon riding high in the darkness makes me lighthearted. I begin to sing softly under my breath. Some old Beatles thing. "Lucy in the Sky with Diamonds." He joins in, and we laugh, trying to remember the words.

"What is it with you and my sister?" he asks after a while.

"You want the long version or the short one?" I say lightly.

"Any one you care to tell."

It takes me only two seconds to decide not to tell him about my best friend, Zoe, getting picked on and me getting into a fight with his sister in the locker room. *But what will I say?*

"We had a falling out," I say at last.

"About . . .?"

"You're persistent, aren't you?" I smile at him. He nods, waiting for me to go on, but I don't. We're almost home now. I can see my parents' light on upstairs. I wonder what's keeping them up so late. At the gate he pulls me nearer.

"You want to go out soon, Rose?"

"Yeah," I say, thinking, *What the hell*. Of course it won't happen because once he's back at the party, he'll find some other, prettier girl. But that doesn't mean I can't kiss him this once, does it? When he pulls me closer, I put my arms around him, push my face into his neck, and take a deep breath. "I'd love to, actually."

"Okay."

That night, on the pathway outside my home, I find out the true meaning, purpose, and *importance* of kissing. I'd kissed one or two guys before, of course, but this is something else. One minute I'm so revved up I feel as though I'm going to burst out of my skin, then I sink seamlessly into this dreamy blissful state of no thought at all. It's like listening to music. All the highs and lows, and little riffs of melody, the low insistent drumbeat under it all. My neck and arms, mouth and face tingle with a million new sensations, hot one minute, chilly, raw, and tender the next. *This is enough*, I think. *Even if I die in an accident tomorrow, I have experienced something wonderful.*

I pass my dad on my way upstairs. He's on his way down but doesn't stop.

"Good party?" he asks, with one of his tired, distracted smiles. I notice the hunched shoulders and dark shadows under his eyes. "There's a message from Zoe on the answering machine," he adds.

"Really?" She wasn't due back from New South Wales until next week. "You look tired, Dad."

But he only gives me a wave and disappears into the kitchen.

I walk back downstairs to the hall phone and press the message button.

"Rose! Couldn't stand it. Came back early. I'm at Mum's now, going out of my mind. I want to see you soon. Can I come over? Ring me back as soon as you get this. As soon as you can!"

I look at my watch. It's after two a.m. I can't ring now. So I decide to ring in the morning. Then I run upstairs to my bedroom, elated. Zoe is back. I'm dying to talk to her. Tell her all about . . . everything.

◆ ◆ ◆

I WAKE UP AT SIX to answer the phone. It's work calling to say they don't need me until midafternoon. *Thanks a lot, guys.* I go back to bed and sleep happily through till ten. When I do get up and go down to the kitchen, I get the weird feeling of being on a deserted ship. The back door is wide open, the radio is blaring about some up-and-coming politician being loyal to the party, there are dirty dishes all over the table, and the garbage can is overflowing in the corner. No sign of anyone. Strange, but it suits me just fine. The last thing I want is an interrogation session about the party.

I shut the back door, turn off the radio, switch on the kettle, throw a couple of pieces of bread in the toaster and start slowly and happily loading the dishwasher. I'm a bit nervous, too. Did all that actually happen last night? I decide I need to talk about it to make it real somehow. *Zoe.* Yeah, I'll ring her as soon as I've had something to eat.

"Rose?" Dorothy's voice calling loudly from upstairs gives me a start.

"Yeah."

"Come up here."

"Why?" I yell back, irritated.

"Just come! *Now.*"

Believe me, I don't normally respond to commands like that from any of my sisters, but there is something about her tone that makes me think that this time, I'd better. I bound up the stairs two at a time.

"Where are you?" I call when I see she isn't in her room.

"Mum's study," she answers sharply.

"What are you doing in here?" I ask, pushing open the door. I stop in the doorway. Mum is curled up in the corner, almost under the desk, hands over her face, sobbing uncontrollably. Dot is squatting nearby, arm around Mum's shoulders, stroking her hair.

"What the hell . . .?" I kneel down next to them. But Dot shrugs and shakes her head. She takes a handful of soggy tissues out of Mum's hands and gives her a pile of fresh ones from the box on top of the desk. Then she just sits there patting Mum's hair.

"Should I get her a cup of tea?" I whisper. Ridiculous, I know, but it's the only useful thing I can think to do, apart from running a bath. Dot nods, so I run downstairs to the kitchen. The phone rings as I busy myself boiling the water and setting out cups, but I ignore it.

◆　◆　◆

The tea goes cold. Dot and I sit next to Mum for more than ten minutes before she even looks up. I have never seen my mother like this. There's drama in our house every day, but this is different. My mind is jumping from one thing to another, and I latch on to the worst I can imagine. Her favorite brother has been killed in a car crash. Mum has three older brothers that she absolutely adores, but Kieran is the one closest to her in age, the one she loves best. Perhaps he's had an accident? Or been diagnosed with some terrible disease?

"We'll help, Mum," Dot murmurs for the tenth time, as Mum pushes her face back into her hands. "Just tell us."

"No one can help!" Mum sobs.

"Yes we can!"

Eventually she sits up. Takes her hands away from her face, leans across for a fistful of tissues, wipes her eyes, and then, with shaking hands, takes the glass of water from me and has a sip. A deep breath and she blows out hard.

"I can't say anything yet."

"Why not?"

"Your father wants us all together!"

"Please! Just tell us, Mum!"

"Well," she manages to whisper, "your father is leaving me. He's in love with another woman, and he is leaving me. Us. He is leaving this family."

Neither Dot nor I say a word. Shock, I suppose. The words just sort of hang there in the air between us. We look at each other without even breathing, then Dot turns back to Mum.

"No," she whispers, quite firmly. "Not true," and I breathe a sigh of relief. Even Dot, who is so susceptible to crazy ideas, doesn't believe it. Mum continues to cry and Dot and I stare at each other, hardly blinking. Mum slumps down again and curls into a fetal position, facing the wall. Then she begins to moan and rock herself like some traumatized kid on television.

"What should we do?" I mouth quietly.

"I'll ring Hilda," Dot whispers.

"Okay. And I'll make fresh tea?" Dot nods. The cups I brought up before are stone cold. But neither of us moves. We both stay sitting there, numbly, for another five minutes, trying to soothe Mum. We rub her back and pat her hair and try to get her to sit up and talk more, but she won't move and won't talk. She lies there, moaning and trembling like a sick animal.

It's a bright afternoon by the time Cynthia finds us. We've drawn the curtains to keep the heat out, but shafts of sunlight sneak in through the top of the window. They bounce off a glass vase on the desk, making fluttering blue-

and-white patterns on the walls. I tell Cynthia quietly what Mum has told us, and she frowns skeptically.

"They've had a row," she pronounces matter-of-factly. Dot and I nod furiously, both of us, I think, hoping that for once, Miss Know-it-all knows something worth knowing. But by this stage I'm seriously freaked out and . . . I'm not so sure anymore that it isn't true. Little glimmers of doubt seep through my earlier conviction that Mum is throwing a wobbly. That she has somehow got it fundamentally wrong. *Could my father really be leaving her? But they've been married forever!* My mind jams up when I try to get my head around it.

Then the door is pushed open, and Hilda is there, a frown clouding her face.

"Dad needs to see us all, urgently," she blurts out straightaway. "I've got someone minding the twins for an hour. Any idea where Mum is?" Then she notices Mum's prone body by the wall and goes still. *"Mum?"* She looks at us accusingly, as though we are the cause.

"What the hell is going on?" she demands.

"Dad says he's leaving," Dot whispers.

"Where's he going?" Hilda snaps.

"He's leaving Mum," I say brutally. "Leaving us."

Hilda's whole body slumps. She lets out a low moan as her legs crumple beneath her. In the process she manages to hit her head on the edge of the heater. When she pulls her hand away, there is blood on her fingers.

"Get some ice," Cynthia orders. Hilda nods but doesn't move. Just kneels there with her hand on her sore head, rocking back and forth. So now it's the four of us with our mother, and none of us has a clue what to do.

That's where Dad finds us, up in Mum's study. As soon as he walks in and turns on the light, I know it is true. I do pray that it might be some other terrible thing making him look like he's just been run over by a steamroller. But I know, even as the words are racing through my head, that things are just as Mum told us.

He stands in the doorway, his face drawn and his shirt and pants all rumpled, like he's been sleeping in the car for a week.

"I'm so sorry, girls," he says in a raw, desperate voice. "There is no easy way to tell you this. But . . . I am going to leave your mother."

Mum hears him, rolls over, stops crying, sits up, and takes another handful of Dot's tissues. She is trembling all over as she stares at him.

"I want you all to know that I'm not doing this lightly. I've thought long and hard about it. But I . . . love somebody else. And in case you're thinking . . . it's just an affair. No. I have found the woman I want to live with for the rest of my life."

Mum gives a low, guttural moan but continues staring at him through her red, wet eyes.

"Dad!" Cynthia stands up quickly and yells, "You can't do this! Not to Mum!"

He holds up his hand to silence her.

"I want you to know that I love you girls very much and I always will and . . . that your mother is a wonderful woman." Then *he* begins to cry. Tears rush down his cheeks. "She *is* a wonderful woman," he says again, "but I don't love her. At least not in the way a man should love a woman."

I am truly amazed by all this. I've never seen my father cry before. Not ever. Not even when his brother died, and that was the saddest I'd ever seen him. There is silence. I don't know how long it goes on. All I know is I can hear Mum's old clock ticking on the desk. I look at my sisters, and they are all, like Mum, staring at Dad.

"Do any of you want to say anything?" he gasps, looking around at each of us in turn. "Ask me anything?" None of us speaks. I think we're all hoping that one of us will say something really sharp and pithy, something that will stun him into seeing reason and make him change his mind. There are a million thoughts flying through my head, but I have no clear idea of what to say. Then a coherent sentence does come to me. *Who is she?* I want to scream, but I can't get my mouth to open around the words.

"Well then, I'll go now," he says quietly, turning away, "but I'll be back soon. I'll ring. I'll see you all *very soon.*" He is almost out the door when my mother scrambles to her feet.

"Don't do this, Justus," she screams hoarsely, beseeching him with both arms. "We have been married for twenty-eight years! I am the mother of your children! I beg you, *please* don't leave me! I'll die!"

I'll die! I'll die! I'll die!

My father stops in the doorway and slowly turns around to look at her. I catch pity on his face, then a flickering mess of sorrow and tenderness. A froth of hope rises in my chest. He is wavering, on the brink of turning back. But he straightens his shoulders and his face hardens.

"You won't die, Patsy," he says quietly. "You're a strong woman. You have many people who love you," then his voice cracks as he whispers the last words, "justifiably. Many people who love you."

Then he's gone.

♦ ♦ ♦

ROAD TRIP

I have my first glimpse of the ocean in more than a year. We're chugging behind an RV through Torquay, and when we round that bend it's there, and I'm surprised at how moved I am just by the sight of it. A shimmering vast expanse of bright blue wedged up against the light sunny sky. I turn to Mum, but she is looking out the side window, her face turned away. I can see by the hunch of her shoulders that something is getting to her, and I have a moment of foreboding. It's been very quiet between us since Geelong. What happened back there after we drank our coffee? Did I miss something? Did I say something?

Only eleven in the morning and it's hot already.

"I'll stop at Lorne," I say, "maybe have a swim. You want to?"

"Yes." She begins drumming the fingers of one hand on her knee. "Maybe I will." She shifts in her seat and keeps drumming with her fingers. It makes me edgy because I know she's got something on her mind. But I stop short of asking because her answer is likely to make me more than edgy. We are crawling along behind the RV and I'm starting to feel claustrophobic.

"Rose, I just wish that . . ."

"Don'tcha just hate RVs?" I cut her off recklessly. "I reckon they should be wiped off the face of the earth!"

We've been behind this monster for about fifteen minutes. There is a pause. I can almost hear her collecting her thoughts to have another go at me.

"We all miss you," she says. "You're living out there in that godforsaken place. With people you don't know or like. And none of us really understands why."

"Us?" I say lightly, but I'm playing for time. *How come I thought I'd be able to evade this? Mum and I locked up in a car for six hours, and we talk about how nice the weather is? Yeah, right. What the fuck was I thinking?* I start chewing the inside of my mouth.

What she says is true, of course. I'm living in a terrible old rundown place, grimy and ugly, with two guys I met at a pub one night. They needed someone to share the rent, and it seemed a good idea at the time. Turned out to be not such a good idea at all, but I don't care that much. I don't care about a lot of things that I used to care about. It's that simple.

"Your sisters and me," she explains, "and your father, too, Rose. He tells me he never sees you."

Even this quick mention of my father triggers an instant ache in my chest. I want to ask her if she talks to Dad often, and what about? What does he say about me? It's true I hardly see him at all anymore. I avoid it.

"Lots of people leave home, Mum!" I try to sound in control. *What was I thinking, letting her come?* "Just because my sisters want to live at home forever doesn't mean I have to!"

"Wanting to leave home is . . . fine," she says carefully.

"So what's the problem?"

She gives me a hard, meaningful look that tells me I'm a completely fucked up person in all kinds of ways that she can't even talk about, which is probably true, but is *not* something I actually want to be reminded of on this beautiful blue summer morning, if you catch my drift. I cringe, in spite of myself.

"Why be a waitress?" she almost whispers. "With your brain?"

"Lots of people take a year off before going to university," I say airily.

Don'tcha just hate it . . . when your family doesn't understand that you've moved out to get away from them? And here they are visiting you with their cakes and potted plants and breezy gossip about the neighbors. Can't they tell you're not interested? And if they're not visiting, they're ringing. All those kind, caring phone calls that drive you crazy!

We're still crawling along behind the trailer, but inside I'm considering the possibility of moving abroad. As soon as I can get the money together! That would get them off my case and right out of my hair. They wouldn't be able to visit me then. Phone calls would be more expensive too.

"So, you're going to take up your place this year?" Mum asks, looking at me hopefully. When I hesitate, she sighs.

"Look!" I snap, "I don't know, all right?"

"But Rose," she exclaims, "it's all you've ever wanted!"

"People change!" I say.

"Have you changed?"

"What do you think?"

"You don't want to do law anymore?" she says disbelievingly.

I don't answer. In fact, I do want to do law. And yet . . . it's impossible now. Even though I only deferred and the place at university is still there with my name on it, I have this weird but very strong feeling that it doesn't belong to me anymore. It should go to someone else. Only fair. I know this doesn't make sense, so why talk about it?

"Rose, it isn't university that we're worried about," Mum says. "We know you're bright enough to do that when you're ready. We're all really worried for other reasons . . ."

"Would you mind speaking for yourself?" I say icily. "I can't stand the idea of the lot of you in cahoots against me!"

"*Against* you!" She sighs dramatically and starts waving her hands about. "No one is against you, Rose. We're all on your side, and—"

"I don't need anyone on my side," I snarl. "Just leave me be! This trip is turning into one big disaster!"

"Oh darling," she pleads loudly, "don't say that. I don't mean to harangue you!"

"Well, that's what you're doing!"

"I'm terribly sorry . . ." she says. "The last thing I want to do is make you feel bad. I just feel so guilty about what happened last year. I know I was a mess. And I . . . I couldn't help you at all. I was hopeless and . . . I relied on you too much. And your sisters! Oh Rose, I so much want to apologize for last year and all that happened!"

"Mum! Just stop it." My mouth hardly moves as I speak. "It wasn't your fault. Nothing *happened*."

"Plenty happened, Rose!"

"But the stuff that happened to me had nothing to do with you!"

"I'm sorry."

All this apologizing is almost as bad as her bringing it up. What am I meant to say? *Oh, don't worry. Let's go on like we used to. The fact that we're missing a few—Dad, Zoe, her father, and Nat Cummins just for starters—doesn't matter! That's beside the point.* Oh yeah? I almost say just that to shut her up. I look down at my hands on the steering wheel, knuckles white with tension. If I grip any tighter, they'll crack and fall right off. We've just passed through the town,

74

the traffic has eased up, and we're coming toward a hill. The RV in front of us has begun to *seriously* bug me. And we're not even halfway there yet!

"So, do you have any other plans for this year?" she asks lightly. "You could, you know, *try* university for six months and see if . . ." And then she stops midsentence because I'm doing something really stupid, but the sudden alarm on her face excites me and, for some weird, sick reason, makes me more determined to keep going.

I've pulled out over the double lines to pass the trailer. Big problem. My van doesn't have a lot of power, and there is a car coming straight at us from the opposite direction.

Mum gives a loud gasp. Then she starts shouting.

"Rose, *don't*! Stop! Pull back."

I have a moment to decide. Continue passing with the risk of a head-on collision or . . . pull back. I keep going, and the car coming toward me has to slow down and dodge onto the gravel and off the road to let me in. We only just make it. Horns blast angrily. In the mirror, I see that the same oncoming car has now pulled over and stopped and behind me the RV driver is shaking his fist and swearing at me. I'm shaking myself as I turn to Mum, who has gone white.

"Sorry," I say.

"My God!" she yells, breathing heavily, tight-lipped and trembling. "What the hell were you thinking?"

"I know. I know." I'm shocked myself, but I try not to let on. "Sorry again."

"If a cop saw you do that," she is screaming at me now, "you'd lose your license. And you'd deserve it!"

"I know," I mutter, the adrenaline still pumping wildly around my system.

"You could have *killed* us!" she adds. "And a whole lot of other innocent people!"

"Look, I know that!" I snarl. "I said sorry. Okay?"

"*Not* okay, Rose!" she fumes, crossing her arms tightly over her chest and hunching herself into her corner, closing herself off from me. "Not okay at all."

We are quiet for a while, both breathing heavily and trying to calm down. At least I am.

Do you have any plans for this year? That was the question I didn't want to answer. If I don't go to university, then the place no longer has my name on it. I'd have to apply all over again, and my future disappears even further into the distance.

◆ ◆ ◆

LAST SUMMER, MELBOURNE

The night before the results come out, I make a bargain with God: as long as Dad comes back, I am prepared to fail every single subject. This is a genuine offer. Not easy to make, either. In fact, I have to struggle with it because my schooling and my future career have been really important to me since I entered high school. I have to dig very deep and get it absolutely clear in my head that I'm not just offering ordinary or disappointing results. I mean out-and-out failure in every subject. I go through all the humiliation and disappointment of this scenario in great detail with every person I know (including Alisha Cummins) as I drift off to sleep. Yes, I decide. I am completely serious and prepared for it all. I will do the year again, or take the year off. I will change direction completely. I will work in a factory or a charity for very little money. In addition to this, I will have both legs broken in a car accident. Maybe one has to be cut off. When I'm over that, I will do whatever humiliating, boring, or soul-destroying job required to make Dad come back. In other words, I will give up my ambition, my dreams, my whole future.

I try to figure out another career path that I start in my thirties (after I've put in ten years at the factory and I'm suffering joint problems), and I come up with nursing, but only if I can keep the legs. By the time I'm drifting off to sleep, it's all starting to feel okay. In fact, I'm looking forward to it. *Please, God. Please.* Send Dad back, and I'll be a really good nurse.

I'm woken up at about ten a.m. on Monday by the smiling faces of my three sisters. I groan and turn to look at the clock.

"What the hell!" I say. Unlike the previous nights, I didn't flake out as soon as my head hit the pillow. My wrestling with God took a lot of time and energy, so I didn't get much sleep.

"Congratulations!" they shout.

Each of them has a glass of champagne in hand. Hilda is beaming and holding out an empty glass for me. I'm still too thick in the head to realize what they're on about.

"A perfect score!"

"What!" I sit up, fully awake now.

"Perfect!" Cynthia says again. "Your headmistress rang Dad. She'll ring you later. You're the only girl in your school who got a perfect score!" Cynthia is sloshing champagne into the glass now and fitting my unwilling hands around the delicate stem. "Only eight in the whole state!"

"Eight what?" I ask, numb with disbelief.

"Perfect scores! Idiot. Wake up."

"The *Age* wants to take a photo of you. They're going to bring some kid down from Echuca or somewhere, get all of you together this afternoon."

"So Dad knows?"

"Your headmistress rang him when she couldn't get through here, and he rang Hilda. He's in court in Sydney. But he's terribly pleased, of course! He'll ring again as soon as he can."

"He was over the moon," Hilda exclaims.

"Jeez!" I shake my head.

The jumble of feelings is indescribable. Acute disappointment because it means Dad is definitely not coming back. But surprise as well, that my offer has *not* been accepted. After all, it was pretty generous and big-hearted of me to agree to give up so much. (Bizarre thinking for an agnostic, I know, but there you go!) At the same time, I'm absolutely delighted. I simply can't help it. The good news zings around my head like a deliciously cold ice cube on a hot day, cooling me right down, making me feel drunk with good fortune, before I've even had a sip of the champagne.

A perfect score! How could I not be pleased with myself! These strong conflicting emotions churn around my guts like soup. One moment I'm euphoric, the next I teeter on the edge of nausea.

Hilda says excitedly, "Why weren't you up first thing to look?"

"Does Mum know?" I ask, ignoring her question. Zoe and I decided a long time ago that we weren't going to look up our results online. We were going to be the cool dudes who wait for the mail.

"We thought it would be better to let her sleep," Hilda says. We are all quiet as it hits us all over again. My three sisters squash onto my bed and we look at each other. Only a few weeks ago, the very idea of Mum sleeping through such good news in the family would have been unbelievable. Mum would have been the one waiting up while everyone else was in bed, then whooping it up outrageously as soon as she had the news.

"Come on," Cynthia says, picking up the bottle of champagne and throwing my old Japanese dresssing gown around my shoulders, "get into gear, girl! We're going to celebrate!" The rest of us follow her downstairs and out onto the steps leading into the backyard.

"Where are the boys?" I ask Hilda.

"A friend came and took them for an hour." She grins and looks at her watch. "So I've got exactly forty-two minutes from now in which to make serious whoopee!"

Cynthia starts down the steps, then turns. "Lets get plastered!" she shouts, holding up the bottle of champagne, and after a few swigs from the bottle, gives a huge, gross burp, which has the rest of us cracking up like mental patients.

"Well, why not?" She has another swig and puts the bottle and her glass on a nearby wooden table. "Come on!"

Dorothy and Hilda go down the steps to join her, but I linger a few moments.

Our yard is huge for an inner-city house. There's a pool at the end, with blue water shimmering in the morning sun. There are loads of big trees all along the back and side fences, flowering gums, jacarandas, and two huge lily pillys, branches heavy with leaves and flowers. Bright sunlight floods through, making dappled patterns on the bricks around the pool and surrounding grass. Everything seems to shimmer, almost dreamlike in the clear morning air. A luxuriant bed of ferns grows under the shade of the old cream-painted wooden toolshed, and masses of bright flowers hang from pots over the shed walls and side fences.

There is a crackling, shiny-green sharpness to everything. A sort of hum of ordered beauty underneath the haphazard way it has all been arranged. Mum and Dad created this. So many weekends they worked together in the backyard. Over all the years, they made this small piece of loveliness happen.

Dot is looking up at me.

"Time to pull out the barbie." She is wistful, as though she knows what's on my mind.

"Yeah." I try to meet her smile with one of my own. At the beginning of every summer, Dad used to make a big deal of dragging the barbecue from the shed. When the weather was good, we cooked the meat and fish outside.

"*Come on!*" Cynthia peels off her nightgown and runs naked for the pool. She does a neat dive and doesn't surface until she gets to the other end. The rest of us look at each other in shocked silence for about three seconds, and then, without a word, we immediately do the same. It's a long pool with plenty of room for the four of us to swim a few strokes, splash around a bit, and dip and dive without kicking each other in the face.

If you're thinking that this is something we ordinarily do—go around naked or swim nude in front of each other—then you're completely mistaken. The four of us are amazingly uptight, considering our easygoing parents. Dot nearly dies if someone sees her in her underwear. Cynthia makes gruesome faces if anyone mentions periods—and she's supposed to be a doctor! And Hilda goes berserk if one of us comes in on her in the bathroom.

We mess around in the water for ten minutes or so. Pushing each other under, laughing, grabbing hold of each other's legs. I'm pretty pumped through all of this. A perfect score. Wow! Can't do much better than that! I want to find out if Zoe has done well, too. But . . . she won't have her score yet and, even though the headmistress phoning with the news had nothing to do with me, I feel bad that our pact to wait for the mail has been broken.

Cynthia is the first to want to get out.

"I'll go get towels," she offers, "if you promise you won't look."

"Well, go on!" Hilda says sharply.

"Do you promise?"

"Who'd want to look at you?" Dot says, making a grim face.

"Bruce does!" Cynthia raises her chin defiantly.

"Bruce!" Dot is quite open in her disdain for Cynthia's simple, good-hearted boyfriend. "I mean someone who counts!"

When we see Cynthia is serious about staying in the water until we all promise to close our eyes, we give her our word, cross our hearts, hope to die, and all the rest of it. Of course, as soon as she's out and running toward the house, we start screaming and pointing, shouting insults until we're blue in the face. Generally trying to make it as embarrassing as possible.

"Had my fingers crossed!" I yell.

"Me too!" Dot screams. "And I can see your enormous bum!"

"It's huge!" from Hilda. "And really wobbly!"

"Ever heard of a bum diet, Cynthia?"

"Liposuction?"

"I hate the lot of you!" Cynthia yells back furiously as she disappears into the house. Cynthia is curvier than the rest of us. Bigger breasts and hips. She's always had this mad idea that her bum is gigantic, which it's not, but . . . of course it's what we tease her about.

She comes back out with a towel wrapped around her head, another around her body, and a smug smile. "Where're ours?"

"Get your own!"

"Anyone ever told you you're a self-centered bitch, Cynthia?"

"Well, now that you mention it!" she giggles. "But luckily it doesn't worry me!"

So the rest of us have to climb naked from the pool and go for our own towels, with Cynthia sniggering insults behind us.

◆ ◆ ◆

"I have a name," Cynthia pronounces victoriously from the doorway. We've been lazing around the pool now for close on two hours, and have drunk two bottles of champagne along with buckets of coffee. Apart from the toilet every now and then, none of us seems able to shift, much less make any decisions about getting on with the day. I suppose we're waiting for Mum to wake. Every half hour or so, someone goes up to check on her, but at midday she's still out of it. We all agree that one of us should go in, have first shower, and start organizing a few things. The answering machine needs to be listened to. Food needs to be bought and prepared. No one has gone shopping for days, and we're getting low on supplies. But still we hang about, soaking up the sun and talking about not much at all. There are coffee cups and bits and pieces of leftover toast, apple cores, and orange peels strewn about.

"It's a start!" Cynthia is holding a piece of paper in her hand and waving it at us. Dot and Hilda are on chairs at the little table under the umbrella, arguing over the crossword. The twins are back and playing happily with some dirt and stones under a nearby tree. They've already had a long stint in the pool with Dot and me, so they're nicely tired out. I'm sitting down at one end of the pool, a little apart from my sisters, legs dangling in the water. I suppose it is just the few glasses of bubbly on an empty stomach—none of us has eaten properly—but I'm still feeling pretty blissed out. Every time I remember my score, this incredible, light feeling invades my brain. I'm going to be a lawyer. *Yes.* Everything else is . . . a side issue. My life is on track, and the surrounding chatter from my sisters and nephews ebbs and flows about my head like a warm, healing bath. I suddenly think of Nat Cummins and wonder if he's rung. I want to let him know how well I've done. Everything is going to be absolutely fine.

"Who?" Dot is scowling.

"Dad's girlfriend," Cynthia says. "I've got her name." We all stop. My wonderful mood simply slides away into a kind of blank sponginess. I look up. At Mum's open window.

"Keep your voice down," I say sharply. Cynthia moves closer to us. "She's still asleep," I say in a softer voice.

"So, what is it?" Hilda asks. She and Dot have forgotten the crossword puzzle now. Like me, they're riveted on Cynthia.

"Cassandra," Cynthia declares. "She's in her thirties, and . . ."

Hilda gives an angry sigh before covering her face with her hands.

"Poor Mum," she moans without lifting her face. The others murmur in agreement.

"And she's a lawyer!" Cynthia declares as though that, too, has heavy meaning.

"What else?"

"Nothing else . . . yet." Cynthia sits down next to me. "But give me time."

"Cassandra," Dot murmurs, a vague, dreamy smile spreading over her face. "Well, we know what happened to *her*, don't we?"

"No," I speak for the others.

"She got done in." Dot's voice is spiky with venom. "Well and truly."

"Done in?"

"Butchered by Clytemnestra, the wife of Agamemnon!" Dot declares triumphantly. "Oh boy, did she cop it!"

"Really?" I say, interested in spite of myself. Dot's regular forays into ancient mythology usually drive the rest of us nuts. But I'm hungry for clues on how to think about Dad's girlfriend. I have to admit that I already hate her, and the very idea of her being "done in" under appallingly violent circumstances is extremely appealing. I know it's insane, but I can tell my sisters feel the same.

"Agamemnon brought Cassandra home as his new woman, and his wife, Clytemnestra, didn't appreciate it."

"Oh yeah?" We all start laughing.

"Yeah." Dot is smiling, now that she has our attention. "When they got there, Cassandra was smart enough to know something was up. She didn't want to go into the house, said she could smell blood. But Clytemnestra stays very cool and entices them both inside. Then she hacks Agamemnon to bits with an axe and chases Cassandra through the house until she finally runs her down!" Dot makes fast chopping motions in the air, her face tight with concentration. "And with the same weapon, kills her. Neat, eh?"

We stare at Dot's beautiful, animated face. This stuff is so real to her! Then we all look at each other and start laughing like gleeful maniacs.

"So no mucking around, eh?" Cynthia says when we're all quiet again. "She just got in there and did what had to be done?"

"A bloodbath," Dot agrees calmly.

"Did she . . . go to prison or anything?" Hilda is the only one who seems a mite disturbed by this twist of conversation.

"Are you kidding?" Dot snarls. "Why should *she* be punished?"

Of course, I should intervene at this point. After all, I'm the one who is going to be a lawyer. But I can't bring myself to ruin her moment, and this story is so attractive. Normally, we just yawn and wait it out when she rabbits on with this stuff. So I laugh along with them, as though I think butchering someone is a perfectly reasonable response to marital infidelity.

"I want to get her!" Cynthia suddenly says, vehemently.

"And do what?" Hilda says in alarm.

"I don't know," Cynthia growls. "Let's just *get* her!"

"Yeah . . . let's capture her," Dot whispers.

"And do what?" Hilda asks again.

We go quiet thinking of the possibilities.

"Hack her to bits!" Cynthia thrusts an imaginary axe into Dot's neck. "Straight through the spinal cord."

"Excellent idea!"

"You're the doctor"—Dot grins—"so you can have first chop."

"I'm serious," Cynthia murmurs, frowning, as she stares into the shimmering blue pool. "Really, I am! I want to kill her."

"Oh, shut up!" Hilda says, and pushes Cynthia into the water. Inside, Hilda's mobile phone rings and rings.

"It's going to be for you," Dot says to me, before diving down and pulling Cynthia's legs out from under her. "Probably Dad."

"He'll leave a message," I say lightly. "I'll ring back."

Dad can wait. I haven't seen him since the day he left, and we haven't actually spoken since the night before, on the stairs after the party. Somehow it wouldn't seem right to hear him say congratulations just yet.

Amid the howls of protest, giggles, and shouts, I realize I'm suddenly wolfishly hungry.

"I'll go and pull some lunch together?"

"Oh, yes, please!" They're all enthusiastic. "What took you so long?"

But when I go into the kitchen, I discover we're out of a lot of things. Most importantly, bread and milk.

"I'm going down the street to get stuff," I yell at my sisters. "So don't discuss anything important while I'm gone!"

"Hey, Rose!" Cynthia yells. "Stop by the hardware store and buy an axe!"

"Will do!" I laugh as I head upstairs to shower and dress, thinking how bizarre it is that the story about Clytemnestra giving Cassandra what was owed her seems to have lightened everyone's spirits.

♦ ♦ ♦

"SO, YOU'RE THE CHICK who bashed up my sister?" Nat sounds baffled.

"That's right," I say, cool as ice.

"Why did you do that?"

"Ask her," I say sarcastically. "You'll get a more . . . creative answer."

I am standing in the street outside the local supermarket. In one hand I have the bag of groceries I've just bought, and in the other, this small, plastic, remarkably realistic-looking axe that I saw in the local thrift store window and bought for Cynthia for a lark. Now I'm feeling unbelievably ridiculous, trying to meet Nathaniel Cummins's full-on stare while pretending I'm not holding a weapon as we talk about me bashing up his sister. The timing is, as they say, impeccable.

Just as I was leaving the supermarket, I felt a hand on my arm. I turned and, much to my shock, it was him, looking down into my face, not smiling. Needless to say I'm now completely freaking. Not that I show it. I'm very good at closing down when I'm in a sticky situation.

I consider casually chucking the axe into the gutter— pretending that I just picked it up out of curiosity—but I decide it would only draw attention to something he hasn't even noticed yet. Maybe he won't ever notice it. But what if he does? I decide I need to get away . . . badly.

"I remember, you nearly got kicked out of school, didn't you?" he says.

"Yeah."

"My parents were really dark, until Dad realized he knew your father from university." He laughs wryly. "Then it was all okay. Apparently Dad stayed a few times with your grandmother down in Port Fairy."

"Really?" I ask, pretending I'm interested, looking over at the cars stopping at the red lights. Right next to us is a neat European sporty number. Why aren't I in one of those? Speeding off to somewhere, loud music blasting and my hair flying?

Nat looks great in his old jeans and sweatshirt, hair still wet from a shower or a swim. I'm not about to ask which. I decide he is altogether too great for me. I know I was kissing him only a few nights ago, but that all feels too weird now. I'm in this tatty old dress of Dot's and I have no idea what to say.

It's true, anyway. Embarrassingly true. During sophomore year, Alisha Cummins started giving Zoe the nasty treatment. Zoe has a good singing voice, and when she won a part in the school musical over one of Alisha's friends, they began to pick on her, big-time. There were snide comments about her weight, and notes in her locker about her clothes, that kind of thing. I took up Zoe's cause with a vengeance and, well, ended up punching Alisha a couple of times. Big mistake! Of course, I got into a heap of trouble. There were meetings. My parents were hauled up to the school, and I had to write apologies to Alisha and her family and . . . all the rest of it. Mum and Dad were amazingly cool about it. Looking back, I think they were secretly amused. I wasn't. It was excruciatingly embarrassing. Even though it's a long time ago, I don't exactly relish being reminded of it.

"I gotta go," I say, turning away.

"So, I take it you had second thoughts about the other night?" he says coolly, not moving, looking down at his feet. I can't very well walk away when he's asked a question like that, so I stop and look at my own feet. He is wearing old flip-flops, too, and one of his big toenails is painted blue. I almost comment, but don't; it seems like a way too obvious ploy to change the subject.

"How do you mean?" I shoot back in my best snooty voice.

"Well, I rang and you never got back."

"Did you?" I say, still not looking at him.

"Don't bullshit me!" he snaps. "You know I did."

"No, I don't, actually!" His anger sparks my defense mechanisms. I forget, momentarily, about feeling so awkward.

"What? You never got the message?" he sneers disbelievingly.

"Right," I say. "I didn't get the message." I'm frantically trying to think of what to say without telling him about our family drama. How do you say to someone, *Oh, my father did a bunk for another woman the day after I fell for you, so the rest of us didn't get around to stuff like phone messages . . .* I can't, somehow. I'm ashamed. And I feel raw, exposed, as though I might burst into tears. The truth is, Dot wrapped up our house phone in an old blanket and stuffed it in a cupboard under the stairs. I saw her do it. She has always had a bizarre anti-phone stance—she is the only person I know without a mobile. But Mum wouldn't take calls, and Cynthia just groaned whenever it rang, then walked out of the room. The sound of it ringing was starting to drive me nuts too, so I didn't object.

Nat looks away, shakes his head, and shrugs. I can tell he doesn't know whether to believe me or not.

"So, you're walking home?" he asks at last.

"Yep."

"I'll walk with you?"

"Okay," I say. We head through crowds of kids just out of school, and then cross the road. Neither of us speaks again until we hit the side street leading up to my house.

"Did you get your results?" he wants to know.

"Yeah."

"Do well?"

"Yeah."

"Well enough to get into . . . law school?"

"Yeah" I nod.

He turns to me with a small smile.

"Congratulations."

"Thanks."

"Alisha did very well too."

"Oh good," I say, because I'm operating on autopilot at this stage. "What course does she want to do?" I'm expecting he'll say art or design. Alisha is really gifted in that area. It used to make Zoe and me puke to see her stuff pinned up around the school corridors, but, once we'd blanked out who did those paintings and clay sculptures, we had to grudgingly admit her stuff was streaks ahead of anyone else's. She's talented, much as it pains me to say.

"Same as you," Nat says.

"What?!" I can't have heard right. "You mean . . .?"

"Arts/law," he says shortly, as though it's nothing.

"But . . ." I can't keep the outrage out of my voice, *"why?"* I am truly horrified by this piece of information. He shrugs as though he couldn't care less.

"Dad's influence," he says, glancing at a car that has just pulled up. "It's sort of a family thing." He grins. "I'm the big disappointment, doing veterinary science."

"She'll do it at Melbourne?"

"Yeah," he says, "assuming she gets in."

I say nothing, but I'm suddenly so . . . unbelievably flat. *Law?* So what's the big deal about that? It suddenly doesn't seem anything special at all. In fact, it seems boring and predictable. Me and Alisha. Two little private school girls doing law like our daddies! *Yawn. Hiss. Boo.* What's interesting about it? Absolutely nothing.

"Hey, Rose?" He stops. We are a block from my house, and I am so dying to get away that I almost walk on and leave him there. There is no point to him and me anyway, so why drag it out?

"Get over it, why don't you?" he says.

"What?" I turn around and look into his face.

"The thing with my sister." He shrugs and gives me one of his charming open grins. "It's in the past now," he goes on. "Forget it. I know she has."

Suddenly, that careless, handsome grin seems so contrived. Like the one his sister used to throw about when she wanted something to go her way. That kind of ploy runs in families, I reckon. *Pretty boy!* He knows he's gorgeous. I make up my mind then and there that I'm going to be the *one chick* in his charmed, predictable life who isn't going to fall for it! It takes me a moment to realize what he has just said. *Get over it. I know she has.*

Oh yeah? I think darkly. *Like bloody hell she has!* What about the party? Staring at me through those slitty, knowing eyes? She hates my guts. There are a few moments of awkward silence.

"Don't lecture me," I say in a low, sharp voice.

"Whoa!" I've taken him by surprise. "Hang on! I'm not lecturing."

"You're telling me what to think!"

There is a stand-off for a few moments. Then he sighs and shakes his head and smiles like he's a bit baffled. "Listen, Rose, I know she's difficult, but . . . she's my little sister."

"Yeah, I understand that."

"So, I can't, like, disown her, can I?"

"I know that," I say shortly, thinking, *Why not? I would if she was my sister.*

"So, what's with the axe?" He grins. "You planning on doing someone in on your way home from the shops?"

I know I should smile and joke back, but I feel too jumpy.

"It's for my nephews," I mumble, feeling the heat rush to my face.

"Gonna put 'em down, are ya?" he jokes again, and I don't even smile. "Well, looks like I'd better go." He shrugs. "If you want to catch up sometime, Rose, you know where I am."

"Okay," I say gruffly, "thanks." I turn on my heel and make my way home, feeling weirdly pumped, as though I've won some kind of victory. Of course, once I'm in the door all that just seeps away, like air from a faulty balloon. I'm left feeling spent and saggy, as though I've just banged the last nail into my own coffin. Confused, too. What the hell was that little episode all about?

◆ ◆ ◆

ROAD TRIP

We are coming into Anglesea now, and a rush of elation washes through me, followed quickly by apprehension when I remember Apollo Bay is only an hour away. How am I supposed to pass the road that leads up to the house in the hills? The house where that sweet nightmare began?

It's at this point I see the hitchhiker. A sloppily dressed guy in flip-flops, dirty jeans and T-shirt, with long dark hair falling in his face and a full backpack at his feet. I hesitate and then slam on the brakes. When she realizes that I'm stopping for him, Mum goes into panic mode.

"Don't, Rose! Please." She reaches out for my arm. "It's not safe."

I shrug her off impatiently, thinking that I'm going to have to do it now. This is *my* van. My trip. I'm the one making decisions. I pull the van over onto the gravel.

"He's got a bag!" she hisses.

"So what?"

"Could be carrying a knife or . . . a gun."

"As if!"

But watching the guy approach in the rear-view mirror, I become nervous myself. The closer he gets, the more he looks like Charles Manson. He's about thirty, short and dark, and surly, like he's got some secret agenda that's making him shitty with the world.

"You hitched when you were young," I mutter to Mum.

"It was different then."

"Oh yeah?" I snap. "How?"

"Lots of people did it then. It was a more accepted way to get about."

"Yeah, well . . ." *I rest my case.*

Shit, I *hate* it. Fact is, I'm just jealous. Everything I hear about the sixties and seventies makes me wish to hell those times could come around again. Imagine being there when The Doors were a hot new band. Or when Hendrix and Janis Joplin were playing little clubs. Or when a song like "Knockin' on Heaven's Door" was on the charts! Then there were local bands like Skyhooks and Daddy Cool, The Easybeats, Billy Thorpe . . . Dad still has all those old albums. That stuff was good! So simple and witty and new. It was okay, then, for a couple of girls to hitch up to Queensland for a holiday—Mum did that when she was nineteen! No computers or mobile phones to tie you down or keep you in your place. And on top of all that, the feeling that you were part of a new, *special* generation that was going to change the world.

Not that they did, of course, but believing that it was possible, even for a year or two, would be so very cool. I don't know anyone now who wants to change the world, much less anyone who believes they can.

The hitchhiker slides open the door and mumbles something that sounds like *thanks*, before hurling his bag onto the backseat. Then he climbs in himself, eyes downcast. A distinct whiff of beer hits my nostrils, mixed with sweat and cigarettes. I immediately feel like telling him to get out again.

"Where are you going?" I ask, sharply, looking at him in the rear-view mirror.

"Apollo Bay." He meets my eyes. "You going that far?"

"Yeah," I say, "but we're going to stop for a swim at Lorne first."

"Surf or swim?"

"Swim," I say. *As if it's any of your business.*

"Lorne's a shit-hole now," he says in this cool, matter-of-fact way, like he knows everything and I know nothing. "You won't get a good swim there. Should go on to Apollo Bay."

"No," I say.

"Why not?"

"Because I want to stop at Lorne," I snap right back at him as I pull out onto the road. He shrugs as though he couldn't care less and then starts rummaging around in his backpack. Mum stiffens and looks nervously at me. I risk a quick glance around. He has pulled out a packet of tobacco and is rolling a cigarette. It takes him about three seconds with one hand.

"Mind if I smoke?" he mumbles, putting it in his mouth and pulling a lighter from his pocket, not waiting for a reply. Audacious prick!

"Yeah, I do, actually," I say quickly, before he can light it. Mum is looking visibly relieved, presumably because it's not a gun. "My mother gets sick from cigarette smoke."

This is true. Mum has never been able to bear being in confined spaces with people smoking. But, to my surprise, she immediately turns to him with an apologetic smile.

"That's okay," she says, nervously. "I don't mind. As long as we have the windows open. Blow the smoke out if you can."

What? I look at her furiously to see if I've heard right. "But you get sick. It's not a good idea."

"Thanks, lady." The guy lights up without looking at me, then mutters, "Some people are cool and some people aren't." He turns to stare distractedly out the window and blow his smoke out.

Shit. I can't believe I heard him say that! What a rude pig! I look over at Mum, but I'm unable to tell whether she heard him or not. I'm on the point of telling him to butt the bloody thing out—I don't like smoking in confined spaces either—but somehow the moment passes. I'm not scared of him. More like I just don't feel like making a scene. Gutless, I know. *Why not make a scene?* I stare ahead and try to concentrate on the driving. *So,* I think angrily, *nothing for it but to put up with this stranger's nauseating stink wafting through my van.* After a few minutes, he turns away from the window and settles himself into the corner. I notice only half the smoke is going out the window now.

"Bit different seeing chicks in one of these shit-heaps," he says in this lazy, confidential tone. "So, where youse headed?"

I pretend I don't hear. *What a dickhead.* He's getting a ride for nothing. So how come he thinks he can insult my van?

"Oh, we're on our way to Port Fairy to see an old lady," Mum gushes. "My husband's mother, actually." *Ex-husband, Mum,* I'm on the point of reminding her. *Your husband pissed off with another woman! Remember?*

"I'm Patsy, by the way, and this is my daughter, Rose," Mum goes on, and then she turns around and holds out her hand! I cringe inside when I see the look of surprise on the guy's face before he leans across and takes her hand in his own grimy one.

"Yeah, well . . ." he says, giving Mum a bemused smile, "I'm Travis."

"So, is Apollo Bay home for you, Travis?" Mum asks sweetly after an uncomfortable pause. This is just like her. *Dippy.* Having decided he's not going to kill her, it's now time to turn on the let's-be-friendly-to-strangers number.

"Nah. I come from Sydney. Apollo Bay is where my old lady lives."

"So, you grew up there?" Mum asks.

He laughs sourly. "My old lady being my ex-missus."

"Oh. I see." Mum backs off, tentatively.

"She's sick, and I've got to do something with the kid."

"Your child?"

"Yeah," the guy sighs. "A boy. He's nine now . . . I think. I don't know whether to take him back with me or try and find somewhere for him to live around there. Not much for him in Sydney."

"She must be very sick?" Mum asks quietly.

"Yeah. She hasn't got long. Only thirty-one. Cancer, you know."

Mum is turning right around now, an open study of sympathy. He's blowing the smoke straight into her face, more or less. This is making me so pissed off that if I weren't driving, I'd turn around and smack the thing right out of his hand.

"You see much of your boy?" Mum wants to know.

"Nah"—he shakes his head—"I've been in Sydney for a long time."

"How will you get him back to Sydney?"

I can tell she's already picturing this guy standing on the road on a dark, stormy night with a badly dressed, cold, undernourished nine-year-old, both with their thumbs out.

"You wouldn't hitchhike with him, would you?" she asks breathlessly, as though this is the biggest concern of her life.

"Look, I don't know." He gestures impatiently with both hands, as though it's all too much for him. "I mightn't have much choice." Then he slumps dramatically, groans, and shuts his eyes. "I had my fuckin' car pinched in Goulburn," he grumbles. "It was a bomb, but it went, ya know?"

Mum nods vigorously, as though she knows all about crappy cars, when in fact she's never driven anything but a prestigious European model.

"And I had everything in the glove box," Travis continues. "Wallet. License. Money. They got the lot."

"Would you mind blowing that smoke *out* the window?" I cut in. He sits up a bit and nods suspiciously, like *I'm* the freak. I hate this guy now. How dare he swear like that in front of my mother. She's an older woman. He should have some respect. Doesn't seem to have affected her, though.

"Oh, Travis, that's just what you *didn't* need!" Mum gives the guy a sigh of pure sympathy, tinged with exasperation, as though the whole sorry tale has just happened to *her*. The guy nods, clears his throat, and looks out the window, not at all embarrassed to have revealed so much. "It hasn't been your week, has it?" Mum sighs coaxingly, turning around to share another isn't-life-damned-hard smile.

"You could say that," he mutters.

"No wonder you're feeling low," Mum declares after some thought. "You've had an absolutely terrible time! How did the car get stolen?"

"I parked it at a service station. Needed to make a phone call. When I came out again, it was gone."

I find myself wanting to caution her, which is ironic, seeing as she was the one who didn't want me to pick up this guy in the first place. My mother has always been like this. Once she gets talking, one to one, her built-in bullshit detector switches off. She gets involved way too quickly. I've seen it happen too many times. Dad used to be the one to haul her back to reality. Then it was my turn for a while. These days, it's usually my sisters playing that role.

How is Mum today? Did she eat? Did she have a shower? Then, when she picked up a bit, maybe three months after

Dad left, *Let's encourage her to go out with her girlfriends this Friday. Will she cope with this? Is that going to upset her? How is she today?*

I don't want to look after her . . . or anyone else for that matter. I can't. I've got too much of my own shit to work out. The guy is drumming his dirty fingers on the backseat now, eyes closed as though he's listening to some song inside his head. And I wonder, *Why the hell did I pick up this . . . piece of human garbage?*

"Did you report it to the police?" Mum asks, and in spite of myself, I crane my neck to hear.

"Nah," he snarls, "it wasn't registered." I almost hoot out loud. That would be right. *Not registered.* I'd like to point out at this juncture that since leaving home, I take no money from my parents. I work as a waitress for fifteen dollars an hour and for that pissant music paper. *And* I am able to register my van *with my own money.* This jerk probably stole the car in the first place.

"So, what are you doing for money now?" Mum wants to know. *Good for you, Mum! Give him an opening to hit on you.* The guy shrugs and looks out the window. Mum glances at me. We're coming into Lorne now, and all I want to do is get rid of him.

"So, Travis," I say, "where do you want to be dropped?"

"You're still going to stop here?" he asks, a note of incredulity in his voice, as though he'd expected that I would have come to my senses and taken his advice.

"Yeah," I say through gritted teeth. *We're still going to stop here, dickhead.*

"Well," he says, shaking his head as though it is the weirdest thing he's heard in all his life, "it's up to you." *Yeah, that's right, buddy! It is up to me.* I don't say anything. I just pull the van into the parking lot in front of the toilet block.

100

"I'll just sit on the beach," he says, "and wait."

"Wait?" I croak. "For what?"

"Till you've finished swimming," he replies curtly. He's meeting my eyes now. Challenging me to tell him he can't. I am momentarily stuck for words because . . . the proposal is appalling. I don't want him hanging around waiting for us!

"I think you should get out on the road again," I say, cool as I can make it. "Apollo Bay is only an hour away."

"But I won't get a ride," he whines. *This type of guy is an expert at playing the victim.* "I was waiting for about three hours before you picked me up. I could be waiting till night-time for another lift."

"Then staying with us sounds like a very good idea," Mum cuts in firmly. "The sooner Travis sees his little boy, the better."

"Oh, jeez," I mutter. *For God's sake, Mum. Get a fucking brain!*

I get out and go to the back of the van, open it, and get out my bag, which is packed with a bathing suit, towel, and sunblock. When the other two have climbed out, I make damned sure I lock the van up properly before heading over to the toilet block to change. Only an hour or two, I tell myself, then it will be over. Come on, Rose. Think positive. Dropping him off will give me something to think about when I hit Apollo Bay. It will divert me. Keep me in the NOW. That's what that self-help book is always banging on about. Stay in the NOW. So this is it. I'm here. Right in the fucking NOW and hating it. So deal with it, Rose . . . just move on to the next NOW.

Don'tcha just hate it . . . when some stranger decides you're it for the day, the hour, or even the next ten minutes. Worse. Maybe it's some guy you met once three years ago and he insists on walking your way when you want to be by yourself. Someone you ended up hooking up with one night because there wasn't a better offer and now you can't even remember his name. He decides you are the one he's been thinking about all these years. You're the one who will take away his pain and make everything right. You're the one who can help. They cling like bloody suckers to your life . . .

My plan is to walk along the shoreline, put my feet in the water and feel the sand under my feet, maybe lie in the sun a bit. Look at the ocean rolling in. Refamiliarize myself with the beach. Get back in the groove, so to speak. It's been . . . a long time. I am aware of a kind of nervous buzz happening in my guts, like when you have too much coffee on an empty stomach. When I come out of the changing rooms, bathing suit underneath my jeans and T-shirt, and towel over my shoulder, I see that Mum is sitting on a small wooden railing next to the van. She is looking up at the hitchhiker, who is leaning against the door, arms crossed and smoking another cigarette, no doubt holding her in thrall about all the hard times he's endured. They're so deep in conversation that they don't immediately notice me.

"So, Mum," I say, ignoring the guy, "coming for a swim?"

"Yes, I might," she says, and then turns back to the guy. "Why didn't she want you to see the child?"

"Well, I wasn't much of a . . . dad." He sighs in this disconcertingly confidential way, and squats down. "You know how it is, Patsy. You get lost in your own trip and forget about—"

"Listen, Mum." I cut across him sharply. "I'll be an hour at the most, so I'll see you back here then, okay?"

"Okay, Rose," she says distractedly. "In an hour. Back here."

"And I'll just be on the beach down there," I add, pointing at the expanse of white sand, the blue rippling sea with its lazy white swell. I notice about four surfers a long way out. Their black insect-like figures are cartoon cutouts against the brightness of the blue, and I am suddenly weak with longing, while at the same time reluctant to leave my mother with this guy. *What's the policy now?* I find myself wondering. Should I ring the sisters? *Oh shit. No.* Not all that crap again. She's fifty-two. It's broad daylight, and I'm only going to be an hour!

"I'll be near the flags, Mum. I'll be easy enough to find when you come."

"Okay, love." She waves me off and turns back to the hitchhiker.

In spite of the heat, the beach isn't too crowded because it's a weekday. I forget about Mum and the hitchhiker when my feet touch the sand. *Oh.* My toes squirm with pleasure in the warm, loose grains. This is so fantastic! I head for the flags and about midway down the beach I select a spot, kneel and spread out my towel, and then take off my shirt and jeans. It's been a while since my skin was exposed like this. I'm thin and white, and my knees and elbows and hands and feet are knobbly—like a boy's. My old spotted bikini is baggy, but I don't care. I look around. No one is looking at me. They are all intent on their own lives: bending over kids, bouncing balls on the hard sand, squinting over newspapers and magazines, dreaming their own dreams as they lie flat out on their bellies or backs in the sun. I get up, walk tentatively down to the water, and gasp at the first delicious touch. The waves lap my ankles, and the sun burns into my back and shoulders like a blowtorch. I forgot to put on the sunblock. Better go back. *Go back. Go back, Rose. Go back and get the sunblock*. But I don't go back. I'm moving forward. It's as though an invisible system of pulleys is tugging me along. One leg moves and then the other. My arms push forward. I just keep moving into the surf. My heart beats hard and my mouth goes dry. I am fearful and full of excitement at the same time. Afraid, too, that this spell will break and I'll lose my nerve. The bubbles of fear rise up from below, but they disappear as soon as they hit the surface. This is so . . . *fine*.

I gasp again as a wave pushes against my hips. This beautiful southern ocean! So clear and freezing. Now that I'm almost there, I turn back to see if I can catch Mum's eye. Part of me is the little kid again. *Look, Mum! See me. Look what I can do*. But she is out of sight. Back up there in the ordinary world that I've just come from. I smile as I dive headfirst into a wave. This is . . . the best. This is bliss.

I swim. I swim. I swim. Freestyle, backstroke, breaststroke. Not out far, but across the beach, amongst all the people. Safe and easy. I keep on swimming. I dip under and open my eyes in the green gloom. Who would have thought it could be this easy?

It's not as though I've forgotten anything. The memories wash in and out with each wave. But just as one covers me and I feel myself sinking, it draws away and is replaced by other images, conversations; feelings jostle for position in my head. But it's okay now. It's all okay. I'm in the water.

◆ ◆ ◆

LAST SUMMER, CHILDERS

Zoe and I had already been in the water for over three hours that morning. The waves were choppy and unpredictable, but it didn't stop us from having the best time. By the time we got out, we were exhausted and hungry.

It isn't till we've climbed the steep steps up from the beach and begun the walk to the secluded parking lot that I decide.

"Just one more," I say, stopping suddenly, turning back to the beach. Zoe looks at me strangely, even though it's something that is understood between us. Every once in a while, one of us isn't quite ready to leave the beach. It's easy enough to get out if you're tired. You pull off your wetsuit, take a swig of water, pick up your board, and start for home. Then, suddenly, it doesn't seem right. All wrong, in fact. You think, *This is too good to leave.* Like leaving half of the most delicious piece of cake you've ever tasted lying on your plate, for no better reason than that it's polite to do so. *Just one more*, you say. One more bite of perfection.

But today she looks at me and frowns, because three hours without a break is a long time and the surf is by no means perfect and I've already admitted to being hungry. More importantly, she knows something is going on. Zoe is extremely sensitive. She can smell the slightest whiff of discord in any situation and often picks up stray notes of fear or discontent in my voice before I know they're there myself.

"Just half an hour," I add. "Your dad won't mind." Her father had dropped us off earlier that morning on the way to see a friend and had agreed to pick us up three hours later. The time is up, but we both know he might not be there yet. And even if he is, Ray is not the sort of guy who'd stress about half an hour either way.

"Okay," she says carefully. "See you at the parking lot, then."

There is no way I can tell her what's on my mind, so I'm putting off the moment when I have to lie.

Nothing's wrong, Zoe. You're imagining it. Everything is cool.

So there I am, paddling out into the distant blue on a clear and perfect day, surrounded only by sea and sky, and on either side by massive jagged outcrops of red and ochre rock. Childers Cove is incredibly beautiful and isolated. There had been a couple of other surfers there earlier in the day, but now I'm in the water alone, and that's the way I want it. I've got things to work out.

I'm trying to loosen up. Asking the universe for answers. And I swear that at that point, the ocean, clear as green glass beneath me, is listening and whispering back advice. Solutions are coming thick and fast, and none too soon. The whole thing has become completely impossible. I know that much. There *is* a way out, the waves are telling me, a way out where no one needs to get hurt . . . *because no one needs to know.* Ever. It can be buried in the bottom drawer along with a few other incidents that I never plan on thinking about again. I can wrap it up in an old sock and stow it, and as the years go by, it will become brittle and dry and absolutely lifeless, like a flower placed in the middle of a heavy book. Some pretty thing that caught my eye one day when I was in the bloom of youth, and I was open to every stray, stupid thing. Something I plucked and smelled, held and enjoyed, before putting it away to keep as a memento. It can become a weird little anecdote in an otherwise blameless and successful life. Yes. I can lock it up in a box and push the whole thing away.

Such relief. Until I feel the rip pulling me out. An undertow, as fast and terrifying as a dozen wild horses, dragging me relentlessly, straight toward a nest of sharp, inaccessible rocks to the left. And I am suddenly helpless against it, this mighty mysterious force under the water. It's happening so quickly that my thoughts collapse in on themselves before they have a chance to register. One thing I do know is that Zoe will probably be sitting in the car with her father now, talking and listening to music and waiting for me. There is no view of the beach from that parking lot. It is a good half kilometer away, nestled between dunes and scrub.

No one will know. My breath gets lost in my chest. The universe has turned on me. I'm going to be punished.

I have a few moments of absolute panic. I will get bashed against the stones. Be cut open and crushed to a pulp. Blood will ooze from my battered limbs, and before anyone even knows I'm missing, the sharks will smell my blood. It will bring them in to feed, and they won't wait for the niceties of death, either. No body, even. No funeral. *Oh shit.* I'd deliberately walked back to this place to surf alone without her or her father or anyone else watching me. Entering the water again, the surf had seemed okay. A little choppier than it had been all morning with Zoe, but more or less the same. Safe enough.

I'm being pulled very quickly toward the rocks. But now I've stopped panicking. That's the trick. Don't fight it. Save your energy. Lie on the board, hang on, and take it easy. Go with it. With a bit of luck, I'll be taken out way past the rocks. Everything is going to be okay. Haven't I been lucky in my life already? I'm the girl with the perfect score. Why should all the blessings cut out now? Why shouldn't my luck hold? Haven't I just decided to take hold of my life again and do the right thing? The swell gets heavier, more wild and brutal as I am dragged out toward the rocks. *I can handle it*, I tell myself. *I've been in some rough water before. What about that time at Portsea when it took me nearly an hour to get in?* Then I . . . lose my board.

I lose my board.

But how? How did it happen? How *could* it happen? I fitted the Velcro strap securely to my ankle, didn't I? *I did. I did.* For a second there, as I watch my board dance off like a kite in the wind, taking away with it my chance to live, I am outraged, livid with fury. This isn't fair. I carefully fitted that thing around my ankle! I'm not stupid. I remember doing it. I can feel that strap still there, so . . . it must have been the other end that came loose. That's the last coherent thought I have.

After that I stop thinking. A mammoth wall of water catches me by surprise and without my board I am picked up like a piece of seaweed and thrown headlong into the deep curve of the wave. It brings me right to the top and then spins me around and I tumble, down down down again. *Crash.* I'm just a small doll in this roiling mass of water. I'm caught, like a piece of undigested food, just a speck in a gush of vomit. As soon as I catch my breath, it is on me all over again. On and on it goes. For how long? I don't know. It seems like forever. I haven't even the energy to wave for help now. Only a matter of time, because I'm vomiting in between fresh intakes of seawater. I can't see. My eyes are stinging, sightless holes in my head. My arms flail about. I splutter, cough, and cry all at the same time. So this is it. This is the way my life will end.

Then I feel something grabbing me, first my arm and then something thick and black and alive around my middle, lifting me up and out of the water. I kick out instinctively, like a frantic insect caught in a web, until I hear the voice in my ear, the wonderful, low, resonating voice shouting above the din right into my ear.

"Stop fighting, Rose. It's me. Stop fighting!" The thing around my middle is an arm. The hard thing knocking my shoulder is a board. The roughness grazing my cheek is a two-day-old beard. Tightly. He is holding me tightly and lifting me onto the board. He has come out to save me.

I wish I could remember what that felt like. Being saved, I mean. I wish I could remember the elation of being slowly pulled ashore, knowing that my life had been spared.

Apparently it took over twenty minutes to get me in, and by that stage he was wrecked too. We both were. But I didn't find out about all that until much later. I was only semiconscious, half-drowned and delirious. The last thing I remember is the sky. I saw the blue, and I remember seeing it slowly fade to black. I can remember wondering about it. Why was the night coming on so quickly in the middle of the day?

◆ ◆ ◆

ROAD TRIP

Last summer fades away as I stumble through the shallows toward the flags. My whole body is buzzing with a fresh, very cool sense of having done something important. *I did it. I went in for a swim.* I vaguely look around for Mum. She loves the water, too. I can't imagine her sitting it out on such a hot day. She's probably somewhere nearby, lying in the shallows, tanning her legs. But although I take a good look around before leaving the water, I can't spot her.

She isn't waiting by the van, either, so I figure I might use the opportunity to head for the shower block. It will be much nicer doing the rest of the trip without salt all over my skin and sand in my bum and between my toes. I unlock the van, climb into the back, and search through my things for soap and a bit of moisturizer. Ah! At the bottom of the bag, my mobile phone. I have a few messages, so I play them back. First one is from Dot, sounding anxious. Gran isn't doing too well. Could I ring back to tell her when, roughly, we might arrive? Then one from Elaine, Zoe's mother, that puts me in a cold sweat.

"*Rose, it's Elaine here. Could you ring me back, please?*"

"I don't think so, Elaine," I whisper. How does that . . . ugly, dumb witch of a woman know *my* number? That whining voice sends dread pulsating through my limbs for moments after the message finishes. *But what if Zoe is . . . She might have taken a turn for the worse. What if she's . . .* I play the message again and sit very still, trying to imagine *that* scenario. Then I play it again. Some gut instinct tells me Elaine is not ringing me with news. She wouldn't. Not me. She is ringing because she wants something, and she wants to make me feel bad in the process . . . all over again. *Well, tough, Elaine! I'm not going to walk into that trap again.* I erase the message.

When I get back from this trip, I'm going to get rid of this phone. I'll drop it into that pile of moldering rubbish in the backyard of the Hurstbridge house. I hardly use it anyway. I don't have any friends anymore, and I hate the fact that someone like *Zoe's mother* can reach me! Not to mention my own family. I don't want to be *available* to anyone. Full stop.

The last message is from Roger the Dodger asking me to call back urgently. I don't, of course. Everything should have been done yesterday with Roger. He's a complete panic merchant who runs on adrenaline. Once you know that about him, he's easy enough to handle.

So, I have my shower and I rub the moisturizer into my shoulders and hope I'm not too burned. Still elated about the swim, I rub myself dry, staring into the mirror. I'm looking a little better somehow. The hair is growing back a bit. I risk a small smile, then go wider. I'm okay. Not ugly. Not beautiful. My eyes are nice. In spite of the Mum factor, this trip is turning out okay. Hey! I've had a swim already. I smile again into the mirror. My teeth are good—straight and white—and the rest of me isn't that bad either. If I'm not dying of sunburn, and if there are waves, maybe I'll go surfing at Port Fairy! Who knows?

Back at the van, I'm irritated to find that Mum hasn't returned. Half an hour late now, and still no sign of her. I pull out the book I've been trying to read for a few weeks and lie out on the grass next to the van. *The Sea, the Sea* by

Iris Murdoch. I can't seem to get very far into it and yet I don't want to give up on it either. I stay with it for ten minutes but can't concentrate, so I get out my MP3 player and play Radiohead loudly, trying to rid myself of the thoughts biting around the edges of my consciousness. *What if he is actually Charles Manson in disguise? My sisters will kill me.* And in spite of erasing her, Elaine is still hovering around, too. It's got to be about Zoe. She's in the hospital, so . . . I turn down the music and close my eyes. What if she is actually *dying* and wants to see me? Wants to give me one last blast before she shoots off into eternity? Suddenly I can hear her again, so plainly. See her, too. Her face contorted in fury, her voice wild with pain.

"Get out of my life, Rose! You slag. I never want to see you again! Remember that. I never, *ever* want to see you again! I mean it. Out!"

I sit up, open my eyes, and pull out the earplugs. Still no Mum, so I call Roger back to see what's eating him.

"Hey, Dodger, it's me."

"G'day, Rose!" He sounds busy, as usual, and flat as a tack, like he's just run a race and lost. "And what can I do for you?"

"You rang *me*, remember?" I say. "You left a message?"

"Oh yeah," he laughs. "Hey, Rose, I gotta tell you something important!" He stops; he obviously can't remember what it is. This makes me laugh. I can see him standing there, screwing up his face and scratching his oily hair, trying to remember what it is he's got to tell me.

"Guess that's why it was so *urgent*, huh?"

"No need to get sarcastic!" he says. "Okay, I've got it. Here it is."

"Do I need a pen and paper?"

"Yep."

Roger and his brother can usually make me laugh just by being who they are. They act like really efficient, tough businessmen, on the brink of making a million bucks, but underneath they're both as soft as mud and pretty *inefficient*, too, if the state of their cars and the café accounts are any indication.

"Those last couple of pieces you did really hit the mark!" he proclaims. "Do more of that *personal* stuff, Rose. It works."

"What do you mean?"

"You know, all that stuff about meeting your dad's girlfriend," he says loudly. "The bitchy sisters, feeling like you want to kill your mother. All that kind of stuff works well for the readers."

"Really?" I'm a bit stunned hearing him put it like that. I'd never actually decided to write about my family. But I suppose that's what I've been doing lately. "Why?" I ask.

"We're getting a lot of feedback about those pieces. I'll print out the e-mails for you when you get back. The readers love 'em."

"Okay," I say uncomfortably, remembering the last few pieces I'd sent in. One was about Christmas last year, when Gran came and sorted everyone out. Another was about my sisters coming unannounced to visit me, bringing cakes and soap and stuff, making me feel like the family's latest lost cause. The last one was about how weird it was to realize that your father is just another boring jerk, when you've spent your whole life idolizing him.

"Yeah!" he cuts in, heartily. "Hang it on your family, Rose! Hang it on everyone you know. Forget about the plight of Africa and Janette Howard's dress sense. Forget about people who insist on chucking rubbish out car windows and boring footballers. The readers love the *family* stuff. It's the way to go."

"Really?" I ask again, stunned. I suddenly imagine people I know reading my stuff, and it doesn't feel so good. *What if my family* . . . Oh no! I really break into a cold sweat this time. Thing is, I really don't think about *readers*. My little pieces are just an excuse for me to let off a bit of steam, to get all the stuff out. Sure, I try to make them sharp and to the point, but *shit*! It's easy to forget there are people out there actually reading them. Ironic, considering that he's just told me I'm doing so well, but I don't feel at all good about this now. Maybe I should resign before anyone finds out that I am the sick brain behind Ms. Angst.

"Everyone hates their family, Rose," Roger adds happily, oblivious to my state of mind, "so they identify with what you're saying."

"Jeez!" I feel a bit sick now. I don't hate my family. Not really. Well, not much, anyway. Maybe I do a bit. Maybe I actually love them. I don't know. *So what the fuck am I doing writing these horrible little vitriolic pieces about them?*

"Make 'em a bit longer if you like," he adds. "Have another couple hundred words. People like it. They read the paper. The advertisers get on board. We all make a buck. That's what it's all about, Rose. Know what I mean?"

"Yeah, I know what you mean," I say warily.

"I'm very happy with you, Ms. Angst," he laughs. "Very happy."

◆　◆　◆

Mum's an hour late now. Where can she be? Can't concentrate on the book or the music. I'm getting tired of sitting around watching other people haul kids and boards and bulging bags of food and towels. All their stupid comments make me wish they'd go drown each other.

Chloe, come here this minute!

It's my turn.

114

Don't forget your hat, Brad!

I'm getting fidgety about Mum. What if that jerk has killed her and the last thing I ever said to her was, "See you back here in an hour"? How will that make me feel for the rest of my life?

Then I start remembering some of my pieces for *Sauce*, and I want to die. What if it comes out? No. It can't. Who in my family would ever read *Sauce*? It's a niche rag for music heads like myself. People pick it up to see where the bands are playing on the weekend. I grit my teeth. *Who am I kidding?* I've already had a close shave.

♦ ♦ ♦

"DID YOU WRITE THIS?" Barry is standing in the kitchen of the Hurstbridge house, holding out a copy of *Sauce*. I'm immediately wary, and then I catapult into full-on panic when I see my logo down in the right-hand corner of the page. "Ms. Angst" is scrawled under the three hundred venom-packed words that demolish a very thinly disguised version of him and Stuttering Stan.

I manage to stay calm—sometimes I think that is my one truly extraordinary gift in life.

Don'tcha just hate people in share houses who always seem to have a good reason why they can't clean up after themselves or buy any food? I live with an ugly red-haired six-footer who thinks it's beneath him to put his hands in a sink of water, and a horse-faced vegan semimute who lives on beans and chick peas and is outraged when I suggest he might like to pick up a broom

"What do you want me *to do with it?" he stutters. It is the longest sentence I've ever heard from him if you don't count the farts.*

"Oh," I say airily, "you could try eating it. My mum makes this fantastic broom stew. If you don't fancy that, you could stick it up your arse . . . I've heard brooms are good for wind problems as well . . ."

So how the hell did Barry get hold of it? He is a Ph.D. student in engineering. The only music I've ever heard him play is boring Latin instrumentals or one hundred times more boring American country singers with a vocal range of

116

three notes. As far as they know, I'm a waitress. Neither of them has ever seemed remotely interested in what I do in my spare time.

"Which one?" I ask coolly, taking the paper out of his hands. "There are three articles on this page."

"The Ms. Angst thing," he mumbles, less sure now.

I feel him watching me as I calmly pretend to read through the whole article, wondering how I'm going to deal with the situation.

"No, I didn't write that," I say, eyeballing him coldly, "but I wish I had!"

"What?" His eyes shift away from mine uneasily.

"Well, it just about sums up the situation here, don't you think?" I say, confident I can say what I like because they won't kick me out. They need me for the rent. I know for a fact that they had difficulties filling the third bedroom. "Neither of you does any cleaning and you barely buy food!"

"We're not here all that much!" he protests weakly.

"Here enough to eat the stuff I buy!" I snap back.

"Ever heard of discussing it?" he shouts back in this weirdly deflated tone. "We could have . . . worked something out." His shoulders suddenly slump, he turns his back, and at that instant a spurt of pure glee fills my head with a mad rush. I have him. *I won.* The whole thing is hitting home! I've got him under my thumb, where he belongs. Then I see that he is on the point of crying . . .

I stop a moment, suddenly appalled with myself. Barry *is* ugly and awkward and mean with money but . . . to *see* it laid down in words would be . . . terrible. *Wouldn't it?* I have to work hard to shrug off my guilt, but I manage. Just. He's hurt? Well *tough*! Me too. Scratch the surface and we're all hurt in one way or another. The truth bites everyone on the bum eventually. Let *him* deal with it!

117

◆ ◆ ◆

I DON'T KNOW whether Barry believed me or not, but probably not. All I know is that after that day, both of them did a little more around the place, and they bought more food, too. But the atmosphere between the three of us changed from friendly-polite to a weird, charged kind of icy indifference. In my most paranoid moments—I mean, late at night with the wind howling around that creaky old dump, and shadows from the trees outside making spooky patterns on my walls—I imagine them sitting out there together in that disgusting little kitchen, eating their canned beans and rice, working out ways to knock me off.

I know I should find another room in some other house with real people. But in some ways, the Hurstbridge place suits me. It's so near work that I can walk, so I don't waste time or petrol. Neither Barry nor Stan is home much, so I don't have to talk to them every day. In fact, most evenings I'm alone in the house until about ten. Barry works evening shifts at a local supermarket, and Stan has some job in a bar.

Even so, after eighteen years of family life in North Fitzroy, my existence in Hurstbridge seems bizarre. It's hard to remember exactly why I moved away from home when I did. *What was I running from? What did I think I'd find?* Partly, I guess I wanted to see who I might *be* away from my family. I wanted to get away from all the pretty wrapping I've had around me since birth. The clever daughter of an eminent lawyer; the dry youngest sister; the niece; the granddaughter; the warm, loyal friend. I'd pretty much burned all those bridges before I left, but still . . . I needed to find out how I was going to survive without it all. Needless to say, when the wrapping came off, there were no nice surprises.

◆ ◆ ◆

I decide I'd better go look for Mum, so I write a message on a piece of paper and stick it under the windshield-wiper. Then I set off toward the main shopping strip just across the road from the beach. Maybe she's in one of the little cafés having another heart-to-heart with Charles Manson. Anything is possible. So I walk up and down the entire shopping strip, peering into the cafés, trying to look like I know what I'm doing and that I have a sensible reason to be staring in at people who are sitting around minding their own business. *God, what if that creep really has done something to her? What if he's holding her somewhere? I was the idiot who insisted on picking him up.*

I sit down in the shade outside one of the cafés, order an iced coffee, and watch everyone who walks past. When a couple of off-duty cops stroll past, I'm tempted to run over and ask them what I should do. I know I'm being stupid; they'd only laugh. She's an hour late! Big deal. There really is no reason to feel so worried. Except I do. Can't she even get it together to stay alive for an hour while I go for a bloody swim? *Calm down, Rose.* But what could have happened? *Get a grip, you idiot.*

This is how I used to feel all the time. For the first few weeks after Dad left, my mother would regularly *go missing.* Sometimes she'd spend all day just walking around our suburb, going from café to park, to café, to the local library, with this dazed expression on her face. She got so thin and wrecked-looking that we honestly thought she might just keel over one day in the street and die. She kept saying she was okay, that she simply couldn't stay in the house, needed

119

to walk, and that we shouldn't worry. But she wasn't okay. She kept losing money and forgetting appointments and being incredibly vague about what she did all day. She'd take the train to Frankston or Werribee or Lilydale, get out and have a cup of tea and come straight home again. I know, because I followed her once. Sometimes she'd be out from early in the morning till late at night. Occasionally, she'd bring home some weird, drunken deadbeat or bag lady to stay in our beautifully set up guest room, and it would be Cynthia's job to get rid of them in the morning. (Something she did with gusto, needless to say!)

My sisters had demanding jobs and kids and boyfriends, but I'd just finished school, so I had more time. Looking after Mum became my job. When she hadn't come back after a few hours, I would be overcome with worry and I'd have to try to find her.

My sisters did what they could. They'd rush home, and sometimes we'd go out on these search parties together. Suffice it to say, all of them were more suited to the situation than I was. Drama queens, the lot of them! By the end of the summer, I'd developed this constant feeling of semipanic. *Where is Mum? Am I going to find her collapsed in the park? Or under a bus? Or with some creep sticking a needle in her arm?* Of course, a lot of other stuff, which none of them knew about, was happening to me at the same time. My sisters would encourage me to head out of town for a surfing break when they could take over the Mum-sitting, but they had no idea what I was actually doing. Minding Mum became a bit of a decoy, a way of not dealing with my own life.

For something to do, I dial Dot at Gran's. I need to share the fear with someone.

"Hello," my sister answers, warily.

"Dot?"

"Rose. Where *are* you?" She sounds pissed off. "Gran is drifting in and out."

"What the hell does *that* mean?"

"What do you think?" Dot snaps back furiously. "And I don't want to be the only one here when it happens! I thought Hilda would be here by now. And you! And Mum!"

"I'm in Lorne, but I've lost Mum."

"What do you mean, lost her?"

"Well, I picked up a hitchhiker and I stopped for a swim and . . ."

"He's run off with her?" Dot jumps in, her mood changing to one of breathless excitement in an instant, as though Mum has suddenly become the main character in a play by one of the ancient playwrights. Sophocles. *The tragic tale of a woman who must suffer the humiliation of being kidnapped by the gods in order to save her family from disaster . . .*

I do have another moment of panic before I remember that I'm talking to Dorothy. Why the hell did I think I'd get any sense out of her?

"I hope not," I say dryly, "but I'm starting to worry."

"Rose, you are not going to believe this," she cuts in breathlessly.

"What?"

"Cynthia *is* coming down tomorrow!" she declares. "And she's bringing Bruce, and I just don't know if I'm going to be able to handle it."

"But I thought she was working the hospitals this week," I say irritably, wondering at my sister's ability to simply change focus. "Cynthia is always saying she can't get time off."

"She got two days!"

"So, where are they going to sleep?" I ask, relieved, in a way, to be diverted from my present dilemma. Gran's place is a tiny two-bedroom cottage. There will be room for Mum and Dot in the spare room and that's about it. I'll sleep in the back of the van.

"In the same hotel as Dad. Who cares?" Dot cries. "Bruce! She's bringing *Bruce*!"

I sigh. Dorothy doesn't so much dislike Cynthia's boyfriend as despise him. Mainly for his ordinariness. Bruce loves his sports and beer. He likes to bet on the races, and he's building a house in Keilor as a property investment. His big passion is bike riding. But so what? As far as I know, he's not seriously horrible, and he puts up with Cynthia. No mean feat.

"Oh jeez, Rose, what are we going to do? How are we going to cope?"

"Dorothy!" I cut in sternly. "I called you because Mum is missing. Just concentrate on that for a minute."

"Oh, she'll turn up," Dorothy declares, dismissively. "She's probably just taken the hitchhiker out for a meal. She'll be listening to his life story and working out how she can help. You know Mum!"

At that very moment I catch sight of Mum walking toward me with Charles Manson behind her. They're both laden with plastic bags. I subdue my sigh of relief because I don't want to give Dorothy the satisfaction of knowing she is right. I watch Mum trying to cross the road. She is looking worriedly around as she hurries over to the van. *Yeah, well, you're over an hour late. Be worried!* I take a deep breath and try not to feel so irritated. What does an hour actually matter? After all, I'm the one who said I didn't want to hurry the trip.

"Listen, Dot," I say shortly, "I've gotta go."

"No sign of her?" she asks sweetly. I just about grind my teeth.

"I see her now. She's over at the car."

"What did I tell you?"

"Shut up, Dorothy."

"You're too uptight these days, Rosie," Dorothy says mildly, and then sighs. "You've got to deal with some of this stuff, you know."

"What are you on about?" I ask, irritated all over again on a number of fronts. I *hate* being called Rosie, for starters. It just isn't me anymore. Rose is bad enough. Apart from that, Dorothy has no right to tell anyone to face up to anything. She is the most unrealistic, impractical, totally vague and dippy person in the whole world! It won't matter, of course, because she's so beautiful. There will always be some guy who'll take care of the practicalities of life for her. But I refuse to listen to let's-be-realistic lectures from the queen of flake!

"You know," she goes on blithely, as though there is no irony in this situation at all, "it's no use hiding away. That doesn't solve anything. Get in touch with Zoe. Work things out, sweetheart! And what about that nice guy, Nathaniel? You should contact him—"

"Dorothy," I cut in before she can say anything else, "when I want your completely irrelevant advice, I'll ask for it, okay?"

I tell her goodbye and hang up.

As I approach the van, I see that Mum is carrying a number of fancy bags, too. She looks as though she's been shopping at a menswear store.

"Mum!" I call.

"Oh, Rose!" She is harried and hot and apologetic. "Sorry to be so late! We got caught up shopping, and suddenly I saw the time."

"We?" I mutter grimly, not trusting myself to even look at the guy. He's sheepish. I can tell by the way he's hanging back.

123

"Travis and I," she says, turning to him with a smile. "Come on, let's put these in the car and we can all get going." She looks at me. "Did you have a good swim?"

"So what have you been buying?" I ask, ignoring the question. I open up the back of the van so they can put the stuff inside.

"Oh, we had something to eat," she says airily. "Then we bought some food to take to the couple looking after Peter."

"Peter?"

"Travis's son. These people have been terribly good and . . . haven't asked for payment." She looks away, embarrassed suddenly. "Just a few things they might not be able to get locally. T-shirts and shorts. A cricket bat."

"Right," I say, turning to stare at the hitchhiker. He is standing apart from us now, lighting a cigarette, frowning and looking out at the ocean as though this conversation I'm having with my mother has nothing to do with him. He feels me looking and turns to face me with this sly smile.

"Your mum is one cool lady," he mutters.

"Is that a fact?" I snarl, slamming the door shut.

◆ ◆ ◆

The next bit of road, cut into the steep cliff face, is very slow and very beautiful. The ocean is on our left, and the rocky cliffs on our right. The traffic is impatient. When I get caught behind a truck, there is nothing to do but slow down and chill out. No more wild risks. I'm not even tempted. Mum is very quiet, and so is the hitchhiker.

Get in touch with Zoe. Work things out. That nice guy, Nathaniel. Dot's words fly back at me on the breeze. Sounds simple, but it's not. Zoe met Nat one night. And that was when things started getting . . . tangled up.

◆ ◆ ◆

LAST SUMMER, MELBOURNE

"I'm a dumb fat-arse and no guy is ever going to like me!"

It's a Friday night, and the excitement over our VCE results is well and truly over. Zoe and I are walking down Swan Street, Richmond, to see a new band playing at the Corner Hotel. She is in a dark mood because some guy she met in the country gave her the flick. As soon as I saw her, I knew the only solution was to get her out to hear some very loud music.

"So you're just the idiot from Bayswater, right?" I follow up, slowly. "Nothing good will ever happen to you from now on?"

She sighs and gives a deep groan.

"Have I got that right?" I add, for good measure.

"Yeah."

"You only made the top one percent in the state with your VCE, but some dumb hick from Albury gives you the heave-ho and you're finished, right? You're the dumb-arse."

"Oh, shut up about the results!" she snarls back. "You with your bloody perfect score! As though any of it matters if no guy will ever want me!"

"Come on, Zoe! You've had loads of guys interested in you!"

"Not for ages and ages!" she moans, and then brightens a little. "But you do like my hair?"

"Yeah, I do, actually," I say, relieved to change the subject. She's had a whole lot of silvery streaks put in and it looks good, but . . . but I'm not in the mood for effusive flattery. We walk along in silence for a while. *Come on, Zoe. What about me?* is actually what is going through my head. I was pretty geared up to tell her about meeting Nat Cummins, about the party and what happened afterward, but her dramas are, as usual, crowding the space between us. She has yet to ask me one single question about what I've been doing while she was away.

Should I contact Nat? is what I want to know. But what would I say? *Things were a bit knotty at home for a while. But . . . I'd like us to go out now . . .* Is it possible to ring a guy and actually say something like that? I am full of doubt. There are probably about five other girls vying for his attention by now.

"Of course *my* life is absolutely perfect!" I cut in with a blunt stab at wit. "My father has run off with a chick nearly twenty years younger than he is. My mum is, like, *dying* of sorrow. Then there are the sisters. The sane, reliable, responsible sisters! The eldest one cries all the time and won't talk to her husband. The next one is plotting revenge and wants to murder the mistress! Don't laugh. I'm serious, Zoe! And the other one thinks that if only everyone would start reading Dante's *Inferno*, they'd see the folly of their ways and all the problems of the world would be sorted out in a jiffy! Hey, it all makes absolute sense!"

Zoe snorts a few giggles, and her mood lifts a bit.

"I can't believe it about your folks!" she moans. "They were, like, my *ideal* couple! They're how I've always wanted to be when I get old! I love them both so much."

"Me, too," I say, pleased with her depth of feeling.

"Who is this other woman? I mean . . ." Zoe is totally outraged with the idea all over again. "I hate her!"

"Yeah, well," I say dryly, "you're not the only one. Hey, come on, let's go. Give me the lowdown on what actually happened in Albury."

◆ ◆ ◆

The pub is packed. Everyone is here to see a new band, Bye Sky Babies. There has been a bit of a buzz about them for a while, so I'm looking forward to it. People our own age, maybe a bit older, are coming in and out through the swing doors. Dressed up. Some a bit drunk already. Yelling out. I begin to feel seriously excited. I haven't been out to listen to a band since my last birthday. Since Dad left last week, since I met Nat Cummins . . . *And* we're eighteen now. We can both legally drink if we want to. When we arrive, there is a boring band playing, so Zoe and I buy the first legal beer of our lives, and stand out in the warm street with a whole lot of others to wait.

When Bye Sky Babies comes onstage, we venture back inside. Standing room only, so we watch from the door as they gear up and launch into their first number. The rest of the crowd is immediately responsive, but I hold back. First impression is of a pretty ordinary outfit. Two skinny guys, a fat, sweaty drummer, and a tall, plain female singer in torn jeans, battered lavender boots, and a paint-splattered black T-shirt. But by their third number, they're warming up, and so am I. It's around then that I start to get a fix on what the lead guitarist can do, and I realize he's not ordinary at all. He's good. He's got this wired-up thing happening underneath the main melody, and he comes in with little playful riffs at the end of each line, as though he doesn't know whether to be sad or happy so he's going to have it both ways.

The female singer has long jet-black hair hanging in greasy tendrils all around her pale face. She looks sour and unhealthy, but . . . she is belting it out as hard and furious as a jackhammer. I find myself lost in admiration just watching her move about the stage, working the crowd with that aggressive, raspy voice and couldn't-give-a-shit attitude. Zoe and I give each other our *hey-this-is-cool* look and sidle up toward the front to find a space for us near the wall. The air is thick with cigarette smoke, booze, and excitement.

When the band's signature tune starts—the one that has been getting quite a bit of local airplay—the atmosphere cranks up a dozen notches, and the crowd loosens up. The rush of crazy-good feeling I get at this point almost blinds me. It's why I'm here. Why we've come. For *this moment* when the music suddenly breaks out of its cage and comes yelling at me through all my senses. It boils over and rolls down from the stage into the crowd, burning everyone in its path. I love it. I love the sharp wild guitar riffs. I love this girl's voice and the hard drumbeat underneath it. I love the way it gets me feeling careless and defiant and loose within just a few minutes. And I love watching other people around me get like that, too.

Everyone is dancing now. We're dancing where we're standing.

Don't call me baby! Make me wait.

Don't give me no reason to play it safe.

No! No! No!

The crowd screams out the song like it's their very own anthem, fists punching the air, lighthearted and aggressive at the same time.

Oh don't call me baby! Let me call you.

I promise I'll call you honey 'cos you make me so so so blue.

The singing is passionate, wild, like everything in the world belongs inside those words. For a few moments, it's kind of true, those ordinary words mean . . . *everything*. The music is holding out its skinny pockmarked arms and pulling us in to where it's hot and dangerous, and hard to move about, and . . . I love it. I love it so much.

Don't give me no reason to play it safe.

Zoe and I are shouting the words out and laughing along with everyone else, and we're both sweating like wrestlers. It feels *so* good.

You can tell when a band is special. These guys have a jumpy, rough feel, but they've got that extra something that is hard to put a finger on. I reckon other people can feel it too. They won't be doing the pub scene forever, is my guess. They're on their way to something bigger and brighter and the rest of us are happy to be seeing them right now, before they take off for another orbit altogether. Well, that's the way it feels, anyway. The number finishes and I edge my way through the roaring crowd back over to Zoe.

"Good, eh?"

She nods without turning around, transfixed by the stage.

"Want another drink?"

She shakes her head. But when I move off toward the bar, she grabs my arm and pulls me back.

"I want to be up there!" she screams in my ear, above the noise, motioning toward the stage with her thumb, to where the lead singer has picked up a guitar and is tuning it. "I really fucking want to do what she's doing, Rose!"

"Me too." I laugh uneasily, but I know Zoe is not joking. She means it. She is dead serious. Whereas for me, being a musician up there on stage is just a wild longing because I know I don't have it in me—I know my limitations—for Zoe, the fact that she *isn't* up there is a sharp thorn in her side. It is at this very moment actually causing her grief. I squeeze her wrist, turn away, and make my way to the bar, trying not to come down too much. But I can't help it. I feel sour. Much as I love Zoe, sometimes she is just too much, with her insatiable longing for . . . just about *everything*. Tonight happens to be one of those times. *Can't you just love the band without wanting to* be *the band?* I want to scream at her. But I won't do that. I know it's the rejection from the guy in the country bringing her down. Tomorrow she'll be okay.

The set finishes, and the band announces a break. I buy another drink and make my way back through the crowd. When I see Zoe talking to a few old mates, I decide to take myself outside.

"I'm out here, okay?" I call to her, heading for the door. I don't know if she hears me or not because she's already turned away.

Outside, the day is fading fast and my spirits rise to meet the still, clear sky. I love nighttime on this street. The buzz, the lights, the crowds of people all dressed up, looking for action. I lean up against the brick wall of the pub and look around. It's good out here. Cool and fresh. Gladness about being just where I am hits me. I forget about my absent father, freaked-out mother, and drama-queen sisters; take a swig of beer; and plunge downward into the memory of that walk home from the party with Nathaniel Cummins, the night before Dad's bombshell. Singing, holding hands, the heels of our shoes clicking against the quietness of the early morning.

Inside, the music begins with the crescendo of a full-on scream and then pulls back into a raunchy, slow number.

I'm trying to find you. You said you'd come.
I'm looking for you, babe . . . don't do a run.

The girl's voice, low now and sultry, thick and sweet as honey, reverberates inside my head. I push my face up into the sky and let a few hot, secret tears of longing leak from the corners of my eyes. Even when everything else has turned to shit, there is still music.

◆ ◆ ◆

"It *is* you!"

The voice has caught me completely unawares. I jump and he laughs. Here I am looking up into the darkening sky, crying, thinking of him, and he appears, as though summoned by my thoughts. *Creepy.* He's standing about two meters away, sweaty and slightly breathless, as though he's been running. Impossibly handsome in jeans and an old T-shirt with holes, he's carrying a tennis racket and ball, of all things. He bounces the ball on the sidewalk.

"Oh, hello!" I say, gulping, hoping it's too dark for him to see.

"What are you doing?" he asks, bouncing the ball really hard and frowning. If he's seen my tears, then he's pretending he hasn't, which suits me fine.

I wave behind me at the music. "I'm here with a friend," I manage, casually enough, "to see a new band."

"What band?"

"Bye Sky Babies," I say. "You heard of them?"

"You know me, Rose." Nat leans against the wall. "I know nothing about *real* music. I only play stupid trance stuff, remember?" He is still bouncing his ball and looking at me. Referring to his party, when I had a go at him about his choice of shitty music, makes me feel embarrassed.

Then he walks over to the roller door and into the back lot. He stays there a few moments, listening.

"They sound okay," he calls back to me with a smile. "Your friend the one singing?"

"No," I laugh. "She'd like to be, though." There is a pause between us. I'm feeling hideously shy to be caught like this. I can't believe I actually pashed this guy last Friday! How did I get the courage for that? What happened? How did it all come undone so quickly? I suddenly don't understand anything that's been happening over the past week, and it makes me feel very thick.

"You been playing tennis?"

"How did you guess?" He grins and begins smacking the ball into the air, then dives around trying to catch it with his racket before it hits the ground.

"Won, too!"

"So the smokes haven't caught up with you yet?"

"Whoa!" he laughs. "Nasty!"

"Just asking!" All the stuff he's doing with the racket makes me feel a bit easier because at least he's not looking at me.

"So, Rose, you never told me your old man was a Queen's Counsel."

"You never asked," I say, wondering why he's bringing that up now and how he found out.

"Pretty neat for you," he says. "Are you . . . close?"

"Well," I say quickly, "he's my dad."

"I heard your parents split up," he says lightly, still bouncing the ball. My whole body stiffens in surprise.

"Where did you hear that?" My tone is unintentionally sharp. He stops hitting the ball and looks at me.

"I'm sorry," he says. "I shouldn't have said that." He smiles hesitantly.

"It's okay."

"My old man told me," he explains, after an awkward pause. "City law circles are tight. Stuff like that gets around quickly. Sorry, again."

I nod and say nothing.

"Must be hard?"

"Yeah," I breathe out.

"So, how is . . . your family doing?" he asks after a while.

"Okay," I say tentatively. I can't work out if I resent his asking these questions or if I actually like it. I suppose at least he's being forthright, but . . . it's unnerving, too. Do I want to discuss Mum and Dad's split with Nat Cummins? I don't think I do. In fact, I'm sure I don't. "Mum's taking it pretty hard," I add, trying to sound as though the whole situation is cool and doesn't have much to do with me. He frowns.

"It's not the worst thing, you know," he says suddenly.

I look at him sharply.

"What do you mean?"

"There are worse things than two people splitting up."

"Such as?" My voice sounds defensive, even to me.

"Such as two people hanging in together when . . . it's all gone."

"My parents weren't like that," I snap impatiently. I'm sick of people pontificating about things they have no idea about. "There was love." A sob rises in my throat. "They were great together. We . . . had the best family." I turn away, embarrassed by the passion that has seeped into my voice. But for some reason, I need him to understand this. My parents' split is not just another separation. I want him to know how tragic it is, but I can't get any more words out. The swell in my chest and throat makes me feel as though someone has slipped a straightjacket around my body.

"Well, my parents are *just* like that," he says quietly. "And they're still together."

There is an awkward pause.

"They don't get on?" I ask after a while.

"They don't even like each other!" he says. Then he stops mucking around with the ball and looks at me straight. "I wish they would split. I'd like my mum to have some kind of life."

"Your father—" I begin.

"Dad is never there," he says sharply. "I'd love to see my mum happy."

I don't know where to look or what to say. Other people might have conversations like this all the time, but not me. I'm not only confused but filled with curiosity, too. How could he possibly want his family to split up? His honesty moves me, but my throat is stuffed with cotton, and my limbs are made of wood.

"Your mum will get over it," he says, beginning to bounce the ball again. "In a year she'll be laughing again. I promise you."

His words make me laugh myself, because it is such a ridiculous thing for him to say, but also because, for just a few moments there, I believe he knows something I don't, and . . . it's such a relief. *Your mum will be okay.* A huge stone dislodges itself and rolls off my back as I go over his words. She will get over it. Nat has just told me so, in very simple terms. As if he knows. As if it's something obvious. No one has been as confidently positive as Nat is being right now, and it's . . . reassuring.

"Well, she's in pieces now," is all I can manage. "We're pretty worried about her."

He nods and we're both quiet. I want to change the subject.

"You want to check it out?" I offer, waving at the roller door.

"Yeah," he grins at me, "why not?"

So we walk back into the pub together and stand watching the band with Zoe. So loud now that talk is impossible, but I don't mind.

When it's all over and we're outside again, Zoe looks at Nat inquiringly. So I quickly introduce them.

"Good to meet you." Nat smiles warmly, holds out his hand.

Zoe looks at me to ask how I've suddenly appeared with this hunky stranger.

"Nat lives near me."

"Oh." She grins, her eyes flashing with mischief. "So, she just saw you passing and hauled you off the street, huh?"

"Yep," Nat jokes, and gives my shoulders a quick squeeze, "and I couldn't resist."

We all laugh. But his brief touch has set off a mass of electrical impulses down my limbs. Every nerve ending seems to have charged up with a fresh bolt of excitement that leaks into the air like laughing gas.

"So, what did you think of the band?" Zoe is flirting now. Flashing her beautiful eyes coquettishly. She is wearing a low top, and her breasts bulge out. Her come-on attitude is a little embarrassing until I see that Nat seems to be enjoying it. Embarrassment jumps sideways into jealousy before I'm even aware of it happening. Zoe suddenly looks so attractive, with her bright smile and blond hair. I must seem insipid next to her. Maybe he's forgotten about what happened between us at the party. Are we just friends now? Maybe he . . . *likes her? What exactly is happening here?*

"I was a small-town boy for too long." He laughs into Zoe's eyes. "I know nothing about music." He turns to me. "Right, Rose?" I nod.

"Well, we'll have to do something about that," Zoe giggles, without taking her eyes off him for one second.

"What have you got in mind?"

Zoe shrugs her plump shoulders and wiggles her hips to suggest all kinds of possibilities. "Why don't you come out with us sometime, and we'll show you?" she adds in a conspiratorial whisper, leaning in close to both of us.

"That would be cool," Nat says immediately, smiling at her and then turning to me. "I'd love to do that."

"We'll show you the funky places," she gushes, "the hot bands and the cool people. Tell you what, Nat, you'll never look back."

"You're on!"

We break up soon after on the understanding that we'll all go out when Zoe and I come back from the coast. I notice the quick flirtatious last look Zoe throws at Nat, and it unnerves me. Do I tell her about Nat and me now? But . . . what is there to tell? It's not as though he belongs to me.

◆ ◆ ◆

ROAD TRIP

It's the hottest part of the day, and we're on the last stretch to Apollo Bay. My T-shirt is sticking to the back of the seat and my jeans are way too hot. Mum has been quiet for ages, leaning her head against the side window. I can tell she's not sleeping because she occasionally fiddles with her hair, examines her nails, and sighs. I want to ask her what's up—it's not like Mum to be so subdued—but I don't trust myself. I would probably end up saying, "It's your own fault," if she said she wasn't feeling well. As soon as we were out of Lorne, the little creep in the back lit up the first of three cigarettes in a row. The spectacular trip along the Great Ocean Road was ruined by his acrid tobacco stink.

Every now and again I sneak a glance back at him. He is leaning against the side window behind me, eyes closed and arms crossed around a few of the bigger parcels, as though he's scared someone is going to take them from him. A few more parcels are beside him on the seat. All that has to constitute more than just a few things for a kid. Mum has probably set him up for the next year.

We pass Wye River, Kennett River, and Skenes Creek, through the rolling hills and big overhanging pines into Apollo Bay. It's a strange feeling passing the exit leading up to the beach house of last summer. *Wild Dog Road*. I suppose my heartbeat quickens a bit, but I don't let myself slow down. It's my only defense against all these memories trying to crowd into my head like a pack of uninvited party guests. Do what has to be done, the book says, and the rest will fall into place. *Okay* . . .

We're almost on the main street now, and on the left is a huge sprawl of grass leading down to the wonderful wide bay. I can see white-tipped waves bobbing gently across the deep blue of the ocean, and they make me think of toy boats and party hats, of all the happy-kid things of childhood. *Okay. Bring it on.* On the right, the string of shops: supermarkets, cafés, and take-out food joints, mixed in with real estate offices, pubs, and arcades. The whole street is packed with vacationers. SUVs vie with sports cars for sought-after parking spots. RVs, sedans, and busloads of Japanese tourists glide past like huge predatory birds. Kids in bathing suits, with bright towels wrapped around their middles, lick on ice cream cones as they casually stroll across the street, just as if there isn't a car in sight.

"Where do you want to be dropped off?" I ask. We're crawling along behind a tourist bus, and I'm anxious to get rid of the hitchhiker at long last so we can vacate this town at the first opportunity. He wakes up, startled.

"Oh." He shakes his head. Then, when he sees where we are, he groans. "Sorry. I fell asleep."

"So, where?" I ask again.

"Man, this is really embarrassing," he mumbles, "but we've missed the turnoff. It's back a bit. Sorry. I should have told you before."

"How far back?" I snap.

"Er . . . it's called . . ."—he rummages in his pocket—"Wild Dog Road. There's a turnoff about three kilometers along . . ."

I grimace with disbelief and try not to panic. *Is this fate?* Then I turn to Mum. *Fuck fate! I don't have to do this.*

But Mum sighs and turns away from the look I'm giving her, gives a little shrug as if to say some things can't be helped. I thump the steering wheel angrily. Does she seriously want me to go *back*, in this heat? To put ourselves way out for an unpleasant little jerk who couldn't even stay awake to tell us where he wanted to be dropped off? *Come on!*

"Mum," I mutter through gritted teeth, "that road is four or five kilometers back."

She tries one of her oh-isn't-life-so-funny smiles, but I don't play along. *She can't be serious!*

"Well . . . it's up to you, darling, you're the driver."

"Okay," I snarl under my breath, "I don't want to."

There are a couple of silent beats while they both take *that* on board.

"All right," she suggests brightly, "so what about *I* drive Travis back and you stay here and have another swim? That would solve everything."

My mouth falls open. *Yep. She actually wants to take this inconsiderate nobody back to a road five kilometers away!* I shake my head, slam on the brakes, and wait until the traffic behind me has cleared before doing a sharp, screeching U-turn in the middle of the main street. No way! After the Lorne "disappearance," I won't risk another one. Mum has never driven this van, and it has a few idiosyncrasies that take a bit of getting used to. Besides, Charlie-boy might take the opportunity to steal it! He'd tell himself he had a right, seeing as his own car was pinched. I'm so angry that all my neurotic thoughts about last summer just dissolve. *Wild Dog Road?* Well, why bloody not? It's not as though the place is infested with rats or bogeymen, is it? I know for a fact that Ray is overseas, so there is no chance of an embarrassing face-to-face encounter.

"Thanks, Rose," Mum says quietly. "Travis has too much to carry in this heat."

Oh, poor Travis. But I don't utter even a word. Since when did hitchhikers expect a ride to the front door? *Whose trip is this, again? Hold on tight, Rose. Hold tight.* As soon as we're out of the main drag, I gun the van back down the road toward Wild Dog at full speed—which in my van means a fraction over the speed limit. But I'm filled to the eyeballs with this greasy, furious feeling that has my blood just off boiling point. I swear I'm going to throw a party when we finally cut this guy loose!

About five kilometers back the way we've just come, we turn left and head up Wild Dog Road—a steep, windy dirt track leading up into the hills behind the town. It's slow and tortuous and at some of the steepest points, the van really starts to struggle. But what can I do at this point? I keep an anxious eye on the temperature gauge, hoping that the engine won't get too hot and give out. Then I swear for the millionth time that I *have* to take one of those mechanics courses that are advertised in the local library. I'm *sooo* sick of not knowing the first thing about engines.

We're well off the main road now. The upside of this little journey off the coastal highway is that, after about ten minutes of climbing, almost every twist in the road gives us a sensational view down the coast. It's dairy country. We pass herds of docile cows feeding in the high pastures, and milking sheds that shine in the sun like silver matchbox toys. The occasional little house or cottage nestled in among bushland or in an open field reminds me of the illustrated books I read as a kid. Some old crone might fly around the corner on her broomstick any minute! Even in summer the countryside is green and luxuriant. But the occasional car or farmer's truck coming down the other way keeps most of my attention pinned to the road. Careering over this steep drop would be nasty in the extreme.

I take the odd glance in the rear-view mirror. Charles Manson is at least alert now. I assume he's going to tell me to stop any minute, that we've reached our destination. But on we go, kilometer after slow kilometer. The van begins to shudder with every gear change as we round the tight little curves and bounce through the gouged-out tracks and potholes of last winter. Twenty minutes in and we come to a fork in the road. I stop the van.

"Which way now?" I ask sharply.

He is frowning, chin in hand, staring out the window, pretending not to hear.

"Do we have far to go?" I ask loudly.

"Don't think it's far." He is biting his lip and frowning hard at the intersection. One fork is a sharp turn, heading higher up the mountain, and the other follows the ridge toward the coast for a while before getting lost again in the hills. I know this last bit. It's been a while, but I'm pretty sure it leads down to the house where . . . never mind. Keep in the *now*. Stay present.

Then, with a jolt, I realize he doesn't have a fucking clue!

"You have no idea, do you?" I ask stonily.

"It's been a while since I've been here," he admits. Then his face suddenly lights up, and he points to the fork leading higher up. "But I *think* it's up there."

"Are you sure?"

"No, I'm not sure," he says in this bored, surly, don't-give-me-a-hard-time voice. "I'm not *totally* sure, okay? As I said, it's been a while."

I boil over at this point and . . . lose it altogether.

"Well, how come you're not sure?" I scream at him furiously. "Why didn't you say so before you let us drive up here?"

"Now, Rose!" Mum tries to intervene. "Just keep calm. I think—"

"Listen," the guy yells over her, one grimy finger jabbing the air two inches from my face, "and listen hard, you uptight little bitch! This is very hard for me! *Very hard.* I'm going to be seeing my kid for the first time in two years! It's a difficult situation, and you're not helping!"

What! I am shocked at the incredible audacity of him talking to *me* like that, calling *me* a bitch when I'm doing him the biggest favor ever! Driving him all this way out here. My mouth falls open and I am momentarily struck dumb. But not for long.

"I'm so *sorry!*" I sneer. "Why don't you get out *now* and see if you can find some nice person who *is* willing to help you!"

"Look, I appreciate the ride," he says in a more subdued way. "Don't think I'm not grateful."

"Oh? Now why would I think that, Travis?" I spit back, my hands itching to grab his scrawny little neck and squeeze the life out of him.

"You gotta understand," he pleads in his best I-am-the-victim whine, "this is a complete freak-out for me."

"But it's not *my* freak-out," I say, my voice still dripping with acid. "Not mine. I have plenty of my own, thank you very much! *Your* problems are not my problems! Can you get your head around that one, Travis?"

"Rose, please"—Mum puts her hand on my arm—"there is no point shouting and fighting like this." Her voice is thin with distress, and a sliver of concern breaks through my fury. There are sweat marks under her arms and beads of moisture on her forehead. My sisters will kill me if Mum arrives drained and upset. "We're here now," she begs, "so let's just see this out, please . . ."

The guy leans over the backseat and taps her on the shoulder.

"I want to apologize for speaking so . . . rough like that in front of you, Patsy," he says gruffly. "You're a real nice lady . . . and I want you to know I really do appreciate everything you're doing for me." Mum nods and smiles faintly. He sits back and gives me a blank stare. "It's up there," he says stonily, pointing to the sharp upward climb again. "I'm ninety percent sure now."

"Right," I snarl, and push the van into first gear.

Ten minutes later, we are crossing a cattle pit and pulling into a driveway that I thankfully don't recognize. For a while there, it was beginning to seem like some kind of nightmare. Part of me half expected we would end up in the same place as last summer for a rerun of events.

At the end of the drive is a simple cream wooden house set behind a white picket fence, dwarfed by six huge pine trees. I look in the rear-view mirror, and Travis is nodding grimly.

"This it?"

"Yeah," he mutters, "this is it."

A shed and garage are visible farther back behind the house. It's all so squat and little and neatly set out that once again fairy tales come to mind. I pull the van up into the cleared space in front of the house, and about five barking dogs immediately rush from all sides and surround the van. They don't look particularly ferocious.

"Kelpies." Mum is trying to be jolly. "Your favorites, Rose."

"Yeah," I reply, but I don't smile. I refuse to be pleased with anything.

Travis slides his door open and gets out immediately and, groaning a bit, stretches in the sunlight. The dogs stop their barking as he bends to pat them, then he pokes his head in Mum's window.

"I'd really like you to come and meet my kid, Patsy," he says gruffly, not bothering to even glance at me.

She turns to me. "We'd better get going, I suppose . . ." she says carefully.

"Go ahead inside, if you want," I mutter, hating the fact that she's asking my permission. It makes me feel like the Gestapo. It's pretty obvious the invitation hasn't been extended to me, and that's fine. I don't want to meet his brat. Anyway, I need a break before heading down that winding road again, so I turn off the engine and stay seated behind the wheel, watching both of them walk toward the house. Travis holds the gate open for Mum, and as she passes through, he turns to give me a cold stare before following her up the path to the front door. I stare straight back and then lift my middle finger.

There are hens, brown and white, having little fights with each other as they peck and scrabble around in the dust for whatever it is they're looking for. There's a fishpond set behind the fence, amid a well-tended garden. I stand with both hands on the top rail, amused by two sleek cats sitting on either side of the pond, moving their heads slowly from left to right, mesmerized by the bright goldfish swimming about. As the quietness settles over me, I start to feel calmer. It's a lovely little place, and I'm sorry for the kid who is going to have to leave it to go live in Sydney with that jerk.

I take myself slowly back up the track to the cattle pit. Two of the dogs are following at a safe distance. When I stop and click my fingers to call them closer, they wag their tails but maintain a wary distance. Even dogs are scared of me. I cross the pit and walk out into the middle of the road we came up, clasp my hands behind my head, and slowly turn on the spot, breathing in the peculiar mix of pungent smells: gum leaves and grass, diesel fumes, cow dung and dust. His house was farther down and along the track a way. But these hills and this view bring up memories so raw that they hurt. I don't want to think about it all again, but I do. I can't help it.

So what was the precise sequence of events that brought me to him? How were they first stacked up, one on top of the other like bricks in a wall, with no cement?

I walk back and cross over to where the dogs are still waiting. This time they let me pat them, and for some silly reason it makes me glad. I bend and rub them behind their ears and tell them they are the nicest dogs I've seen in a while, but that they had better not give me fleas or they'll get what's coming to them.

◆ ◆ ◆

LAST SUMMER, APOLLO BAY

It was my first long trip in the van, and I was proud of myself, excited to have made it at last. Zoe's instructions were not all that easy to follow, and I'd missed a couple of turnoffs.

I'm late, but I'm here. At least I think I am. I stare across at the house nestled between a few big peppermint gum trees. There is a garden and a paling fence all around. Trees and birds. Not exactly the romantic little run-down shack I'd heard about over the last four years. Nice. But when I see the word *Serendipity* written on the gate leading into the property, I know this has to be it. I cross the cattle pit, pull up outside the front of the house near a couple of old cars, and look around. I jerk in startled surprise when I see a lone guy peering suspiciously out from under the hood of a car at my approach. No sign of Zoe. She promised she'd be waiting for my arrival with flags and balloons and bated breath, so maybe this isn't the right place after all. The guy is dressed in oil-stained work clothes, an old flannel shirt over jeans and big boots. He straightens up and, still unsmiling, leans one arm against his car and watches me get out. The Sex Pistols are blaring out from speakers inside.

"Hello," I say tentatively, moving across to him. "I'm Rose, Zoe's friend." He has a thin face with a long, beaked nose and heavy brows over the same almond-shaped green eyes that make Zoe's face so intriguing. He's probably in his mid-forties, and he's very good-looking in a lean, weather-beaten, cowboy kind of way. Short sandy hair, flecked with gray. He is thin, with well-defined muscles and tanned skin.

"Well . . ." he says in a lazy, slightly amused tone, "Rose. It's good to meet you at last." He rubs his oil-covered hands on his trousers and holds out his hand formally and we shake. "I'm Ray. Zoe will be back soon," he says, walking over to the house to open the door for me. "Come in."

"Thanks," I mumble, and walk past him through the door and into the music. The Sex Pistols are crap, but I sort of like them anyway.

Once inside I can't help smiling. I'm in awe. The music is loud, and the big central living room is lined with original rock posters from the sixties and seventies. Not only all the big bands like the Stones, Zeppelin, the Grateful Dead, and The Who, but lesser-known artists like the Doobie Brothers and Crosby, Stills and Nash. It's completely covered in these very cool old posters, some of them frayed, torn, and dirty, but . . . oh, trust me, it's impressive. Very. Even the ceiling is covered. The stereo takes a place of pride on a wooden cabinet. Two huge speakers blare from either side of the room. The track ends with a long clashing chord, and almost immediately The Cure starts up, with one of my favorite tracks from their late-eighties album *Disintegration*. Suddenly I'm in a trance. There is no tomorrow. This is *cool*. I'm really intrigued. Zoe told me her dad was into music, but I had no idea it was so . . . over the top!

"Wow!" I say when I read the 1973 poster advertising a Van Morrison concert in London. "Did you actually *go* to this?"

Her father looks to where I'm pointing and nods but says nothing. He remains expressionless as he goes over to the turntable and turns off the music, creating a sudden sharp silence. Then he points to one of the old armchairs.

"You want to sit down?"

It feels as if I've been asked to sit down for an interview.

"No, I've been driving. I'm okay," I say, going over to the big front windows that look out over the sea. "Great view."

"Yeah. It's not bad."

The room is messy, but not overly so. The floor is on different levels. There is a big, comfortable lounge setting around a television, and a few other easy chairs set down in one corner. Up higher is a big table and chairs. A little home office in the far corner. Desk. Filing cabinet. Phone, fax, and small computer. A corkboard stuck to the wall. Zoe's father heads toward the double doorway leading out to a small kitchen.

"A drink?" he offers.

"I'm okay," I say shyly. "I'll just wait here. You go back to work if you like."

"I'm going to make coffee," he says, glancing over at me as he reaches for the coffee plunger. I feel him take in my bare legs in the too-short denim skirt, the pink tank top pulled tightly across my chest, and my long hair pulled up at the back of my head. "It's no trouble."

"Then I'll have one, too." I pick up a Doors album cover, and walk through to join him in the kitchen. I wish he hadn't turned the music off, but I'm too shy to say so. "Nineteen sixty-nine," I say, putting the album cover on the table. "Recorded live in front of twenty-five thousand."

He's leaning over the sink, his back to me, and it gives me a spurt of satisfaction to see him stop what he is doing as he takes in what I've just said. He turns around slowly and looks at me again.

"Not as good as the studio version, though," he says seriously.

"Don't agree." I shrug.

He grins and turns back to fill the kettle.

"But I *know*," he says, still grinning.

"How come?"

"I was there."

"You . . ." I'm at a loss for words. "At the concert where they recorded it?" He nods and I shake my head, tongue-tied with awe. "So how was it?" I ask eventually, laughing a bit.

"Ah, not bad."

"Just not bad, eh?" And we both laugh.

"So, Rose"—he hands me the mug of coffee and sits down at the table—"Zoe told me you did well in the exams. What's next for you?"

"Law," I say without hesitation, coming away from the window and sitting down at the opposite end of the table. He smiles and shakes his head.

"Just like Dad?"

"Yeah, I guess."

"That van won't fit," he jokes.

"So, what sort of car should I have?" I pretend to be miffed so I don't have to look back into those oddly watchful eyes.

"Some girly European shit-box!"

"Well, thanks a lot!" I can't help laughing. "But I don't have that sort of money."

"Your old man would buy one for you, wouldn't he?" he asks with a sly smile, like he knows all about my family being well off and that he kind of approves and disapproves at the same time.

"Nah." I shake my head with embarrassment, remembering Dad's check still pinned to my wall. After everything that happened, it hadn't felt right to cash it. "Anyway, Zoe and I are going surfing. We need the van for our boards. Hasn't she told you yet?"

"Yeah, she's told me"—he shakes his head and looks into his coffee, frowning—"and I'll believe it when I see it."

"What do you mean?" His tone disconcerts me; it's like he knows something I don't.

"Well . . ." he drawls slowly, "there's a new bloke on the scene. And you know Zoe. Everything else has to fit around that."

A new bloke? I take a sip of my coffee, my mood suddenly edgy and poised to spiral downward. I know Zoe rang Nat and that they went to hear a band on Saturday night. She asked me to come but I couldn't. I figured she'd tell me if anything happened. She always has in the past.

"So, the new bloke got a name?" I try to make my voice light.

"I'll bet you anything he has"—her father shrugs dryly—"but I don't know it." He turns to the window, listening. "That's her now." He smiles when he sees that I hear nothing. "I've got good ears for an old rocker."

A couple of minutes later, Zoe bursts in.

"Sorry! I got caught up with some old fart in the supermarket who knows you, Dad." Still holding plastic bags full of groceries, she rushes over to me and gives me a big apologetic hug before she chucks them down and turns to her father with a beaming smile. "At last you get to meet Rose! Isn't she fantastic?"

"Yep"—her father nods slowly, looking at me—"no question about it. She's fantastic."

We all laugh, but his words make a fizz of excitement pulse through me before I can think. There is something odd going on here, and I don't know what it is. For no good reason, a nervous tingle spreads down from my chest into my belly and legs.

The rest of the afternoon is spent surfing. We pile our boards into Ray's minivan, and the three of us hit the waves. Zoe and I head out together, and her father takes a spot farther up the beach. The wind is up, it's a bit choppy, and I miss quite a few because I'm so out of practice, but it's still wonderful. Actually, after the last couple of weeks, it is total bliss. I decide not to ask Zoe about the new guy until later.

I love the way time loses its chokehold when I'm surfing. Not that you don't think about things when you're paddling out or you're up there riding a wave. All kinds of stuff slide into your head, but everything is knocked back down to size. Who cares if you're late or early, if it's three or six o'clock? Who cares about some weird vibe between you and your best friend's father? I mean, how crazy is *that*? You want to laugh out loud. Such bullshit. With a big sky surrounding you, spreading up and out as far as you can see, and this water the color of fresh mint biting into your skin, you feel cleaned out from the inside, cool as a slippery fish inside your wetsuit. You're just one of the sea creatures going about their business, and it makes absolute sense to be right where you are.

The sun will tell us when our time is up—the sun and my own belly, growling for food. Out here on the waves, the knots untangle all by themselves.

Zoe is the first one out. I see her sitting halfway up the beach, out of her wetsuit, and I'm surprised she hasn't lasted longer. There is no way I'm ready to come in yet. I wave, and she waves back. If she wants me out for any reason, she'll have to come and get me.

When I do come in, at least an hour later, she's lying on her back with her knees up and eyes closed. Her father is sitting next to her, staring distractedly out to sea.

"Hey!" I say, all breathless and enthusiastic, shaking my hair about like a puppy. "I'm completely wrecked!"

Her father smiles at me as I unzip my wetsuit and begin pulling it off. I wrap a towel around me, then plonk myself down next to Zoe.

"You got out early."

Zoe groans and sits up.

"Got a headache," she mumbles.

"You didn't have anything to eat, Zoe," Ray chides quietly.

"I'm on a diet."

He and I share a bemused smile. Zoe is always doing something mad with food. Starving herself on some stupid low-this or low-that plan that she can never stick to for more than a day, or else she's on a total pies-and-chocolate bender.

"You've got to eat," her dad says, stroking her head a couple of times, "or you'll have no energy and you'll feel sick."

"Hunger doesn't give you a *headache*, Dad." Zoe sniffs mournfully.

"Yes it does!" I say. "If I'm hungry, I get a headache."

"Yeah, but you're a weirdo!" Zoe laughs quietly and covers her eyes as though in pain. "Sorry, but I'm going to have to pike out . . ."

"You want to go home?" her father asks.

"Yeah, I'm feeling putrid," she groans. "Sorry."

We get up reluctantly and begin to pack up our things. I slip on my little skirt, aware of the other two watching me as I zip it up.

"I bet Rose doesn't go on crappy diets," her father says approvingly.

"So?" Zoe gives me a jab in the ribs. "She's a skinny arse!"

We begin to make our way slowly up the sand to the car. It's true, I don't diet. I'm naturally slim. I don't think about what I eat, and I reckon that is the key. But I don't like her father comparing us, making out like I've got it all together while she hasn't. I don't know what I'd be like if I was naturally big. I'd probably be on stupid diets and crap, too.

"I've got other problems," I say weakly.

"Oh, yeah?" Ray says, amused. "Such as?"

"She's one big problem!" Zoe cuts into the odd moment between her father and me with a giggle. "Just look at her."

And so it goes. Easy enough, but as the day proceeds and we make our way back to the car and then to the house, the weird undercurrent surfaces again. He takes my board from me to put in the car—Zoe's board is already in, and she's waiting in the front seat—and there is a moment's hesitation, with us both holding the board. We stand there at the back of the car, inside the open doors, not looking at each other, just breathing. It's as though he's waiting for something to happen, or for me to say something, at least. I pull away feeling totally wired up.

Two minutes later I find myself sitting in the backseat leaning forward a little, staring at his hands on the steering wheel, at the strong, blunt fingers still faintly covered in oil stains. I make myself sit back and look out the window, but the lines at the back of his neck and the way his hair is flecked through with gray catch my attention. *This guy is old.* But when he puts one of those hands out to caress Zoe's knee as he explains something about road rules (Zoe has only just gotten her license), I am breathless for a moment as though it's me he's about to touch, and I'm walking a tightrope, waiting for it. *What is going on?*

◆ ◆ ◆

"Hey, Rose!" Zoe calls from where she's lying on her bed. "There's stuff I've got to talk to you about."

I'm off to the bathroom for a shower, but I stop in the doorway of her room, a towel hung around my shoulders.

"Oh, yeah?" I say. She looks back at me with this weird, sheepish expression on her face but doesn't say anything. Suddenly I *know*. Nat Cummins is the new bloke. Has to be. A flare of anger ignites in my chest. She wants to get it all out, then hear me tell her it's all just fine with me. Nothing has happened between them yet, but she wants to tell me now how keen she is to push it. *She knows . . . she knows I like him.* I don't know how I know this last bit, but I do.

"Can it wait till after my shower?" I say lightly. "I feel too gross to talk right now."

Grains of sand swirl around the drain before disappearing. Come on, be fair, Rose. How would Zoe know about me and Nat? Stop being paranoid. *Unless he told her . . .* but I can't imagine him being that uncool. I mean, nothing really happened between us. *Be fair, Rose.* I told her it was fine to ask him out, even though I couldn't come. I turn off the shower and stand naked, drying myself slowly. I hear her father moving along the hallway whistling "Wish You Were Here," and it sends a sudden, sharp shiver right into my guts, and my head catapults off in another direction altogether. I put on my clothes and decide that all the crap happening at home is making me crazy. I console myself with that thought as I tousle my hair in front of the mirror. When I bend to search for lipstick in my toiletry bag, I stop for a moment before applying it. *Lipstick?* Why am I so desperate to look nice?

◆ ◆ ◆

ROAD TRIP

"Dorothy has gone completely nuts."

I'd been about to walk around the back of the house with the dogs to see if there was a view of the sea, when my phone started ringing. It was Cynthia in army general role, getting the troops into line.

"What are you talking about?" I ask. The reception isn't good. All the hiss and crackle is making my sister sound like a foreign correspondent reporting from Iraq.

"Have you still got Mum?" she wants to know.

"What do you think?" I shout impatiently.

"Don't shout!" she shouts back.

"May I speak to her please?"

"Not really."

"What do you mean, *not really*? Dot said you left her with some hitchhiker! Why on earth did you pick up a *hitchhiker*, Rose?"

"You're breaking up, Cynthia," I say. Not true, but I'm not about to admit any hitchhiker regret to her. I walk over to the house now, and it's sounding clearer.

"I can hear you very well!" she snaps back. *Damn.* "So where are you," she wants to know, "and why aren't you there already? Dot is going berserk! Dad has arrived. And guess what? He's got Cassandra with him. They're staying at the Stump."

"You're kidding," I say, shocked. "Why would he bring her?"

"Who knows? But I want to warn Mum."

"Is she—Cassandra, I mean—hanging around the house with Gran and Dot?"

My mind boggles trying to imagine that cool, glamorous, red-suited woman in Gran's cluttered kitchen.

"No. But it's still awful. Ring Dorothy, Rose. Let her know what's happening!"

"Nothing is happening!"

"Well, things are happening here!" she declares. "Hilda and David are fighting again, and . . ."

I let her ramble on with the latest details about the state of our eldest sister's marriage, which has apparently taken some kind of dive, but I refuse to get involved.

Don'tcha just hate it when you've left home but your family expects you to join all their squabbles and dramas? Just ride the surface, *you tell yourself,* and think of something else while they're yabbering on at you. *The moment you start to think about what they're saying, you're gone. Feels like standing on a cliff that is slowly giving way beneath your feet . . . There you go, sinking back into the spot where you were before.*

We are both quiet for a moment.

"So, where *is* Mum?" Cynthia wants to know.

"I frankly don't know if I'll ever see her again," I say, just to irritate her. Cynthia always has to know where everyone is at any given time of day or night. But her view of how life should proceed just begs to be ruffled occasionally. "I'm in a tiny remote house in the hills at the back of Apollo Bay, and we've just driven the hitchhiker out to see his son, who he hasn't seen in two years. Mum has gone inside with him and they've been gone for *ages!*"

There is silence as Cynthia churns this over.

"Go inside and get her at once," she orders sharply. "You know what Mum is like, Rose! She's probably signing away the house or something, as we speak. Get her. This isn't funny."

"I can't," I say.

"Why not?"

"I don't trust myself with the hitchhiker."

"Jeez, Rose!" She gives one of her deep, exasperated sighs.

"Look, I'm joking," I say. "They won't be long. He just wants her to meet his kid."

"I hope you are going to university next year?"

"What?" But I shouldn't be surprised by this turn in the conversation. It's so like her to change the subject, just as I'm getting comfortable.

"Well . . . you've got a brain," Cynthia declares. "Someone told me they saw you in the State Library recently. You looked very involved. They said you were definitely writing something. See . . . that says it all. You're destined for serious study, Rose, whether you like it or not—it's in the family."

The family! Jesus, I hate the way they all have this strong belief in *the family*, even though we don't have one anymore, well . . . not a proper one. Just because they're all high achievers doesn't mean I have to be one. There are some days when I actually like being a waitress and I don't want to be anything else.

"It must have been someone else," I mumble as a shiver of dismay goes through me. "Gotta go now, Cynthia."

"Rose, answer me!"

"Sorry, Cynthia, you're breaking up."

Just then, Mum, the hitchhiker, a young boy of about ten, and a very fat middle-aged woman I've never seen before come out the front door. I decide not to tell Mum about Cynthia's call. Why get her upset before she has to be? We'll be there soon enough. I'm introduced to Marion, the woman who has been looking after the kid, and then to the kid himself. He is a surprisingly nice-looking boy with dark curly hair, deep brown eyes, and a serious expression. I like the way he looks at me curiously when we shake hands, as though he's expecting me to tell him something interesting. *Sorry to have to disappoint you, kid.*

"We can give Travis and Peter a ride back into town, can't we, Rose?" Mum smiles anxiously, her hand on the kid's shoulder like he belongs to her or something. "Seeing as we've got to go that way?"

"What?" Haven't we just taken an hour out of our time to drive him out here to see his son? So *why* the hell are we driving them back in again? I sigh pointedly, raise my eyebrows, and look away. Will this fiasco ever end?

"They want to take Travis to see Peter's mother in the hospital," Mum explains quickly, just as though she knows what I'm thinking. "Marion's husband will pick them up from there."

"No problem," I say, letting my voice teeter on the edge of sarcasm. "Anyone else want to go somewhere?"

Without another word we all pile into the car, Mum and me in the front and the other three in the back. We strap ourselves in. I put the key into the ignition and turn. Nothing. I try again. I pump the gas. And again. And . . . *nothing*. The engine is absolutely dead. I don't believe this. What now?

I turn around and look at the three faces staring at me from the backseat and shrug.

"Sorry," I mutter, "it won't start." The hitchhiker gives a loud, exasperated groan, slides open the door, gets out, and lights a cigarette. I seriously do want to kill him at this moment. *Oh, sorry!* I'm on the point of screaming. *Sorry for not having a better car for you to take a free ride in, you bloody jerk!*

Mum and the other woman exchange glances. The kid's eyes stay on me. I roll down the window. "Don't suppose you know anything about cars?" I snap at Travis's back. He turns around and shrugs without meeting my eyes.

"Go figure!" I snarl under my breath as I try again.

"Well, never mind!" Marion says cheerfully, giving the boy's shoulders a little squeeze with her fat fingers. "Ross will be home soon."

"Does *he* know anything about cars?"

"Oh yes, love," she declares mildly. "He'll fix it. No worries."

"So when will he be home?"

"In an hour."

So we all pile out again. They invite me in for something to eat, but even though I'm hungry, I'm feeling so shitty about everything that I refuse. Watching them go through that gate again, I'm tempted to pick up a stone and chuck it at Travis's back. *What the fuck am I doing here?* What if Ross—whoever he is—can't fix my van? We'll be stuck here forever!

I wander around, kicking things and swearing to myself about the mistake of bringing Mum. After a while I calm down. There is nothing to do but wait. My spirits revive a bit when I remember the packed lunches stashed in the van.

I'm sitting on the ground with my back up against a tree, eating the sandwiches, when the kid approaches.

"You want this?" he asks, holding out a can of Coke. He startles me a bit because I'd been looking the other way, but I take the can gratefully, break open the top, and take a long guzzle. He stands there looking at me.

"You want to see the calves?" he asks after a while.

"Okay." I finish off the drink. "What is your name again?"

"Peter."

He ends up showing me all around the little dairy farm: the hens, the dogs, the cows, and about a dozen glossy-coated, tottering, black-and-white calves. So pretty. He's a quiet kid but turns out to be amazingly knowledgeable. I can't help being impressed. He knows how many cows there are in the pasture, and how many liters of milk they give each morning and night, and what prices the calves are likely to bring when they're sold in the spring. He tells me when they need rain and when they don't, and what the government's milk policy is, and what's happening with dairy exports. At first I think I've happened upon a genuine eccentric, a kind of quaint anachronism from another age, but after a while I start listening to what he's actually saying, and it's interesting. When he's not at school, he works alongside Ross, the owner. He proudly shows me the new posts they put in the day before, where the cows had trampled down a section of the fence. He is just a young boy, but his serious attitude is surprisingly refreshing. After about half an hour, I realize I'm actually enjoying myself. *What an excellent kid!*

He's curious about me, too, but it takes him a while to get over his shyness. His first question makes me laugh.

"Why is your hair like that?"

"Just a crazy idea I had one day," is my answer. "Don't you like it?"

"It's okay." He grins shyly. "Can I feel it?" So I let him run his two hands over the top of my bristles. "At least you don't have to comb it," he says thoughtfully.

"That's right."

We walk down the hill to a dam that is surrounded by trees. I squat down under one of them and watch this odd, skinny, self-contained kid skipping stones across the gleaming brown water, and I try to imagine him suddenly transported to Sydney. How will it be for him?

160

"Do you like my dad?" he asks suddenly, without looking at me.

"I don't know him," I reply, avoiding the boy's direct look. "What about you? Do you like him?"

The kid shrugs and looks away, and I immediately want to kick myself. What a stupid question for me to ask! He hasn't even seen his father for two years.

"My mum is dying," he says, still not looking at me. I knew this already, and yet his words chill me. I look at his thin legs and his raised, bony arm in the big T-shirt, about to throw another stone, and . . . something unfamiliar stirs inside me. What? Sympathy? I don't know. I can't put a word to the feeling. *My mum is dying . . .* I don't know this kid. So why do I care?

"You'll miss her," I say. And, when he nods, "What is she like?"

"She's got black hair," he says, "and brown eyes."

"She sounds nice," I say encouragingly, thinking he'll continue with a more detailed description, but he doesn't. I'm suddenly curious. I want to ask him what kind of person she is. Does she laugh much or get mad easily? How tall is she? Does she ever get angry that she is going to die?

"My dad might get another car," he says suddenly.

"Do you want to go back with him to Sydney?"

"No." He shakes his head.

At that point we both hear a car arriving up at the house, and the boy's eyes light up.

"That's Ross," he says. "He'll fix your car, no worries."

◆　◆　◆

Marion's husband, a huge gentle man with a kindly manner, had the battery recharged and the wire causing the problem sorted out within about five minutes of him opening the hood, and now we are traveling back down to Apollo Bay

161

with Travis and his son Peter. Ross will go down and pick them up again in a couple of hours.

As we pull up outside the hospital, I look at my watch, amazed to see it's nearly three p.m. Mum sees too and smiles.

"We'll be on our way, then." She turns to the two in the back. "We've still got a ways to go." Travis gets out and comes around to Mum's side and pokes his hand through the open window.

"Thanks for everything," he says. "I won't forget you."

"Oh Travis"—Mum shakes his hand warmly—"you're more than welcome."

"I'll keep my eye out in the local paper," he goes on, still holding Mum's hand and looking earnestly into her eyes, "for when the old lady dies. Maybe me and the kid will send a card or something?"

"That would be so nice!"

I turn around when I feel a tap on my shoulder.

"Want to come and meet my mum?" the boy asks shyly. I only just manage to hide a shudder of distaste. *No offense, kid, but dying mothers are not on my agenda of things to see and do today.*

"Thanks, Peter, but . . . we'd better get going," I mumble.

About to go on, I hesitate because I can see that this nice kid who made the hour or so of waiting pass quickly and pleasantly really does want me to come in and meet his mother. Pretty simple really.

"She'll like you," he adds seriously, before I can utter a word.

"Yeah?" I can't help smiling.

"Yeah." He smiles back. "She used to do stuff with her hair too."

On the one hand I'm touched, but . . . I simply don't want to go in there. I've never even seen a seriously sick person before, much less someone who is dying, and considering my present state, I figure it makes sense to leave it that way. After all, I'm going to see Gran soon. If she's still alive when we get there—which I'm secretly hoping won't be the case—I'll do whatever I'm supposed to. She's my grandmother, after all. I'll kiss her, say goodbye, all the right stuff. Not exactly my thing, but . . . I'll do it. *And what about . . . Zoe?* I suddenly feel like such a creep, and the kid is still looking at me, waiting for my reply. What can I say?

"Okay," I say casually, "just for a few minutes, I'll come say hello." I turn to Mum sitting next to me. "You coming too?"

To my disappointment, she shakes her head.

"No, darling," she says wearily. "Not appropriate for me."

So, if it's not appropriate for her, why would it be for me?

◆ ◆ ◆

"How is my best buddy?" the shrunken figure in the bed whispers. The kid props himself behind her on the bed and puts both thin arms around her frail shoulders.

She smiles hello when we're introduced, her eyes like huge dark pools in her pale face. Every bone is visible. Such an elaborate structure, with the skin like the finest parchment stretched across it. It's odd, but she looks younger than me. Doesn't even look twenty, much less thirty.

"Is it a nice day outside?" she wants to know, caressing her son's arm. "Did you go to Adam's party yesterday?"

How can I describe the next ten minutes? Meeting this woman is so unlike anything I've done before. She is so young and weirdly *alive*! Hearing the gentle rebuke in her voice when she tells Peter he must speak to the teacher if he's having trouble with his reading. Asking what the heck he has done with his good sneakers. What fun it will be getting to know Dad again. All the obvious stuff.

I watch Travis's eyes well up, in the face of the enormity of what is going to happen. It's the first time he's seen her since she was diagnosed, and he is shocked. I can hear it in his voice. The really odd thing is that I came in expecting to feel awkward and out of place, but I don't . . . and I'm not sure why this is. Okay, it's sad, but I'm also thinking how cool, how brave she is, just staying . . . ordinary.

When Peter happily suggests that his mum feel my bristly head, she laughs and reaches out both of her clawlike hands.

"Come here, Rose!" she says as though she's known me all my life. "Give me a feel."

And it is at that point, as I'm leaning forward, her bony fingers caressing my skull, the three of them—mother, father, kid—laughing around me, that I feel something give way. The hard rock cemented in place since last summer begins to shift about a bit, it creaks and groans and tries to roll forward.

I don't know what's going on exactly, or what to say. But I feel *blessed*. I know no other way of putting it. It's a strange feeling and only lasts a few seconds, but it's like the inner core of me, held secret for so long, wrapped only in old rags and left to rot in some forgotten dank corner, has been pulled outside and exposed to the sun. The warmth and light come rolling in . . .

I leave soon after. Shake hands formally with Travis, without either of us actually looking at each other. Then I shyly take the woman's hand and wish her well. When it comes to Peter, I hold out my arms for a hug, and he hugs me back tightly with both arms.

"Thanks for bringing my dad," he says.

"That's okay."

164

We smile, and he runs his hands over my head one last time before I leave.

I find the toilets on the way out, lock myself into a stall, sit down on the seat, and cry for a long time. Then I splash my face in cold water again and again and wipe it dry with the paper towels. I don't think Mum notices when I eventually get back out to the van. If she does, she doesn't say anything.

I turn the key and the engine fires up first go. *Thank you, Ross!* I pull the van out onto the open road, glad to have the diversion of driving.

We're traveling west, and I'm anxious to get to Port Campbell before the sun begins to set, or I'll be virtually driving blind. Mum and I don't speak. She hunches up in the corner almost as soon as we're out on the highway.

After half an hour I turn to her, about to ask what she thinks the odds might be of the kid being allowed to stay where he is, happy with Ross and Marion, but her eyes are closed. Her whole body seems tense, her legs are twisted up in what has to be an uncomfortable position, and her head is at an oddly stiff angle. Every now and again she drums her fingers on her knees, too, and I wonder what the hell she's thinking about. Am I supposed to say something here? Do something?

Don'tcha just hate it when you're supposed to say something and you can't because . . . but the sun is in my eyes and Peter is on my mind and the sentences don't flow the way they normally do, so I put on an old Eric Clapton CD because we both like listening to those low blues riffs. We drive along without speaking.

Mum stirs herself when we get to the Lavers Hill sign. "Dot called when you were in the hospital."

"Oh yeah?" I tense up.

"Your father is staying at a hotel," she continues in a bland tone, barely above a whisper, "with his . . . girlfriend."

I look at her, but she is staring straight ahead. On the point of asking her how she feels about it, I hesitate. I have no idea if Mum has met Cassandra yet, or how she feels about the situation now. Since leaving home, anytime my sisters try telling me the latest development in the Mum-and-Dad saga, I tell them I don't want to know. Now I wish I knew more. But something about the way Mum is sitting tells me not to pry.

"Ah well," she sighs after a few moments.

"Have you met her yet?" I blurt out.

"I've seen a picture of her," Mum says. "It's going to be awful."

"Mum, she's ugly . . ." I say, meaning it, even though I know it's not true. "Honestly. She is a nobody, compared to you!"

"A nobody," Mum repeats softly with a grim smile, and then she reaches out and pats my leg as though she doesn't believe *that* for a second.

When I next sneak a look, I can't see her face because her hair has come loose from her bun and she has turned away, looking out at the coastal scrub. I try to concentrate on driving. It's hard, traveling into the sun.

It's not long before I'm wrapped up in myself again. Almost against my will I find myself chewing over the remnants of last summer as I drive. Why *didn't* I go out that night with Nat and Zoe when she rang to ask me? It was so obviously what I should have done. If I had, then . . . maybe the rest of it wouldn't have happened.

♦ ♦ ♦

LAST SUMMER, MELBOURNE

It's my turn to get lunch. When I call my sisters into the kitchen, it's after two in the afternoon. They wander inside carrying towels and sunscreen, newspapers, and bottles of water, all of them bleary eyed and a bit cranky. Summer has come early this year. The four of us have been sitting around the pool, discussing Mum, who still isn't up, yet again.

Cynthia has a short blue sundress over her bathing suit. Her legs and feet are bare and her short hair is curling up into a kind of frizz from the pool in just the way she hates. Hilda is in one of her white cotton sunfrocks, her hair hanging in loose tendrils around her neck. And Dot, who is holding the sleeping Cormac in her arms, is dressed only in her swimsuit with a towel wrapped around her. Even so, she manages to look like a Madonna figure in a Raphael painting. She settles the little guy on the couch under the window, head to toe with his sleeping twin, who conked out half an hour before.

"I think we should wake her," Hilda says, filling a glass with water and cracking ice cubes into it. "It would be good for her to come down and eat something."

"Let her sleep," Cynthia orders. "It's the body's way of dealing with shock."

"It's the body's way of dealing with that bloody strong sleeping pill you gave her!" Dot snaps, slumping down at the table. "Are you sure they're not for horses?"

Cynthia gives a deep, exasperated sigh. "We'll have to get her to a shrink soon," she declares imperiously.

"Who will only give her drugs!" Hilda sniffs dryly.

"So?" Cynthia shakes her head impatiently as though the rest of us know nothing. "Every drug on the market has been well tested. And, believe it or not, they really help in these kinds of situations!"

"*These kinds of situations*," Dot mimics, rolling her eyes at me. "Madame Expert knows all about *these kinds of situations*!"

"She's not sick"—Hilda is literally wringing her hands—"she's just . . ."

"Listen, Hilda" —Cynthia starts banging the table with her fist—"Mum is not eating! She is not sleeping. She has dropped a stone in weight. She is unable to work. I call that being ill!"

"It's only been a little over a week since her life fell apart!" Hilda's eyes are bright with tears. "Of course she can't cope with anything. She's in a state of grief!"

"Call it what you want." Cynthia sighs impatiently. "Extreme psychological states adversely affect the immune system. She might very well be on her way to becoming seriously ill. Some kind of intervention is needed, and a doctor who specializes in her condition would be a good start!"

"Shut up, all of you," I intervene, bringing a bowl of chips to the table. "Let's just eat." I'm getting very sick of these discussions that go round and round without getting anywhere. None of us knows what to do, except maybe Cynthia, who would probably have her admitted to the hospital if it weren't for the rest of us.

I've already set out some bread and cheese and pickles and a roasted chicken that I'd bought down the street.

"Any salad?" Cynthia snaps.

"Nope," I say, handing her the cheese, "and no fruit, either."

Our meals are getting worse and worse. I don't care that much. I sit down with my sisters and try to summon up a bit of enthusiasm for the food.

◆　◆　◆

We have nearly finished eating when a couple of sharp knocks at the back door make us all go quiet.

"Let's not answer it," Dot mutters.

"Let's just leave it," Hilda agrees under her breath. But there is the sound of a key being slipped into the lock, the creak of the back door opening, and footsteps. Then our father is in the room. He is dressed in old, comfortable clothes, and is carrying a big bunch of flowers. He is trying hard to smile.

"Hello, you lot," he says, standing in the doorway. "Lunchtime?"

"Daddy!" Hilda is the first to rise, her face soft with pleasure. She throws her arms around his neck, and he puts the flowers down on the table and embraces her.

"Hello, Hilly, my sweetheart!" He spies the twins asleep on the couch over her shoulder. "And the terrors," he laughs, "having their sleep here?" The surprise in his voice is understandable. Hilda is usually so particular about getting the twins back to her house for their afternoon nap. I have this sudden, mad impulse to tell him that he wouldn't believe the changes over the last week; that it's nothing now for the twins to have ice cream for morning tea, to wear grubby clothes, and to watch television. All complete no-nos before . . . he left.

"We've had the boys in the pool."

"Good idea. Lovely weather for it."

Dorothy moves in. "Hi, Dad!"

"Dotti!" Dad hugs her tightly and then looks at Cynthia, who hasn't risen. "And how is my mover and shaker?"

Cynthia doesn't smile. Nor does she get up. She allows him to kiss her cheek, but pulls back from his hand on her shoulder, her mouth grim. It crosses my mind that Cynthia is going to have to watch that mouth. When she gets older, it could turn into one of those dog-bum numbers that old people get after years of frowning and disapproving and being concerned.

My turn. Whatever the rightness or otherwise of Cynthia's plan to be tough, I don't remember anything of it now. I simply can't help myself. Tears well up in my throat as I move toward him. He takes a step back, opens his eyes wide, then holds both arms out.

"Rose," he says softly. "Rosie. Rosie. Rosie. My clever girl!" Before taking me in his arms, he picks up the beautiful flowers, does a silly bow, and hands them to me. "I am so proud of you," he says seriously, putting both hands on my two shoulders and looking me straight in the eye. "Just had to come and tell you how very proud I am."

"Thanks, Dad," I say.

He looks around at the others. "What do you all think? Incredible, isn't she?"

"Yes!" They all nod. "Absolutely brilliant."

Then he hugs me and dances me around the room a bit, and I'm laughing before I know it, and crying a little, too. I've always loved the smell of my father, the feel of his rough face on my cheek. I love his voice and the way he laughs and pushes my hair back from my face with his hands.

"So, Rosie girl," he murmurs, wiping away my tears with his two thumbs, "it's all going to plan, love. Not long now and you'll be at the bar . . . killing 'em dead."

"You think so?" I laugh.

He looks around at the others with his mouth open, feigning outrage that I would even ask.

"Do I *think* so?" he exclaims. "I *know* so. The world is your oyster, girl. Mark my words! I'm getting nervous already!"

The greetings over, a weird awkwardness sets in, but it isn't too bad. Cynthia remains cool, but the rest of us can't help rushing off at the mouth whenever he asks a question. We pour him a beer and he sits with us at the table and we talk over each other and drink and laugh. It feels like he's just home from one of his overseas trips and we're all catching up on the news.

"You haven't opened your card," he says when there is a lull in the conversation, pulling the large square envelope from the paper around the flowers and handing it to me.

"Oh. Thanks, Dad," I say, and immediately tear it open. Inside, a short note. *Love and congratulations from Dad*, and . . . I gasp . . . a check for five thousand dollars.

"Dad," I say in protest, and try to give it back, "I can't take this!"

"It's for the van"—he smiles, putting his hands behind his back so that I can't make him take it back—"so you and Zoe can go do your surfing."

"But . . ." I protest weakly, "I nearly have the money saved myself. By the end of January I'll have it. Honestly."

The check is overwhelming. It makes me feel awkward. My parents have never been into big gifts. Sure, we have parties and the house is open to all our friends at any time—booze and fine food laid on—but they've always made it clear that they didn't believe it was their role to hand the big stuff to us on a plate. Instead, they let us know that they gave money to overseas aid organizations, to the Salvos and

171

to the St. Vincent de Paul Society. Too many people in real need not to give it away, we were told. And the other message was that there are way too many pampered, spoiled-rotten kids of wealthy parents who are completely stuffed up because they've never had to work for anything. So, in spite of our being very well off, it's always been understood that we have to save up for things like cars and overseas holidays.

"It's instead of a party," he says shortly, as though he, too, is suddenly embarrassed by the gift. "The others had parties when they left school."

"Thanks, Dad." I try to repress the feeling of being bought off in some way, but I can't help it. This amount of money jars. It's too much, and we both know it. But I don't want to hurt his feelings either.

"Anyway, you deserve it," he mumbles.

"Not really." I am suddenly close to tears again, so I tuck the money back into the envelope, stand up, and pin it up on the notice-board near the fridge, then go to the sink and get a glass of water. I make myself take a few deep breaths before turning around again. Thankfully, by this stage Dot is telling him when she'll be starting back at university, so the moment passes.

Dad is exactly the same: warm, funny, and ironic. And yet . . . being with him now is totally different. It's not only the cool undercurrent coming from Cynthia that makes things awkward. It is more about the chasm of unspoken subjects that is lying between us. I want to ask him where he is living and who is he is living with, and yet . . . I desperately don't want to know.

After about forty minutes, there is a lull in the conversation.

"So, girls, how is your mother?" he asks at last. There are a few moments where none of us says anything. I look at my sisters, only to find Hilda looking away uncomfortably, Cynthia staring at her hands, and Dot switching her gaze from Cynthia to me to Hilda.

"Why don't you ask *her*?" Cynthia's voice is icy.

"Well, I will, Cynthia, I will," Dad replies mildly, "but I'd still like to know how things are from your point of view."

"Well then, *things* are awful." Cynthia looks around at the rest of us for confirmation. "Bloody awful, if you want the truth. Mum is not coping. She can't eat or sleep. She does nothing all day and cries continuously . . . I personally think she should be hospitalized—" But Cynthia doesn't get to finish her sentence.

The door from the hallway suddenly opens, and there is Mum, in her old, very beautiful green dressing gown, looking absolutely . . . terrible. Distraught. Crazy. Completely freaked. I hadn't realized how much weight she'd lost! I see now that she's changed from being a pleasantly plump, curvy woman into a thin, pale, and washed-out one. The dressing gown, made of thick silk, was a present from Dad years ago. I remember him bringing it home from Paris in the fanciest gold box I'd ever seen, when I was about ten. It used to suit her perfectly. Cut on the cross in that flattering forties style, with a pointed waist and soft gathering on the bust and hips, the soft color gave her fair skin and red hair a luminescence that made everyone who saw her in it suggest she get more clothes in the same shade. Not now. Now it drapes around her like a piece of old curtain, and the subtle green only accentuates the transparent quality of her skin, making her look ill.

Obviously shocked too, Dad doesn't quite know what to do. He goes to stand up but then thinks better of it and remains seated. Mum has stopped in the doorway, and they stare at each other for close on half a minute. The rest of us sit still, not knowing where to look, barely breathing.

"Hello, Patsy," Dad says at last, but she doesn't even nod, much less acknowledge his greeting in words.

"What are you doing here?" she demands in a hoarse voice that doesn't even sound like her. She is standing tall and very still, her chin held defiantly as though she's about to prove something.

"I came to see the girls," Dad says simply, then with a small smile he motions to the bunch of flowers on the table. "And, of course, to congratulate our Rose on her wonderful results."

"Get out!" she hisses. Dad winces as though she has struck him. His face drains. Hilda stands up, puts a hand out toward Mum, opens her mouth to say something, but then thinks better of it. None of us has ever seen our mother like this. Not with anyone. I remember her getting mad once when some guy wrongly accused her of smashing into his car. She really let him have it—but it was nothing like this.

Dad nods and slowly stands up.

"I think it's pretty legitimate for me to come and congratulate our daughter on her VCE results," he says, "but if you would prefer . . ."

"You no longer live here!" Mum yells, cutting him off. "It is no longer your home! You have no right to come in the door!"

Dad's mouth tightens angrily, but he swallows it and merely shrugs. "I did try to ring," he says in this strained, put-upon way, standing with his arms folded tightly against his chest, "a number of times. I left messages." He turns around to us. "But no one rang back, so . . ."

"So you decided to just come in anyway!" Mum interjects.

"Well, yes."

"How dare you treat me with such contempt!"

"Now, Patsy," Dad cuts in forcefully, "I have *never* treated you with contempt. Would never . . . do that. Quite the wrong interpretation of events."

"You have treated me with *absolute* contempt," she screams straight back. "You have shamed me terribly!"

"*Shamed* you?" He is genuinely bewildered.

"Utterly shamed me!"

"Patsy, for goodness' sake!" Dad is genuinely at a loss. "This is not the nineteenth century! You have a job and your children. This house. You will not be left destitute! There is plenty of money." He pauses. They are still staring at each other. Dad lowers his voice into a more kindly tone. "You're an attractive woman. After some time . . . I don't see why we can't be friends again. Good friends. I know I want that. You are dear to me, Patsy. The girls are dear to me. I have never said I want you out of my life . . ."

Then Mum does something that is so shocking I can barely believe it. Even when I see it with my own eyes, it's as though it happens in a dream. She picks up the vase from the nearby dresser, a quite large, ornate vase that Grandma Greta gave them eight years ago for their twentieth wedding anniversary, and she throws it straight at his head with all her might. Dad manages to duck in time, but only just. Honestly, it could have killed him! The vase slams into the wall and smashes into tiny pieces. Dot screams, the rest of us gasp and leap to our feet. We are standing there, breathing quickly, shaking a bit, staring at the large half-moon shaped hole in the plaster. Mum moves quickly to the table. She picks up the plate of chicken bones and hurls that, too. The twins wake up, with a sharp cry from each of them, and then they are silent and watchful, as though they understand intuitively that a huge drama is happening and they'll miss it if they don't keep still.

"Patsy, stop this!" Dad shouts, deeply distraught. He has always hated violence of any kind. "Stop it at once!"

"Don't tell me what to do!" Mum screams, grabbing a jar of chutney. "Just get out!"

Hilda rushes over to the twins, pulls them protectively onto her knees, and starts sobbing loudly as the chutney jar smashes against the wall. Dad makes a move toward Hilda, then stops when he sees Mum is all set to throw something else. He retreats to the door, his face twisted up with utter bewilderment and pain.

"Okay, Patsy!" he calls shakily, pointing at Hilda and the twins. "I'm leaving right now! I beg you not to do this in front of our children. You'll . . . be so sorry later!"

"Will I?" she screams. "Will I really? *I'll* be sorry, will I?"

"Yes. I think you will."

"Don't you dare tell me what I'm going to feel!" she yells. "Did you tell your children that you've been seeing this woman for *two years*?" Mum adds sarcastically, *"On and off."*

Dad groans and shuts his eyes. There is an awful, sharp silence as those words settle over us. I don't know why, but this information takes everything that has happened down to a new level of awfulness.

It feels as though someone is up there tightening the screws on all our lives and there is nothing any of us can do.

"Her name is Cassandra," Dad says in a low, desperate voice, "and I thought we agreed it was not necessary to disclose these kinds of painful details to our children."

"So *you* won't appear in a bad light!" Mum hits back savagely. "Well, fuck you, Justus! I've changed my mind! I'm going to tell everybody!"

Another first. My mother rarely swears. If she's seriously angry or stressed, she might say *damn* or *bloody*, but never *fuck*. I don't think Dad has ever heard her use that word either, because he gives an almighty shudder of distaste before he opens the door and walks out.

Mum stands there for a few moments, staring straight in front of her. Her hands, still holding a couple of bowls, begin to shake violently. Without looking at the rest of us, she suddenly puts the bowls down again, turns around, and disappears through the same door she came in. Back up to her room, I guess. The rest of us stand looking blankly at each other, except for Hilda, who sits crying on the sofa.

The phone starts ringing.

No one moves, and it rings and rings and . . . *rings*. The three of us keep looking at each other like zombies as Hilda continues to sob on the couch. We're all waiting for the appalling shrill noise to stop. After it rings out once there is a short wait, and it begins all over again. Oh shit. Someone must have accidentally unplugged the answering machine.

I come out of my shocked stupor and pick up the receiver.

"Can you come out?" It's Zoe, in breathless mode.

"When?"

"Now!" she says. "Jane Morton just rang me. Peeping Tom are playing the Social Club in an hour. Last gig before they go overseas. There's a group of us going down. Come on!"

"Zoe, I can't."

"Why not?"

Why not? Just, everything, and . . . no good reason at all. I really like Peeping Tom. Then I look around. My three older sisters are staring at me blankly. I'm the sane, sensible one that they're all counting on.

"I just can't, Zoe," I say again. "Not tonight."

"Well, do you mind if I ring him?"

"Who?"

"You know! It would be such a cool band for that guy to hear!"

That guy? She means Nat Cummins. *Do I mind if she calls up Nat? Well . . . yeah. Of course I do. I mind very much.*

"Oh, course not."

"Are you sure?"

"Yes, it's okay," I say, actually trying to inject enthusiasm into my voice. *Why?* I realize I'm not thinking straight, but I don't know what to do about it. This is ridiculous, I know. I should say something right now. Crazy not to. Zoe would back off if she knew . . . *She would, wouldn't she?*

"Rose," she says, "tell me! Do you mind if I ring him?"

But I suddenly don't have the energy for anything. Not for Zoe or for whatever she has going, or wants to have going, with Nat. There is this low buzz of misery bubbling in my ears, and I am looking at my life from a distance. What will be will be. I say goodbye and put the phone down listlessly.

◆ ◆ ◆

LAST SUMMER, APOLLO BAY

If Zoe hadn't gone to bed early that first night, none of it would have happened. That's what I often tell myself when I'm looking around for someone else to blame. What happened next seemed like fate . . . but I don't believe that, either. I've always thought that believing in fate was a coward's way out. I reckon we've got to take responsibility for what we do, or give up altogether.

I feel better after my shower, and it's easy for a while. Ray makes us all a snack, which Zoe won't eat, but he manages to talk her into some fruit and yogurt, and she picks at it a bit. Ray heads out to work on the car he is fixing for her, and Zoe and I play cards and listen to music. She seems to have forgotten that she wanted to discuss something important, so I don't ask. It's all okay. In fact, all the weird stuff fades into the background, and before we know it, the day has all but disappeared.

At about seven, Ray comes back inside and washes his oily hands at the kitchen sink.

"So, what's for tea, girls?" he jokes. But of course Zoe and I haven't thought that far ahead. We look at each other and shrug.

"Just as I thought!" He pretends to be angry as he pulls open the fridge, takes out a big fish, and holds it up by the tail. "Okay, smarty-pants Rose, what are you gonna do with this?"

"Me?" I squeak. Hasn't he heard? I'm the worst cook in the world.

"Yes, you!"

"Er . . . well," I say, "I guess I could . . . *eat* it?"

"This girl has her wits about her!" He chuckles, whacks the fish down on the table, and selects a couple of sharp knives. "Come on, you two, I need helpers. We're gonna have ourselves some fancy frog soup."

So he shows us both how to make bouillabaisse. It's the three of us in the kitchen, with Zoe and me taking direction. We chop, slice up the fish and vegetables, and joke around in French. He spent time in Paris as a young man and so has the accent down pat, along with a few key words and phrases. Zoe and I aren't too bad either. Our French mistress at school was a native speaker and a good teacher, and we both did well. But by the time the dish is ready and smelling absolutely divine, Zoe is feeling pukey again.

"Do you mind if I just go to bed?" she asks.

"After dinner," her dad insists.

"I can't eat, Dad," she says, holding her head. "Honestly, just the smell is making me feel sick."

"You can go to bed if you eat a sandwich."

Zoe raises her eyebrows at me, as though this is the most unreasonable thing she's ever heard.

"Okay then."

◆　◆　◆

As soon as Zoe is in bed, I go out to the deck with a magazine. I pretend I'm reading it, but really I'm watching the light fade and wondering why I feel apprehensive, as though I should make some excuse and head off to bed too. It would save feeling . . . so jumpy and awkward. The door slides open behind me.

"Hey, Rose, the soup is nearly ready. You want wine?"

"Okay. Thanks."

He brings me a glass of red and then disappears back inside again to see to the food. When he doesn't come out to join me, I am . . . *disappointed*.

We sit across from each other at the table in the fading light, two large bowls of the delicious-smelling, steaming fish soup in front of us. Behind him the kitchen light has been turned off, but through the windows we can see the blue tinge of twilight sweeping over the fence and garden. The sounds of the sea are rushing and pulling in the background.

"We need a bit of light in here," he mutters, getting up and going to the side dresser. He lights one of the big candles and carefully brings it over. The dinner table is suddenly bathed in a cocoon of soft, warm yellow, and his face looks so . . . interesting. Old, but handsome in a way I don't understand. I'm embarrassed. Something tells me he wouldn't bother lighting a candle if it was just him and Zoe sitting down to eat. Then again, I could be wrong. Some people light candles every night, don't they? But what if Zoe came out right this minute? Would she find her best friend sitting like this across from her old man a bit weird? *Or not?*

I look over at the TV. I'm on my second glass of wine, but I know that's where we should be. Zoe is in bed, so her father and I should be sitting on different couches, eating our soup, laughing at some dumb American sitcom, not look-ing into each other's faces across a narrow table. But my hair is hanging just so, in freshly washed, gleaming curls, and I'm wearing my best tight mauve top and light cotton pants that fit snugly around my hips. I have on the high-heeled sandals that Zoe made me buy only the week before. I've had a glass of wine and I feel . . . *I feel beautiful*. For the first time in my life I feel beautiful and grown-up.

"You have beautiful eyes, Rose!" Ray says, squinting at me. "I've been trying to work out what color they are. Brown, I thought at first. Then hazel, this afternoon on the beach. But in this light they look almost green!"

"Brown," I say shortly. Feeling myself flush, I turn back to my soup. "That's what it says on my passport, anyway!"

"Well," he laughs wryly, "they *must* be brown if it's written on your passport."

"So, how come you have all these posters?" I ask brightly, trying hard to keep things ordinary, to sound like an ordinary eighteen-year-old talking to a much older man. "Did you go to all those concerts, or did you get them from friends?"

He doesn't answer immediately. Just cuts a few slices from the warm bread and hands me one. Our fingers touch, and I recoil as though I've been stung, but he doesn't seem to notice, so I put the bread on my plate and reach out for the butter. "Thanks."

"I went to most of them," he explains softly, looking up from his soup, letting his eyes wander briefly over the walls before coming back to my face. "I was a roadie for years with a number of bands."

"Really?" I ask. Did Zoe tell me this? I don't think so. No bells are ringing. Zoe only ever spoke about her father in a very vague, offhand way. "Which bands?"

"Oh, famous ones and some . . . not so famous." He smiles slowly. "I started off with Manfred Mann. You probably haven't heard of them." *Yes I have! Of course I have!* "But I suppose my big claim to fame is that I was with the Stones for a while."

182

"The *Stones*!" I say excitedly. *Why didn't Zoe tell me this!*

"One summer I lugged their equipment around, Rose"—he grins at my enthusiasm—"with a whole lot of other guys. I didn't play music with them, and it wasn't all that glamorous, to tell you the truth! I was a nineteen-year-old kid carting stuff around, and that was about it."

"But you would have met them and heard them play a lot?"

"Oh, sure, yeah." He bites into his bread. "And I got to go to a lot of free concerts, too. And sometimes we got in on some of . . . the action."

"The action. How do you mean?"

He looks away a moment as though slightly embarrassed at having mentioned it.

"Oh, you know"—he shrugs, with a diffident smile—"the booze and the drugs and the . . . pretty girls." He hesitates. "Some of it wasn't all that nice."

I nod, remembering those old vintage *Rolling Stone* magazines from the seventies that Zoe and I pored over the summer before. The journos covering those big tours wrote some pretty hairy stories of what happened. Amazing to think I'm sitting across from someone who was there!

"So, who else?"

"Well, in my early twenties, I went to America for a while, and I learned a bit about sound. For a time there I was a mixer at some of the big concerts. Neil Young." He frowns, trying to remember. "Then Jackson Browne and Emerson, Lake and Palmer. I had my own mixing company with another guy." He looks away for a few moments, then muses, "We were with Joni, too, for one summer."

"Joni Mitchell?" I whisper, in awe. He nods and frowns as though embarrassed. "What was she like? Did you get to know her?"

He smiles and shakes his head. "Not really, but we . . . worked up close for a while. She's a nice woman, but I don't pretend we were ever friends. I wasn't friends with any of these people." He smiles in a self-effacing way. "Sorry to disappoint you."

"Oh no. Don't be sorry!" I laugh. I like his honesty. It means whatever he tells me will be the truth and not a beat-up. "You haven't disappointed me. It's enough that you met them and worked with them and *heard* them play so often."

"Well, I certainly did that," he sighs, as though it is all a bit boring to him. "Now, how do you like that soup?"

"Fantastic," I say, and take a few more mouthfuls. "Did you ever, like, *talk* to Jimi Hendrix?"

"No," he laughs, "but I did pass him on the back stairs once coming offstage, all dressed up and on his way to the toilet."

"God, you must be so old," I say in awe, without thinking. Then I flush with embarrassment. "I'm sorry. What I mean is that you must be so much older than you look?"

He laughs, but pauses before he continues eating his soup. "Well, I dunno, Rose," he says guardedly, "I'm pretty old."

We get seriously stuck into our soup and bread and continue talking. Mainly about music and the people he met in the early days. I'm awestruck and keep coming back with more questions. How many hours a day would Eric Clapton practice? Was he really good friends with George Harrison? Was Led Zeppelin easy to deal with, or were they crazy? He has all kinds of little anecdotes and stories that I lap up. The bottle of wine disappears, and he opens another. I refuse any more because I know I'm a little drunk already. Besides, I feel totally easy now. All the nerves and jumpiness have gone.

We're onto coffee and ice cream when he tells me about the work he is presently doing. Zoe was never quite able to explain, so I'm interested. For the last ten years, he's been a buyer for a small chain of shops in the city that sells Eastern clothes, jewelry, and artifacts. It involves being away a lot, traveling throughout India and Indonesia, choosing and buying the stuff to be shipped home.

He tells me funny stories about some of the characters he meets year after year, the stall owners and village entrepreneurs and artisans, who lie and bargain and get under his skin in all kinds of ways. I forget about Zoe in bed down the hallway. Her father is so nice, kindhearted, and funny all at once.

"So, you like it?" I ask shyly, when there is a gap in the conversation. He is over at the fridge, serving us both more ice cream.

"It's a living." He shrugs, coming back with my refilled bowl and setting it in front of me. "But to tell you the truth, I'm always so glad to get home." He sits down and suddenly reaches out and briefly covers my hand with his own and gives it a squeeze. "We're so lucky here in Australia, Rose," he says earnestly, looking into my eyes, "having all this sea and space and clean air. So many people live such cramped and busy lives that they never even get to see the stars."

"Yes." I nod breathlessly. Him touching my hand like that has sent my head swirling off to another place altogether. I daren't move and certainly don't breathe until he moves it away again.

"Would you like to see the sort of stuff I buy?" he asks, pushing back his chair when we've both finished. "Give you some idea of what I'm talking about."

So we head out into the dark night, along a concrete path to a large back shed that I hadn't noticed before. He unlocks it with a key hanging inside the doorframe, pushes the door open, and turns on the harsh fluorescent light hanging from the ceiling.

"After you," he says politely, standing aside for me to enter.

I step into what I guess is a small warehouse, full of all kinds of bright, exotic Asian stuff. The walls have been roughly lined in white ply board and they're covered in gold-threaded wall hangings, brocaded curtains, weavings and mats—a mass of rich color. There are tables lining the walls as well, covered in carved wooden statues, ivory knickknacks, batik paintings, all kinds of toys and jewelry and furniture. A couple of racks of bright, beaded clothing, too. I smile as I begin to wander around and look through it all, touching things, amazed at the variety of textures and workmanship.

"So, this gets sold in the shops?" I ask.

"No. This lot is mine," he says, pulling himself up onto a side bench, watching me move around.

"Why isn't it in the house?"

"I sell it from here," he explains, his eyes shifting away uncomfortably. "Most of what I buy ends up in a warehouse in Melbourne, of course. But I keep a few bits and pieces for myself, on the side."

"I see," I say, wondering if that means he pinches it. But I decide I don't need to know.

Outside, it is still mild with not a cloud in the sky. The moon is a deep, buttery color and almost round, and the endless swathes of stars light up the night like so-many-billion silver pins stuck into a huge dark cushion.

"Fabulous, eh?" he says, walking in front of me out to the side gate. "The best place to see the stars is here." I follow him along the path and we stand together, leaning on the gate, craning our necks upward.

"Ah, I never get sick of it," he mumbles, then he moves away a bit, leans his elbows on the fence, and looks out into the distance.

"Zoe told me your mum and dad have split," he says.

"Yes."

"That's hard," he says softly. "Always sad."

I nod, and then, I'm not quite sure why, but pinpricks start in the backs of my eyes and my throat clams up. I gulp a few times, but the tears form anyway, and within no time, they are spilling out, down my cheeks. Oh hell. I gulp again. *Stop this.* Maybe it's a reaction to his kind tone, or maybe it's all to do with the wine I've had, or with the enormity of the night around us. All the indifferent beauty of the stars makes me feel so small and insignificant and lonely. Maybe it's because I don't have Dad anymore. At least, not the way I used to. Ray doesn't notice at first, but when he asks me something else, I mumble my reply in a hoarse voice and gulp a couple of times.

"Rose?" He reaches out and puts one hand to my cheek. "You're crying," he says simply. "Why?"

"I'm okay," I bluster, "it just hits me sometimes."

"What hits you?" he asks gently.

"The sadness of it."

"Hmmm." He breathes out a couple of times. We are very near to each other, one of his hands still on my cheek. I'm not jumpy now or nervous.

"Life is sad," he says gently. "As you get older, you learn that."

He pulls me to him, and I take that as a cue to cry a bit more into his shoulder. But very soon I'm laughing, apologizing for getting upset, and he's chuckling a bit too, telling me that it doesn't matter at all, that everyone needs to cry every now and again. Why not cry when a marriage breaks up? It *is* sad, he says, for everyone and especially for the kids. I try to pull away but he doesn't let me move, continues to hold me, talking soothingly. His hands move up and down my spine and over my shoulder blades. One of them kneads the back of my neck while the other continues to massage my shoulders. We are like that for ages. I let myself slump into him, shyly put one arm around his waist, telling myself nothing is happening. This man is my best friend's father, so now he's a good friend to me, too. He is holding me because I feel sad, and I love this feeling of his arms around me.

"Ah, Rose," he sighs in this very gentle way. "You are a lovely girl."

He bends down and kisses me quickly on the mouth. Once, twice, three times. I open my eyes, too surprised to know what is happening. *A lovely girl*. Is that what I am? It makes me feel relaxed and calm, as though I don't have to think anymore. I'm lovely, so . . . I'll do. Then he carefully kisses each of my wet cheeks, and next my neck and ears. I feel cherished, adored, and very special. Then he kisses my mouth again. This time it lasts longer, and soon his tongue is in my mouth and I'm overwhelmed. I don't respond, but I don't pull away, either. This all lasts for probably no more than a minute. When he pulls me tighter and begins to kiss me more insistently, I do pull away. We look at each other, both breathing heavily.

"I've got to go to bed," I say with a gulp.

"Okay then, Rose," he says gently. "It is pretty late."

I run inside.

◆　◆　◆

I lie awake for ages, appalled by what has just occurred and, at the same time, longing for it to continue. I lie there fantasizing about him coming into my room and us making love that very night, with Zoe in the next room. How quiet we'd be! How sweet and strong would be those kisses. Just once, of course, and then the next day it would all be over and no one need know. We could forget all about it. That's what I tell myself. I have never felt such intense desire before. I lie naked under the sheet, longing for a tap on my door, to hear the mumble of his voice asking if I'm awake. I'll go to the door and open it. Say nothing, just take his hand and lead him over to my bed like they do in the movies. It feels like I've never wanted anything in my life as much as I do now.

I do go to sleep, but my dreams are murky and troubled. I wake late and very confused. Where am I, again? Did I dream the whole thing?

When I eventually get up, Zoe is out in the kitchen eating toast. She grins at me affectionately and points at the teapot.

"Just made!" she exclaims. "It's ten o'clock. You must have been wrecked."

"Yeah." I ruffle her hair as I go past toward the bread and the toaster. "Are you feeling better?"

"Loads! I'm wonderful."

She tells me that her father has gone out fishing for a few hours. We eat breakfast and then we go down to surf all day.

It could have ended there. Died a natural death. Fizzled out like lemonade left in the glass too long. He gave me that option. By coming back late that day with two fresh bream in a plastic bucket and three DVDs, by treating me like the kid, the friend his daughter brought home for a few days, joking about my bad cooking and calling me "Your Honor" and "Ms. O'Neil, Queen's Counsel." He was saying exactly that: *Forget it ever happened, Rose. Leave it be . . . Let's just cook and eat and joke and tease each other.*

I leave the next day, with Zoe and me having planned a Christmas shopping day soon.

Don'tcha just hate the way you get caught up in stuff without really wanting to? You make a wrong move and before you know it, you're committed. You've locked yourself in a box and there is no way out. You're in some shitty, weird scene that isn't you, but . . . how do you get out of it?

Maybe you lied, maybe you stole, maybe you betrayed your closest friend?

Hey Saucers! Let's get specific. Who among you has never made eyes at your best friend's guy or chick? Harmless enough? Yeah. Until it goes a bit further. Then suddenly you're one of those pricks you hate because . . . you can't be trusted. Now let's go down a notch or two. Anyone out there ever gotten involved with someone from the totally—and I mean totally—no-go basket? Someone like your stepfather, an underage girl, your best friend's old man? Don't laugh! It happened to someone I know . . .

◆ ◆ ◆

ROAD TRIP

We are driving through the Great Otway National Park, still more or less in silence. Not much traffic, no beach to look at, just the curves of the road to negotiate, the trees and scrub on either side.

"You're very quiet," I say, after about an hour.

"Feeling a bit . . . tired," Mum mutters shortly.

"We'll stop in Port Campbell," I say. "Get out. Have a break."

"Okay."

I take a few quick glances at her after that, but her face is averted, staring out the side window. Her quietness freaks me out a bit. It's not easy somehow. She is probably thinking about Dad and how she will cope with him and Cassandra. Or maybe I've said something to piss her off.

Once we're back down on the coastal road again past Lavers Hill, it seems better for some reason. Even just being near the ocean has a soothing effect on me. We pass the Twelve Apostles turnoff and then the sign leading to the Loch Ard Gorge. There is a lot of traffic now. Tourist buses and RVs. I'm on the point of asking if something is troubling her, when she speaks first.

"This is where it all happened, isn't it?"

"*What?*" My shutters immediately come crashing down and I recoil, as wary as a kitten approaching water. *Don't even try that, Mum . . .*

She turns to me.

"Around here? You nearly drowned somewhere around here?"

"Yeah." My voice cracks.

"Where exactly, Rose?" she asks quietly.

"A place called Childers, on the other side."

"So, you want to stop here for the night, maybe?"

I shrug and continue to stare ahead, grim-faced, as the silence settles again between us.

"I tell you what," Mum says matter-of-factly, after about five minutes. "I'd like you to drop me at that central motel on the beach in Port Campbell. I'll ring through and make a booking. You'll probably want to stop here for the night, too, won't you? Considering . . ."

My jaw drops. *What the hell?* "I haven't decided what I'm going to do yet," I say gruffly. *Considering what? If you don't mind!*

"Fine," she snaps, "but I'm going to stay there tonight."

"Why?" I ask, looking at her. "What's wrong?"

"Nothing is wrong," she says, "but if you want to go on, I'm sure Dorothy will come and pick me up tomorrow."

"But she's looking after Gran!" I protest. *This is my van. My trip. You have to fit in with me.* "Don't you want to get there before Gran dies? I mean, that was the idea, wasn't it?"

The truth is, I'm not so sure I want to spend the night in the van now. It might turn into one big freak-out. The more I think about it, the more I think it would be better to head on through to our destination, but I'm too embarrassed to tell her this.

"Look, Rose," Mum says, exasperated, "stop trying to organize me. I'll get there when I get there. It doesn't matter *how*, really, or when. She's not *my* mother!"

192

"But Mum!" I am almost wailing now, and I loathe myself. "Isn't she why you came?"

"Well . . . sort of," Mum says irritably. "I don't know. I wanted to come to be with you for a while, too."

We stare at each other for about three seconds as I take that on board. She came to be with me. Well, of course, I knew that, I just wish she wouldn't say it! It only puts more bloody pressure on the situation and makes me feel guilty that I haven't been nicer and *opened up* more. That's what she was hoping for, and that is exactly what I've avoided.

"Dorothy is there to look after Gran," I shoot back sharply, ignoring the stuff about her and me, "not to come traipsing after you."

"It's only forty minutes away," Mum says. "It's you who should get there, Rose. Gran wants to see *you*. You go on if you want."

◆ ◆ ◆

We roll into the pretty little coastal town of Port Campbell, tense and hot and out of sorts. Like so many others along the Shipwreck Coast, this former fishing village is hell-bent on turning itself into a tourist center. There are a couple of smart cafés, motels, and real estate agencies in place of the shabby old milk bar and hardware store of yesterday.

"Look at that sky," Mum mutters as we round the bend and come down into the street leading onto the beach. "The weather has turned on us."

She's right. Out over the two rocky points framing the small ocean beach, the clouds have darkened to a menacing gray, and a strong wind is making the water choppy.

"It's that one over there," Mum says, pointing to a modern, low-lying building. I pull the van over. Mum immediately opens the door, gets out, and pounds off toward the office, as though she knows exactly where she's going and is longing to be free of me. Well! Suits me! I sit back a moment and watch hordes of people clutching bags and towels as they hurry in from the beach. It's now nearly five, and I wonder how things have changed so quickly. The day has turned sour. Then I remember that this was forecast.

"You need a hand?" I ask, getting out. She's back at the van with her room key, trying to lift the back door open. I unlock it for her, and she starts searching around for her bag. I jump up into the back and haul it out from under some of my junk, and walk with her past the small office to find her room.

It's small and sparse and ordinary. There is one big double bed, a single as well, coffee- and tea-making facilities, and a little bathroom off to the side.

"I need to lie down a while," she says, as though completely exasperated with everything, including me. *What the fuck did I do?* "I've got my phone. Just ring me in a couple of hours and we'll go have dinner. If you want to," she adds wearily. I almost tell her I'm sorry. Sorry for being a horrible person, for disappointing her yet again. But I don't. I didn't ask her to come, I remind myself. She suggested it. I'm going to hold my ground.

"Sure."

Right on cue, her phone rings. She waves for me to take it while she goes to the bathroom.

It's Hilda ringing from Melbourne. "Rose, how is Grandma?"

"We're not there yet."

"Why not?" She sounds bewildered. "You should have been there ages ago. Did you have car trouble?"

"No," I say. "Well, sort of."

"How is Mum?"

"She's tired."

"Can I speak to her?"

"No, she's in the bathroom."

"What bathroom?"

"We're in Port Campbell and Mum is staying overnight in a motel, and I'll either go on or sleep in the van near the beach," I say, exasperated myself now. Why should I have to give my sisters an account of my every move?

"Why would you do *that*?" Hilda explodes. "Everyone in Port Fairy is waiting for you to arrive!"

"How do you know?"

"They've rung me. They don't know where you are."

"Mum is tired and she doesn't want to talk to anyone," I snap, "and I don't think she's all that keen to get there."

"Why not?"

"Cassandra will be there."

"Why should Mum care about that?"

I stop a moment to marvel, yet again, at the stupidity of my sweet-natured, good-hearted, utterly pampered and childlike eldest sister.

"Well? She must have known it would be in the cards." She's genuinely puzzled. "Why did she go if she doesn't want to get there?"

This is typical Hilda. She means well, but she is sort of dumb. She can't think around corners. Sometimes I think her thought patterns fit in way too well with the neat, swish, expensive hairstyles she insists on getting every six weeks.

"Try not to be so *thick*, Hilda!" I say eventually. "As a special favor to me, eh?"

"I suppose it *might* be uncomfortable," she concedes with a sigh. "David and I are departing in about an hour."

"Are the twins coming?"

"Yes, of course!" she snaps irritably.

"Okay, okay."

"Well, David thinks we should leave them here, but I don't want . . ."

"It's not a bad idea, Hilda."

"Look, I don't care what you think! My children come with me, or—"

"Okay! Fine." I cut her off from the rant I know she is simply dying to embark on. All about how society is so antichild these days, that parents are made to feel uncomfortable for bringing their little kids anywhere.

"I've changed my mind," I say. "I agree with you, they should come. Gran will want to see them."

"Okay," she mutters. My change of attitude catches her off guard, and she is quiet for a moment.

"We've booked into the pub, and we'll see you . . . tomorrow, if you're staying there too," she says.

"I'm sleeping in my van, remember."

"Rose! Don't do that!"

"Why not?"

"It's not safe . . . for a young woman."

"And what would you know about . . . *not safe*, Hilda?" I say nastily. I'm deliberately having a go at her cushy, wealthy lifestyle in just the way she hates. Like most wealthy people, Hilda has no idea that she is so well off. She snaps back something about me being "so far out of touch that it doesn't matter . . . ," but I don't listen because Mum comes out of the toilet drying her hands on a towel and slumps onto the bed.

"Mum, do you want to talk to Hilda?"

She shakes her head vehemently, then, in typical style, changes her mind and takes the phone. She listens to Hilda a while, then draws her knees up, sighs, closes her eyes, and leans against the cushions, murmuring *yes* and *no* a few times.

196

"Oh, Hilly," she butts in eventually, "don't be hard, darling! David *adores* you and the boys! He wants some time with just you . . . and remember this is about Gran, too . . ."

Oh God! The Dave-Hilda soap opera has begun! For the past year everyone's ideal happy couple have been at each other's throats, on and off. To be fair, it's mainly been Hilda finding fault with David. It's amusing, hearing her complain about him being too goal-oriented, impatient, and rigid when those were exactly the characteristics she was lauding last summer!

Time to depart. Get out of here before I get embroiled in one side or another. After all, *I have my own life.* Sometimes it's hard to remember that. My own life! I motion to Mum that I'm leaving. She waves me off out the door.

"Call me," she says, "and let me know what you're doing."

"I will," I say, forcing myself to be cheerful.

I move the van and park it in front of the beach. The sky is black now, with deep purple patches, like it might just break open any second. The waves toss about angrily on the mucky green water. But, with luck, I'll have time to walk along the pier before the storm starts.

I take off my canvas shoes and slip my jacket on again, although it's not cold. I jump down onto the sand and make my way toward the pier. The beach has virtually emptied, only a few stragglers about now, peering up at the sky and holding their hands to their faces against the stinging sand. I hang about on the edge of the pier for a while, watching a couple of old guys, completely unfazed by the weather, haul in their lines and reposition their bait. Their catch, of about six midsized bream, is in a bucket between them, and I wish I could ask them stuff about fishing, and life in general, but after turning over a couple of opening sentences in my mind,

197

I back off, scared that they'd find me intrusive. I return to the van, get in, and sit a while, trying to decide what to do.

It doesn't take long.

I'll have to at least go out there to that beach. It's why I came, though I never admitted it to myself. Only twenty minutes away, and there is still light in that gloomy sky.

◆ ◆ ◆

LAST SUMMER, MELBOURNE

Zoe is such a good Christmas shopper. Astute in a way I'm not. She knows where to go for the good stuff, and she knows if you can get it cheaper somewhere else. Every year I write myself a list before I hit the shops, but it never goes according to plan. Even when I've got something for everyone, I find myself wandering around, feeling desperate about whether anyone is going to like what I've picked out. Mad, really, because every year it turns out fine.

Having Zoe with me has made everything so much easier. We've had a great day together. Done loads of shopping and had lots of giggles, trying stuff on and working out what to buy for everyone.

We're standing under the clocks at Flinders Street Station, both laden with parcels, about to say goodbye, when she hits me with it.

"I went out with that guy again the other night," she says casually, then she looks at me directly. "Saw a movie."

"Which guy?" I ask, but of course I know.

"Nat Cummins." She turns away abruptly, as though she is already regretting bringing it up. "I rang, but you weren't home. A few of us went to a movie. But him and me ended up having coffee together. He talked about you."

"Me?" The idea of the two of them talking about me is disconcerting. Humiliating even. *God, what about? Maybe they were discussing how to break the news gently!*

199

Weird, I know, but for those few hours shopping, I'd forgotten all about this crap. Zoe and I had been back to how we used to be. Joking about the guys we passed on the street, the crappy music in all the department stores, how hard it was going to be to get down to studying again next year, all the usual stuff. We were mooning over the fancy clothes we couldn't afford and working out some of the details of going surfing after Christmas.

So I guess it *was* Nat she wanted to talk to me about down at the beach house when I fobbed her off.

"Yeah, you." She smiles uncertainly.

"What did he say?" I ask, feeling my mouth move into its thin-as-a-piece-of-string pose. I look over her shoulder at some guy playing the violin, badly, so I don't have to meet her eyes. I want to get away. *How long is this going to take?* Of course, at the same time, I'm curious as hell.

"Oh, he just . . . said he met you at some party and that he thought you were great, and . . . I agreed. I told him you were my very best friend." She suddenly moves in close, links arms with me, and smiles right in my face. "'Cos that's right, isn't it? We're best friends?"

"Yep." I try to smile. *What is going on underneath all this?* She is holding something back, that's what I don't quite understand. I feel sort of sick. But maybe it's just jealousy.

"So, did you . . .?" I step away, out of her grasp, and shrug, as though I don't care either way. "Did you and him hit it off?"

"Well," she giggles, "we had a bit of a pash in the car when he dropped me off."

Oh! Her words make something inside me crash to a halt, but I manage to meet her smile with one of my own. Just.

"He drove you home?" I feign incredulity, as though this is what I find interesting, when all I'm seeing is them together in that car, his hands on her, their faces and mouths locked. "All the way to Bayswater?"

"I know!" she gushes. "It was so nice of him! Said he didn't mind, he wasn't doing anything. God, Rose, he's . . . *yummy*! What . . . do you think?"

Is she asking my permission? I have to look away. *Nat? Does she have any idea how I feel about . . . this?* Zoe and I are best friends. And he didn't bother to call me again when I didn't return his calls, so he's moved on to her! Okay. It's fair enough, isn't it? Why am I shocked? I had my chance with Nat, and I blew it.

Anyway, my time to speak has gone. The truth of my own position sinks into my head as sharp as a blade into a soft sponge. What right do I have to judge *her* after . . . *kissing her father*!

She takes a quick look at her watch. Her train is due in about three minutes, but she continues to stand there with that expectant look on her face, waiting for some reaction. There *is* stuff I want to say, a lot of stuff, but I can't seem to open my mouth. Time is running out.

Zoe blows out impatiently and squeezes my hand.

"Let's talk later, eh?" she says in a nervous, slightly patronizing tone. She turns away and bounds up the steps to the railway station.

"Hey, Zoe!" I yell after her. I am desperate for her not to get away with this so easily. My inability to say anything in the face of her buoyant high spirits feels so weak, so *infuriating*. *Something* has to be said. She stops and stands looking back down at me, this strange half smile on her face.

"Yeah?"

I have a moment of confusion, almost panic. The crowd ebbs and flows around me, the noise of the pre-Christmas traffic fills my ears with the discordant, chaotic sounds of an orchestra tuning up before a concert. I don't trust myself.

"Wait." I run up the stairs to join her. "I'll come see you off."

We dash through the entrance and, because we both have student passes, run straight through the turnstiles, down the ramp, and onto the right platform. We're both gasping. A loud announcement tells us that the train is about to leave, the doors are closing. She must know why I have followed her down to her train.

"I think he really likes me!" she suddenly blurts out.

"Yeah?" I call back, coming in closer, hating her suddenly, but kind of loving her too, almost at the same time. There is something genuinely over the top about Zoe that makes love and hate sit alongside each other quite easily. Well, no! Not easily. Envy floods every pore of my body. *Why can't I be like her? Why don't I know who I am? How come I've turned into this little pissant loser who can't even stick up for herself?* But Zoe's confidence is mesmerizing.

"And it's up to me now to . . . you know, to *do something*. Don't you think?"

"*Do* something?" I repeat weakly, feeling myself pulled in by the whirling gravity of her energy. She breaks up laughing, her face bright and lovely inside that frame of wild, dyed-blond curls.

"Oh, you know!" She giggles. "I'll ask him out again. On his own this time. That's if . . . you're okay with it?"

She is not even pretending to be concerned now. *Zoe goes for what she wants. So what else is new?*

I plaster an encouraging smile over my face and give her a thumbs-up sign as I step back from the train.

"Sure," I say quickly. "Go for it, Zoe."

◆　◆　◆

I'm on the way to my platform when I suddenly turn around and run back out of the station, down the steps, onto the street, and into the sunlight. The handles of my shopping bags are cutting into my hands, and I'm crying. Crying. Crying. Crying. It's so embarrassing. The tears are just pouring down my face because . . . *I want Nat Cummins. Why do I mess everything up? Why does she have to have everything in my life?* People turn and stare with quizzical, sympathetic expressions as I rush past them. I feel like a dizzy soap star, but I can't seem to stop it. *Just stop this right now*, I think. *Stop it. This isn't you. You are behaving like . . . one of your sisters. Worse.*

I must see my father. I have to talk to Dad about . . . everything. I am filled with a new kind of manic energy as I melt into the crowds.

I swing left and make my way to Elizabeth Street, and slowly, I calm down and stop feeling so crazy. Then I hop on a tram and travel up a few blocks to Lonsdale Street, where I get off and walk two blocks up to William Street. On one corner is the Family Court, over the road is the County Court, and on the adjacent corner is the Supreme Court. I'm pretty sure Dad is appearing in the Supreme Court on behalf of a corporate client. It's not yet three o'clock. I should be able to catch him before he goes back in for the afternoon's proceedings.

I climb the sandstone steps and walk through the complicated security system into the middle courtyard. Small groups of wigged and gowned attorneys cluster together like a strange species of birdlike insects. They talk earnestly to each other and with clients, pull apart and come together, calling out final messages and terse goodbyes before disappearing down various corridors to separate courts. I head for the wooden library doors and push through into the round space under the central dome, and . . . I am in another world. I look around and take a few deep breaths. This is familiar territory for me. Sunlight streams down in great square shafts onto the polished wooden bookcases, the tables, and the worn flagstones. Roughly a dozen people sit, alone or in small groups, working quietly. Solemnity of purpose prevails. I scan the room for my father. He will be here or somewhere close by. I'm sure of it. Another deep breath as I wait for the atmosphere to work its magic.

But nothing happens. I'm standing there like a dumb, awestruck geek, feeling completely out of place in my jeans and tight top. I look around enviously at the small groups of people who know what they are doing with their lives. For years, the belief that I, too, will be able to make my mark in this place has sustained me, given me purpose, a reason to study hard, an anchor to pin my life to. And now?

I see now that this place has nothing to do with me. The very idea that it ever did makes me want to burst out laughing. What an egotistical little shit I've been all my life! I can't believe I was so sure about my place in the world. The lawyers with their wigs and gowns, the heavy bound books full of dense language and weighty knowledge—all those judgments and precedents and detailed cases have been written by people who know who they are and what they are doing in this world. None of that applies to me. Maybe it never will.

I need to talk to my father. He will be able to tell me who I really am. I walk over to the wooden pointers and note which corridors I have to take.

I'm through the door and heading toward Court Five when I see him. He is in the middle of a group of about five other lawyers. All men, except for one woman. She has fair hair and is dressed in a cherry-red suit. The suit is conservatively cut and beautifully tailored. They are all talking and laughing, walking toward me. I move instinctively to the wall and watch them walk past into the front vestibule. They shake hands and begin to break up, calling about catching each other at a later date. Feeling shy, I wait for Dad to move off, figuring he'll either go back into the library or out onto the street. I'll catch him either way. But, although the other three lawyers have scurried away, my father continues to stand there with . . . the woman.

It must be her. They are standing close together, smiling into each other's faces, without speaking. Then his hand reaches up and he brushes a strand of hair from her face. No doubt. It's her. I watch as he holds her lightly by the elbows, bends slightly to listen as she says something to him. She is almost as tall as he is. Straight and slim with short, well-cut fair hair. I can't see much of her face.

In less than two minutes my father has changed from the one person I wanted to see most in the world, to the one person I really don't want to see at all. I'm longing to escape. Longing for them both to turn away and walk out the front of the building, or at least disappear into one of the nearby courtrooms or offices. Then I'll make my run for it and they never need know I was here. I will be able to push that image of him smiling down at her from my memory. In my head, I'm already on my way back through the crowds, down to the train station. Home. That's where I want to be. I want to get home.

So, it's true, I keep thinking stupidly, feeling as though a limb is being slowly ripped from my body. It's really true. He has this other life, this other woman not our mother, who he loves. How incredible that it takes so long to sink in. I feel tainted, in a way, because I have witnessed my father touching another woman. I need to shower, change my clothes. It feels like I am now a part of his betrayal.

But they don't turn for the street or disappear into a nearby office. They talk a little more and then spin around together and walk back toward me, holding hands. I cringe, push myself nearer to the wall, and shut my eyes. Just like a little kid. *If I can't see them, maybe they won't see me.*

"Rose!"

I open my eyes and try to smile, but I can't. My mouth doesn't work. I can't meet his eyes or even look him in the face, so I concentrate on the point just over his left shoulder. He moves and stands in front of me, waiting for me to look up.

"Sweetheart?" he says softly, perplexed. "What are you doing here?"

"Nothing," I manage weakly. "I just . . . came to see you."

"I'm so glad you did, pet!"

I look over his shoulder and catch the moment of shock on the woman's face.

"Meet Cassandra, darling," he says, taking the woman's elbow and pulling her forward. "Cass, this is my youngest daughter, Rose."

"Hello," I say. She holds out a soft white hand, and as we make eye contact, her smile becomes bigger. She has lovely, creamy skin—nicer than Mum's—small, bright eyes, and a wide, voluptuous mouth painted dusky, matte pink.

"Well, hello, Rose." She squeezes my hand without shaking it. "I've heard so much about you!"

"Have you?" I ask warily. It suddenly doesn't seem possible. How could she have heard about me? What would Dad have told her? I pull my hand away, shaken in some deep way.

"Your results," she says, as though reading my mind. "Justus is . . . Your dad," she corrects herself, "is so very proud of you!"

A bemused smile hangs on the edges of her mouth. She is taking in everything about me, from my tight, slightly grubby jeans to my cheap, bright earrings and my sweaty, sandaled feet. I've never felt so young and hopelessly transparent before. She can see right through me, and I know nothing about her.

But she is waiting for me to say something. What? Something sassy and witty to show what a cool and hip eighteen-year-old I am? Then we'll all be able to laugh together. Most of all, she wants to laugh. I know this instinctively. We'll laugh and everything will be hunky-dory.

"But what brings you to the city?" Dad cuts in, embarrassed by my hostile stance and refusal to meet his girlfriend's eyes.

"I've been shopping with Zoe," I say, indicating the bags at my feet.

"Did you have any luck?" he wants to know.

"A bit," I mumble. "I got a few things."

"Aren't you wonderful?" Cassandra coos, as though we're best friends already. "I haven't even started my Christmas shopping yet!"

"Listen," Dad takes command, "why don't we all go to a café?"

"I don't think so," I say. "I'd better get home."

"But why, darling?" He puts his arm around me. "I'm so pleased to see you."

"I've got to do . . . things." I shrug and try to move out of his reach, but in the process I stumble over my bags. This makes me feel doubly stupid. More than anything, I want to get away.

"Please," my father pleads, "we'll just go and have some coffee."

So even though sitting with them in this trendy little low-lit café is the last thing I want to do, it's exactly what I'm doing. This is my dad, after all. I'm confused as well as miserable because I know there is no legitimacy to my feelings. My position is . . . ridiculous. I am not a little kid whose life has been turned upside down. I am not going to be neglected or wrecked in any way. My whole future is assured. And yet . . . a mass of raw pain, like strong acid, bubbles and ferments in my chest. I swallow and gulp and try to breathe it away. But there doesn't seem to be anything I can do to ease it. *This is not like you, Rose,* I chide myself. *Dramatic mood swings are not you. You are, and remember this, the queen of calm.*

We sit down together and order coffee and cakes. The café must be a favorite haunt of the legal fraternity, because every second person seems to know Dad. They stop by our table in droves for quick chats, congratulating him on recent wins and commenting on current cases. I remember how I loved this kind of attention only a few months ago. And now? Who are these sycophants? With their soft handshakes and polite voices. All the knowing nods for Cassandra and the careful fake smiles for me! I am the sour-faced bitch of a daughter. And they remind me of dead fish. Stuff them all.

Cassandra bubbles on about her time in Italy, when she put on three stone because all she ever ate was cakes and pasta and crusty bread. I guess I'm meant to find this amusing. Dad seems to. He smiles at her and touches her hand every now and again as she blathers on. I hate to see him pandering to this woman. I can see, now, under the glamorous clothes and fancy hairstyle, that she is not all that young. There are lines around her mouth and eyes. I am longing to know if she, too, has a family, that she has left. *Exactly how many lives have you wrecked?* is what I want to ask her.

"I just couldn't resist all those divine cheeses!"

Why on earth does she think I'd be interested in listening to this crap? Why doesn't she shut up? Dad has his arm around me the whole time. Through my misery I see that he seems genuinely glad to have me there.

"So how are things at home?" he asks me when, at last, the woman stops and there is a gap in the conversation. I glance up at him in surprise. Surely he doesn't expect me to go into details here.

"It's okay," Dad says, frowning deeply and briefly taking the woman's hand. "Cassie knows things are tough. They'll get better though, pet. I promise you, they'll get better. Your mum is a . . . sensible woman."

I glance at Cassandra. Her eyes are downcast. She has a sympathetic expression plastered across her face and . . . I am filled with such a burst of sudden hatred that my breath gives way again. What was it that Cynthia had planned for this woman? I try to remember the Greek story Dorothy told us but I can't recall any details. I want to pick up the small knife on my plate and stab it through her little white wrist. Pin her to the table and then run away.

"A sensible woman?" I repeat lightly.

"Well, what I mean is," he mutters uncomfortably, taking a brief look out through the lace curtains, "your mother is strong. She's one of life's survivors." He gives a short, dry laugh that means something, but I refuse to consider what.

"A survivor?" I choke on the word. *Is that all you can come up with?*

I decide that I've had enough. The half-eaten cake and unfinished cup of coffee sit in front of me like a couple of glaring mistakes on an exam, too late now to try and correct them. I've run out of time. I push my cup aside and get up.

"Sweetheart?" Dad looks alarmed.

"I have to go," I say shortly, picking up my bag from the table.

"Oh, Rose." He half stands, sits, and then stands up again, looking perplexed and utterly miserable. "I'm sorry if I've said the wrong thing. I know this whole business is all so . . . fraught and terrible for you girls."

"Justus," Cassandra insists softly, pulling the sleeve of his jacket, not looking at me. "Rose wants to go now." She looks up at me coolly and holds out her hand. "Nice meeting you, Rose."

"Yeah." I take her hand. It feels soft and slightly clammy.

"See you again?"

"Yes," I say weakly. *I hope not.*

For a brief moment, I see myself picking up the cup of coffee and sloshing it out onto the stiff white tablecloth in front of her. Then the half-eaten slice of blueberry muffin from her side plate, I'll mash it up before dropping it over her expensive red suit, and what's left into her hair. I don't, of course. I just stand there and let it run through my head like a sick little movie.

◆　◆　◆

Don'tcha just hate it . . . when you meet your father's new girl-friend and you have to shake hands and be polite, when all you really want to do is cut her throat? I mean, it's not her fault, and it's not his fault, and it isn't your fault, but hey! That doesn't mean you don't want to see everyone dead . . .

It is only when I am halfway down the street that I real-ize I've left all my shopping bags under the table at the café. Damn. No way can I go back without losing face. My hard-earned savings have gone on presents that no one will get. Right! Well, that seems to be in keeping with the rest of my life at the moment. I decide it doesn't matter. This year I want to forget all about Christmas.

I stare out the train window, watching the shops and houses roll past, wondering if all those ordinary-looking people out there, the guys in suits, the mothers with their prams, the old codgers shuffling along with their walking sticks, have secret lives too. Weird desires they don't understand Would theirs be as bad as mine? I pull my phone out of my bag and stare at it awhile. Then I flip through the numbers and laugh to myself in this black, totally nonsensical way.

Zoe gave me his number when I drove down to see her.

"Ring my dad," she said, writing it out on a piece of paper and handing it to me. "If you get lost, just ring him."

You see, I haven't forgotten. I've been thinking about it: the soft candlelight, his hands on my neck. That deep, murmuring voice. *You're a lovely girl, Rose.*

I punch in a quick text message. *When can ICU?*

He calls back within five minutes.

"Hey, Rose, I'm going to be in Anglesea on Boxing Day."

"Right," I say breathlessly.

"Feel like a surf down there?"

"Sure!"

◆ ◆ ◆

And so we arrange to meet in Anglesea after Christmas. It's only days away. His friend owns a place there but is overseas. So it's Zoe's father and me meeting in an empty house. *Use your brains, Rose.* And yet, I don't admit to myself what's going to happen. No way. For a start, he's got some other reason to be there. He has to pick up something for the car he's fixing . . .

Anyway, there is still time, heaps of time, to call the whole thing off. There are a few days to get through before Christmas. I don't even have to talk to him. I can send a text message any old time. Anything could happen between now and then.

And anyway! Why shouldn't I hook up with an older guy for a while? It's not like I'm going to *marry* him. He . . . made me feel good, alive somehow in a way I've never felt before. I shiver, thinking of his voice, those hands on my back, rubbing my neck, his tongue probing my mouth. And I decide I want more. More, more, more of everything! No one needs to know. *It's my turn now.*

◆ ◆ ◆

I let myself in. My mother is sitting at the table alone, drinking tea. It's five o'clock in the afternoon and she's still in her nightgown. My irritation intensifies. Can't she get it together enough to just get dressed? Yesterday, she seemed so much better, and now . . . it's back to square one. What am I meant to do here? Where the hell are my sisters? How come all this falls to me?

"How did your shopping go?" Mum asks. I can tell she is trying to sound bright and cheery and, in spite of everything, that tugs at my heartstrings. My mother, who has always been so naturally bouncy and loud and full of beans, has been reduced to this! Trying to be cheery. Trying to sound normal. Angry tears well in my throat, but I don't let them come any farther. I take a few breaths and close down. I'm an expert at this, I remind myself. Remember, Rose, *the queen of calm.*

"Just fine," I say sharply, "except that I left it all in a café."

She looks up quickly. I see my tone surprises her, but I don't care. I can feel her eyes following me as I get myself a glass of water from the tap. She is waiting for me to turn and smile and tell her something about my day out shopping with Zoe, but I suddenly can't stand it.

212

"Gotta check my e-mail," I say, and leave the room.

I check the paper, and note that the surf is likely to be good. The van needs a long run . . . I'll have a day on the surf. Cynthia will be home, so she can look after Mum. That's what I'm going to tell everyone. We'll meet up by accident. *Yeah right, Rose!*

That evening, when dinner is over and Mum is taking a bath, I begin a blow-by-blow description of my hour with Dad and Cassandra for my sisters. What she looked like and sounded like. What she was wearing, and everything else I can think of. But an important part of me isn't even there. *I'm going to escape all this*, is what I'm thinking, underneath. I have a sudden image in my head of the ocean swelling, back and forth along the shoreline, and I'm filled with longing. In just a few days I will be hurtling along the highway in my van, toward . . . the rest of my life.

Who knows what will happen?

The next morning I find my parcels outside the front door. No note attached, but there they are in a neat pile. Dad, I guess.

◆ ◆ ◆

ROAD TRIP

It's only just after six when I pull into the little car park above Childers Cove, but the darkening sky makes it seem later. I turn off the engine and sit awhile, brooding over this beautiful, secluded little beach where everything fell apart last summer. The choppy green water is held by two mammoth, jagged arms of dark cliffs. When the sun is out, these rocks are all the many shades of earth: ochre, bronze, almost fire-orange in parts, and punctuated with tufts of green where the coastal scrub has found dirt in which to grow. But in this light, they are ominous, like two heavy piles of rusting war machinery, great black monstrosities of destruction. I shiver as I get out of the van and slide the door shut. The wind has died down, and the air is very warm but thick now, heavy with the promise of rain.

The track that descends down to the steps that in turn lead down to the beach is only a few meters from the car park. Now that I'm here, I guess I'll go down, but I wish I'd arrived earlier, and I wish there was someone else about.

Once down the steps, I pick my way through the rocks, testing each one for slipperiness and stability before I jump. In this rapidly dimming light, it would be easy to break an ankle. Every now and again I stop and straighten up, look out at the sea rolling in, hungrily beating, sucking the shoreline. Against the black sky, hundreds of white gulls wheel and dive like maniacs, their shrill screeches filling the air with wild discord. They must be able to feel the approaching storm. *Go home*, they're telling each other. *Something might happen.* I feel like I'm being warned.

This is where I almost drowned. It's where he saved me and where that crazy, doomed love came undone. How tightly it held me in its fist. I couldn't move. *Oh Zoe . . .*

When I got back in the van after leaving Mum, I found another message from Zoe's mother asking me to call back. I deleted it straightaway. It was basically the same as the last one, *"Oh, Rose, it's Elaine here . . ."* in that clipped, annoyed tone of hers. Like *I'm* at fault for not being there when she wants me. Hasn't she twigged yet that I never want to have to think about her again, much less see her, much *much* less talk to her? *But what if Zoe is . . . in a bad way? What if she's . . . really sick and . . .?*

Slowly and methodically, I start to dial the number, dread pumping into my heart like poisonous gas, but when my finger hesitates over the last digit, I take it as a sign. Whatever that horrible woman wants to say to me will be encased in her agenda of trying to make me feel as bad as possible. *Do I need another dose of that?* No. I clear the punched-in numbers, snap shut the phone, and slip it into my pocket. If there is big news, I'll find out soon enough. *It's not like I'd be welcome at any funeral, anyway.*

I take off my shoes and walk slowly down the sand to the water. But I don't stay there long. The tide is coming in, and every now and again a maverick wave crashes higher than the rest and catches me unawares. By the time I've moved up to the dry sand, my jeans are soaked through to the knees.

I see a man in the distance, near the rocks up on the other end of the beach, throwing sticks to a large, playful dog. My mouth goes dry because, for a second there, I think it's him. It's the angle of the shoulders, the profile against the sky, and the way he lifts his arm to throw. The dog is running in circles and bouncing up and down as it waits for the man's next move. My heart begins to beat wildly as I watch the stick being thrown again and again. Each time, the dog careers off as though its life depends on bringing it back. The man begins to prance about, sprinting after the dog, calling to it as he runs a few feet into the surf and out again. At one stage, he does a couple of cartwheels on the sand, just for the hell of it, and my throat contracts again, this time with a hard, stinging joy. *I'm glad.* In spite of everything, I'm glad I was drawn into that dark, murky world of strange houses and shady bedrooms, of hours snatched here and there, of my own helplessness in the face of the avalanche of desire. Sorry, too, of course . . . but inside a few short weeks I lived a whole life and so *how can I be sorry for that*?

The dog stands by, watching the man, barking loudly with excitement. Ray was like this, so ebullient and strong. Once, when I complained that the hot sand was burning my feet, he insisted on giving me a piggyback ride all the way up from the water to the car.

"You're no burden, Rosie girl," he said, when I suggested I might be too heavy. I remember laughing all the way and planting one of my shy kisses on his ear when we reached the car, my heart nearly bursting with the whole business of loving him . . . Zoe was back in Melbourne with her mother, so there was no one to see us.

It's not him, of course. Ray is overseas again. It's over and it's gone and it will never come back. The last time we spoke, he told me *no, he didn't think it was a good idea for us to meet again*, that things had now become *uncool* and that we both should *get on with our lives*—along with a few other clichés I can't remember, but that basically amounted to *piss off*.

A rough sob pushes its way out from my chest and into my throat before I find the will to gulp it away. *Enough tears. I've cried enough.* He collapsed on this beach after rescuing me and was put in the hospital for a few days. Although he didn't have an actual heart attack, the whole exercise had strained his heart. I walk toward the stranger and his dog, glad for their presence on this lonely beach. There isn't another soul about. The man smiles at me as we pass. He looks nothing like Ray. He's much younger, only about thirty.

"Might have to go back for your umbrella," he calls cheerfully, pointing at the sky. "It's gonna let loose real soon."

"Yeah." I bend to pat the dog, who is sniffing me curiously. "Sure looks that way."

The first raindrops splatter and sizzle against my face and arms as I come at last to the rocks at the other end of the beach. *Okay, here it comes.* Better find somewhere to shelter. I feel a bit daft that I didn't think to bring my raincoat because it is actually sitting rolled up on the front seat of the van. I could head straight back, I suppose. But I don't want to return just yet.

◆ ◆ ◆

LAST SUMMER, ANGLESEA

"I hope you're not regretting this, Rose."

He is peering out the window through the slatted blinds, frowning thoughtfully. It's just Ray and me in this huge old ramshackle house at the back of Anglesea. I shake my head and whisper, "No," but his back is still turned to me, and he gives no indication he has heard. I don't repeat myself. Does this mean *he's* regretting it?

I'm lying on top of the unmade sofabed against a couple of grubby cushions, naked except for a cotton Indian bedspread that I have pulled up to cover myself. I stare at the bike poster on the opposite wall: a man dressed in leather with a girl dressed in not much at all sitting behind him. She is pouting like crazy and holding a can of bike oil in her right hand. I want to ask him about his friends. What kind of people would have such a tacky image on their wall? But there are more pressing things to think about, such as what to say, exactly. And how to get to the bathroom without him seeing the blood on my thighs?

We've just had sex in this strange room, after a crazy couple of hours of talk and laughter, a bit of drinking, and some wild dancing. I'm feeling dazed, I suppose. Stunned might actually be a better word, and I'm on the verge of crying. *How did I get here, again?* I can hardly bear to admit the next thought that runs through my head, because it indicates just how seriously crazy I've become within a matter of a few short weeks. *Nat Cummins. It should be him standing naked by the window. I wish I'd just had sex with Nat Cummins.*

"I want you to know," Ray turns around and folds his arms across his chest and looks at me seriously, "that I didn't plan this. In fact, I was thinking I must not let it happen." He looks away. "I'm so much older than you, and when I invited you for lunch, lunch was all I had in mind . . ."

My mouth falls open in surprise. *He's got to be kidding!* But he throws both hands up in the air and the towel slips off from around his waist and I don't know where to look because . . . I've never really seen a naked man before.

"Of course I'm attracted to you," he continues, "and I like you and—"

"I know." I cut across him impatiently. His sincerity is obvious, but it is also baffling. I might be only eighteen, but I knew what was happening when he invited me in for lunch! After all that flirty talk on the beach, the swimming together in the surf, the quiet lying side-by-side in the glorious sunshine, the music and the dancing . . . this was the next thing. I knew what was happening when I walked through the door. So why pretend?

"Good."

There is an awkward pause.

"So are *you* sorry?" I ask, sitting up straighter and pulling the sheet more tightly around my breasts. "Because . . . if you are, just say so. I mean . . ."

"No!" he says. He comes across from the window and sits down at the end of the bed, then reaches out and picks up my foot, which is poking out from under the covers, and settles it on his knee. "I just hope you feel . . . okay," he says, rubbing my foot and smiling in this tense way. "We both got pretty . . . carried away there, and you seemed to want to go ahead with it, and . . ."

"I *did* want to go ahead with it," I cut in sharply.

He is frowning and still seems troubled because he sighs a couple of times as he caresses my foot.

"So, you didn't feel pressured?" he persists. "Because that is the last thing I'd want, Rose. I'm so much older. I'm not sure if it was the right thing . . . to do." His voice trails away.

"How old are you?"

He hesitates a moment.

"Nearly fifty-four," he mumbles with a rueful smile.

"Really?" I whisper wonderingly. *Fifty-four!* Then I start giggling and I can't stop. I flop back on the pillow and let the laughter hoot and bubble out of me. I'm shaking with it. It's coming up from my toes. He is older than my father! *No. That's got to be wrong!* I wriggle the toes he's holding, wanting him to join in my laughter, for the tension to ease. He doesn't, so I eventually stop laughing, sit up again, and look at him directly. *Yeah! He's older than Dad!*

"I just want to be sure I didn't push you," he mutters.

"Don't treat me like a child," I say, reaching for my skirt and top, which are lying at the end of the bed, then add for good measure, "You didn't push me into anything. I might be young, but . . . I'm old inside."

"Are you?" He seems amused by this idea.

"Yeah," I say, and I mean it seriously. "I was born old."

"Well then . . ." It's his turn to laugh. "That settles it."

◆ ◆ ◆

We came in from the beach, and after an hour of sitting at the kitchen table, talking easily, having a couple of drinks, and getting on like a house on fire, he turned on the music and suddenly . . . it was impossible not to dance. We had this incredible half hour or so of dancing together in the living room to an old Elvis Costello record. Then, sweaty and breathless and laughing, we retreated hand in hand to the back bedroom, as though it was the most natural thing in the world. As though it was something *I'd* done many times before, when in fact I'd never done anything even remotely like it. Our clothes were off within half a minute, and we fell laughing like drunken sailors onto the bed. But I wasn't drunk, and neither was he. And within a few minutes, things got a bit awkward, a bit messy for both of us.

Now we're both too shy to talk about it. I was a virgin, and that fact is lying between us like a package we're both too embarrassed to unwrap.

"Do you want to continue?" he asks quite formally.

"Continue?" I don't understand.

"After this?" he says.

"Yeah," I say, not exactly sure that I do, but it seems the right thing to say under the circumstances. I shyly raise both arms and slip on my top. "If you want to?"

"Well." He looks genuinely overwhelmed, and it is his turn to fall back on the bed. "I suppose I do." He is looking at the ceiling thoughtfully. "Yeah."

"So, when?" I say. "When can we see each other again?" I pull my skirt over my head, zip it up, and when I next look at him, he's grinning. I can tell he's getting right off on my forthright attitude, so I crank it up even further.

"Whenever you like," he says, leaning forward to push my hair behind my ears. "You're pretty wonderful, Rose. I know there is this age difference between us, but as soon as I met you, I sensed that you're much wiser than your years. I feel like I'm talking to a very mature woman."

"Yeah," I say, "so I'm always being told." Which makes him laugh again. But it's true. People are always telling me that. Maybe it's because I seem so sensible compared to my sisters. "But I'd better go now." I edge off the bed. "I'm worried about getting home. My mother hasn't been . . . well."

"Okay." He catches me by the arm before I can get up, pulls me back to him and kisses me softly. "Ah, little Rose," he mumbles into my neck, "no need to worry about anything, sweetheart." Then he begins to caress me very slowly and tenderly, while continuing with the lingering hot kisses. This time it is much better. So languorous and slow that I become weak, only half-conscious. I feel like I might be swimming in slow-motion underwater, every part of my skin alive and singing out for more. We push and slide, roll forward and back in it, like sea creatures moving through the still, warm, dark waters toward light.

When it is over, I decide that this must be love. There are no more thoughts of Nat Cummins or anyone else. In the space of an afternoon, we have woven a soft, delicate cocoon around ourselves, him and me. Or that's what it feels like, anyway. We're outside time and apart from anyone else. All I want is for it to continue.

Hand in hand we walk out toward the front door.

"Are you going to tell anyone?" he suddenly asks, opening the door and stepping aside for me to pass. I stop.

"Well . . . no," I say. Then I remember Zoe. The perfect warm bubble that has held me spellbound for nearly three hours breaks open with a splash of ice to my face. He notices and is immediately concerned.

"What is it?" he asks. "Is something the matter?"

"Zoe is my best friend," I whisper.

"Rose," he mutters into my hair, "she needn't know."

"But what if . . . ?" I am suddenly overwhelmed, not only because of what I've just done, but because I'm going to keep such a huge secret from her, *my best friend*. I slump against him, longing to be taken back to our private no-man's-land, back into the hot, thoughtless space of locked torsos, skin and heartbeat, away from ordinary life and

222

everyone else. He smiles and grabs me by the shoulders and tries to lift them, makes me stand up tall again. I raise my eyes and we look at each other quietly, and I know I can't give him up.

He puts two fingers gently over my mouth.

"We'll fit this around your friendship with Zoe," he says, slowly and very firmly. "Trust me, Rose. I love her too."

So I do. I trust him, and I walk out of that room and get in my van and I drive home, buoyed up with excitement and my own set of grown-up secrets.

◆ ◆ ◆

ROAD TRIP

I scurry about on the rocks, looking for somewhere to shelter as the wind starts to blow up again. The temperature drops farther and the rain begins in earnest. Eventually I find a little cranny between a few big boulders. Not perfect, but there is a dry space in there, so I bend down and crawl through, feeling pleased with myself. This should do until the storm passes. Lightning crackles and I can see across the sand where I've just walked, and over the ocean, too.

There is not much room to move, though. Whenever I want to straighten out my hunched-up legs, I have to put them out in the rain. And the rock is so hard. I peer out at the pounding rain and wish again I'd brought the coat, if only to put under my bum.

It's not so bad at first. I quite enjoy sitting there, watching the heavy rain in the thickening darkness, thinking back over the day, feeling quite proud of myself, actually. First the swim in the ocean, then the kid—for some reason, I feel quite good about Travis, his ex-wife, and Peter—and now this. I've come back to the scene of the nightmare to lay a few ghosts to rest. Isn't that what you're supposed to do? Pretty stupid to let past events, or places for that matter, have too much power, so . . . this is my way of *dealing* with it.

But after a while, I begin to feel weirdly stuck, as though I'm caught in someone else's little groove. Elaine's voice keeps diving in from nowhere, playing around my consciousness like a tune that I don't like but can't get out of my head. *Oh, Rose, it's Elaine here . . . I wonder if you could call me, please . . .* The answer is to move, but I don't. All I have to do is get up and out and walk back along the beach in the rain and up those steps to my van. And yet something holds me back.

The storm shows no sign of giving up, and although it couldn't be later than seven in the evening, and with daylight savings that should mean at least a couple of hours of light, the low black sky seems to have set in for the night.

As much as I try not to, I begin to freak out. It doesn't help that I'm so bloody uncomfortable. Water drips in from one corner. The rock I have to lean on has a jagged surface. More water seeps up the bottom of my jeans. My feet and legs are numb with wet and cold.

I am alone on a lonely beach at night, watching the sky go crazy, hearing rolls of ominous thunder as the rain slants down. The horrible voice of my ex-friend's mother squeaks and bites into my brain. This whole fucking display of storm power is aimed directly at me. That's what it feels like, anyway. The cramped shelter will soon be my tomb and I'll be buried alive. So I hunker down and shut my eyes and wait for it to be over.

◆ ◆ ◆

LAST SUMMER, MELBOURNE

I didn't know anything about Ray's collapse until I was back home with my family in North Fitzroy. They'd been called to come and get me when I was pronounced fit after only an hour in the local hospital's emergency room.

The next morning, there is a very short message from Zoe's mother on our answering machine, telling us that Ray is being kept in the hospital for a few days' observation and that Zoe is now back in Melbourne. I replay it a couple of times. Her tone is cold, rushed, slightly hysterical, as though she rang to say something else entirely but didn't have time. Why didn't *Zoe* ring? I batten down my worst fears, chock it up to Ray being in the hospital. And I feel bad because, of course, I'm the cause. I insisted on going back into the water. *Poor Zoe must be worried about her father.* Even so, when I pick up the phone a few times and try to ring her, I end up chickening out before I get through the numbers. What am I going to say? *I'm so sorry that your father had to save me?* But it's . . . *too close* to the rest of it, somehow. Too close to the secrets I'm keeping from her.

On the third day I'm home, Mum and Cynthia come in from shopping to find me standing listlessly by the phone, trying to work out what to do. Mum is convinced that the best thing would be to go to Zoe's house with some flowers. She offers to drive me.

"Don't ring," she says. "We'll just land up there with flowers and you'll stay for five minutes or five hours. Whatever seems right."

"But they might not want . . . *outsiders*," I whisper.

"Darling, you're not an outsider!" Mum hugs me. "Your best friend's father has taken sick after helping you. Of course she's worried and she'll want to see you."

◆　◆　◆

Zoe answers the door. She stands there and just stares, mouth open and face blank, for about half a minute before her mother comes and stands behind her. And then, unbelievably, Nat Cummins appears behind them both. The three of them, standing there looking at me, completely stone-faced. There is no hint of acknowledgment. It is like they don't know who I am anymore.

"I got the message about your dad," I manage to mutter. "Is he home now? Or still in the hospital? How is he, Zoe?"

My voice triggers something in Zoe, because her face suddenly contorts into the ugliest sneer I've ever seen. Her hands dart out and she grabs the flowers I'm holding, all those beautiful roses and lilies that mum helped me buy, and she throws them to the ground. Never one for half measures, she then stomps on them furiously, kicking them about with her high-heeled sandals.

"How *could* you come here," she screams into my face, "after what you've done? Get out of my life, you fucking slag! I never ever want to see you again! I mean it. Do you hear me? *Never ever!*"

I go back to the car, shaking, and get in. Mum doesn't say anything, just squeezes my hand briefly, fires up the engine, and takes me home. I have no idea if she witnessed what happened, but I think not. She was in the car, after all.

At this point, I'm not quite sure what happened myself. I'm just thankful for the silence.

I get home and go straight to my room, lie on my bed, still with a sliver of crazy hope that Zoe might not know the full story. I am clutching at straws, I know, looking for any way to believe the worst hasn't happened. It could be that she blames me for going into the water again that day, causing her father to have to save me. Maybe she doesn't know about . . . the rest of it. We have always been so careful, so discreet.

But two days later, her mother rings again, to make sure I know they have the full picture. Her light, sarcastic tone is as bad as Zoe's anger. Did I know that Ray made a habit of seducing young women? He'd been doing it all his life. *Admittedly none as young as you, Rose, but there you go. There is a first time for everything, isn't there?* They'd been through his things. Found a note from me in the pocket of his jeans. Other stuff, too, so there is *no point denying it*. Zoe had been unwilling to believe it until it was confirmed by the owner of the house in Anglesea. Ray had apparently been *talking up some little chick called Rose* . . . to anyone who'd listen. I might be interested to know, too, that the whole sorry business had brought her and Zoe closer together. They were getting over things *together* by having *a good laugh* and, just in case I interpreted that as meaning that they were going to treat it lightheartedly, she made it very clear that what I'd done was . . . *unforgivable*. I was no longer on their radar. I didn't count. *Don't write and don't ring. Don't bother us again. Just stay away forever . . . it's best that way.*

I listen to all she has to say without uttering a word, then I just put the phone down. I go into shock. Or I think that's what happens. My legs melt away beneath me while I stand next to the phone. I am in a limp heap on the living room floor when my sisters find me. So Ray has been *talking up some little chick called Rose*? Me. That's what I was to him. *A little chick called Rose.* Believe me, that was the hardest part to hear.

◆ ◆ ◆

ROAD TRIP

The rain starts to ease. I watch as the wind begins to clear the heavy black clouds away, letting through broad horizontal patches of deep blue. A crescent moon emerges, hovering like a magical good-luck charm in the twilight sky, sending down tracks of silver-bubbled light to play over the black water. This all happens within about fifteen minutes, and I'm totally mesmerized. After a while, I crawl out of my shelter and stretch. My limbs are stiff and my clothes and shoes sodden with rain and spray. It's a relief to be standing again. I walk back across the beach toward the steps. Behind me, the sinking red sun sends streaks of gold and crimson across the twilight sky. It is the last hour of summer evening light, before the day finally signs off. I've always loved this time.

A sharp breeze nips around my face and neck. The sand is soggy between my toes in these completely stupid canvas shoes, making me feel like I'm walking on iron filings, and giving me blisters.

Way up ahead, I suddenly see three black figures with boards making their way down the steps toward the water. *Are they serious?* I quicken my pace and then stop, a few meters up the sand, to watch as they enter the water, fall on their boards, and begin paddling out. Three guys. I can hear them yelling over the roar of the ocean, joking and laughing and scoffing at each other. I am completely riveted, in awe

230

really, as I watch them go way out into that watery darkness, making themselves almost invisible.

Then, one by one, they come riding in. Moonlight catches the middle one's blond hair, making the tendrils around his head stand out like golden spikes. For a few moments, the three of them seem like young gods, gliding across some jeweled landscape. It's so fantastic, so bizarre, that I wonder if I'm imagining it. Envy starts to bite in hard. *How would it feel?* To surf the black ocean under moonlight instead of the harsh, bright light of day. To skim across the ocean's surface like a night bird on a secret mission, unseen by anyone in the real world. *Oh shit! No.* It would be too scary. I wouldn't be able to see a thing. Not at night. Not here. *Especially not here!*

Hey, Rose . . . don't even think about it!

But I've already quickened my pace, and now I'm running. I figure it will take me ten minutes to get to my van and into my wetsuit, and maybe another five to get back down to the water with my board. By then there won't be much light left, maybe none. So I have to hurry. Suddenly it seems like the most important thing in the world to join those guys on the water. To catch just one wave before night finally falls . . .

◆　◆　◆

It is not quite dark as I feel the sea slapping around my knees. The waves crash against my belly, and that is my cue to sink forward into the inky black chill and start paddling. I'm laughing like a maniac now, scared as hell. *No rip*, I try to placate my jumping nerves. It's my mantra to quell the rising fear. *See those guys, Rose. They're doing it. No rip. You'll be okay.*

And I am. I get out to where the swell is rising like silver froth in the dim light and I wait for my chance.

I miss the first one entirely. The next dumps me like a sack of potatoes.

"Hey!" a friendly voice shouts. One of the guys is right nearby, and he's suffered the same fate. But I don't have a chance to return his greeting. Both of us are paddling frantically toward a beautiful new white crest. Then I'm up, I'm riding my board in the semidark at Childers Cove. Afraid, yes, but totally alive. My feet lock that board, my arms stretch out like wings, and my eyes sting with salt and breeze. It feels for those short few moments—maybe half a minute—exactly like I'm flying.

I am skimming over this water like a bird.

I only get that one wave. The next few just dump me, and when I see the guys hauling themselves out onto the sand, I do the same. The courage I found to go in doesn't extend to staying out there on my own at night. The light has totally gone now. Even so, I paddle in reluctantly, gasping with the cold, my legs trembling with exertion, wishing it could have lasted longer.

Before getting out, when it's waist deep, I let myself fall under the surface of the waves. Facedown at first, legs tucked up. Then I flip onto my back and spread my arms and legs out as far as I can. My mind cuts loose in the drifting silence. So many stars out now! I feel the dark currents ebb with secret life around my head and limbs. I can imagine the shadowy, gliding shapes of fish and seaweed and a million other living things beneath the surface of this water.

"Wow," I whisper, and then again, louder, "Thank you. Thank you, thank you." I have no idea who I'm talking to, but . . . I am overwhelmed with gratitude.

"Cool or what?" one of them calls over as I approach, clutching my board. The three guys, huddled together on the shore, have turned to watch me curiously as I come out of the water.

"Yeah!" I smile and wave as I pass them on my way toward the steps. "Very!" I'm feeling too shy to stop and talk, even though I feel strongly that I'd be welcome.

In spite of climbing all those stairs, I'm still shivering when I reach the van. I get out of my wetsuit and rummage around for some dry clothes in my bag. I pull on jeans and a long-sleeved T-shirt. Not anywhere near warm enough, but it seems to be all I've brought. *Damn.* Then I open the door and slide onto the torn plastic seat behind the wheel, feeling high as a kite. *That was . . . special! And I'm alive to tell the tale . . . Hey, Rose!*

I turn on the ignition and try to get the heater working, but the noisy vents only blow out intermittent rushes of freezing cold air. *Damn it. Just my luck.* I mess around with it for ages in the semidark, trying to remember the trick that the service guy told me, wishing I had a flashlight. I'm shivering uncontrollably by now and swearing furiously through my chattering teeth. *Why didn't I listen properly? And why the hell didn't I pack a really warm sweater?* Truth is, I'd forgotten how cool summer nights sometimes get on the coast. I groan when I remember that I'd only packed Cynthia's crummy light sleeping bag, too. Couldn't find mine and thought hers would do. *Not* smart, Rose!

I give up on the heater and turn on the radio, flicking through the stations furiously. Nothing but crap! All the easy-listening shit. In desperation, I switch over to AM and Bruce Springsteen's old hit "Dancing in the Dark" suddenly fills the cabin. Well, okay . . . it will have to do. But it takes only one line of the song and a sliver of memory lobs in from left field and sets up camp right under my rib cage.

When Ray and I got together, we'd usually end up dancing. We'd put on some music, have a couple of drinks, talk, make some food. Then we'd turn up the stereo, switch off the lights and . . . start dancing, just the two of us, dancing in the dark.

I shake off the memory as I watch the three surfers making their way to their vehicle around the other side of the car park. Their loud voices are muffled in the night air. Doors slam, an engine fires up, and the taillights shine like small red eyes in the darkness. They reverse and beep the horn as they pass me before heading out toward the exit. I feel strangely bereft when the sound of their motor finally dies away.

I'm sitting there staring out into the night at nothing, shivering, feeling myself slide downward like a kid on one of those high water slides, wanting to stop but unable to do so. *So I went for a surf under the stars? Well . . . great. But it doesn't exactly solve everything, does it?* Like, what to do now? And how to deal with the sisters tomorrow and . . . This small secluded parking lot suddenly seems creepy.

I turn around, look at the jumbled mess in the back of the van, and try to get enthusiastic about bedding myself down in there for the night. But why should I crawl into that miserable, inadequate sleeping bag and toss and turn all night, chewing over the same old boring stuff of last summer, just because I decided I would twelve hours ago? I don't really want to stay here. No way. Everyone is allowed to change their mind occasionally. I straighten up and start the engine.

Once up on the main road, I turn right at the intersection, rev up hard, and gun the old van toward Port Campbell. I pass no one else on the road. Halfway there, I slip on a Kyuss CD. A bit of desert rock will do the trick. Gotta keep the devils onside.

The downfall of Ray and me didn't hinge on Zoe and her mother finding out. That is just the official line, the one I tell myself, because all through this past year I've wanted like crazy to believe that we were meant for each other, and that we were stymied by brutal outside forces. But it wasn't like that at all.

◆ ◆ ◆

LAST SUMMER, APOLLO BAY

I wake up early to the chortling of the magpies outside. I slip
out of bed and pull on my jeans and the thick plaid shirt of
Ray's I sometimes wear. Then I go out onto the veranda.

The branches and leaves of the native oak near the gate
stand out against the soft pink light of the rising sun in the
most breathtakingly lovely way. Not a hint of wind. I slide
my feet into a pair of old rubber flip-flops and take myself
off down the track, away from the house. I walk quite a way,
past the first curve in the road, and the second. I turn around
. . . wham! It is as though someone has turned on the celes-
tial glory just for me. The sea, bright green with flashes of
shimmering pearl, pushes up against an endless sky. It is like
a magical backdrop to an important religious event, almost
surreal! A figure wreathed in glowing white is going to
descend from the stratosphere any minute now, accompanied
by a host of winged angels!

I stand awhile, lift my face to the sky and laugh. My
heart is full to bursting. You can send the hurricanes in now,
if you like, I whisper to whoever might be listening. An avalanche of snow or ice. An army of barbarians to pillage and
burn. I don't care what happens. This is it. I've seen all I need
to see.

Of course, that's all bullshit. I don't want anyone to
come in and change one thing. Ray and I have been alone
together for three days, and I'm due back home tomorrow

and I desperately don't want to go. Why would I? I don't want to see my family. I don't want to see friends or take phone calls or go to work. I don't want to go to university, either. Future plans have faded into the murky haze of boring background. The very idea of career ambitions seems ludicrous and beside the point. We've been sitting around for three days: reading, watching the sky, talking, having the occasional swim, eating and sleeping, dancing, and making love over and over again. I'm only eighteen, but I've already found what everyone else spends their lives searching for.

I run back to the house, eager to share my revelation. But he isn't in the kitchen or the bedroom and not on the back porch, either. Eventually I find him out in his office storeroom, marking up orders, frowning over sheets of paper covered in numbers, a pen stuck behind one ear and the fax machine purring.

"Rosie girl?" he says, looking up with a preoccupied frown. I'm leaning against the big open doorway, my arms folded, watching him work. I smile but don't move. He returns my smile and picks up a fresh pile of papers and positions them in the photocopier. Suddenly I'm overwhelmed. All of it seems like a kind of miracle. Him. Me. *Us.* Tears come to my eyes. I stand in the doorway, laughing a bit at how ridiculous I am being, at the same time letting them trickle down my cheeks, aware of their dramatic effect. No one could possibly love anyone more than I love him right at this very moment, and that's what he needs to know.

"Baby?" He looks up, concerned, puts down the papers and moves toward me. "Has anything happened?"

"No!" I fall into his embrace and continue to cry and laugh at the same time. He rubs my back and keeps murmuring that everything is absolutely fine, and that I'm not to get upset or worried. Between gulps I tell him that I already know that, and he isn't to think I'm upset or worried about a thing . . .

At last, I am able to blow my nose and find my voice, although I can't find the exact words I need. I start rambling on in this gushy, vague way that probably doesn't make a lot of sense, but I can't seem to stop. I try to describe what I've just seen, all the stunning subtlety of color, and the grand, magisterial wonder of the sea and sky. I rave on and on about the magic of *everything* when we're together. He listens, says nothing, only smiles occasionally. When at last I stop, I am a little fearful. What if me putting it into words is against the rules in some way? *What if doing that makes it all . . . disappear?*

You see, my head is full of all the possibilities for our future together. That's what I really want to talk about.

"Do you believe in heaven?" is how I broach it. He doesn't laugh at me or tell me I'm silly. In fact, he doesn't say anything at all for some time. "I sort of feel like I'm there," I say shyly, "when I'm with you."

"Do you?" he whispers into my hair.

"Yes," I say, then pull away a bit and look up into his face. "Do you know what I'm talking about? Do you believe we're in heaven too?"

"No, baby," he interrupts me softly, shaking his head. "No, I don't."

"What do you . . ." I can feel myself starting to crash inside, because his face is telling me things I don't want to know, but I try like crazy to hide it. "What do you believe in?" I whisper.

He smiles in a weary way and shrugs. "I don't believe in anything," he says, his eyes drifting away from my face, "except that every good thing will end and that everything holds the seeds of its own destruction."

My skin starts contracting, and the goose bumps rise, and it is like being dunked into ice-cold water against your will.

"You're reading too much into all this, baby," he goes on gently, still stroking my hair. "You need to know none of it is all that important. You're young. You'll meet other people."

"But Ray!" I recoil from him. "You're . . . I love you!"

An ache rises up from my belly to my chest and throat whenever I think of his words. *I don't believe in anything.* It makes me feel so sad. For him and for myself and for what happened . . .

◆ ◆ ◆

I didn't accept it, of course. Instead, I took on the role of his personal savior. My love was going to single-handedly lead him back to a full and happy life. I was going to make him *see.*

I rang, e-mailed, and wrote notes to him constantly, with small snippets of good news about the world.

> *Oh, Ray, you should have seen the baby ducks on*
> *the pond this morning! They were so pretty . . .*
> blah, blah!
> > *So much love from your Rosie girl.*

> *Ray, you wouldn't believe the funny thing I dreamed*
> *last night . . . you and me in Washington as special*
> *guests of President Bush. We were discussing the*
> *state of the world. Bono was there. Bush was really*
> *impressed with your suggestion to . . . etc., etc. . . .*
> > *Your Rosie girl.*

(I made up the bit about Bush being impressed with him!)

*Hi, sweet man. Just a note to let you know that
although I'm serving ice cream today, I'm actually
down on the coast watching the sunset with you!*
        Love you forever . . . Rosie girl.

I also constantly brought him gifts and offerings: books
to read and other little things I'd found, like flowers and the
superfine black ink pens he loved. Dad had left a very special pen behind, given to him by a childhood mentor. I stole
it and gave it to Ray. Once I spied a tiny bird's nest perched
up in the fork of a tree. I actually climbed the tree and prized
it away from the branch. Inside were four speckled eggs.
Two traumatized parents screeched and fluttered around me
as I committed this crime, but do you think I cared? I didn't
give a shit! As long as I could give this perfect thing to Ray.
It was my job to light up his life. I was desperate to make him
love me in the way that I loved him.

◆ ◆ ◆

ROAD TRIP

"Mum, can I come in?" I knock on the door again, this time more sharply. "Mum, you there?" I wait a few seconds and then close my eyes with frustration. I haven't got my watch, so I have no idea what time it is, but when I drove back through the town, the pub lights were out, so it has to be after ten.

"Mum!"

Nothing. Then it dawns on me that she might not even be there. Maybe she went out to eat in some local restaurant; met up with someone she knows. (Mum is forever running across people she knows.) They will have invited her back to their place for coffee. Right at this moment, she'll be chatting on in some warm, dry, comfortable living room and has probably agreed to spend the night there instead of heading back through the storm to this ratty joint! That means no way in for me, unless I dare to wake the manager. *Damn!* I'm not up to that, so I'll have to sleep in the van after all. I'm chilled through, my teeth are chattering, and I have blisters on my feet from sloshing around through the rocks in these light shoes.

Hang on. Was that some kind of rustling inside? I lean up against the door and knock again.

"Who is it?" comes this suspicious, low voice through the keyhole. *Oh God.* I almost collapse with relief.

"Mum, it's me, Rose!"

"Do you know what time it is?" she grumbles.

She sounds really cross.

"Just let me in! Please."

She begins fiddling with the lock and then swears when it won't open. A yellow light suddenly spills out through the cracks above and below the door. It is all I can do to stop myself from yelling, *Hurry up!*

At last, the door opens and I fall inside. For one confused moment I hardly know where I am, or who exactly. Rose, yes, but at what age and who have I come to see? I might be a kid of five knocking on my parents' door in the middle of the night. *Mum, I've had a bad dream! Can I get into bed with you?*

Or come to find Ray after I hadn't heard from him for a week. I will never forget the look on his face as he opened the door, as though I was some silly little girl he only vaguely remembered.

Sorry I didn't call, baby. Had so much work on . . .

As though he'd already begun the next phase of his life and I wasn't part of it. At that point I became terrified because I realized my life wasn't my own anymore . . . I'd given it away to someone who didn't want it.

"Rose!" Mum stands aside. "You're freezing and . . ." She tries to put her arm around my shoulders, but I push past her into the warmth of the room. "What happened? I was worried. You were going to ring me!"

"Nothing," I say, gulping. "I forgot. Sorry." Her hair is loose, and she is in a cotton nightgown with a panel of lace around the neck. She looks warm and soft and a bit bleary-eyed. I obviously woke her.

"You mind if I take a shower?"

"Now?" She seems baffled more than anything.

"Well, look at me!" I say.

"It's two a.m., Rose!"

"Is it?" *What the fuck do I care what time it is!*

"Well"—she smiles—"of course you can take a shower." She yawns, walks past me to the little bathroom, and opens the door. "So, what happened? You went out to the beach and . . .?" She takes a couple of steps toward me, but I back away. I've come onto her territory, so it's important to keep my distance.

"I'm okay, thanks for letting me in," I mumble in this surly keep-your-hands-off-me way. Much to my annoyance, it makes her laugh.

"Oh! Like I was going to let you stand wet and dripping outside?"

"Well, thanks anyway," I say, reaching to the side table for tissues and blowing my nose. She dives over to the spare bed, plucks a towel off the end, and pushes it into my hands.

"Go on!" she orders. "Have a warm shower. You'll feel better."

When I come out of the shower, Mum is sitting up in bed with the bedside lamp on, her knees up, reading a book. She has turned down the single bed for me, found a couple of extra pillows, and there is a glass of water on my table. I stand there, wrapped only in a towel, trying to work out how to hop into bed without taking off the towel and letting her see me naked. I know it's ridiculous, but I'm in a completely unplanned-for, up-close situation with my mother. We haven't slept in the same room since I was about eight.

"I've got a spare nightgown," she says.

"Thanks." I watch as she gets up and pulls it from the little case at the bottom of her bed and throws it to me. I slip it over my head while her back is turned. "Is there anything to eat? I'm starving!"

"There's a cardboard breakfast over there," she says, pointing to a tray near the door with a small packet of cornflakes sitting in a white bowl. "Milk in the fridge, and I think there is a banana left in that bag of fruit we brought. Bread, too. Don't make toast, though. It will make the room smell all night."

"Thanks," I say gruffly, emptying the cornflakes into the bowl and reaching into the fridge for the jug of milk. With sliced banana on top, it isn't bad. In fact, it tastes absolutely delicious.

"So, Rose," she says, "what happened?"

"Nothing happened," I snap, continuing to eat the cornflakes hungrily. "I just got caught . . . in the rain." She sighs and gives me a meaningful look but I turn away. "I just . . . didn't feel like sleeping in the van," I add weakly. I toss up whether to tell her about the night surfing and decide against it. She'll only think I'm crazy, and anyway it's hard to believe I actually did it now. Maybe I am crazy.

I finish the cornflakes and go brush my teeth. By the time I come back from the bathroom, she has the light off. I get into bed, thankfully. I can tell she's cross with me for keeping her at a distance, but I'm not sure what to say. Even though I'm so tired, I don't immediately curl on my side to go to sleep. I lie on my back and look up into the darkness. I owe her something.

"It's good being here," I say awkwardly, at last. "Thanks, Mum."

She murmurs, "That's okay," and, "Goodnight," then shifts around a bit, getting comfortable.

I think that she must have decided to go off to sleep because she turns her back to me and doesn't say anything. I just lie there, staring at the yellow streetlight pouring in around the edges of the curtains, knowing that I've been a rude pig but not knowing what to do about it.

"You know that we all *know*, don't you, Rose?" she says softly across the dark space between our two beds. My breath catches in shock. "That you and Zoe's father had a sexual relationship?" she adds, as though I might not understand her meaning.

My response is to become instinctively still. I'm lying there, stiff as a mannequin, a rabbit in the headlights. I want to run and hide, but where would I go to at this hour? The quietness between us becomes so heavy, so pregnant with unsaid things, that I have to sit up a bit because it's hard to breathe.

"No," I say at last. "I didn't know that."

"I suspected, after we dropped off those flowers," she tells me quietly, "and your sisters knew it intuitively even before that, so . . ." She rolls onto her back. I watch her profile against the window as a flood of raw emotion fills my chest. Shame, anger, and then a weird, cocked-up kind of relief are vying with each other for first place.

"So why didn't you say anything?" I ask, utterly confused.

"I should have," she replies quickly, "but I was so furious. I didn't know what to say. I couldn't trust myself."

"Furious?"

"I wanted to kill him." Her voice is low, barely above a whisper, and full of raspy venom. "I actually worked out a plan. Ask your sisters! Cynthia found me out. First I was going to knife him. Then I was going to run him over. Pretend it was an accident. I had it all worked out. I was at the point of hiring someone to track his movements. They . . . your sisters cottoned on and . . . talked me out of it."

Kill him? Run him over? What the hell is she talking about? I'm so shocked at this that I can't speak. My mother is the most peace-loving person I know and also the most kind and compassionate. She sends cards and flowers and takes around casseroles, not only to friends who are having a bad time, but to *friends of friends*! To anyone she hears about. She is always phoning people, driving them somewhere, *helping* in some way, *and* making excuses for their bad behavior. She was the one who got Dad involved in all the social justice stuff, all that prisoner advocacy, the refugees and the abused women. Dad gets the credit, but everyone close to our family knows it was Mum behind it all.

In short, my mother doesn't *do* violence.

"*You* were planning to *kill* Ray?" I say, just to make sure I have it straight. And it is suddenly such an outrageously horrible thing to say that I feel sick. I want to chuck something at her. That familiar profile looking up at the ceiling is driving me crazy. So self-satisfied and middle-aged! "You had no right to . . . even *think* that," I splutter, "much less plan it or—"

"*He* had no right," she cuts me off fiercely, "none whatsoever! At his age it was *evil* of him to seduce you." She stops for a bit and shifts about angrily in her bed. I think she has turned to face me, but I stay rigidly on my back. I won't turn and look at her. "How dare he do that to my . . . beautiful daughter!"

I gulp down my anger. *So keep it to yourself!* I want to yell, *because I don't want to hear your opinion of him or your beautiful daughter or . . .* I can't cope with any of this. I feel like I'm drowning in something thick and black and stinking. But I hold it together. Just have to because . . . I owe it to Ray.

"He didn't seduce me, Mum," I manage to say very slowly. "I loved him."

"Of course you loved him," she snaps back, "but it was still wrong!"

"I know it was wrong!" I say. "I should never have . . ."

"I don't mean *you* did wrong!" she bursts out angrily. "It wasn't your fault! He is the guilty one. That . . . *creepy* old bastard!" She begins to sob, and I feel absolutely terrible because I can't move now, much less speak. I'm breaking in two.

You see, I can understand this from her point of view. I can. Her eighteen-year-old daughter was sleeping with a guy *older than the husband who left her!* How upsetting, not to say humiliating, that would be! But I can't move, and the words won't come.

"I *still* want to kill him!" she shouts through her tears, sitting up, reaching for the tissues. "With my bare hands, and . . . so does your father!"

"Dad?" I say weakly. This is rock-bottom. Never in my wildest dreams did I imagine Dad learning about Ray and me.

"You should have seen your father when he found out! He was livid . . . I have never seen anyone so angry. Once the girls talked me out of my plan, he and I joined forces. We were going to have it out with him together, take out a court order, anything, but . . . Anyway, the girls talked us out of that, too. They said that you must be given . . . space and the respect to work things out for yourself. But I'm still not sure if we should have confronted that bastard or not! We both felt so helpless." She stops to cry some more, and I lie there like a block of wood.

Shit! This is *so, so, so, so* excruciatingly horrible. So humiliating! The whole friggin' lot of them know *everything!* So what must they think of me? The weirdo youngest sister who can't cut it with guys her own age so she has to go off chasing men old enough to be her father? And I'm going to be seeing all of them tomorrow. *Oh Christ!* I turn on my belly, hide my head under the pillows, and tell myself that I will never, *ever* come up again.

Dad! My mind goes numb. I haven't spent more than an hour or two with Dad in months. Since leaving home, it's been easier, somehow, to just avoid him. All my sisters see him regularly now, and Cassandra, too, but I never go. He rings me most weeks and he's always inviting me out for lunch in the city, or coffee if I don't feel comfortable going to his new home. *But you're always welcome anytime, pet . . . just give me a ring. Cass gets in most nights at six. I won't be much later.* Right! As though I would willingly spend one minute alone in a room with her!

The one good thing about this conversation is it's happening under the cover of darkness. Mum can't witness my leaking eyes or choked-up throat. *How dare she? How dare either of them judge Ray?* I will never blame him for what happened. Never!

"Mum, you don't understand!" I try again from under the pillow in my wrecked, croaky voice, because it is very important that she understands this. "Honestly, I was as into it as he was. I was . . . *more* into it than he was!"

"Believe me, I understand."

"I was crazy for him," I blunder on miserably. "I wanted it to go ahead. I . . . rang him all the time . . ." It is so bloody humiliating admitting all this to her, of all people, but she has to understand the truth. I did ring him all the time. And by the end, he wasn't ringing me back. I was driving him crazy. That's the truth of it. I am on the point of telling her this last bit when she cuts me off sharply.

"I *do* understand, Rose! The same thing happened to me when I was your age, with a much older man. Believe me, I understand exactly how it happens, and it *doesn't* change

248

the fact that I hold him totally responsible!" She spits it all out furiously.

"What?"

"He is totally responsible!"

"What do you mean, *the same thing happened to you*?"

"Look, it happens, Rose"—she gives a deep sigh—"all the time. One of my freshman-year university lecturers hit on me when I was eighteen or nineteen. I was so flattered. Before I knew it, I was in up to my eyeballs in an affair with a married man over twice my age. I came to the university a bright, sparkling girl, full of confidence, and by the end of the first year, I was a mess. I failed every subject . . . everything. It took me years to recover! I'll tell you all about it sometime . . ."

I am so shocked that I can't even nod.

"But listen, darling, we've got to see Gran tomorrow and . . . your father, too," she continues gently, "so let's just give it all a rest now, and get some sleep. Okay?"

"Okay," I say meekly. "'Night then."

I stay awake long after her breaths become deep and even. The occasional noises she makes in her sleep, the little sighs and snores, are more comforting than anything. At one point I think she must be awake too, because she calls out, "Rose," quite loudly.

"What, Mum?" I ask softly. "What do you want?" But she's asleep and doesn't answer. *Ray saved my life*, I want to remind her. Don't forget that, Mum. He saved my life. *Don't hate him . . . Don't wish him dead . . . It happens, Rose . . .* That is the line I keep coming back to. It makes me feel easier somehow, not so lonely.

I find myself wondering, *What would Roger make of it all? Is this the kind of family stuff he wants me to write about?* I laugh a bit to myself as the silly sentences for my next column pile up in my brain like clumps of soggy seaweed.

Don'tcha just hate it . . . when you're on the brink of a big discovery and the person you're getting the mind-blowing piece of information from suddenly decides to . . . shut up? Your mother lets slip that she had this past you had no idea about. It has everything to do with what is happening to you and . . . she decides to go to sleep!

◆ ◆ ◆

WE DON'T WAKE UP until after ten. By the time we're out of bed and dressed and packed, it's nearly midday and we're both starving. Mum pays for the room. We pack her gear into the back of the van, wander up the street to a local café, and take a table overlooking the beach. Amazingly, the only signs of the storm of the night before are great clumps of black seaweed all the way up the sand, and a certain drenched look to everything that is kind of invigorating. I think of myself down on Childers last night and it still seems vaguely unreal, like one of those weird little dreams you have in that time just before waking, especially the surfing. *Did I actually do that?*

We order eggs and bacon, mushrooms, orange juice and coffee. The service is good and the food is better. I look at my mother as she talks to the waiter, a pasty-faced young English kid about my own age, with dyed blond hair and silver rings in both ears. She is asking all the usual, tedious stuff about where he comes from, what the weather would be like in Britain at this time of the year, and how Australia is treating him. The guy prattles on in his chirpy London accent, and I have a rush of pride in her. She is always so warm and friendly to everyone.

Then I remember last night in the motel room, and my mood shifts sideways and down a notch or two. *She wanted to kill Ray!* I shudder, hearing again the way she spat the words at me. The depth of passion in her voice was unusual for Mum. I could tell it was coming from somewhere very deep inside. *So what happened to her?* We grew up on stories of Mum and Dad meeting each other and falling in love and getting married. Crazy, I know, but it's shocking to think there was someone else in Mum's life before Dad.

She looks really good in her sky-blue dress. Her dark red hair, down and freshly washed, is pushed back from her face with combs. She looks younger, more vibrant than I think I've ever seen her before. After getting so thin and pale and freaked-out looking when Dad left, she is now back to a good weight. But not so plump and motherly as she used to be. Being this slender suits her. She looks fit and her skin is glowing. We're both quiet, tucking in hungrily. I keep picturing her young again, with her arms around some older guy, in some seedy, half-lit bedroom, having strange hands undo her bra, her jeans pulled off before they even reach the bed . . . I shake myself. *God, Rose! Cut it out. This is your mother!*

"So, off to see Grandma?" I say, putting down my knife and fork for a moment. "Will you be able to handle it all, Mum?"

"Well . . ." She shrugs. "I guess I'll have to try, won't I?"

◆　◆　◆

Before long, we're back in the van, hurtling along the coastal road toward Port Fairy. It's only forty minutes away, on flat land covered in coastal scrub. The day has opened up for us, warm, and light, layered clouds skim in careless threads across the blue sky. She leans over and begins to fiddle around with the radio buttons.

"I wouldn't mind hearing the news," she mutters. "Okay with you?"

"Sure."

I wind down my window and let in some of that fresh, warm air from outside. The careful tones of the radio announcer tell us that there has been a murder in some small town in Gippsland and that there is a danger of bushfires. Also that the temperature will reach eighty-one degrees. Perfect. Mum and I smile briefly. We both think that eighty-one is the perfect temperature for a summer's day.

"You don't need to worry about meeting his girlfriend," I say casually. "You look really great."

"Well, thanks, Rose." She gives a small smile. "But apparently this Cassandra woman is a good fifteen years younger than me, so I can't really compete, can I?"

"It's not a competition, Mum!"

"Oh no!" she says with a wry laugh. "Of course not!"

"I mean it," I say awkwardly. "You're much nicer looking than her!"

"Thanks, but . . . I'm nervous."

"Don't be!"

She's going to come face-to-face with her ex-husband and his new woman. I want to tell her again how there really is no competition, that she's already the winner. He'll see that. The days of her being a vulnerable mess are over. But how do I tell her that without sounding like a complete suck?

"You will be okay, Mum," is all I can manage. "You've got us, remember."

Mum doesn't reply, but she gives me a little smile, reaches out, and briefly squeezes my hand.

"Anyway," she says gamely after a little while, "I've decided to get back on the horse when I get home."

"What do you mean?"

"I'm going to go out more," she says, and then adds, "I'd like to meet a new man."

My mouth falls open before I can think.

"Well, why not?" She seems surprised by my reaction. "Your father and I will be divorced soon."

"It's too fast, Mum," I say quickly. "You're only just getting over . . . everything. It wouldn't be a good idea to hurry into that kind of thing. Honestly . . . everyone will tell you that." Just the idea of her going out and *meeting men* makes me feel . . . ill.

"I'm not looking for someone to marry!" she continues cheerfully. "I just want to test the water, see what's around."

See what's around? Jeez! This puts me seriously on edge. If it was hard imagining her years ago with some older guy, then it is doubly awful trying to imagine her in that situation now!

"Have you spoken to any of the others about this?" I ask, thinking it would be just like my crazy sisters to encourage her.

"No, I haven't asked their permission yet," she jokes. Then, when I don't laugh, "You, Rosie, are the first to know that your mother is about to go out on the tear!"

"How," I ask, trying to sound casual, "are you going to go about meeting a new man?"

"The Internet," she says calmly, as though this is an obvious and reasonable answer. "Apparently there are all these sites you can clock into that offer . . ."

"Mum!" I protest loudly before she can go on. "You can hardly work your mobile phone! You go to pieces if you have to send an e-mail!"

"It's time I got over that." She waves one hand airily. "Veronica is going to help me. It is how she met Frank, you know."

"Really?"

Veronica is Mum's oldest friend. Her husband was killed in a road smash about three years ago, and within a couple of years, everyone was marveling when Veronica turned up at a function with a new bloke. I guess he's still on the scene.

254

"She is going to come and stay with me for a few days," Mum says, "and explain it all."

"You should think seriously before you go on the Net. I've heard all kinds of stories. It could be dangerous!"

"No more dangerous than driving with you," she mutters, and then turns and smiles to let me know she's joking.

"You'd be a sitting duck," I warn, still feeling weirdly unsettled. "Those sites are riddled with creepy old men."

"Creepy old men, huh?" she repeats lightly.

"Yeah." I turn and look at her. She is staring straight out the front window, but I can tell she is trying not to laugh. The words sit between us for about five solid seconds before I find the grace to give a grim smile.

"Okay. Okay! I get your drift. *Touché.*"

Mum takes this as her cue to let the giggles rip.

"Shut up!" I try not to smile. "I'm serious."

She leans over and skims her hand across the top of my hair. "Rose, will you do something for me, please?"

"What?"

"Grow your hair back."

"I'm trying!"

"It looked so much nicer before."

"I'm trying, okay?"

"I'll pay for the extensions," she laughs.

"Oh, shit no!"

"Remember Dot?"

We're both laughing now, remembering how Dot had to get hair extensions last year when she got a part in a TV series. She'd had her hair cut stylishly short just the day before being offered the part, and the producers weren't happy. They insisted she get extensions. The process was so time-consuming and tedious that Dorothy had a tantrum every hour for the next few days about how unfair it all was.

How come men can wear their hair any way they like? Blah, blah . . . *How come women have to tizz up?* All the usual stuff. When she turned up for the first day of filming, the director changed his mind and had a hairdresser brought in to cut them off again! Dot was so mad that she went around threatening to quit.

"Seems like such a long time ago," Mum muses wistfully.

"Only last summer." I take a swift look at her, trying to gauge her mood. But she's looking out the side window. I can't see her face.

Dot's big about-turn from classics scholar to television star began just before Christmas last year. I'd only just met Ray. And it was way before I'd decided not to go to university. Way before I'd thought about moving out of home as well. So much has happened since then . . .

I take another glance at Mum. She has pulled down the sun shade and is busy very carefully applying lipstick. I suddenly want to talk to her about some of the stuff that happened last summer, but we're only a few kilometers from Port Fairy, and I can tell she's apprehensive about getting there. Now might not be the best time to bring it up. She's come a long way. The last thing I want is for her to do a nosedive back into despair . . .

◆ ◆ ◆

LAST SUMMER, MELBOURNE

Only days before Christmas and I'm with my three sisters in the kitchen, trying to work out how we'll manage the big day. Gran has insisted on seeing us all together, as usual. Because she's so old, and because it might well be her last Christmas, Mum and Dad have agreed to a shared lunch, in the family home in North Fitzroy. None of us feels it's a good idea, but we can't think what to do to get out of it. Cynthia is giving us a lecture on staying calm, when the phone rings. I'm the nearest, so I pick it up, glad for a diversion.

"It's for you, Dot," I say.

Dot frowns and takes the phone, says who she is and yes and no a couple of times, and the rest of us go on with our conversation in low tones, waiting for her to finish.

After a while, her tone becomes animated, almost excited. She turns her back to us so we can't see her face. The rest of us watch as she leans across to the table, picks up a pen, and begins to write something down on an old envelope. At last she says goodbye and hangs up, but she doesn't turn around immediately. We're all curious as hell now.

"Dot," Cynthia ventures at last, "who was that?"

Only then does Dorothy turn around. Her exquisite face is a picture of delighted surprise. Those brilliant, lavender eyes shine like gas lamps in the twilight of her creamy skin.

"I got it," she whispers. She is standing erect, arms straight down at her sides, clenching both fists, hardly managing to contain her glee.

"*What?*" We're all concentrating now. "What is it? What have you got?"

"I can't believe this!" She begins to hop up and down. "I just can't believe it!"

"Dot! Tell us!"

"I got the part of Chloe Preston in *Time and Tide!*" she suddenly shouts. "I got it. I got the bloody part!"

"*What?*"

"Penny what's-her-name is being phased out and they're bringing me in!"

"*You?*"

The rest of us stand there completely stunned. No one, at this point, understands exactly what she means.

"You're going to . . . *act* . . . on TV?" Hilda gulps.

"Yes!"

"You're kidding!" Cynthia frowns in disbelief.

"No, it's true!"

"But *how?*" Cynthia starts jumping up and down herself. "I mean, how did you get it? Did you go for an *audition*, or . . . tell us what happened!"

"I was approached by this guy in the street. He gave me his card." Dorothy suddenly puts out both arms and pulls us around her. "Don't be mad!" she pleads. "Please don't be mad! I never thought anything would come of it. I only went along to those auditions for fun. That's why I said nothing."

"I'm not mad." I begin to smile, feeling absolutely . . . *glad*.

"Me neither!" Hilda giggles.

"I'm furious!" Cynthia chortles, and we all start laughing. Well, why not? This is so far outside the square of anything that has happened in our family. It's like one of us has been chosen to go to the moon.

"Tell us more!"

"Well . . . this guy gives me his card and asks me to ring and arrange to come in for an audition. I was about to throw it away, but my friend Alana told me I should have a bash. So . . . I rang and I did an audition. They liked it and asked me back. So I went, and then I had to go back a few times . . ." She looks embarrassed again. "But . . . it was for fun, really. I never thought I would actually *get* it."

Ours is not, and never has been, a big television household. We only ever watch the ABC or SBS and not much of either. And I'm sorry if that sounds snobby and elitist, but it's just how things are. So, as well as being in complete shock, we're all standing about feeling totally ignorant. *Time and Tide*! Well, yeah, we've all heard of it. It's just that . . . I look at the others and suddenly we're giggling like maniacs again, trying to get our heads around the fact that our sister is going to act in a popular soap opera!

"When do you start?" Hilda gasps.

"Right away!" Dot shouts gleefully. Now that she can see we're pleased for her, she begins to dance about from one foot to the other. In fact, she can't keep still. She runs up to the old couch under the window and begins to bounce up and down in exactly the way that we used to get into trouble for when we were little kids.

"Tomorrow!" she shouts again. "They want me in there tomorrow."

"Will you be on TV next week?" I ask naively.

"No! Of course not." Dot laughs at me. "My character won't be seen for about three months. They're going to build her up slowly into one of the main roles."

"Shit a brick!" Cynthia grins.

"Is it full-time?" Hilda wants to know. "Will you be able to finish university? What about your master's?"

"No way!" Dot says with a deep, delighted chuckle. "The hours are long. I'm going to give up university."

"Forever?" I ask, trying not to sound as stunned as I actually am.

"Maybe." Dot giggles and shrugs. "Probably! I don't know."

I gape at her, openmouthed. It's hard to take in. Dot has always been so uninterested, so *scathing* about television. About all forms of contemporary popular culture, actually: TV, pop music, films. Up till now, her devotion to the ancient classics has been all-encompassing.

"Stop *looking* at me!" she gripes. "Stop disapproving!"

"Of course we disapprove!"

"We're outraged! You've let us down completely."

"You are such a disappointment, Dorothy!"

We're all amazed and thrilled and delighted. But considering Dorothy's former interests, I think it's only natural that we are also a bit surprised.

The transformation to television actor suits her. The excited pink flush on her cheeks makes her look even more gorgeous than usual. No wonder they want her! She leaps off the couch and the four of us stand looking at each other.

"You do realize," Cynthia declares, grabbing our hands, "that this calls for bubbly!"

"You're turning into an alcoholic, Cynthia!" Dot is looking at her watch. "Let's have it in front of the telly, then," she says. "I've got a tape of the last eight *Time and Tide* episodes they want me to watch."

"Oh, yeah. Let's do that!"

So that's what we do. The four of us sit together in the living room, drinking champagne and giggling like idiots, watching *Time and Tide* tapes. And loving every minute of it, I have to say. At the end of about two hours, we've all become converts, and promise to watch it every night from now on. This obviously means a lot to Dot, because she starts crying. The rest of us join in, raving on about how excited we are for her and how proud, and, well . . . the whole scene degenerates into an emotional sobbing and giggling session that I won't inflict on anyone. Suffice it to say, it would make your average chick flick look cool, subdued, and intelligent in comparison.

"What about Mum?" Dot suddenly says through a mouthful of pizza. *Time and Tide* is well and truly over. David has come and, after a few terse words with Hilda, has taken the twins home. The four of us are a bit drunk. Hilda ordered pizza just to show David she's not about to come at his beck and call, and we're stuffing our faces.

We all look at each other guiltily. Incredibly . . . we have forgotten about our mother, who is still upstairs. The thing is, she spends so much time in her room since the split, we've become used to her not being around during the day.

"I'll go," I say, getting up.

"Let's all go," Dot says, "and tell her my news."

We switch off the television and head upstairs.

I knock on the door tentatively.

"Mum," I say, "can we come in?"

But there is no answer, so I push open the door and we all crowd in.

We don't see her immediately. The bedroom she used to share with Dad is huge, covers most of the top floor. It's full of all the furniture, artifacts, and knickknacks collected over their years together. Tapestry-covered chairs, antique lamps, woven rugs, original paintings, family photographs, and books. Their enormous carved walnut bedroom suite is set against the far wall. Even though it's late, the curtains have not been drawn over the wide window, which looks out onto parkland below. The first thing I'm aware of when I walk into the room is the deepening blue sky outside and the mass of European trees crowding below it. The first few stars are out.

Then I see Mum. Wearing, yet again, her lovely green dressing gown, she is only partly visible. She's kneeling in front of the big polished-wood wardrobe, pulling clothing from the bottom drawer and stuffing items into a plastic bag, working at a frenzied pace.

"Hi, Mum." I am the first to speak. "What are you doing?"

She jumps a little, startled by our entry, then turns back to the job at hand.

"Clearing his stuff out," she says breathlessly. "I want all traces of him gone by the end of the day." She points to at least half a dozen full bags under the window. "I've made a start."

Hilda switches on the overhead light, and Mum stands up and blinks. The bright spots on each of her pale cheeks tell me she is either upset or angry. Maybe both.

"We've got news, Mum . . ." Cynthia begins.

"I could do with a hand, actually." Mum waves impatiently that she's not interested in anyone's news and kneels down to continue the job. "I'd be grateful if someone could clean out that top drawer," she mutters, motioning toward a small chest. "And someone else the top of the wardrobe. Fill those two cases and the plastic bags over there."

In silence, we guiltily set about doing as she asks.

"Just get rid of everything of your father's," she orders, "then I'm going to wash the room out thoroughly."

I almost gag. *What a horrible thing to say!* I don't dare look at my sisters, but I know they must find it awful too.

"Dot's got a role in *Time and Tide*," I say suddenly. Mum doesn't react. At first I think she doesn't hear and so I say it again. "Mum, Dot is going to act on television."

"Well, my, my, my!" Mum blinks, stands up, and looks at Dot wonderingly. It is almost as though she can't quite figure out who she is, or what she or the rest of us might actually be doing there in her bedroom. Then she gives a strained smile.

"Acting, you say?"

Dot nods and smiles shyly. Mum shakes her head. She is staring down at a pair of my father's shoes, old brogues that he used to wear around the house. She puts one hand out tentatively to touch them, and then in a fit of fury picks them up and throws them at the pile of loose things under the window.

"But you're *not* an actor, Dorothy!" she says scornfully. "You have no training as an actor."

"I went for the auditions, and . . . they want me to do it." Dot tries to sound careless, but Mum's reaction is hitting home. I can tell by the way that rosebud mouth is quivering slightly.

"How can you possibly contemplate doing *that*, Dorothy?" Mum asks quite seriously after a few moments.

"*W-what* . . ." Dot stammers. "How do you mean?"

"I mean, associate yourself with that kind of rubbish."

"Easily Mum," she says defensively. "It's a job."

"But what about your university work?"

"I'm going to . . . let it go for a while."

"Let it *go*?" Mum is suddenly outraged.

"Yes."

"This is your father's fault," Mum explodes, chucking another pair of shoes, which hit the wall with a thud. "This is what happens when parents break up. The children get involved in all kinds of ridiculous things. Acting in some idiot show! This is just the beginning, I suppose!"

"For Christ's sake, Mum!" Cynthia interrupts angrily. "Dot's not sixteen. She's already been at university for five years! She has an Honors degree. It will be easy to defer. She *wants* to do something else for a while. This has come up, and . . ."

"I'm excited about it, actually," Dot says, but her voice is thick with hurt.

"I see," Mum says grimly, turning back to sort through the clothes. "Well, I can't say *I'm* excited about it."

We all look at each other. None of us can believe this. It's like our mother has swallowed a nasty pill or something. She ties up the top of another bag and then stands, picks it up, and dumps it under the window.

"Hilda," she asks out of the blue, "shouldn't you be home with your husband and children?"

What? The four of us stop what we're doing and look at her.

"I've had the twins all day, Mum!" Hilda says through gritted teeth.

"So where are they now?" Mum snaps.

"Dave has just picked them up, and . . . I'm going home soon."

"Good." Mum hurls a fresh bundle of Dad's clothing at the other bags under the window. "It's where you belong. Poor Dave will be tired after a day at work."

Poor Dave? Yeah, well . . .

We finish the rest of the tasks more or less in silence. At the end of an hour, there are nearly a dozen bags and cardboard boxes filled with Dad's things. Oddly enough, I don't feel much of anything as I'm piling it all together. I can tell it's really hitting the others, though. Hilda is quietly crying as she kneels in front of a chest of drawers and empties the contents into a bag. Cynthia and Dot look really upset as they fold up Dad's shirts.

"So, where should we put this stuff?" Cynthia asks tersely, after a while.

"I don't care!" Mum says. "Just put it outside somewhere. And if he doesn't come and pick it up very soon, I'll burn it." We watch as she slumps down on the bed, lies flat with her arms across her chest, then curls up and closes her eyes. "I'll burn everything," she mutters again.

The rest of us begin lugging the bags and boxes downstairs. On the way up again to collect the next load, Hilda, Dot, and I meet Cynthia coming down.

"I'll ring Dad," she says in a conspiratorial whisper. "Tell him to come and get it tonight, otherwise . . ." She rolls her eyes, waves her arms, and makes a big whooshing noise. "It's all gonna burn!" We start to laugh.

Within a few moments, we're hanging on to each other, verging on hysterical but trying desperately not to make noise in case Mum hears. But that only makes it harder to stop. Dot collapses onto the top stair and the rest of us fall on top of her. Tears run down our cheeks and we hold our bellies. I'm not sure why I'm laughing so hard. It's not as though anything about this situation is even remotely funny. But I have to cross my legs so as not to wet my pants.

◆ ◆ ◆

ROAD TRIP

We come into town on the golf links road. As soon as I see the bridge and the pines and some of those squat nineteenth-century buildings, my guts start churning. I love this town. It's the place of so many childhood summers, so many memories. Gran's house was way too small for the six of us, but we used to pile in anyway. When we got older, Dad would put up a tent in the backyard, and we'd have friends down as well. I turn the van into the packed main street.

"You want to buy anything?" I ask, pointing to a parking spot.

"Let's just go to the house," Mum says anxiously. "Get it over with."

"Cassandra?"

"Yeah."

"It will be okay, Mum," I tell her. "You'll be fine."

"But . . . what will I *say*?"

"Just say 'hello' and 'nice to meet you.'"

Mum thinks about this for a while.

"*Hellooo,* Cassandra!" she practices in a gushy mock whisper. "I'm so *thrilled* to meet you."

"Well done," I say approvingly.

Mum lets out a tortured groan.

"But Rose . . ." she wails, "I don't want to meet her!"

"Then it's, '*Hellooo,* I've been so *dreading* to meet you!'"

266

After an initial giggle, Mum looks even more anxious. I drive past the buzz of the holiday crowds and turn into Cox Street. Gran's little house is right at the end, just a short walk from the beach.

"She might not even be here," I suggest, trying to be optimistic.

"If only," Mum mumbles, and closes her eyes. "Please God, make her have taken to her bed with gout, or sore feet, or food poisoning." She turns to me, suddenly looking wildly hopeful. "She might have the flu?"

"A definite possibility," I agree. "She could be getting it as we speak."

Mum murmurs, "Yes," longingly, as though this would be the best thing ever.

"Just remember, she might be younger," I say, "but you're way better looking. Seriously!"

"Oh Rose, I'm not!" she groans. "I've seen a photo, and she's . . ."

"She's more *glamorous*," I cut in derisively. I really mean this. "But only in a superficial, cheap, completely meaningless way!" Mum begins to laugh, so I continue. "Her eyes are piggy small and her hair is a shitty sort of dyed straw, and . . . she's got short legs."

"Really?" Mum whispers, as though she can't believe the good news, because she herself has long and well-shaped legs.

"Absolutely!" I say. "Her bum is way too near the ground. Didn't the others tell you?"

"I thought they were just trying to cheer me up!" she exclaims. "Whereas I know you . . ." She stops awkwardly.

"You know that I *never* try to be nice!" I say bluntly.

"That's right," she smiles, "and it's very reassuring."

"I'll keep that in mind."

"Good."

We pull up under the tree by the curb.

"Well . . . here goes," she mumbles.

I turn off the engine, feeling strangely torn myself. Gran's little cottage, set behind a picket fence, looks so pretty from the road, with its slate roof, deep veranda, and small windows on either side of the open front door. I haven't seen it for a couple of years, so part of me is longing to go inside again, but . . . it's been months since I've been with my family en masse. Now that we're here, I want to turn the van around and drive right back to the city. I think my mother is feeling something similar, but she's braver. She grabs the door handle and pulls it open.

"Let's go, Rose," she says, stepping out.

◆　◆　◆

Hilda is sitting on the front lawn, watching the twins play with the hose and a bucket. When she sees us, she stands to wave, and the little boys come running toward us.

"So you're alive?" Hilda calls.

"Not only alive"—Mum kneels to hug the boys warmly—"but kicking."

"Kicking butt," chirps Cormac, and the two of them break up with wicked giggles and start shouting it over and over again. *Kicking butt!* Hilda is dressed in tailored shorts and a cotton blouse. Her hair has been cut into a sharper bob than I remember. Very straight. She pulls one of the twins back from the road and peers at me incredulously.

"Wow, Rose! Your hair!"

"Yeah," I say. "It seemed like a good idea at the time." I'm feeling so . . . self-conscious. All the conversations that must have gone on behind my back! It's weird coming face-to-face with my eldest sister, knowing *she knows*, and that basically she's known all along.

"Er, how's Gran?"

"Okay now. She had a little turn last night, so they decided to put her in the hospital . . ." Mum and I look at each other.

"I like it," Hilda says suddenly, touching my hair.

"Do you?"

"Well . . ." she laughs, "the cut could have been better! But it looks good short." Her eyes shift over to Mum. "What's up, Mum? You've got your twitchy face on."

"Is *everyone* here?" Mum asks tentatively, looking toward the cottage as though some alien is going to appear at any moment.

"Dorothy and Dad are sitting with Gran," Hilda explains confidingly, taking her arm, "and Cassandra isn't here, so relax. *She's* back at the hotel doing work or something, so . . . don't worry!"

"Oh, I wasn't *worried*," Mum says, embarrassed. "Just feeling a little . . . jumpy, you know?"

Hilda and I raise our eyebrows behind her back.

So what the hell was I doing living out in a miserable dump in Hurstbridge for the last ten months if they all knew everything anyway? is what I'm thinking as I follow them up the little path to the front door. This whole business would be funny if I didn't feel so freaked out about it.

Don'tcha just hate it . . . when you find out that all your dirty secrets are public knowledge? You go around thinking your life is private, that no one knows your business. Well, I'm here to tell you, you millions of multitalented, meat-eating, hoodwinked, rock-loving Saucers, that not only do the banks, the tax department, and the credit companies have all your details on file, more than likely your family knows a lot more about your every move than you do. Yep, that's right! Face it! Your mother reads your diary. Your siblings trawl through your e-mails.

Your friends, hungry for contact with warm-blooded creatures after a day in front of the screen, spread your private confidences like preachers at a religious rally. Don't blame them. Privacy is dead. Get used to it! But how does it make you feel? Huh? Tell me, how does it make you feel?

I follow the others inside, down the central hallway, past the two front rooms, and into the back kitchen, where a hive of activity greets us. Cynthia, complete with rubber gloves and a scarf tied around her hair, is on her knees pulling stuff out of Gran's shabby cupboards. Old papers, dirt, and mouse shit are piling up around her.

"At last!" she proclaims before turning back to her work. "So, is the hitchhiker with you?"

"Good God, no." Mum smiles at me. "He had more important fish to fry."

"Well, there is heaps to do here," Cynthia says sternly, her head disappearing into the cupboard again.

"Not before I have a cup of tea," Mum laughs. Cynthia is trying to make us feel guilty for not getting here sooner, but we're not biting.

Bruce is up a stepladder, piling old newspapers, jars, and plastic containers from the top of the cupboard into garbage bags. He jumps down, wipes his hands, and comes forward with a smile.

"Hey, Rose." He motions at my head. "Someone get at you with an axe?"

"Something like that." I grin back and feel myself blush a bit as he runs one hand over it. *Maybe this isn't going to be so bad. No one is treating me like a freak . . . not just yet, anyway.*

Nothing much has changed about this kitchen except that it seems smaller and grimier than the last time I was here. There is the little window overlooking the backyard. The chipped green dresser with worn canisters sitting on top—flour, sugar, salt. The small yellow stove fitting snugly in between sink and counter. I walk over to the two sleek black and white cats sitting side by side on the table, watching everyone suspiciously. Gough and Margaret, an old sedate couple that've been with Gran forever. I can just remember Margaret as a new kitten when I was about eight.

"Hi, Gough," I say, as I give the larger one a pat. "You're even fatter than when I last saw you."

"He'll die of a heart attack soon," Cynthia pronounces disapprovingly from the cupboard.

"You don't know that," I say, just to annoy her. "You're not a vet."

"Well . . . he's obese, and he's at least twelve years old."

"Obese?" I croon, continuing to pat him. "I wouldn't take that sitting down if I were you, Gough! Have a go at her!"

I needn't have worried, Gough isn't in the least concerned. He looks up at me disdainfully through half-closed eyes, as though he understands exactly what we're saying and discounts it absolutely. He's as wide as a football and, in this position, with his legs tucked under him, almost the same shape. Bored with me, he gives a wide yawn and hops daintily (for a cat that wide) from the table and makes his way slowly to the open back door. I reach out to tickle Margaret behind the ears, and she swipes at me casually with one open claw, as though to say *piss off*, before settling back into exactly the same position on the table.

"What was that for?" I chuckle. She blinks back at me innocently and growls when I put out my hand again, warning me not to push my luck.

"Don't take it personally," Bruce laughs from the top of the ladder. "Margaret's furious."

"Why?"

"Oh, you know . . . females!" Bruce says blithely. "So moody!" Everyone groans and laughs, except Cynthia, who gives him a sharp, shitty look.

"What will happen to Gough and Margaret?" Mum is filling the kettle and getting mugs down from the cupboard. "I mean, when Gran dies?"

"Harry is going to take them," Cynthia replies, "and Hilda and I are going to toss for Hawke"—she looks around—"but he seems to have done his usual flit."

Harry is the eighty-four-year-old widower from two doors down, and Gran's best friend. They've known each other since they were at school in the twenties. They're always arguing (Harry is an archconservative and Gran is a leftie), but they are very close and have relied on each other enormously over the years.

"You're in an unstable situation," Cynthia preempts me casually. "Cats need a firm home base."

I shrug as though I couldn't care less, when, in fact, I do. I've always secretly thought Hawke would be mine. He is my favorite, and my sisters know it. Small, jet-black, and very much a loner, he hangs around only if he's interested. I really like his style. Gran said that his independent streak came from his mother, Germaine, who used to hunt snakes and leave them dead on the mat, until one got the better of her. But Dad always maintains that Hawke's independence has more to do with Gran forgetting to have him neutered when he was young. But how can I object? Cynthia's right. (When is she ever wrong!) I have no idea where I'll be living in six months' time.

"What we're all concerned about is the Collection," Cynthia declares, getting up from the floor and fixing me with a fake innocent look. "Have you heard anything?"

"No," I say shortly. "Have you?" There is an uncomfortable silence as they all look at each other.

"We think *you're* going to get it, Rosie!" Bruce grins at me.

"But why me?" I protest. "What did I ever do to Gran?" I groan, walk to the back door, and look out. Gough and Margaret are sprawled out in the sunshine now, with Gough licking Margaret's ear tenderly, and I have this intense, sudden rush of envy. I wish I were a cat! I mean a real one. *Not* one of those tacky cheap porcelain things sitting on Gran's crystal cabinet that I am apparently destined to inherit, but a warm-blooded, sleek, well-fed one who can lie around in the sun all day being licked.

"The Collection is very special to Gran," Cynthia adds encouragingly.

"Gee, Cynthia!" I don't bother to turn around. "Aren't I the lucky one?"

"Why not be honored, Rose?" she adds censoriously.

"Oh, I am," I say sarcastically. "Deeply."

"Come on, Rosie!" Hilda puts an arm around my shoulders. "We'll make it up to you, won't we Cynthia?"

"Of course we will!" Cynthia chucks some rolled-up cleaning rags at my back, then she starts laughing. Whatever can be said about Cynthia's officious nature, she does have the best, most infectious laugh. It gets everyone else going too.

"We'll come and help you look after it," she yells. "I'll bring my duster and my polish!"

"I'll bring food!" Hilda squeals.

"I'll take them to see football," Bruce chimes in.

Everyone is laughing now, so I have to join in.

Everything in this room must be at least fifty years old, most of it older. No microwaves or juicers or electric grills, not even an electric kettle. The walls need painting, and dirt and grease are caked in around the stove and sink. Maybe it was always there and I never noticed. I watch Cynthia pile even more old ice-cream containers, egg cartons, and empty jars into the mountain of rubbish in the middle of the room, and it hits me that all this might be a wee bit premature.

"Did Gran ask you to clear out the kitchen?" I ask.

"As if!" she mutters, energetically pushing stuff into garbage bags.

"But what if she comes home?" I'm suddenly appalled. "She might like it just the way it is!"

"She's not going to come home, Rose," Cynthia declares, carrying right on with her cleaning. Mum raises her eyebrows as she hands me a mug of tea, and I grimace. Okay. Neither of us is surprised by Cynthia's matter-of-fact attitude toward our Gran's imminent demise, but even so . . . does she have to be so blunt about it?

"Want to go up to the hospital soon?" Mum asks me. "See Gran?"

"Sure." I slurp down some tea and then wander out of the kitchen, up to the front room to check on my inheritance. "I'll just drink this."

Here they are, all twenty-three of them, sitting where they've been ever since I can remember. Nelson Mandela. Julie Andrews. Clark Gable. Normie Rowe and Dennis Lillie. Muhammad Ali. Olivia Newton-John and Pope John XXIII. Bert Newton. Gran named all her real cats after people she admired in politics, sports, and entertainment, and here they all are in porcelain cat form on top of her crystal cabinet. Only one is missing: Harry Belafonte, smashed when a window was left open during a storm in the sixties. Most of them are sitting up in some cute pose, washing their faces with one paw or waiting to be patted. "Oh, shit!" I groan as I stand looking at them. The cats look weirdly alive in the light streaming through the gap in the closed blinds. How unfair that I should have to have them! And how weird to think that my poor old Gran has to die and these things will go on, into eternity, their smug little faces looking out onto the world like benevolent plaster saints! I wish I could say that there was something about them I secretly liked, but the reality is, I don't like anything about them. In fact, I associate them with Gran's long-winded stories about the past, and although I know you're not meant to think this, much less say it, those stories were so boring. Especially when it's hot and you're thirteen and you just want to get down to the beach!

I pick up Ben Chifley, the big, ugly olive-green one sitting at the back of the collection. He was the first, I think. Named after the wartime prime minister, the workingman's hero who'd begun his adult life as a train driver. Grandpa gave him to Gran early in their marriage when her real cat of the same name died. I turn him over to check. Yep . . . the name is still there, written on masking tape in Gran's black scrawl, and the year the cat died, *just in case anyone is confused.*

Still holding Chifley, I look around the little room and try to imagine life here over the years. I cross to the piano to check out the photos of Dad. Only three, and I know them so well already, but for some reason I like looking at them. Each is in sharp black and white, apparently taken with Gran's old Brownie box camera. The first is of him as a little boy of about eight, playing with two kittens out on the back step. The larger one is of a surly teenager in his high school uniform. We always used to tease him about this one because he looks so much the grumpy adolescent. And the third is a really good shot of him as a longhaired university student in the seventies, standing with a mate on the grass outside the Melbourne University Law Library. I used to stare at this one a lot when I was younger because both guys in the photo look so happy, so much like they're enjoying their lives. As much as anything else, this photo hooked me into the idea of university. Even at ten years old I wanted to go to a place where I could be like this, too, smart and carefree and easy about my life.

It's my favorite of the photos, so I put Chifley down and take it over to the window to scrutinize it a bit more. When I move my eyes from Dad to his mate, I suddenly have a weird sense of recognition. But . . . I don't know the guy. How could I? I've been looking at this photo for years. Why would this old friend of Dad's suddenly ring a bell with me, decades later? I can't remember Dad even telling us his name.

I push the curtains back and squint more closely, and it suddenly dawns on me. *Nat Cummins!* God. But yes. Same eyes. Same jaw. I smile to myself as it becomes clearer. That slightly raised chin as he faces the camera! Like he's a bit shy but determined not to show it. Even the way his arms are crossed. The guy in this thirty-year-old photo would have to be his father!

"Rose, where are you?" Mum calls. "I'm ready to go see Gran!"

"I'm in here," I yell, placing the photo back on the piano. I pick up old green Chifley and slip him back into his rightful position. At the doorway I turn and take a final look at the Collection. *Oh God!* I wonder darkly what it would feel like to go out to the shed right now, pick up a hammer, and come back and smash the lot of them.

◆ ◆ ◆

I SEE DAD through the glass. He is sitting on a hard-backed chair close to the bed, holding Gran's hand, his head thrown back, eyes closed. He looks dead to the world, but as soon as we come in, he is on his feet.

"Patsy," he says formally, with a relieved, but very strained, smile, not letting go of his mother's hand. "So good of you to come."

"Hello, Justus," Mum greets him just as carefully.

I step between them and kiss Dad awkwardly. Dad smiles at me and runs his hand across the top of my head.

"You a skinhead now?"

"No."

"I'm not sure the judge will agree when you're making an urgent plea for clemency." He laughs softly, then pulls over a couple of uncomfortable chairs from a far corner for Mum and me, and we park ourselves on the opposite side of the bed. Gran grumbles a bit at the commotion but doesn't open her eyes.

"Is she conscious?" Mum asks, kissing Gran's brow before she sits.

"She is quite lucid when she's awake." Dad sighs, and looks at his watch. "But she slips away every few minutes."

"How long has it been like that?"

"Days." He shrugs and smiles wearily. "I've lost all sense of time."

"What do they say?"

"Any time now," he says matter-of-factly. "Her heart is very weak."

I'm shocked by how terrible Dad looks, and for the first time in ages, I feel a pang of concern for him. Apart from having lost weight over the last year, his hair is now almost white and his skin is ashen. Whereas Mum's weight loss makes her look younger and healthier, Dad looks simply scrawny inside his clothes, his face uncharacteristically lined and old.

Mum must be thinking the same thing.

"Justus," she whispers, "you look . . . *terrible.*"

Dad smiles apologetically and shrugs.

"You do look shithouse, Dad," I chip in bluntly.

"Well, thanks, you two." He grins good-naturedly. "Just what I needed to hear."

"Would you like to go to your hotel and take a nap?" Mum suggests. "We'll stay with her."

"No," he sighs. "I want to be here when . . . "

"Yes." Mum nods. He doesn't have to say any more. Although Dad hasn't always been the most consistently attentive son, his ties to his mother go very deep. We grew up on stories of how she used to take in washing to feed them both. How she nagged him to use the local library. How she scrimped and saved for his school uniforms and encouraged him to go into law. I guess it's only right that he sees her out.

I end up sitting there with them for most of the afternoon. Dorothy comes back, grinning sheepishly, from her interview with the reporter from the local paper, bringing coffee and cakes for us. She has just had her photo taken outside the post office, and next week she's going to be on the front page with an accompanying article: "*Time and Tide* star returns to look after Gran."

The hours tick by slowly. It's weird being stuck with my estranged parents like this. Initially they're very careful with each other, making only neutral comments and boring chitchat. But after a while, the odd joke bubbles through, and I can feel them both start to relax. Gran's heavy, slumbering old body between them probably helps. It's okay having Dot there too; it takes the spotlight off me.

Soon they are like old friends with a lot in common. Mum tells him about the hitchhiker. Dad teases her about her propensity to pick up lost causes. When he and Dot relay some of the outrageously horrible things Grandma has been saying about the nurses and the hospital food, Mum and I crack up laughing.

At different times through the afternoon, I have this weird sensation that the past year didn't actually happen. That it's all been a figment of my imagination.

"So, where is Cassandra?" I whisper to Dot at one point.

"Back at the hotel, apparently," she replies. "She's got a big case on."

"What bad luck!" I grin sarcastically. Dot giggles.

"So what do you think of her?" I ask. All my sisters have spent more time with her than I have, and I'm suddenly interested in Dot's opinion.

But she only shrugs and makes a bored face.

"She's okay."

Gran begins to shift about a bit like she is trying to wake up. Dot and I turn to see Mum and Dad exchange a worried glance as they prop her up in the bed.

"Poor old Gran," Dot murmurs sympathetically. "She must just hate this. Stuck in bed, not able to move or talk . . ."

"Or boss people around," I add softly. Dot giggles again.

"Remember Christmas last year?" she whispers conspiratorially, nudging me, making sure Mum and Dad can't hear. "Remember it, Rose?"

"Jeez!" I reply dryly. "How could I ever forget!"

♦ ♦ ♦

LAST SUMMER, MELBOURNE

I wake up, wondering what the sinking feeling in my chest is all about, then remember that it is Christmas Day. The first since the split, and Dad is bringing Gran over for lunch.

I have to make myself throw back the covers, crawl from the bed and into the shower. Then I pull on the clothes I wore the day before. A weirdly apt Paul Kelly song pulses out from some other room: "If I Could Start Today Again."

Oh yeah. I know what he means. I want to flip right into tomorrow *now*. I listen more closely to the lyrics, and I find myself wondering which day I'd choose if I wanted to take back one day and start again. *Will it be tomorrow?* My arrangement to meet Ray in Anglesea is only a day away now. I can't work out if the mass of strange knots in my stomach is about that or about Dad and Grandma coming.

When I get downstairs, I find the others gathered in the kitchen, drinking tea and looking as freaked out as I feel. Dave and Hilda and the twins. Cynthia and Bruce. Mum. When they see me, they all rouse themselves, trying to appear cheerful.

"We've been waiting for you!"

"Happy Christmas!"

"Now we can open the presents!"

We take our cups of tea into the living room, to where all the presents have been arranged under the tree, and proceed to do what we do every year. Give and receive presents,

280

all of us pretending not to feel the enormous empty space that Dad's absence creates. Mum, now so thin that she looks frail, nods and smiles vaguely as she opens presents but puts them aside, without interest, as soon as she can. One of her brothers rings from overseas. Then a neighbor drops around the back with two pots of homemade marmalade. When the doorbell rings on the dot of twelve thirty, my sisters all look at me.

So it's my job to get the door! I get up reluctantly, knowing Hilda will only burst into tears and Cynthia will get all icy and distant. Dot has already run upstairs to avoid the situation, and Mum looks completely unable to do anything. She's clutching the arms of her chair with bony fingers, looking almost sick with anxiety.

"Hi, Dad," I say, cautiously opening the door, "and Grandma!" Dad looks incredibly tense. Apart from a brief phone call, we haven't spoken since the city meeting with Cassandra.

"Merry Christmas, Rose." He tries to smile. Dressed casually in light pants and a plain red shirt, he is holding a bunch of bright flowers in his left hand, bottles of wine and two plastic bags full of brightly colored parcels in the other. He looks like he hasn't slept.

He steps forward, kisses me on both cheeks, then puts all his things down carefully on the doorstep and pulls me close. His skin against my face feels slightly damp, and I catch a whiff of alcohol.

I move on to my grandmother, who is dressed in the lavender dress she always wears on Christmas Day. Blue-rinsed hair and four strings of heavy pearls around her neck, her skin as thin as parched white paper and amazingly unwrinkled for someone her age.

"Happy Christmas, Gran!"

"Ah Rose!" she kisses me sternly. Her smell, sweet and slightly musty, catapults me into another time altogether. For a moment I feel like I'm about ten years old.

"I heard you have a boyfriend!" she exclaims.

"What?" My head swarms briefly with panic. *Ray? How could she know about him?*

"The Cummins lad!" she declares cheerfully. "I know his father well. He came down to stay with Justus."

"Really?" I say in relief, and then I'm curious in spite of myself. "So, does he keep in touch?"

But Gran has lost interest. She is sizing me up critically.

"Never mind him," she sniffs. "What the devil have you got on?"

"Oh." I look down at my completely inappropriate old jeans, T-shirt, and rubber flip-flops. *Damn.* I'm still in the clothes I threw on that morning. I forgot to change.

"You're planning to change before Christmas lunch, I hope?" she booms. "You won't impress anyone like that!"

"I'm just on my way," I say meekly, thinking, *I'm not exactly trying to impress.*

"Is everyone here?" Dad asks, taking hold of my arm in desperation before I can escape.

"Yes," I say, thinking for the hundredth time that this has to be a big mistake. I should have quashed it as soon as it was brought up. Stupid. Crazy. I step aside and motion them in. But Dad is bending, fishing in the bag of presents nervously.

"I have something for you, darling," he says.

"Justus, leave the presents until later," Gran orders imperiously. "I need a drink. Now *where* is everyone?"

◆　◆　◆

At last we are all there, sitting around the beautifully set, polished wood table. Grandma is in pride of place, just under the window. Hilda and Dave are on her left, Cynthia and Bruce down the other end, and Dorothy and me between Mum and Dad. Tension sits in the air like a big cat lurking behind foliage, eyes on unknowing prey, waiting for the right moment to pounce. Needless to say, by this stage I've changed my clothes.

"Happy Christmas, everyone!" Gran declares defiantly, raising her glass. "I'm so glad to be here."

"It wouldn't be Christmas without you, Greta," Mum responds quietly. The rest of us murmur our agreement, and I have a moment of thinking that the whole thing might work out fine after all. There is a lot to be said for protocol and for *not* speaking your mind.

But I have it wrong, of course. Gran is simply biding her time. The polite conversation finishes almost as soon as we are all served our food.

"I want to shake your father until his bones break," is her opening line, as she unfolds her napkin and spreads it carefully across her lap. Spoken calmly though, as if Dad isn't sitting right next to her. The rest of us simply stop. Hilda's mouth drops open. The color drains from Mum's face. And Dad's mouth sets into a grim line. Dot breathes out to calm herself. David and Bruce pretend they don't hear. Thankfully, Cynthia is in the kitchen getting something, or she'd be sure to inflame the situation further. "The only thing I can think is that he's taken leave of his senses," she adds mildly, picking up her knife and fork and looking around at the rest of us, who are all simply staring at her. "Well, am I the only person interested in this delicious food?"

In unison we all pick up our silverware and begin to eat.

"These are not the actions of the son I brought up to be loyal and true," Gran says through a mouthful of succulent roast turkey.

"Well, I'm afraid they are, Mum," Dad says coolly, putting down his knife. "I am that son. So, now, why don't you concentrate on your meal? Everyone is very pleased to see you. It's Christmas, after all." He holds up his glass of wine and gives a tortured smile.

"Happy Christmas, everyone," Dad says, not meeting anyone's eyes.

"Yeah," we all say miserably, clinking glasses. "Merry Christmas!"

Mum doesn't even pick up her glass.

"You need some kind of . . . help," Gran persists, frowning at Dad. "Some of that counseling business that everyone has these days."

"No, I don't," Dad says shortly with a sigh. "I'm fine."

"Fine!" she exclaims. "I don't think you're fine! You're far from fine. Why would a man in full command of his senses leave his lovely wife and family?"

She looks around in bewilderment at the rest of us, as though we might have the answer, then she snorts derisively. "For some little flibbertigibbet on the make?"

"That's enough, Mum!" Dad explodes.

Good for you, Gran! is what the rest of us think.

◆ ◆ ◆

The meal lurches along at its own pace. Both my parents remain very quiet. I take surreptitious glances at my watch every now and again and see my sisters doing the same.

The twins, Cormac and Ryan, are the only ones to break the awkwardness. They have their lunch near us at a small table and chairs. After a few bites, they are careering around the room, chattering happily, their eyes blazing with mischief.

"Look!" They hold out their new toys for Dad to see. "Look what we got from Santa!"

Dad's face melts into a study of joyful tenderness.

"What have we here?" he says, taking a car from Cormac and a gladiator figure from Ryan and putting an arm around each of them. "Can you show me what they do?"

Both little boys become engrossed as they demonstrate how their toys work. Hilda doesn't tell them to let us eat in peace. I think she senses that everyone is relieved to have the distraction.

By the time the lunch is over, Gran has managed to sort out most of us. As usual, she's blunt, verging on rude, and, as usual, by the end, we all hate her vehemently and love her in roughly equal proportions.

"Cynthia, you are wasting your time with that young man," she begins mildly, hardly waiting for poor old Bruce to be out of earshot. "You need someone with a brain, dear!" There is no sarcasm in her voice. It is more like she's stating an obvious fact that Cynthia has simply overlooked.

"Gran!" Cynthia counters sharply, under her breath. "Bruce is a very talented person! He not only rides, but he is involved in—"

"I'm sure he's a perfectly decent young man!" Gran ignores Cynthia's stricken face as she attacks her last roast potato with gusto. "But he's not right for you. You're going to be a doctor. You can get someone a lot better than him!"

Cynthia looks around to the rest of us for support, but we all refuse to meet her eyes. Mum is staring into the far distance with this weird, fixed smile on her face. Dad is looking down at his meal—hardly having said a word since Gran attacked him—and Dave, with a twin on each hip, simply looks toward the kitchen, concerned that Bruce might have heard. Dot, of course, is nodding and smiling with gleeful agreement.

When Hilda gets up from the table some time later and goes to the window, irritated because David is taking too long to fetch something for one of the twins from the car, Gran snaps at her to sit down.

"He's not your servant, Hilda."

"I know that, Gran," Hilda says defensively. "It's just that—"

"Then don't treat him like one."

Gran has picked up on the Hilda and David situation intuitively, inside the space of an hour.

"What do you mean?" Hilda is turning bright red.

"You glare at him whenever he opens his mouth," Gran declares.

"No I don't!"

"You do," Gran counters firmly, "and it has to stop."

"But Gran!" Hilda wails. "He can't find the most simple thing."

As the first, most-favored grandchild, she is more used to Gran's unequivocal support and approval for everything she does, so her nose is out of joint.

"Men never *can* find anything!" Gran declares with all the force of someone who knows an irrefutable fact. "But that's no excuse. David is your husband. Treat him with respect."

"Well, sometimes it's . . . very difficult," Hilda mumbles defensively.

"Just think of the money he earns"—Gran sniffs—"and it will become less difficult, I assure you."

If it had been anyone else telling us these things, the house would have been in an uproar. It would have descended into a screaming match, fisticuffs, or something worse. But we all just cop it from Gran. Mum and Dad, too. If she'd turned up sweet and docile, like a proper old lady, most of us would have been disappointed.

"So, Dorothy, I want to hear all about your show!" Gran declares. She's sitting at the head of the table, tucking into the pudding, brandy cream, and homemade ice cream that Cynthia and Bruce slaved over all morning. For an old lady, she sure can put the food away. "I've told all my friends, and they are blind with jealousy!"

"I started last week," Dot says shyly.

"And how was it?"

"It was . . . hard," Dot says, frowning. "I have to be there at six in the morning!" Dorothy absolutely hates early mornings.

"Did they send a limo?" Gran wants to know.

"No!" Dot grins. "But they do send a taxi."

"How wonderful," Gran murmurs thoughtfully as she pictures this. "You must be enjoying it?"

"Too early to tell." Dot gives a deep sigh.

"You must be!" Gran insists.

"Well . . . I can't say I'm actually enjoying it . . . yet," Dot declares. "I'm not used to such long hours and dealing with so many people. Learning lines is hard, too. The others seem able to do it so quickly. No one thinks to tell me anything. Most of the others have been there forever, and they've done other acting. It's really hard working out what they want me to do . . ."

Cynthia, Hilda, and I exchange surprised looks. Poor Dot is just running off at the mouth. Until now she hasn't said much about her first week on the *Time and Tide* set. Surprisingly little, actually. I feel guilty that I haven't asked her more. As far as I know, none of us has even mentioned her new job since she started, except to be sarcastic.

"It's not you, Dot," Mum declares firmly. "It's the silly show." There is an awkward silence. *Oh no, Mum, don't!* I look quickly at Dad, but he is frowning down at his plate.

"Whatever do you mean by that, Patsy?" Gran snaps. "The poor girl has barely had a week to settle in. Anyone would need time to get used to it."

"I know my daughter, Greta," Mum continues quietly, "and she is better than *Time and Tide*. Way better!"

"Mum!" Cynthia exclaims hotly. "Give her a break!"

"Dorothy just said as much herself," Mum exclaims.

"I did not!" Dot says, upset, her face set into a stubborn grimace.

"You are not enjoying it," Mum declares forcefully, "and I can tell you *why* you're not enjoying it. Because it's a shoddy show that panders to the lowest common level—"

"Patsy!" Dad says, unable to contain himself. Thick silence descends among all of us. Mum turns to him furiously, her face suddenly scarlet with suppressed emotion.

"Yes?" she shrieks, picking up her bread knife. "You want to say something to *me*, Justus?"

"Well I . . ." Dad falters.

"Go ahead," Mum commands, still clenching the knife threateningly.

Dad gulps. Silence seems to crash about the room. On this warm, sunny day, chunks of gray ice are being thrown over us all. I want to run. I look from one to the other, from my mother to my father, and then to my sisters and grandmother. I feel myself teetering on the brink of something. I wait, breathless. Is she going to try and stab him or start throwing things again? One second. Two second. Three . . . How long can a person live without breathing? I'm a bird about to fall from the sky. I hover up there in the wind, but the pull of the ground is strong. I have to use everything to stay in place.

I imagine myself driving down to the coast the next day. The rattle and pull of the old van as I crash into the gears. *Oh, how good it is going to be . . .*

Dad is the first to speak.

"I don't want to say anything," he says.

288

Just shut up, everyone, I want to yell. *Just shut the hell up about everything.*

"It's an absolutely wonderful opportunity for Dorothy," Gran persists firmly. "And I find your attitude very hard to understand, Patsy."

"But you don't even *like* television!" Mum exclaims weakly, looking around the table at us for confirmation. I notice that now she at least has some life and animation in her face. "Isn't it true? Gran has been so . . . inspirational in her refusal to watch rubbish!" Gran simply ignores Mum and reaches over to take Dot's hand in her old gnarled one and rubs it protectively.

"I've changed," she says in a low, intimate voice that excludes everyone else in the room. "As soon as I heard your news, I began to watch the show, and now . . . now I'm a complete convert! I won't answer the phone or go anywhere in the evening until it's over!"

"Really?" Dot laughs in spite of herself.

"And once you come on, I'll take out an advertisement in the local paper so everyone knows you are my grand-daughter."

We all laugh at that, except for Mum.

◆ ◆ ◆

At last it is over. Five minutes before the two hours are up, Dad suddenly rises from the table and touches Gran's elbow. "I think it's time we went, Mum," he says.

"Yes." Gran nods and, to everyone's surprise, gets to her feet almost immediately. Gran is not known for doing what she is told. Dad escorts her to the door, then turns to look directly at Mum.

"Thanks so much, Patsy," he says quietly and sincerely, his voice strung out with emotion. "It . . . was really good of you to have us."

◆ ◆ ◆

ROAD TRIP

Late in the afternoon, just as I'm deciding that my bum is going to stay numb forever, my Grandma wakes. Dad bends forward immediately.

"Hey there," he whispers, gently lifting her up onto a pillow. "Guess who has come to see you?" He motions to me to come nearer. So I make my way around to the other side of the bed, and Dad gets out of the way.

"Hi Gran," I say, bending down. "It's Rose."

Gran stares at me as though she isn't sure who I am and isn't all that interested either, then she gives a big groan followed by a sigh and waves one hand dismissively.

"What day is it?" she asks sharply.

"Tuesday," I say.

"And I'm still here," she says crossly. "Damn it."

This makes us all smile. It is so Gran. Always practical and to the point, she'd expected to be dead by now and it's pissing her right off that she's not.

"Rose has come to see you," Dad tries again.

"I don't want to see anyone!" she grumbles crossly. "I thought I'd be gone by now. Why doesn't God take me?"

"You wanted to give something to Rose?" Dad persists. But the old lady shakes her head.

"No, no," she mutters, "I'm too tired." Her whole faces droops a bit then, and sort of closes down. Her head lolls to the side and she's gone again, back into deep unconsciousness.

Mum and Dad look at each other worriedly, and although I'm feeling a bit awkward, I can't help finding it a little funny, not to mention a relief. *Maybe I'll be spared after all!* I was secretly expecting a big dramatic moment where Gran handed over the Collection into my safekeeping, and I'd been practicing sounding sincere as I uttered my words of gratitude. Now it looks like I'm going to be let off the hook. *Yippee!*

But when Mum's phone suddenly rings, Gran jerks awake again. Her eyes are clear as she watches Dot dithering around in Mum's bag trying to find the phone, and she's annoyed.

"Who is that ringing?" she asks grumpily. "Don't they know you're visiting someone in a hospital?" But after saying, "Hello, Dorothy here," Dot immediately frowns and turns her back to us to take the call.

Gran turns to me.

"People can be very inconsiderate, can't they, Rose?" she says really clearly.

"Yes, they can," I say, surprised, and pleased, too, that she actually does know me.

A nurse bustles in and excuses herself. She needs to check Gran's temperature and blood pressure. We smile politely and pull away from the bed to allow her access.

"It's for you." Dorothy holds the phone out to me. I don't immediately take it. There is something about Dot's expression that warns me off. In fact, I have a strong premonition that there is trouble on the other end. *Don't take the phone, Rose!*

"Who is it?" I ask suspiciously.

"Just take it," she snaps.

"Hello," I say cautiously. There is a second or two of silence and then a voice I don't immediately recognize.

"Hello."

"Who is this?" I ask, but then suddenly *I know*. I can feel it, and after one moment of pure relief . . . *so she's not dead* . . . I am immediately on high alert, wary as hell. My skin prickles with it. The small black phone I'm holding feels dangerous, like a lethal weapon. I am tempted to hurl it from me before it explodes.

"Why are you ringing me?" I ask loudly. Mum and Dad, Dorothy, and even Grandma and the nurse look up. So I turn my back on them.

"I just thought I would," comes the uncharacteristically calm reply. "My mother has been trying to get in touch . . ."

"Tell your mother not to do that," I bark loudly. "Never again, okay?"

"Yeah, well . . . okay," comes the mild response.

"And there is something I want to clear up with you!" I spit the words out without any clear idea of what I'm going to say. I swear I have not planned any of this. It all just spills out of my mouth.

"You *knew* about me and Nat Cummins last summer!" I snarl. "And you pretended you didn't because, well . . ." Here I let my voice drop into a very sarcastic tone. "Whatever is mine is yours! Isn't that right, Zoe? Including the *one* guy that I liked . . . who was interested in me."

"Right," she cuts in, "but nothing happened really . . ."

So nothing happened between them? I try to feel some pleasure, some satisfaction, but . . . it's all too late now.

"I don't care!" I say loudly. "You *wanted* it to happen! You were all geared up for it to happen big-time. Don't deny it!"

"It's true," she admits.

"Because you're so *greedy*!" I'm shouting now, and shaking. "You want everything! From the beginning of freshman year you wanted my clothes, my homework, my family, my money! Everything that was mine you thought you could just take!"

"Well . . . yeah," she agrees with a sigh.

This rage is making me pant. Maybe I'm hyperventilating because, at the same time as feeling insanely powerful, I also feel a bit light-headed, like I might faint any minute. *She agrees! So this is real. I'm not just making this stuff up.*

"You even let me take the rap for hitting *his* sister that time!" I scream. *Now I'm dredging up stuff from four years ago! How fair is that?*

"I went to bat for you when Alisha was giving you a hard time. When the shit hit the fan, you just left me to cop it. I almost got expelled because of you. Did you help in any way? No! You were too busy with the play. Let Rose do it. My parents split up and where were you? Did you even once ask me how I was feeling?"

I stop, feeling spent and wrecked and nervous all at the same time. I would like to continue screaming at her, but I can't think of anything else to say. What *did* I say exactly? Was it even *true?* Should I put the phone down right now? I look out the window at the little garden, mortified because it is only now that I fully comprehend that I'm speaking to a sick person, maybe a very sick person. *Jeez.* Something chilly crawls around my neck and ears and head as it sinks in. I haven't even asked her how she is, or where she is, or if she's going to get better or . . . I haven't asked her anything. I open my mouth. But I can't, somehow. I just can't. I turn around to the others helplessly.

Dad is standing now. He comes over and stands right next to me. Mum and Dot, still sitting on the chairs, are staring at me blankly. So is the nurse. Even Gran looks alert. Dad puts his arm around my shaking shoulders. "Come on now, Rose," he murmurs gently. "Maybe you should finish up? Say goodbye."

"Okay." I nod. But I continue to hold the phone tightly to my ear, breathing into it. *Let her hang up. I won't.* But she doesn't either.

"Zoe?" I say eventually in a calmer voice.

"Yes?"

I still have no idea what to say next. I don't get how quiet and controlled she is being. This isn't the Zoe I know. She must be on some kind of medication.

I hear faint music from her end. A mad part of me wants to ask what she is listening to now. Has she heard the latest Wicked City album? And what about that new band, Fire Witch? Just when I think I will have to hang up, she speaks.

"You got your own back, Rose."

This pulls me up. Something heavy jams its way straight through the center of me, and I'm stuck, legs and arms and head flailing around like an insect caught live on a pin. This is it. No way out of this one.

"With my father," she adds slowly.

"Yes, but . . . I didn't mean to . . . let it happen," I whisper. *What are you talking about, Rose? That's not even true! Stop being so gutless!*

She sighs softly. "I know you didn't mean to hurt me."

"So . . ."

"I'm in the hospital again, Rose," she says in a more normal way, "and I miss you. Will you come and see me?"

"Well . . . I don't know."

"Don't think about it. Just come."

"Okay," I say. "I'll come."

◆　◆　◆

On the way out of the hospital, we run into Cassandra coming in. I'm feeling so wired up after the conversation with

Zoe that I don't immediately recognize her. I do vaguely notice this very attractive woman dressed in a conservatively cut summer dress and high heels, walking briskly along toward the hospital entrance as we make our way out toward the car. It goes through my mind that she's probably not a local. Way too glamorous.

"Hello, Cass," Dad calls out reluctantly.

She stops, sees us, and walks carefully over the grass. She's holding her head high, but I can see she's nervous. She wasn't expecting to meet up with *the family*. It's a weird moment as Dad introduces her to Mum. It had to happen. After all, it's been over a year.

"Er . . . Cass, I'd like you to meet Patsy."

Dot and I instinctively draw closer to Mum. All the sadness, the crying, and the fury our mother went through, trying to come to terms with Dad leaving her for this woman. Now here she is, standing before us, squinting nervously through her small, pretty, almond-colored eyes.

"How do you do?" She nods politely, then, about to hold out her hand, suddenly changes her mind and doesn't. It gives me some satisfaction to see how uncomfortable she is. It is probably the first time in her life she hasn't known how to deal with a situation.

Mum is nervous too, but touchingly polite.

"Hello," she says in a weak voice. Then she holds out her hand and gives a tentative smile. Cassandra flushes as they shake hands briefly, then she turns to Dad.

"How is your mother, Justus?" she asks in this sharp, strained voice.

"She has actually picked up a bit," Dad says with a smile. "The nurse told me that everything is better than it's been in weeks."

This makes us all laugh a bit.

"Maybe she'll make it after all," Cassandra says carefully. *As though she cares!*

"Maybe," Dad says wryly, "but I don't think so."

"I've got to get back to town," Cassandra says, looking straight at Dad so she doesn't have to look at the rest of us. "There has been an adjournment."

"Really?" Dad slips into instant lawyer mode. "So they got the hearing?"

"Yes."

"Well done!" He smiles at her. "When will you go?"

"Well . . ." Cassandra shakes her head uncomfortably. "Within the hour, I guess." She hesitates. "I'm sorry, but I have to."

"Of course you do." Dad puts a hand each on my and Dot's shoulders. "I'll just see this lot to the car, Cass. Be right back."

"So pleased to have met you." Cassandra gives Mum one of her icy sharp smiles and backs off. "Goodbye, Dorothy and Rose."

"Yes," Mum replies faintly. "Me, too."

At the car, Dad is strangely reluctant to let us go. He seems preoccupied, troubled.

"Listen," he says, "how about we all have dinner tonight?"

"I thought you wanted to sit with Gran?"

"I'd like a break for a couple of hours," he says. "The nurse can ring me if . . . things change."

"Okay, Dad." Dot and I are in agreement. We look at Mum.

"All right." Then she looks away into the distance, very strained.

◆ ◆ ◆

AT AROUND SIX a.m. the next morning, when I'm out on my board, catching my first wave of the day, my grandmother dies. Not that I know it then, of course. I find out later.

There are about eight of us out that morning, and I'm the only girl. Early on, I have a short conversation with the guy nearest to me when he makes room on a nice, low swell and lets me ride across his path, but after that it's just me and the waves.

Two hours into it and I'm so thrilled to be back out there on the water again, in daylight, that I don't notice much at all, certainly not Dad waiting for me on the beach. In the still, gray, early-morning light, the ocean is perfect, green and clear as glass. Within an hour, I'm a mass of aching muscles. My left wrist hurts from a massive tumble I took early on, and my eyes sting like crazy, but I don't stop. As soon as I surf in, I paddle right back out again. Time ticks away.

This has to be the best thing in the world! Of course, I'm out of practice, and when the easy ones slip away, I curse and swear like anyone else, but . . . the joy factor is immense, believe me. Immense. Ray and Zoe, Dad and Cassandra, Mum, university and the rest of it float into consciousness occasionally, but they slide out again before anything like worry can take hold. Just being here charges me right up.

Eventually, I get out, completely exhausted, and stumble through the shallows to collapse onto the sand. When I sit up again, I see Dad coming toward me. I had noticed a lone figure in black, strolling along the shore earlier, and I'd idly wondered if he was okay without realizing he was my own father.

As he gets closer, I see he looks even worse than the day before. Strained and pale, his face so lined and thin it makes me want to yell out some joke to make him smile. *Hey, Dad, aren't you getting fed these days?*

"How long have you been down here?" I ask as he sits down beside me, my teeth still chattering a bit.

"Ages." He smiles. "I've been waiting for you to get out."

"You should have called out, waved."

"No." He shrugs, and when I stand and unzip my wet-suit, he gets up too. "How was it?"

"Fantastic!" I say, drying myself. "Did you see me?"

"I did."

"You see that last one?" He nods, and I laugh, pleased. The last one would have to be my best ride ever. "Thought I'd leave on a high note!"

"Always a good idea." He smiles, then takes my arm suddenly, not looking at me but at his feet, frowning. "Now listen, Rose, your gran died this morning." He is trying to sound easy and matter-of-fact, but the strain is evident in the slight waver in his voice and the way he turns away abruptly to look at the car that has just pulled up. "Three hours ago, to be exact."

"Oh." I'm rudely catapulted out of my present happily exhausted state to stand looking at him, trying to comprehend what he has just told me. My mind immediately goes into overdrive. *So what now?* I start calculating. There will be a funeral in a couple of days, so that means I'll have to stay here. When I was out on the waves, *Go see Zoe* regularly flashed across my mental screen. Her way-too-calm voice has been playing away in my unconscious all night. *Go see Zoe.*

God, I'm nervous just thinking about it. Why the hell did Gran have to die today? It means I won't be able to get back to town until after the weekend and . . .

Then I actually *see* my father, the slump of his shoulders, the red exhausted eyes, his tight mouth trying to hold in the sadness and . . . I'm ashamed. Gran was the rock on which Dad built his life. And now she's gone.

"Hey, Dad."

"Oh pet," he says, putting one hand on the back of my head, holding me close as a couple of deep sobs wrench through him.

"Dad," I say again, tears stinging my eyes. "Don't be sad. *Please.*"

"Okay," he murmurs, but continues to hold me tightly, like he really needs to.

What a totally stupid thing for me to say! Why shouldn't he be sad?

"Disregard what I just said, Dad," I murmur. "Be as sad as you like!" He laughs and holds me tighter.

It feels good to have my arms wrapped around my father after all this time, even though I can't remember his shoulders and chest ever being so bony before. I smile to myself. He's probably thinking the same about me. *Who is this bony, sharp, shorn-off girl who used to be mine?* Eventually we pull away, he kisses me on both cheeks, and we laugh a bit. Without another word I finish getting dressed and we walk up through the sand to the van together, arm in arm.

Don'tcha just hate it . . . when you realize that you are a jerk too? For years you'd thought that "jerkiness" was a trait that belonged to other people. Then you find yourself in a situation that calls for more. Maybe it's only a bit of empathy and kindness . . . And your immediate response? You behave just like all the other self-centered arseholes on the planet! Oh, how inconsiderate of my grandmother to die just when I needed to get back to town!

"Were you there?" I ask.

"No."

"How come?"

So he tells me how, after our dinner, which we ended up having at the cottage because the restaurants were fully booked, he went back to the hospital to spend the night with his mother. But the nursing staff suggested he go get some rest. They were all joking about her being stronger than she'd been in weeks. Why not come back in the morning, they suggested, after he'd had some sleep? So, after kissing his mother goodnight, he went back to the hotel and got his first good night's sleep in more than ten days. He was woken up by a phone call from the hospital at five thirty. Mrs. O'Neil had taken a "turn" and he should come in quickly. By the time he got there, she was dead.

"Does that upset you, Dad?" I say, unlocking the van door. "I mean, that you weren't there?"

"Well . . . I suppose it doesn't matter." He shrugs, and I see immediately that it does matter, a lot. "She went peacefully, apparently."

"Do the others know?"

"Yes, I called in to the cottage, then walked down here to you."

"Want me to drive you back there?"

"You know, Rose," he says quietly, "I'd just like to sit with you a while."

"Okay," I say a little awkwardly. *Me?* I get in and lean across and open up the other door for him. Then we sit together in silence, watching the surf roll in.

I can't remember the last time I was alone with my father. I switch on Classic FM low because it's his favorite station and settle back behind the wheel. After a couple of minutes, the quiet, cultivated voice of the announcer tells us that they are beginning a special on Haydn. *What luck.* I turn to Dad with a smile. That's his favorite composer. When a lovely joyful quartet starts up, I sneak a look at him. He is sitting with his head against the side window, staring straight ahead, both thin hands on his knees, very still.

"Is this too . . . much?" I ask, meaning, is it too bright and cheerful for how he feels?

"No," he murmurs. "I love it," and then adds wryly, "and it's going to change into something somber pretty soon."

"Want it up a bit louder?"

"Yeah."

He's right. The next movement plays with the original theme but it's much darker, and more sorrowful, exactly right, in fact. It's fantastic music, rich and tender in a way that pulls me right into its core.

I don't have my watch, so I don't know how long we sit there. But I figure that it's getting on a bit because people are starting to arrive at the beach for the forecasted hot day. Mothers with little kids in tiny bright pants, towels slung over their shoulders, all the colorful hats and balls and bags. Fat middle-aged men with hairy bellies. My own belly is rumbling but I'm determined not to hurry Dad. *His mother has just died*, I tell myself sternly, so sitting with him is the least I can do! The quartet ends, and they read the news. More terrorist bombings in the Iraqi capital have killed seventeen people. Then some poor girl has been taken by a shark off the West Australian coast. The dollar is losing value. *Life goes on.*

Should I be trying to cheer Dad up, or asking him how he feels? Maybe he wants to know about me? The last three hours of surfing have cleaned me right out; I feel like I've got nothing to hide anymore. I almost wish he'd ask me something. I never discussed with him why I deferred university, and I refused point-blank to talk about what had happened with Zoe when he tried to broach it. My present life in Hurstbridge as a waitress, living with those two odd-bods, has likewise been off the agenda. I can't remember even one conversation with my father in the past year. And we used to talk all the time.

But he remains silent and so do I. The beautiful music rolls out between us, and as the minutes push by, I sort of space out. I find myself hanging on to the edge of each dramatic crescendo as though to a cliff face by my fingertips, then I dive with the musicians straight into the wild, painful bits and crash like a mad girl into the finales, as if my whole life is there, depending on each note. And I want to cry out loud for every bloody thing! The girl taken by the shark. Ray, of course. My gran and her hard life. That special gift that never came my way. Listening to music is a bit like mind surfing. It picks you up and chucks you around inside your own head. You lift and plunge back and forth into loosely connected thoughts and memories that hold you in place, and all the while you live and breathe right alongside the sound.

But my stomach is rumbling again and I can't stand it much longer. I need to eat or I'll go completely spare.

"You had breakfast?" I say, trying to sound casual.

"No," he murmurs, shaking his head indifferently.

"Feel like a drive in my *hot* machine?"

He looks up then and smiles, puts one hand out and runs it over the top of my sawn-off hair.

"I was wondering when you'd ask."

So I take my father to Warrnambool for breakfast.

◆   ◆   ◆

He seems to really enjoy the trip. "God! I haven't been in one of these things since 1975!" he mutters as I pull out onto the main road. It loosens him up. All the rattles, clunking gears, and screeching brakes have him grinning with pleasure.

We buy some egg-and-bacon rolls and hot coffee and take them to the main city park, where there is a wooden table with seats. He eats a few bites and then seems to lose interest. This is my dad, I remind myself. Until recently he was so handsome, a brilliant lawyer, and the most cheerful, intelligent father in the world. He was my mentor and my idol. *So what happened?* How does all that equate with this thin, old, wretchedly sad man sitting across from me, trying to pretend he is interested in eating the rest of his toasted sandwich? But maybe I got it all wrong . . . *maybe he never was what I thought he was.*

"Are you happy now, Dad?" I ask. It's unfair to ask him this, but I have to know if he thinks it's all been worth it.

"What a question!" He smiles and looks away. He's not being evasive. It might take a while, but I know he'll give me an honest answer.

"Well," he says after a while, "Cass and I are right for each other, so I am happy in that respect, but . . . I had no idea I'd *miss* everyone so dreadfully."

I turn away, self-conscious and guilty.

"Me?"

"You and all the others."

"But you see them," I protest. "Cynthia told me that she sees you at least once a week." *And what did you expect? I* want to add but don't. *You chose to leave!* He must be able to read my impatient body language, because he suddenly reaches out and touches my arm.

"I'm not blaming anyone, pet," he says. "You asked. I'm just answering the question."

I think back to the evening before in Gran's backyard, Dad cooking those fresh fish over the grill, laughing and talking. Him and Mum pretty relaxed together, considering everything. Then the speech he made to us all.

"Thanks for coming. The last year hasn't been easy for . . . anyone here, and it means so much to me to have all of you around with my poor old mum, your gran, on her way out." He looks at Mum. "Patsy, you particularly. Your generosity is absolutely"—his voice breaks—"overwhelming. Thank you so much."

"I wouldn't want to be anywhere else, Justus," Mum replies quietly. "I've known and loved your mother for over a quarter of a century."

"Mum was in good form last night," I say slyly now, not looking at him. Mum *was* in good form. The strained look of earlier in the afternoon had disappeared, and by the time we all got together to make the food and eat, she was laughing and joking like the old days. I want to see if he noticed how pretty she looked in her tight cream pants and soft silk matching top. I want to rub it in and make him sorry that he left. Actually, what I *really* want to see is my father begging Mum to take him back, leaving Cassandra out in the cold, with egg on her face. But he either doesn't pick up on the intent of my question or pretends not to.

"Yes," he says mildly, "but she was always a lovely woman."

Well why leave her then? I want to yell at him. *Why leave a lovely woman who also happens to be your wife!*

"I fell in love with Cassandra," Dad says, as though he can read my mind, "and it was the most powerful thing I've ever experienced. All-consuming. So . . . I had to leave."

"Right," I say cynically. *He fell in love!* God, how many people through the ages have used that excuse for bad behavior?

"Like you did," he adds mildly.

What? I jerk away from his intense look. But he's right, of course! And I'm thrown back into the confusing morass of my own life, not daring now to ask if he thinks it has all been worthwhile. That would mean asking the same question of myself. *Was the whole thing worth it? Was Ray worth it?*

The gray morning cloud has cleared and the sun is coming out. It's got some real bite in it, too. With the food sitting comfortably in my belly, I suddenly want to laugh. At myself, mainly, because I've only just worked out that life isn't an exam, and there is no way I can get a perfect score. Unfortunately, it's not an investment portfolio, either. You can give it everything you have, and more, but there are no sure returns. I grab Dad's wrist and look at the time. Nearly eleven already! The sun is climbing high in the blue sky, and my sore eyes are dazzled by its brightness. Time to go.

"Dad, it's getting hot. I'll get burned."

"Yeah. Let's go."

He nudges me, smiling, suggesting I take a look at the group of about eight teenage girls passing our table. They are all dressed in either tight jeans or tiny denim skirts and halter tops that expose backs, cleavage, and brown bellies. Their long hair falling about, tied up, bunched and braided with bright little scrunchies, baubles, and bands. A couple of them hold mobile phones to their ears and joke and yell into them . . . then turn to relay to the others whatever important information they are getting. This brings on bursts of helpless giggling, falling over, tripping, whispering, and then shouts of "Cut it out!" and "Behave!" I glance at Dad and smile because he is obviously finding it so funny.

"They remind me so much of you girls," he says, chuckling and shaking his head.

"I was never like that!"

"Yes, you were," he laughs.

"Bullshit!"

"And your sisters, too!"

I make a face and stand up, suddenly touched because I'd forgotten Dad's appreciation of . . . things. That fantastic ability he has to find the spark of joy in whatever he's doing. I manage to hold the lid on the tears that are threatening, thankfully. I haven't turned into one of my sisters just yet!

"Come on," I say gruffly. "Let's go."

He stands and puts an arm around me.

"It's early days yet, pet," Dad says, as though he knows how I'm feeling. "Things will work out. Honestly, I believe they will."

"Do you?" I ask, frowning because I'm not at all sure myself.

"I've got to," he sighs, in a way that makes me think he's not that sure either.

I open the van and we both get in. I settle myself behind the wheel and start the motor.

"So, back to the cottage?"

"Yeah," he says, "I've got a funeral to organize." Then he grins, in just the way he used to. "That is, if Cynthia hasn't done it already."

◆　◆　◆

When we pull up outside the cottage, Dad hesitates.

"I forgot this." He pulls a small envelope from his pocket. "I found it in Gran's things. It's for you."

I take the letter but don't open it immediately, because seeing my name written in Gran's fat, shaky scrawl is making my heart do a dive. Just when I thought I was off the hook!

"What is it?" I ask, but I know of course.

Dad shrugs, slides open his door, gets out and stretches, before giving me a tired smile. "Why don't you open it and see?"

I watch him walk off into the house and then sit there skimming through six pages of almost indecipherable scrawl before I get to the crunch. Yes, just as we all thought, the Collection is mine. Mine, all mine. *Damn.*

THAT NIGHT, after the funeral arrangements are more or less worked out, I go into the front room with a big cardboard box and a few reams of that plastic bubble packing stuff. I start with old Chifley and move up through the politicians, religious leaders, sports stars, and entertainers, all the people my grandmother loved and admired through the decades. I wrap them carefully and place them side by side, one on top of the other, in the box.

When my sisters come in to offer help, I tell them to go away.

"She's bonding," Dot whispers, and they all immediately collapse into hysterics. I push them out, shut the door on them, and go about the business. For some weird reason, I do need to pack up this horrible inheritance all by myself.

When it's done, I secure the box with tape.

Don'tcha just hate the way we're all so hung up on surfaces? We read all kinds of positive value into what is sleek and new and pretty, yet the ordinary, cheap, ugly things often sing a deeper note. Think about your dad's old suede boots sitting in the closet, the ones he wore when he taught you to ride a bike. The big, stained green teapot from Coles. That wrecked old pillow that you cried yourself to sleep on every night last year. Stuff that holds secrets about us that the lovely new things will never know . . .

Ah, that's crap. A piece for Roger has been bubbling up all afternoon, but I haven't got a proper angle on it yet. Until I do, I have to keep turning the sentences over, churning through them, trying to see if there is any halfway interesting idea under all the rubbish. I never know if Ms. Angst will turn out or not, and that's what makes the whole business so tricky and interesting. If I do manage to nail this one, I have a feeling it might be good. The hard ones nearly always turn out better, unfortunately. That's just the way it goes.

When everyone else is in bed, I sneak out into the dark, star-filled night and wedge the cardboard box holding the Collection between the spare wheel and a pile of clothing and wetsuits in the back of the van. I feel a little spooked, like I've just shut away my grandmother's life, so I close the van up quickly and rush back inside. Maybe I won't unpack them, ever.

In bed, I pick up the letter again and read to the end.

. . . *When I heard from your father that you almost drowned, I decided that you should have my precious collection, Rose. Your grandfather drowned over fifty years ago and I still remember that day as though it were yesterday. Oh, the tears I shed. All you girls are lucky to be here because I almost forgot to feed your father! He was a baby at the time and a hard one to rear, and I'm ashamed to say I lost interest in everything, even my baby son. I didn't seem able to move, much less look after anyone. A neighbor—you remember Eunice Simpson with the crook knee who used to live at the end of James Street?— came in and helped me cope for a few weeks. I always tell her that she saved both our lives. Your father's and mine.*

How lucky you were to survive. And all thanks to that brave man who saved you! I've been trying to get his address from your mother and sisters so I can write and thank him personally, but no one has it. They don't seem to even want me to have his name. But why not? Surely a letter from a grateful old girl in Port Fairy wouldn't do any harm? But when you're my age nothing is surprising. You never know with people. You never know when you're stepping on toes. And you never know what else has gone on before. All I do know is that I wish some-one like him had been there the day my Des lost his life . . .

Thanks Gran, I whisper. Thanks for the gift that I don't want. Maybe I will unpack that box one day and find some place in my life for it.

◆ ◆ ◆

A LOT OF GRAN'S FRIENDS have already died, so there is not a big crowd at the funeral. Probably sixty or seventy people at most. Most of them old, although a few of Dad's lawyer friends and their wives have made the trip from Melbourne, and there is quite a contingent of cousins from Gippsland. The rest are locals, neighbors, and fellow volunteers from the Red Cross shop. There are also quite a few from the bowling club and the local Labor party.

I sit between Mum and Dorothy in the front pew, watching the four candles flickering around my gran's honeywood coffin. Every now and again I have to remind myself that she is actually lying in that box, only a few meters away from me. But where is her tough old spirit after eighty-six years? *Where do people go?* Dad is the only one among us who actually knows the hymns and the responses to the prayers. It touches me to hear his thin voice belting them out.

When the long service is over, Dad gets up to join Gran's old friend Harry and four other younger men as a pallbearer. Mum takes my arm, and along with my sisters, we follow the coffin slowly down the aisle to the back of the church. I study the lovely mosaic floor, feeling shy in front of the rest of the congregation, who are standing to watch us before following us out. I'm also scared I might make eye-contact with Cassandra, who has come back for the funeral. I saw her standing alone at the back in her crisp black suit and high heels when we walked into the church. Hilda and Dot went up especially to speak to her, but, I decide, that doesn't mean I have to.

St Patrick's is an old bluestone building on a rise near the edge of town. I hold back a bit on the top step as Mum and my sisters move forward with the rest of the congregation to watch the coffin being put in the back of the hearse.

"Rose?" comes a male voice from just behind me. I turn quickly. There he is, standing arm in arm with a faded blond middle-aged woman dressed in a linen suit. He looks very different from how I remember him last summer. He's in a badly fitted suit for starters, and his hair is cut very short. He looks older and more serious. "G'day, Rose!" he says with a warm smile.

"Hello, Nat," I say, furiously trying to stop the heat from rising to my face. "How are you?"

I am conscious that I must look a bit weird myself in this sleek, very conservative blue dress that Cynthia wore to her graduation, complete with pantyhose and high heels and an ugly handbag. Not me at all, but in the end it was the only outfit I could cobble together that my sisters thought was in any way appropriate for a funeral. I just toed the line and did what I was told.

"Good, thanks," he mumbles, before turning to the woman next to him. "Mum, this is Rose." I can see that my awkwardness has made him embarrassed, and that makes me feel worse. His mother gives a strained smile and holds out her hand.

"Pleased to meet you, Rose," she whispers in this very breathy way. "So sorry about your grandmother." Her hand is unbelievably cool for such a warm day. And so is the smile.

"I'm standing in for my Dad," Nat explains uncomfortably. "He really wanted to come, but he couldn't. Work in

Sydney, you know. Mum doesn't drive much, so . . ." His voice dies away, and there are a few moments of silence while we all try to think of something to say.

"Ah, Mum, Rose and Alisha went to school together," he says, sparking up. I immediately curl up inside, and at the same time want to clock him. Of all the stupid things to bring up! Why remind her I was the one who hit her daughter? I think the irritation must show on my face because he immediately tries to undo what he's just said by acting like it doesn't matter. "Long time ago, of course," he mumbles distractedly, looking away.

"I know that, Nathaniel," his mother says in her crisp, unfriendly voice. Thankfully someone intercepts our uncomfortable little triangle, and his mother moves away. Nat and I are left looking at each other. I gulp self-consciously and say the first thing that comes into my head.

"So . . . what's with the suit?"

"It's not mine." He smiles uneasily. "Mum insisted. Funeral. You know."

I nod carefully and take a better look at him. He is standing with his arms crossed, looking away at the rest of the crowd. His whole stance reminds me so much of Dad's friend in the photo on Gran's piano that I want to laugh.

"Whose is it?" I ask.

"My old man's." He makes a rueful face and jokes, "I wouldn't buy something like this!"

"You look like him," I say.

"When did you meet him?" He grins curiously.

"Gran's got a photo of him with my dad."

The ice has melted between us and we're both smiling now. He is about to say something else when his mother edges back from whoever she was talking to, taking his arm again.

"Rose, you'll have to excuse us," she says, "but Nathaniel and I can't stay for the afternoon tea. We must get back to the city."

"Well, it was very good of you to come," I say politely.

Nat gives me an apologetic smile and allows his mother to pull him away. But at the last minute he turns back and gives me a grin that really warms my heart.

"Hey, Rose?" he says mischievously. "What happened to your hair?"

I shrug, momentarily stumped for words.

"It's okay." He gives me another warm smile, turns his back, and walks off with his mother.

For the rest of the afternoon, right through all the introductions, the polite chitchat and cups of tea, I keep coming back to that smile. At the same time as giving me a bit of a warm buzz, it makes me oddly frustrated. The conversation was just getting started when his damned mother pulled him away. I would have liked to ask him about Zoe. Does he still see her? What should I expect when I visit her? And what about *his* life? That whole thing on the church steps was a missed opportunity, but there is nothing I can do about it now.

◆ ◆ ◆

IT IS LATE afternoon, and Mum and I are driving back to the city after the funeral. Not much traffic. We're taking the inland route and have just passed through Camperdown, heading for Colac, going through the slightly spooky country they call the stony rises. It's all undulating green fields edged with low stone fences, trees in the dimming light like black ghosts against the wide streaky-pink sky. The night slowly closing in like this has me feeling washed out and empty, ready for something new. Good. For the last few mornings I've hit the waves for at least three hours, and just thinking of it gives me a rush of pleasure.

Mum is alongside me, asleep, leaning her head up against the side window on a couple of rolled-up towels. I'm sitting up with both hands on the wheel, feeling pretty cool. Pretty on top of things. Pretty much like everything is going to come out right in the end. *Dangerous!* I almost hear Zoe's voice. *Could mean you're due for a big crash, kid!* Yeah, I agree. But why not enjoy it while it lasts?

I switch on the headlights and slip in the cheapo CD that Mum bought earlier in the petrol station when we were filling up.

The Harder They Come. Jimmy Cliff. Nice. *Good one, Mum.* I look over, wanting her to wake up to enjoy it, but she's dead to the world. We were out late last night at the best restaurant in town. Dad's shout, in honor of Gran, he said. Bruce and David stayed in and looked after the twins, and the rest of us got stuck into the wine—and into each other—in the usual way. It was good. Got to bed about three a.m. Mum had to get up early because she promised one of Gran's old friends a ride to church. Typical. It's why she's tired. The rest of us didn't get up until after midday.

I look at my watch. If we're back in a couple of hours, I should just make it. I'll drop Mum off and then go straight over to the Royal Melbourne. They wouldn't give out much information about her condition or treatment, so . . . I guess I'll find out the details when I see her. Visiting hours are from seven-thirty to nine. I've got the floor and the room number.

The closer I get to the city, the more that hospital visit starts to loom as an ordeal that I've got to get through. There is a very real risk of me being hurled back into the events of last summer with no way out, and I'm dreading it. I know it will take only a look, a word or two, or a flick of her wrist to put me back there. But I said I'd go, so I will. It would have taken a bit for her to ring me. This is something I have to do.

"You think we'll be back by eight?" I ask. Mum stirs and wakes.

"Oh, I think so," she mumbles, looking at her watch. "It's only an hour from Geelong." She cranes forward suddenly, and I can see what has caught her attention. There is a dark figure standing up ahead by the side of the road, and for just a moment, it's an image from a fantasy movie, the tall spooky stranger come to change our destinies forever. Hairs rise on the back of my neck. But as we hurtle toward him, I see it is only a man wearing dark clothing, with one arm extended, a hitchhiker no less, and not a particularly tall one either. He'd been standing on a rise in the road, and for a couple of moments had taken on a stature that he didn't possess.

"It's not . . . *him*, is it?" Mum asks, turning to me.

"Who?" I ask, puzzled. "Do you want me to stop?" I take my foot off the accelerator but don't brake. We're about to pass the guy now and I'm hoping Mum will tell me to keep driving, because I want to get back to the city.

"He probably only wants a ride to Geelong," Mum says. I sigh and step on the brake.

"After he murders us," I mutter.

"That's my line, Rose," Mum laughs.

I pull over onto the gravel and wait as the dark figure lurches up behind us. He is carrying some kind of heavy pack, and I sense something familiar about his gait before the full realization hits home. *Oh shit!* The door slides open.

"Thought it was you guys!" he puffs. "Recognized the van."

"Well *hello*, Travis!" Mum turns around with the biggest, most delighted smile. "What an amazing coincidence!"

"Yeah." He grins at her as though he was kind of expecting it all along. "Knew I'd see youse again somewhere." Then he looks at me and I can almost hear his brain clicking through all the negative data stored there against me. *Well, ditto mate!* I want to say. But he nods in a perfunctory way and raises one hand in salute.

"How are you doing?" he says briskly.

"Great," I say, not bothering to smile either. "How are you?"

"Not bad."

I watch in the rear-view mirror as he settles in like he's been there all his life. Pushes one of my bags to the floor so there is room for his on the seat beside him. Takes off his jacket and pulls out his tobacco and rolls a cigarette.

"Funeral yesterday in Camperdown," he explains shortly in response to a couple of questions from Mum, blowing the smoke straight into her face. "I stayed on at a mate's place for the night. Hey, you got any other music? This is shit."

"Oh my," Mum says breathlessly. "So she *died*?"

"Yeah." He nods, expressionless. "On Saturday."

"I'm so *sorry*, Travis!" Mum gushes. *Ex-wife*, Mum! I want to remind her. *Ex-wife*. He probably doesn't care that much, actually!

"And what about your . . . old lady?" Travis asks after a pause.

"She died last Thursday," Mum replies. "We buried her yesterday too."

I listen to them settling into the funeral talk like old friends, and I wonder what the odds are of me coming across him on the road again. *Maybe next week*, I think darkly, *I'll be traveling back down the coast to surf and . . . there he'll be. Travis the dickhead.* Shit! Just the possibility of it makes me want to stay home. I *would* like to know about his son, though. I'd like to ask him how the kid is doing and what's going to happen to him next, but I don't. I let my guard down with a guy like Travis, and he'll be walking all over me.

"Hey, you got anything else to listen to?" Travis asks again. "You had Pink Floyd last time, didn't you?"

"Yeah." I nod sharply. *No way am I taking this off!*

"I'm actually loving this, Travis!" Mum intercedes brightly, saving me the bother of telling him to go fuck himself. She throws her head back and starts tapping her fingers on her knees. "I haven't heard Jimmy Cliff in ages."

"Ah well," Travis sighs miserably, and winds the window down. "Each to his own, I suppose."

Mum asks all the questions and I find out everything I want to know anyway. He tells us the kid is fine—not that Travis would know, I have to remind myself. But the really good bit is that Peter doesn't have to leave Apollo Bay, at least not straightaway. Travis is on his way up to Sydney for a quick visit to "tie up a few loose threads," as he puts it, and finish up with "a dumb little chick" that he had been breaking up with anyway before "all the shit" happened. (Lucky escape for *her*, is what goes through my mind!) Then he's coming back down to try to get work in Apollo Bay.

"Oh, what a great idea!" Mum is over the moon about all this. "I'm so pleased to hear that you've made that decision." Her belief in people should be bottled. It amazes me. It doesn't even dawn on her that he might, in fact, be making all this up and doing a flit. As far as I'm concerned, the odds that he'll even bother coming back for his son are small.

But I don't say anything. After about fifteen minutes the conversation runs out of steam and silence descends. The kilometers pile up and I start loving everything again, the drive and the quietness and the low sun outside. We sail through Colac and Whittlesea and before long we're coming up to Geelong. My mobile flashes blue and gives that irritating little jingle that tells me someone has left a message. I reach to pick it up, but Mum gives me a dirty look so I leave it. She's right. The road between Geelong and Melbourne is alive with cops at this time of the year.

I play Jimmy Cliff through again just to make my point, but when we're coming up to the West Gate Bridge I figure I'm ready for something else.

My hand hovers over Pink Floyd's *Wish You Were Here* album, and I think, *Oh well. What the hell! Give Travis a thrill*. I slip it in and turn up the volume and I'm rewarded with a nod and a smile in the rear-view mirror, which is oddly pleasing. Considering how I feel about him, I mean.

◆　◆　◆

Being up on the bridge at dusk is magical. I'm sailing through the air. Below us the boats and the water gleam. In the soft light, all those factories and refineries and city offices have come alive. I wonder how it will feel walking into that hospital room in less than an hour. What state will she be in? Who will be there?

That fantastic old Pink Floyd song goes on and on and it makes tears well up in my throat. Wish you were here. After a while, I don't know whether I'm thinking of Ray or Nathaniel or my old friend in the hospital.

On the Bolte Bridge now and turning onto Racecourse Road. We've made good time. I'll make visiting hours for sure.

"You going anywhere near the Hume Highway?" Travis suddenly asks.

"No," I say, immediately wary.

"We are going through Parkville though, Rose," Mum chips in. "We have to cross Royal Parade, so we can let him off there." I look at her blankly. I know that letting him off in the middle of busy Royal Parade will *not* happen. It will be too inconvenient. As soon as we get there the pressure will be on to drop him farther out.

"That would be really good," the little punk says enthusiastically. Mum looks at me inquiringly.

"Sure," I say. "Why not?"

Don'tcha just hate . . . the way you can never do enough for some people? It's like they really believe life owes them, big-time, and because the big, bad world isn't exactly listening . . . then you'll have to do. You can be the one to fill in the bits that they're not getting, until someone better, richer, and more important turns up . . .

But no, I can't get excited about this one either. Nothing about driving Travis out of my way seriously bothers me at this point.

◆ ◆ ◆

WE'VE JUST dropped Travis off at a northern suburbs petrol station where he'll have a good chance of catching a truck going all the way through to Sydney. We're heading back down Sydney Road when Roger calls me on the mobile. I've been working on a new piece for him in my head, so it's annoying being interrupted. I had the feeling I was running with a good idea, and now I've lost it.

"I'll answer it." Mum grabs the phone before I can reach it first.

"Hello. This is Rose's phone," she says politely, and waits a moment. "Excuse me, *who* do you want to speak to?" Then, "This is Rose O'Neil's phone." She listens for a few more moments, then shakes her head. "He says he wants to speak to *Ms. Angst*," she whispers, raising her eyebrows like she's got a crazy on the other end. "What should I say?"

"Oh," I reply. "That's for me." I grab the phone. "I can't talk, Roger. I'm driving," I say bluntly.

We're in Parkville now, heading down the Royal Parade avenue of trees, past the university. There isn't much traffic on the road, but even so, Mum is giving me that look. I know I shouldn't be taking this call.

"Okay then. Got your message," he says quickly. "*You okay?*"

"Yep. Thanks." I don't think he's ever asked me *that* before.

"But I'll be very disappointed if you miss a week, Rose . . ."

321

"Uh-huh," I say. *Lay the bullshit on with a shovel, why don't you, Roger!*

I'd left him a message earlier in the week, telling him that, due to the unforeseen circumstances of my grandmother's death, my next column won't be ready in time for this week's paper. We'll have to skip a week.

"People are really enjoying your stuff," he goes on edgily.

"Well . . . I'm sorry about that, Roger," I say, "but it can't be helped."

I'm not sorry at all, actually. I know he's deliberately putting it on me because last time we spoke, I asked for more money. I mean, fifty bucks for all that work! This is his way of putting me in my place so I won't ask again.

"I just hope you can get something from it," he says.

"What do you mean?"

"The funeral."

"I don't think so," I reply shortly. "Nothing happened."

"Everyone can connect with their grandmother dying, Rose," he says patiently. I don't answer because I'm actually thinking *seriously* about the illegality of taking this call while driving, and the fact that if a cop saw me, I'd lose my license on the spot, so I put on my blinkers and pull over into the service lane.

"Didn't *anyone* behave badly?" He goes on. "There must have been some excruciating or embarrassing moments?"

"Oh . . ." I sigh. "Let me think."

The fight Cynthia and Hilda had half an hour before the service about who was going to read the *prayers of the faithful* comes to mind. And then there was Dad's surprisingly woeful speech. Everyone was expecting a pithy, funny, and succinct few words from the important city lawyer, and instead he was sentimental and long-winded. Not that anyone really cared about that. *The other woman* was another issue.

Cassandra. All the locals were interested in her. My sisters and I were sniping all afternoon about her looking like a crow in her stupid black suit and spiky heels. What was she doing there, for God's sake, hanging on to Dad's arm like someone had glued her there? She and Mum kept out of each other's way. I eventually made it my business to go and talk to her, for Dad's sake. She told me about the case she's working on and . . . well, it was okay, all very polite. I'm not saying she's my new best friend, but being nice to her pleased Dad so much that I'm not sorry I made the effort. I could write about all that. Make something twisted and bitter and funny from it. But the very thought of delving into it all is boring me to tears.

"I've actually got this problem, Roger," I say mischievously.

"Yeah?" he says eagerly.

"Nothing much is pissing me off right now!" It's weird but true. I look out at the wide leafy street and smile at Mum, who is sitting alongside me, good-humored now because I've stopped driving, but with an increasingly puzzled look on her face.

"What do you mean?" he exclaims, pretending to be outraged.

"I'm just not particularly pissed off at the moment!" I say.

"But that's *terrible*!" he yells down the phone at me. "Get back to the city and you'll be feeling *bad* in no time!"

Now we're both laughing. I tell him I've got to go. He tells me to sit down and work on a piece as soon as I get back. Have it to him by the morning and we won't miss a week. Concentrate on all the shit that went down at the funeral, he orders. I tell him to get stuffed and to start paying me more if he wants that kind of effort.

"Important not to interrupt the momentum you've got going, Rose."

"I've been driving for four hours, Roger!" I blast him. "We've just dropped off a hitchhiker. I have to take my Mum home, and I have to see someone in the hospital. *If* that is okay with you?" I add sarcastically.

"So, what's in all that for you?" he yells straight back. "Dropping people off! Driving people home! Visiting the sick. Shit, Rose, I hate to break it to you, but you're *not* a nurse!"

This hits my funny bone because I remember deciding I would be a nurse last summer. I can't stop laughing, and I turn to Mum, who is looking even more bewildered.

"Got to go now," I lie. "Call you tomorrow."

"Remember, you would be an absolute disaster as a nurse!"

"Thanks Roger!"

"So, who is Ms. Angst?" Mum asks curiously.

"Oh, it's just . . . a silly nickname," I say, clicking my phone off and putting it back on the dashboard. I push down the blinkers. No way I'm going to tell her about writing for *Sauce*. Not tonight, anyway. No doubt someone in my family will find out, one way or another, so I'll explain when I have to.

◆ ◆ ◆

We round the corner into Alfred Crescent. Our house looks dark and quiet from the street. The others aren't back yet. Mum has always hated going home to an empty house. She never mentions it now, but . . . I feel for her as I pull up outside the front. It's wrong that she should have to, I think. After nearly thirty years of being married, she shouldn't have to be alone like this. It makes me pissed off with Dad all over again.

324

"So who was that who calls you . . . Ms. Angst?" Mum frowns.

"It's a joke," I mumble.

She is quiet for a minute.

"You are the only one of our children whom we didn't flip and flop about with trying to choose names," she says. "Right from day one you were Rose!"

I'd heard this before, but it still has me flummoxed.

"But what about *now*?" I ask shortly. "Dorothy is more a Rose than I am! And I'm more a . . . *Dorothy*." My voice peters out. I know I must sound like such a *dick*. What the hell is a Dorothy meant to be like, anyway?

"Absolutely not!" Mum says fiercely. "You are definitely Rose." She frowns, puts her hand out, and runs it a couple of times over my stupid, hacked-off hair, not smiling or even looking at me. "You are my tough and shining Rose," she adds quietly.

My tough and shining . . . Rose!

"Mum!" I burst out laughing. "Roses are *not* tough, and they don't shine!"

"Wrong!" she says. "Roses are very tough. You've got to look after them, cut them back, water them and feed them, but if you do, then they go on and on. They're tough, and in certain lights they shine."

"Do they?"

"Yes."

"Well." I try not to sound as pleased as I feel. "You're the gardener."

"That's right"—she slides open her door—"I'm the gardener. I know!"

I open the back of the van and help her get her things out, and we walk together to the front gate.

"You're going to see her now?" she asks lightly.

"Yep." I nod and look away. They all know about my plan to see Zoe, but I have deliberately played it down. What is the point of making a big deal out of something that might not work? A lot of time has passed. A lot has happened. With the best will in the world, it might not be such a good idea for Zoe and me to try to patch things up. You can't make something dead come alive again.

We stop at the front gate. Mum puts down her bag.

"Good luck then," she says, grabbing me by the shoulders and kissing me on both cheeks.

"Thanks."

"Working in the café tomorrow?"

"No," I reply. "I've got one more day off."

"So, why not stay here tonight?" she suggests lightly, taking her bag from me. "After such a long drive, why go all the way out to Hurstbridge? Go see Zoe, then come back here."

"Thanks. I might," I say shortly. "Bye, Mum."

I watch as my mother turns and begins to walk up the steps to the front door. Something sort of melts inside me as I watch her fiddling around with her key and slipping it into the lock. She looks strong and purposeful and vulnerable all at the same time.

"Hey, Mum!" I call out, without knowing what I want to say. She turns around and my insides heave to a halt again, because right at that moment, in the dim light, she seems so utterly . . . special. Her hair falling out of her bun, all untidy. Her clothes crumpled and a bit grubby from the long trip. This expectant smile on her face as she waits for me to speak.

"Thanks for coming with me," I call, "and . . . everything."

"Oh, Rose!" She gives one of her airy laughs and a little wave. "Thank *you*, darling! Thank you so much for all the driving and for everything else, too. I absolutely loved it." Then she disappears inside.

I watch from my van as the hall light is switched on and a flood of yellow light pours out onto the front porch, then the front rooms light up too. A warm yellow glow spills from the kitchen window, and I picture her walking through the house, switching on the lights, washing out the teapot, refusing to be mournful. Making the best of things. Seeing our house all lit up like that gladdens me somehow, makes me feel lucky. Even though I don't live there anymore.

WHEN I GET OUT of the lift on the eighth floor, I'm feeling jumpy in the extreme. What if she's changed her mind about seeing me? I should have rung. Told her I was coming tonight. What if she is too sick to talk? What if she tells me that she's going to die? What do I say to that? How do I behave? What if her mother is here? Shit! I could make a run for it . . . right now.

But I seem to be stuck on autopilot. I cross to the desk and ask the nurse for directions. I walk off like a docile zombie down the white corridor. It smells of disinfectant, and it's filled with shiny, complicated equipment and bustling staff, none of whom look like they've ever been confused about anything, ever, in their lives. From the young doctors with the stethoscopes around their necks to the smiling nurses to the old guy collecting used linens, they all know what to do in every situation. I'm sure of it.

I see the room number on the half-open door and I'm suffused with panic all over again. *What if . . .?* But there is nothing for it now. I'll have to go in.

◆　◆　◆

Zoe is lying alone, eyes closed and earphones in, with two empty beds on either side of her. I stare. There she is, my ex-best friend. The same wild, dyed-blond hair, broad brow, and wide mouth, but . . . thinner, I notice. I tiptoe in a little farther. She's in a white hospital gown, and there is an IV hooked up to one arm. I move closer and she opens her eyes. They are exactly as I remember them from when I first saw her freshman year: startlingly bright, green, and lovely, but now with what looks like a black shadow smudged all around them. Initially startled, her face soon breaks open into one of her smiles, and I am suffused with the feeling that it is absolutely right for me to be here.

"Hey Zoe," I say softly. I'm standing quite a way back from her bed, waiting for her to give me a signal to come closer.

"Rose." She pulls out the earphones, lifts up the arm connected to the IV, and motions me forward. I notice a lot of bruising, all the way up from her wrist on the inside. "God, you look . . . *wild*," she murmurs wonderingly. I'm immediately bamboozled. *Me?* I look down at my ordinary old T-shirt and jeans and sandals, wondering what the hell she means.

"Oh." I smile, running a hand across my head. "The hair."

"You do it yourself?" she asks approvingly.

"Yeah," I admit ruefully.

"God!" she laughs admiringly. "I love it."

"Thanks."

She motions to the end of the bed. "Take a pew, why don't you?" So I do. Up close, I can see she's pale and sick, that the black shadows around her eyes have nothing to do with makeup.

"So . . ." I begin, on the point of asking her how she's feeling and what exactly is going on with her illness and treatment, but I . . . don't. Some instinct tells me she doesn't want to answer those kinds of questions. Instead I point to the earphones lying on the bed. "What are you listening to?"

"You heard of Nunchukka Superfly?" Her smile breaks out again when I shake my head, and she hands me the earphones.

"Well, get a load, Rose! They're fantastic!"

"Okay!"

So that's what we do. Listen to music and talk about it. Music and bands. Who is hot and who is not. All the gossip we've heard around the traps, about what bands are breaking up and who is playing where and who has a new album out. Neither of us speaks about parents or families or funerals. Nothing about sickness or friendship, either.

But after little more than half an hour, I can see that she's flagging, so I don't stay long.

"I'll go now," I say, standing up. She nods. Her mouth trembles a little, and I think she might be going to cry. But she doesn't. She looks away toward the window and at the same time reaches for my hand.

"You'll come back?" she asks, holding on tight. There is a self-mocking smile around her mouth, but her green eyes are dead serious.

"Of course I will," I say.

"When?"

"Tomorrow?"

Her face relaxes, she nods, and we say goodbye.

◆ ◆ ◆

I'm fine going down in the lift with all the other people. I feel relieved and pretty much on top of things, like the whole visit worked out way better than could be expected. I walk through the hospital foyer, past the raffle stand and the florist, and then past the café. The smell of coffee and food reminds me that I'm ravenous. I stop and walk in but see straightaway that they're closing up. There isn't much left to eat except some old sandwiches, curling up at the edges. I decide I might as well wait till I get back home.

On the way out through the front doors I see the Ladies sign and I think, *Oh yeah, I need the toilet*. So I go in and push my way into a stall. I close the door. I undo my jeans, sit down, and . . .

And then I crash into a heap. I cry and cry and . . . cry. So much so that it feels like it's never going to end.

Fuck this! I think angrily as I grab another handful of toilet paper to soak up my streaming eyes and nose. *What is this about?* Last time, at least I knew that kid's mother was dying! There was a reason. I don't know anything about what's going to happen to Zoe. Maybe it's all going to be fine. They might be expecting her to get completely better and go on to live a long, happy life. So until I find out otherwise . . . *cut the drama queen crap!*

But I can't seem to. I keep seeing that IV sticking into her, and the half-filled soft plastic bottle above. I see the big black bruises running up and down the insides of her arms. I see her, lying alone in that strange bed, in her white hospital gown, with her bright eyes and her wide, hopeful smile and . . . it just breaks me. It makes me want to howl like a dog for the rest of my life.

Eventually I venture out of that stall, wash my face and dry it with a few rough paper towels, trying not to meet the eyes of a girl about my own age who is talking into her mobile phone. She must have heard me crying because she breaks off her conversation to watch me a moment.

"You okay?" Her voice is full of fake concern.

"Yeah. Thanks," I mutter. She starts applying mascara and then lipstick while she talks, checking me out surreptitiously all the while, like I'm some kind of freak who might do something dangerous at any moment. I splash more cold water on my face, dry off again, and straighten my shoulders.

She is applying gloss now. One layer and then another, and another! She twists this way and that, preening in front of the mirror. Checking out how flat her stomach is and how far her bum sticks out and how much of her boobs are on show. I head for the door, yelling at her in my head. *I might be a freak, but I'll bet anything I'm a more interesting freak than you are . . .*

◆　◆　◆

It is a relief to get out of the hospital and into the soft, still evening, but all that crying has left me disoriented. I've come out on the other side of the building, and I panic momentarily. Where am I? Where the hell did I leave the van?

Then I recognize the Royal Parade and Grattan Street corner, and I relax and start walking, feeling clearer with every step. I reach the van and try to decide where to go. I'm starving. It would be so easy and convenient to head back to Fitzroy, raid the fridge, and stay the night. But something tells me not to. Something tells me to sit still with my lonely life for a bit longer. My mother and sisters want me and Zoe to be unknotted and ironed out and put back in place as soon as possible. Fair enough, but I don't know if that's going to happen, or even if it's possible. If I go back to Fitzroy tonight, then I know I'll be in for an interrogation session like no other. They'll come flying in from all corners of the house, desperate for news, full of all kinds of advice and arguments. I smile to myself as I unlock my van. I don't need questions and comments or advice tonight. My family can wait.

I get in and start up the engine, then notice my mobile pulsing red. Someone has rung and left a message. I pick up the phone and click the button and wait, still smiling to myself as I try to guess who it will be. One of my sisters for sure! I can predict the message, too.

Hi, Rose! Just wondering how you got on with Zoe. Call us.

Hi, Rose! Just wanted to check if you're coming back here tonight and . . .

But it is a male voice. I'm puzzled at first, because whoever it is doesn't identify himself, and I don't immediately recognize the voice.

Hey, Rose! I've been wondering about the girl who sings on her bike. She still around? Call me. I've moved house. New number . . .

It takes me longer than it should. But when the penny drops, I replay it again and again.

After all this time, after all the shit that has gone down . . . *this* one is truly a surprise.

Suddenly I am wild with delight, jumping out of my skin, picturing him at the funeral in that daggy suit of his father's and the warm smile. *G'day, Rose!* Whatever is rushing around my system feels like it might be dangerous, so I turn off the van, get out again, lean up against the hood, and try to calm myself by checking out the stars. But it's hopeless. You can't see much at all in the city.

I take a few deep breaths and get back in again and fire up the engine.

THERE IS NO ONE HOME in the Hurst-bridge house, so I bounce in and switch on a few lights. I go to the kitchen and unpack the things I bought on the way home—bread and butter, cheese and apples—and start making myself a few toasted sandwiches. When they're under the griller, I look around the funny little kitchen. It pleases me that someone has cleaned up a bit and bought milk while I've been away. Must be Barry. Stuttering Stan doesn't drink milk. Hey, things might be on the improve.

When everything is ready, I take my supper to my room at the front of the house. I open the door and stand a moment. Every single thing is as I left it. A straight, well-made bed, a neat desk, a chair, and one of those collapsible canvas wardrobes with six little cubicles down the side for undies and folded things. There is no print on the wall, or rug on the floor, or cushion. The only real splash of color is the navy and pink floral bed cover. It suddenly amuses me to see the dozen books from the library stacked so neatly in their separate piles on the floor by my bed: fiction, nonfiction, crime, schoolbooks. My shoes, too, are lined up under the window like soldiers waiting for orders, and my clothes hang in sober straight lines from the flimsy railing. All very commendable, but for some reason part of me wants to mess it all up tonight. Somehow I don't feel like the same girl who went to great trouble to get her room looking like this before she went away.

I decide there might be a better use for this wild burst of energy than messing up my room, so I settle myself down at my desk. Why not have a go at making Roger's morning deadline?

I pull the scraps of paper from my pockets and bag, those few notes that I made while I was away, and start reading through them, wondering if there is anything that I can use.

Don'tcha just hate the way . . . There are half a dozen of them and some have distinct possibilities, but not one of them feels urgent. I know if I'm going to work all night, then that is what I need. It's got to sing out and beg to be written.

At that point, I start mucking around with a different start.

Don'tcha just LOVE the way life messes with you! One minute you're on the fast track to success, sure as hell you'll get there, and then . . . wham! It tosses you off course and you're flailing around like a piece of stray gunk from an old, rusty fishing hook. You surface, gasping, half-blind. What's the point? you ask. Friends let you down. Your family drives you nuts. Your career is so far off the rails it doesn't matter and . . . even your name seems like a sick joke! For years you've wished you'd been called something different.

Then something happens and you suddenly see it from a different angle. You start appreciating it. You start loving it. Once that starts, you're off. It's like being on a wave. You hook into the swelling energy below and start gliding. Nothing can stop you now . . .

Ah shit! Roger will have a fit if I go down that track. He'll be howling like a dog. Crying for mercy. *Come on, Rose!* I can hear him shouting down the phone at me. *Where is the spite? Where's the venom?* Sauce *doesn't do . . . nice!* Do I want to stay up all night working on something he's going to chuck right back in my face? I sigh and put the pen down, stand and have a long stretch. Well . . . I'd better think about that one.

I go into the grimy bathroom and check on the rate of hair growth since this morning. Miniscule. Damn. Why did I do it, again?

The girl who sings on her bike!

He was probably just being nice at the funeral when he said my stupid hair was *okay*. Anyway, *okay* isn't good, is it? It's not fantastic or pretty or beautiful. It's not overwhelming in any way. I turn this way and that, trying to see it from his point of view. Guys don't like girls with weird haircuts like this . . . Do they?

Hang on a minute, Rose.

I've got some real color in my face after my week away. My eyes flash back at me, my cheekbones are sharp and . . . interesting. I pick up an old tube of lipstick sitting on the sink, plaster a bit on, and rub my lips together. There, that's better. A faint resemblance to Audrey Hepburn, maybe? Yep, for sure there is. Unmistakable. *Breakfast at Tiffany's*. I laugh to myself. Or maybe breakfast in Brunswick Street on Saturday morning? Why not? I'll ring and ask. I smile at my own image. *I'm tough and shining Rose . . . who sings on her bike.*

Well, okay. I can live with that.

I decide to take a punt. No harm giving it a go. I'm way too revved up to go to sleep anyway. Whether Roger wants it or not, that piece *is* calling out to be written. *Don'tcha just love the way* . . . I turn off the bathroom light, get myself another coffee, wrap myself in a blanket, and hunker down at the desk. It's going to be a late night. But I can live with that, too.